ASCENT INTO HELL

Andrew M. Greeley

ASCENT INTO HELL

WARNER BOOKS

A Warner Communications Company

A
BERNARD GEIS ASSOCIATES
BOOK

29216

C-1

Warner Books, Inc., 666 Fifth Avenue, New York, NY 10103

A Warner Communications Company

Printed in the United States of America

First printing: June 1983
10 9 8 7 6 5 4 3 2 1

Designed by Giorgetta Bell McRee

Library of Congress Cataloging in Publication Data

Greeley, Andrew M., 1928–
Ascent into hell.

I. Title.
PS3557.R358A8   1983   813'.54   82-61879
ISBN 0-446-51254-0

For Dan Herr
May he never
"Stop Pushing"

April is the cruellest month, breeding
Lilacs out of the dead land . . .

T. S. Eliot

NOTE

This is the story of why one man became a priest and why he left the active priesthood.

Hugh Donlon is a product of my imagination and is not based on any priest I know. I do not intend to suggest that his story is typical either of men who become priests or of men who leave the active priesthood. Nor is his wife intended to be typical of the women who marry priests who have withdrawn from the ministry. I am not writing a sociological study about marriages between priests and nuns.

Father Donlon, his family, his friends, and everyone else in the novel are creatures of my imagination. Those who love to search a novel for traces of a roman à clef or a "thinly veiled autobiography" are perfectly free to do so, of course, having paid their money and perhaps even having finished the book. A search for "real" counterparts of the characters of my story, however, tells more about the searchers than it does about the story.

Nor should it be assumed because Hugh Donlon is a priest and I am a priest that his voice is my voice. Only Maria speaks for me. Moreover, like God, I refuse to assume responsibility for the moral behavior of my creatures.

Background information about the workings of the Chicago Board of Trade was furnished by Robert Brennan and Richard Mortell. They are not responsible for any inaccuracies in my description of what might have happened at that splendid institution—but in fact did not.

Guilt-ridden priest, after his sexual
involvement with a nun, leaves the
priesthood to become a successful but
unhappy stockbroker.

PASSOVER

There are three experiences that are at the core of the religion (or religions, if you prefer) of Yahweh—Community, Freedom, and New Life. Both the Christian and Jewish Passover commemorate these three experiences, the Christian Passover adding (perhaps) a new overlay of meaning on that which was already contained in the feast. In both festivals the dinner of Unleavened Bread represents the experience of Community, the Paschal Lamb represents the experience of Freedom, and the Fire and Water represent the experience of New Life. In the Christian Passover Thursday is the day of recommitment to the Community, Friday the day of celebrating Freedom, and Saturday the Festival of New Life.

In both Christian and Jewish traditions the Paschal Lamb wins forgiveness and thus freedom; it is the innocent victim who stays God's wrath, the loving one who reveals God's loving forgiveness. Good Friday, then, is especially a feast of forgiveness, a feast of dying to the old in order to be able to rise, free once again, to the new.

The followers of Moses recounted their experience of Freedom in the story of Exodus, the going forth of a slave people who in their going forth became a free people. The followers of Jesus, caught up in the powerful energies of their experience of Freedom in their contact with the Still Living Jesus, described it through two stories that had great resonance to their contemporaries—the ransoming of military captives (salvation) and the buying of slaves to set them free (redemption). Perhaps we would obtain the same resonance today if we told it as a story of an army general liberating a concentration camp or the leader of a rescue party saving survivors of an avalanche.

Or perhaps the story of men and women who have spent much of their lives in the misguided crucifixion of themselves with misunderstood passions, discovering at last that their God is not a God of rules but a God of love, a God whose forgiveness cannot be earned since it is already given.

The seven passages from scripture quoted in this story are the seven last words of Jesus on the cross, around which the Tre Ore (three hour) service, popular with Catholics before 1960, was constructed.

PROLOGUE

1933

"Woman, behold, thy son. . . . Son, behold, thy mother."

On Good Friday night Thomas Donlon knelt in the sacristy of the chapel at Oak Park Hospital. He had come to bargain with God.

A nun unlocked the door to the sanctuary so that he could pray for his wife in the presence of the Blessed Sacrament, hidden away until Holy Saturday morning. He turned off the single electric light and knelt on the hard wooden prie-dieu in front of the fussy old sacristy cabinet with its many little drawers and panels. The flickering red sanctuary lamp bathed the room in a bloodred glow— the blood of Jesus who had died for Thomas Donlon's sins, the blood of his wife Peggy who might die before the night was over, perhaps a punishment for his sins.

When he met her, only a year ago, Peggy was a lovely girl, dressed in white, standing next to the pergola at Twin Lakes after Mass on a Sunday morning in June, sweet, innocent, and radiantly beautiful. His father, a wealthy, dishonest, and penurious police captain, was dead. At twenty-five, Tom Donlon had inherited the family money and the string of family apartment buildings, a position in a prestigious Loop law firm, and a promise from the Organization that he would eventually be slated for a place on the Cook County Superior Court.

He had spent the previous year in Europe, at first a lonely exile wandering amid the ruins of a collapsing banking system and an eroding social order. Then in Salzburg he met a young music teacher.

But the girl would not come home with him, fearing, perhaps rightly, that she would wither in the harshness of a nation she did not know. Tom Donlon instead went to Twin Lakes looking for a wife.

And he found one, a sumptuously beautiful young woman with buttermilk skin and thick, jet-black hair—a Black Irish Venus.

It was a speedy courtship. The Curtins were delighted that such a fine young man wanted to marry their Peggy. Even if she was only eighteen, he was too good a catch to pass up, especially since it seemed that the Depression might never end. Peggy thought she was in love, but was in fact an innocent traded by her family to a lustful young man for veiled promises of political advantage and financial rewards.

He swam with her the afternoon they met, discovering that in a white swimsuit she was every bit as enticing as she was in a white dress. He kissed her in the mysterious, humid darkness of the golf course that night, after a dance at the Red Barn, held her close in his arms, and told her, honestly enough, that she was the most beautiful woman he had ever known.

She trembled when he caressed her, but her lips were firm and generous in their response to his. Dimly he realized that she was too young to marry and that her parents should delay the match for a year or two. Yet the Curtins wanted his clout, he wanted Peggy, and she wanted to be in love, even if her intended was a slight, bookish, reserved young man—except when his hands were gliding over her body.

Tom Donlon was a man of stern principle, in reaction perhaps to his father's total lack of principle. A voice in the back of his head told him softly that his courtship of Peggy was little more than an exercise in the buying of a wife and that he was violating all his principles by exploiting the Curtin greed. Yet his lust for her was so powerful that he turned off the voice the way he would turn off his Philco radio.

On their wedding night he discovered, as he should have foreseen, that she was altogether unprepared for marriage. Instead of being angry at her, Tom Donlon was furious at himself for forcing her into his bed, innocent of both reflection and freedom.

At that moment love replaced lust. He rearranged her rumpled nightgown, straightening out the white lace and the whiter limbs, patted the hand pathetically clutching a pearl rosary, and told his bride not to worry, their love would triumph. Several days later at an Ozark honeymoon hotel, Peggy had insisted they consummate their marriage and she had done her best to cooperate. Months after that, when their first child was beginning to stir in her body, his patience and sensitivity were rewarded, aided considerably by magic words he had found in a booklet called "An Examination of Conscience for Catholic Married Women." The words were "In matters which pertain to the rendering of the marriage debt, the good Catholic wife trustingly follows the lead of her husband." The formula, repeated mysteriously and with no explanation at the Convent of the Sacred Heart, where Peggy had attended high school, sufficed to legitimate passion. Peggy discovered that she enjoyed sex, perhaps not as much as he did, but enough to admit guiltily that she liked it and to wonder if she were "abnormal." Tom suspected that eventually, with patience and love, his woman would become more of a wanton than he.

In their few months together, Tom found that his wife was not merely a pretty girl with firm breasts, long, straight legs and a promise of blossoming sexuality. Peggy was fascinating and unpredictable—the kind of woman who unveils some of her mystery and then retreats into yet deeper mystery.

Prudish in her opposition to smoking and drinking ("Not in my house, whatever Governor Roosevelt says"), Peg nevertheless was the life of the somewhat stuffy parties organized by the wives of Tom's law partners. She would sing the latest Broadway song in a clear, pretty voice after only a hint of an invitation, and after a few parties, with no invitation at all.

She was talented with a watercolor brush but afraid to show the results of her work. When Tom took a painting from her by brute force and exclaimed in surprise at its pastel loveliness, she forbade him to tell anyone that she painted, much as if it were a secret vice. Yet she clapped her hands in happiness when he insisted that she go to the Art Institute for the lessons that Maude Curtin had sternly forbidden.

Peggy was rigid in her pieties and deeply believing in her faith, afraid of God's punishing wrath, and confident of His generous love. She was absurdly modest with her own body, though it was Tom's whenever he wanted it, but almost persuaded him to take her to Sally Rand's show at the Century of Progress World's Fair.

And now she was close to death.

She had gone to bed early, pleading a faint headache. About midnight she had called for him. He was curled up in the parlor with a book of medieval history, a passion that had now taken second place to another in his life.

"I'm scared, Tommy, I think the baby is coming."

"A week early?"

"I know . . . the pains are regular . . . and they hurt."

Dr. Walter Mohan, cheerful and indulgent, was waiting for them in the empty Emergency Room at Oak Park Hospital. One look at Peg and his demeanor changed.

Hugh Thomas Donlon was born seven hours later, a six-pound, five-ounce baby boy, healthy and screaming. Doc Mohan, a thin, red-haired man in his early forties with a trace of the brogue, was grimly serious when he discussed Peg's condition. "We have a hemorrhage problem, Tom, and I don't like the looks of it. The next twenty-four hours will be touch and go."

Her skin parchment pale, her voice weak, Peg was calm and brave. "Everything is in God's hands, darling. We'll have to pray for our own resignation to His holy will."

Desperate with fear, Tom stumbled into the bloodred sacristy of the hospital chapel.

I'd be here even if I didn't believe a thing, he admitted finally to the Deity. For hours he'd pleaded, begged, implored. Now he remembered his mother's custom of making promises to God. Captain Daniel "Dollars" Donlon of the Chicago police had had little patience with Harriet Donlon's promises; in fact he'd had little patience with anything about that vague and wistful woman, especially her attempts to teach their only child the moral principles that the captain ignored all his life. Tom had never made a "promise" before. It couldn't hurt and it might help.

What could he give?

"Look, if you want the boy to be a priest, I won't oppose that. I promise you. Leave me Peg and you can have Hugh."

A damn fool thing to say. Peg had once remarked that it would be wonderful "if God blessed us with a vocation for one of our sons." Inwardly he'd been revolted at the idea, then upset with himself. God knows the poor Church needed good priests.

"I hope your intelligence isn't insulted by such a promise." He addressed the Lord much as a good lawyer with a weak case would address a distinguished federal judge—the kind of judge Tom wanted to to be someday. "It was a stupid remark. Don't blame Peg for my stupidity. If you want my son, now or later, you can have him, regardless. If you want Peg now too, you can have her. Only please don't want her."

At some point even the most penitent offender has no recourse save to throw himself on the mercy of the court.

Finally he slipped out of the chapel and ran down the empty corridor to her room. Doc Mohan was smiling.

"I hope you were in the chapel praying for me, Tommy," she said weakly as he took her in his arms.

"I was, very hard." His breath was coming in gulps, as though he'd run many miles on a humid August day.

She seemed surprised. "That was so good of you. I was ready to die, but I asked God for more time so I could thank you for all the love. . . ." Her voice trailed off.

"Still pretty weak," said Mohan, "but out of the woods, thank heaven. So young. . . ."

"Too young," said Tom Donlon, turning away to hide his tears.

Several weeks later, Tom Donlon thought about the Fireside Chat he'd listened to before going to bed. He had turned off the radio as soon as Roosevelt was finished, so that it would not wake Peg, though he knew that once she was asleep a Big Bertha shell would not wake her.

They were living in a small and rather stodgy furnished apartment in one of his buildings on Austin Boulevard. He'd argued that they ought to save their money so they might eventually buy a house and furniture for it, instead of wasting money on new furniture for a small apartment. Maude Curtin was outraged, having expected that her princess would promptly move into a palace, at least what passed for a palace in North Austin.

Peggy merely laughed, refusing to take Tom's financial caution seriously. "I like living here," she insisted. "I want my husband close to me whenever he's in the house. If I get tired of it, I'll buy a house."

He did not doubt that she meant it. An obedient and docile woman she was. Yet when she soon became weary of riding the Austin and Washington boulevards bus to the Loop, she went to a Packard agency in Oak Park, wrote a check for $750, and presented him with the car as "a birthday present."

He almost read her a lecture on the value of money, thought better of it, and took his place in the plush driver's seat of the Packard. A good lawyer knows when to plead "nolo contendere."

It had been a year since he'd cast his vote, for Franklin D. Roosevelt. In the twilight between waking and sleeping he calculated that Peggy would vote in her first national election three years from now, in 1936; and it would be the off-year election of 1954 when Hugh would cast his first vote. What would the country be like then? Would the Depression last that long? What kind of world would Hugh face in his young manhood?

He'd do all right. A tough young man, putting on lots of weight, although he looked so small it was difficult to imagine him walking into a flag-decorated polling place as a member of the Democratic Party.

Tom Donlon laughed to himself. Of course, he would be a Democrat. He was a Catholic, wasn't he?

That night created wonder and mystery that would fascinate and trouble Tom Donlon for the rest of his life.

He woke suddenly from a deep sleep. Peg was nursing their son, who required but one feeding a night and then quickly went back to sleep. Tom had assumed that his wife, both prudish and fastidious, would put the baby on a bottle as quickly as she could. Again he'd underestimated her. She loved providing her own milk for the adored boy child.

His heavy eyelids closed. Go back to sleep. Then he forced them open again. There was something strange. . . .

Peg was sitting next to the bed, Hugh in her arms. A light was radiating from them, soft and misty and very bright. She had slipped the straps of her nightdress off her shoulders and the baby's skin and her own cream white body seemed to blend into one. Her eyes were afire with infatuation, possession, delight.

She saw him watching and smiled at him too, inviting him into their communion. "I saved some of my milk for you."

"What . . . ?" he stammered.

"You've wanted to taste it and were afraid to ask." She drew his head firmly to her nipple.

Her milk was sweet and warm, like Peggy herself. She was administering her sacrament to him. The light crept around him too.

"I have enough love for both of you," she said complacently.

No longer a child bride with a live doll, Peggy was age-old woman, mysterious, absorbing, life-giving, totally captivating. She put the sleeping Hugh back in his crib, patted Tom's head, turned off the light, and cuddled next to him. Father and son had both been nourished. Mother and wife could sleep.

The next morning, a Sunday—Mass at St. Lucy's, Father Coughlin and Walter Winchell on the Philco—Tom tried to tell himself it had been a dream. Yet Peg was next to him in bed, the straps off her shoulders, her nightdress hanging from her waist, her breasts strong and reassuring.

Had the light been real?

Was that kind of ardent, physical love between a mother and son dangerous?

He brushed his lips against hers and touched lightly the breast from which he'd drunk as if it were a chalice from which a priest might say Mass. She continued to sleep.

I'm not sorry I bargained with God for you.

BOOK
ONE

"I thirst."

CHAPTER
ONE

1954

The girl who opened the door just as Hugh was about to put his key in the lock was so disconcertingly beautiful that he stepped back abruptly, as if to shield his eyes from a blinding light.

She seemed to be about twenty, pale burnished hair, an expressive and mobile face with a clear suggestion of barely suppressed comedy, a figure slim rather than voluptuous in bermuda shorts and print blouse, feet in sandals, both hands jammed jauntily into her pockets.

"Hi," she said, light blue eyes dancing with fun as she stood in the panel of light in the doorway.

"Hi," he said, his voice unnaturally thin. "I'm Hugh Donlon."

"Course you are." Her face crinkled.

"I live here."

"Course you do; would you like to come in . . . ?"

"You live here?" he stammered with minimum understanding.

Her head tilted to one side, her smile amused yet tolerant, she regarded him with the benign grace of a wealthy countess.

"Sure. . . . It's all right for you to come in. I'm not dangerous."

I'm staring at her and acting like a clod, Hugh told himself. But I don't care. She's gorgeous.

He stepped through the doorway into the small parlor of their summer home. "Do you have a name?" he asked.

The room was comfortably ugly with mismatched old furniture and threadbare rugs. His mother had won the argument about a Lake Geneva summer home, as she always won the mild disagreements between her and his father, but the judge had made his point that the home ought not to be ostentatious. Ezio Pinza was singing "Some Enchanted Evening" from *South Pacific* on a record player of dubious vintage.

"Doesn't everyone?" There was a flicker of intelligence as well as humor in her rapidly changing eyes. This one is smart too, he thought. She's got me on the defensive and is going to make the most of it. That's all right, pretty lady. With you I don't mind being on the defensive.

In one graceful movement she crossed the room to turn off the record player, crumpled a bubble gum wrapper into her pocket, and hid a copy of a film magazine under a newspaper on the many-spotted coffee table.

Seminarian or not, Hugh exercised a young man's right to consider carefully what it was about a young woman that made her beautiful.

Her smile came first. Not quite a smile, really, half smile, half grin, hinting at amusement, confidence, sophistication, mischief— and assuming as a matter of course and a matter of simple justice that she saw right through him.

He felt his face grow warm.

And her eyes. Soft blue like the waters of Lake Geneva. Changing rapidly as the lake did on a windy day when small cumulus clouds raced across it trailing lights and shadows as if it were momentarily Holland instead of Wisconsin and the lake was on loan for a Rembrandt painting.

Her face was a little too thin perhaps and the nose a little too long. Yet her fair skin was flawless and her delicate facial bones promised loveliness that time would not alter. Her slender body suggested femininity rather than flaunting it; breasts small and perfectly shaped, as if a sculptor had molded them to make men clench their hands; slender waist; a pert rear end. Hugh cut off the flow of his imagination. He was, after all, studying for the priesthood.

"Do I get to learn what the name is?" he said, trying to sound cool and collected.

"If you've decided that I pass the exam." She sat on the couch and gestured toward the decrepit easy chair next to it, all confidence.

"With highest honors," he said.

"I'm Maria. In fact, I'm Maria Angelica Elizabetha Vittoria Paola Pia Emmanuela . . . almost enough for a baseball team."

And now, astonishingly, he saw a touch of vulnerability, perhaps even a little fear in her Rembrandt eyes. Why should you be afraid of me, pretty countess?

"I should know you, Maria?" he asked cautiously.

"You've known me for a long time." Shaking her head in mock displeasure, and then in a total transformation, she ceased to be a countess and became a waitress. "You want a beer . . . ? I know what you want. Don't go away."

He followed her with his eyes as she rushed from the room, then reproved himself sharply. He'd given up girls four years ago when he'd entered the seminary. Young women like Maria could make his heart pound, but they must be kept at a distance, especially after the four depressing weeks at Holy Family Orphanage. He wondered what had happened to his own family.

He was glad to be home, sitting in a warm and familiar room with its mixture of white wicker chairs, beige couches with broken springs and torn fabric from his grandparents' house on West End, and the rag rugs that were in the house when the Donlons bought it and tended to skid on the slippery wood floor. Golf clubs, tennis rackets, swimsuits, and laundry were heaped in various empty places and the lightbulbs were always too dim because no one could remember to buy stronger bulbs on their trips to the store in Walworth.

The only bright colors in the room were his mother's latest watercolors, hanging by family insistence on every available wall space, including that above the rarely used fireplace.

The dominant colors were blue and gold, blue skies, gold waters on the lake, blue like that in Maria's eyes, gold like that in her hair.

"*Eccolo.*" Maria returned. "Raspberries and cream. Your mother insisted that we must lay in a great supply of raspberries for the return of the firstborn."

"Maria who?"

She sat cross-legged on the couch. The clouds wiped out the sunlight in her eyes. The game was over and she was sad. "Maria Manfredy, who else? I'm your sister's classmate at Trinity, the daughter of the shoe repairman on Division Street. . . you know, the handsome man with gray hair and the pretty wife who speaks hesitant English."

Not twenty, but sixteen or seventeen. Hugh was furious at himself. Taken in by a kid and a shoemaker's daughter at that. Countess indeed. The orphanage must have been worse than he thought.

"I'm sorry, Maria," he said. "I guess I don't remember you; people change."

Her wonderful eyes could not stay cloudy for long. Sunlight flooded back in.

"I might have changed a *little*." With the return of sunlight came both mischief and intelligence.

Hugh revised his opinion again. Seventeen all right, but no ordinary seventeen. She can be any one of a number of people and she's trying to find out which one I like the most. All of them, I think.

"Don't you remember the time you carried me home?"

Now she was shy and winsome. This Maria is the most appealing of all. When her eyes plead with me that way, she owns me.

"How could I forget something like that?"

"Well. . . ." She took a long breath, like a diver before a leap into a pool. "I was a proud little girl going to St. Ursula's on a Sunday afternoon in my First Communion dress for practice of the May Crowning procession. It had just stopped raining and there was even a rainbow in the sky. Some big kids chased me and called me a little Dago and shot rubber-band guns. I fell on the curbstone and cut my knee and got my dress all muddy. Then the big kids ran away and left me there sobbing and I was sure I was going to die of disappointment and disgrace. The captain of the patrol boys came by and cleaned my dirty face, wiped away my tears, fixed the cut on my knee as best he could. Then he took me by the hand and walked to Division Street with me. So I started to cry again, because my mother and father would be so disappointed that their only child couldn't march in the May Crowning.

"Now do you remember? You had to carry me the last half block to the store, because I didn't want to go home. My father said that Judge Donlon was the best man in the parish, even if he was a politician, and my mother—not knowing what your mother would think about such a terrible thing—gave you a glass of homemade red wine and you drank most of it, without even making a face. Then you and my mother and father made me laugh and you went to see Sister Cunnegunda and even though I missed practice I was still in the May Crowning."

Tears were streaming down her face. He wanted to wipe them away again.

He took her chin in his hand and turned her head in his direction.

She was intrigued, a little frightened, and unresisting.

I'm going to kiss her, Hugh thought. I have to kiss her.

There was a noise outside.

"Car door, your parents," Maria whispered.

He barely heard her.

"Don't," she said, pulling away from him.

His mother saw them sitting together on the couch and there was a hint of unease in her smile of greeting.

"We didn't expect you home so soon . . . we went to the movies."

His father covered his concern more skillfully. "You were right, Maria. *The Robe* is an excellent film."

"Are you here all alone?" his mother asked. "Where's Marge?"

"She's out with Joe Delaney," Maria said timidly.

"And I don't suppose Tim has showed up yet," Judge Donlon said. "Mother, father, brother, sister, all somewhere else when you come home."

"Maria was here," Hugh said.

"And you didn't have the slightest idea who I was, kind of thought I might be a glamorous thief." Before the judge and Mrs. Donlon had a chance to examine their son's face more closely, Maria took over the party.

She served up "another round of raspberries and cream on the house" and told the May Crowning story again, this time as high comedy, ending with Hugh staggering down Division Street after drinking a bottle of the "Manfredy's bathtub grapa."

Despite herself, Mrs. Donlon laughed till she cried. "You look happy and relaxed, Hugh," she said when she recovered. "The time at the orphanage must have been good for you."

"I feel fine," he said, not wanting to admit that the happiness and peace had come only when Maria appeared in the panel of light at the front door.

"I tell you what." Maria never seemed to wind down. "It's so warm and stuffy . . . why don't we poor stay-at-homes go for a moonlight swim . . . ?" Then her voice trailed off and she did wind down. Fragility and fear returned to her eyes.

Worried that she might have gone too far with the proper Donlons? Hugh thought not. You could never go too far, Maria. We're not like you but you're what we think maybe we could be, if we ever got time after our serious responsibilities are fulfilled.

His mother was the first to succumb to Maria's fading voice, his mother who had probably never gone for a midnight swim in her life.

"That's a wonderful idea, dear. I was thinking the same thing myself."

His father managed to keep a reasonably straight face.

Maria was silent, almost invisible five minutes later, as, wearing a modest black swimsuit and a sweat shirt, she walked after the elder Donlons to the edge of the pier. Hugh followed behind her, still yearning to touch her lips with his.

The humidity was so thick that it seemed to be a physical presence, like a ghost with clammy hands and hot breath, a heavy sinister spirit, lurking in the moonless sky, too elusive to be illumined by the faint glow of starlight.

Peggy dove off the pier gracefully, quite unafraid of the darkness. The judge followed her.

Maria hesitated. "I can't swim very well."

"It was your idea and now you're scared." Hugh taunted her gently.

"A woman can have second thoughts." She pulled off her sweat shirt and dropped it on the pier.

Too dark to see her shoulders, merely a pale white gash in the night.

Hugh pushed the pale white gash off the end of the pier.

He half expected that she would be furious. Instead, she popped to the surface laughing and spitting water. "It's great, fraidy cat, come on in."

Hugh dove in and swam out to the raft with his mother, while the judge kept Maria company.

"Why have we never done this before?" Peggy asked. "I think I might be able to paint the scene . . . swimmers on a moonless night."

"How was *The Robe*?" Maria asked Peggy shyly when they were all together again at the pier.

"It was very moving," Peggy replied solemnly, "to see our Lord and Savior's life portrayed on the screen, even indirectly. The movie will give me a lot to think about."

"A tremendous number of historical inaccuracies," the judge commented. "For example, the legionnaires in Palestine were unquestionably Syrian, not Italian."

"I wish I were as pretty as Jean Simmons," blurted Maria, definitely a teen-ager now.

"You're much prettier, dear," Peggy said generously, "and you'll be pretty all your life. . . . I sometimes wonder what He thinks about us. Nineteen centuries later and we're still selfish and unkind and resistant to His Holy Will."

"I bet He's much happier with us now than He would be if we hadn't gone swimming tonight . . . hey, where's the pier?" Maria, having floated too far away, flailed in the water. "I'm not too good at this swimming thing. . . ."

Hugh grabbed her arm in the darkness and pulled her toward the pier. She brushed against him for a delightful moment.

"I'm going to learn to swim, just you wait. I'll be as graceful as one of those cute dolphins." She eased out of his grasp and reached for the ladder, breathing hard as she tried to catch her breath. "Anyway, He made the lake and the moon and this night for us— He even made the pier for me to cling to—and we should be grateful."

My countess even preaches sermons, Hugh thought. And when she brushes against me I think I'm going to die.

"And we should be grateful to Him for sending you to make us appreciate the night," his mother said, even though Maria's theology was foreign to her own somber vision of the Deity.

"Now you'll make me cry, Mrs. Donlon." Maria lost the pier again. But this time, alas, she did not need Hugh's help to find it.

And he could hardly put his arms around her, even in the dark, with his mother and father floating beside him.

Walking up the lawn to the house, Hugh and Maria fell behind his parents. In the distance lightning cut jagged lines in the night sky. Outraged crickets continued their protest against the heat. Hugh and Maria paused, in unspoken agreement, underneath the tiny light at the entrance to the gazebo that served as Peggy's studio.

Hugh tilted her chin up so he could look into her eyes, mischievous, mocking, yet so easily hurt. Wet hair glued to her head, water still on her face and shoulders, Maria was a piquant little slave, utterly his if he wanted her. In the heaviness of the summer night she seemed to promise an eternity of sweetness and life if only he would take her in his arms.

"You're an amazing person, Maria," he said lamely, his fingers feeling the pulse racing through her throat.

"Not bad for a high school junior, huh?" She giggled.

Hugh knew with total clarity that he had the power at that instant to decide for or against the priesthood. To envelop Maria in his arms would be to repudiate his priestly vocation.

Why did temptations have to be so pathetic and so lovely?

And was she a temptation? Perhaps, after all . . .

Hugh decided for the priesthood. "We'd better go inside . . ." he said, releasing her chin.

"Too many mosquitoes out here." Maria laughed. "A guy could get badly bitten."

CHAPTER
TWO

1954

Later that night, Hugh knelt in his shorts at the side of his bed, saying his night prayers. He prayed for Tim that he would stay out of trouble, for Marge that she would be protected from harm, for his parents that they would worry less about their children, for his classmate and friend Jack Howard who was thinking of leaving the seminary.

And thank You too for sending Maria to bring us some laughter.

The sheets were clammy, the air was still, crickets were buzzing outside. Maria was in the bedroom next door, alone till Margie came home. His parents were sleeping down the corridor. A thin wall between him and the lovely Maria.

Father Meisterhorst would be horrified. The spiritual director of the seminary had harassed Hugh for three years about the girls he had necked with and petted when he was in high school. There would be bad thoughts about these "sins of the past," the old man had thundered, and powerful temptations to seek out his "partners in sin" and begin again.

Hugh was not convinced that his sins were that great, though he regretted them. He felt no inclination to seek out his high school sweethearts, some of whom were engaged, a few even married, and one a mother. He had no trouble containing his fantasies about the mild conquests of his teen-age days.

Maria was another matter. No older than the girls he'd passionately kissed in high school, but more threatening and more appealing. It was a test of his vocation he didn't need.

But he wasn't going to leave his own home to escape from her.

Life consisted of hard choices, for the love of God. There would be other attractive women who would force him to make difficult decisions.

He was at an age when a man looks for a wife, unless he is committed to something else. The juices of his body made Maria attractive. To resist her appeal was a measure of his character.

Besides, she chewed bubble gum.

Peg Donlon's hand tightened its hold on her husband's. He felt the familiar reassuring pressure of the pearl rosary beads. Twenty-two years and he loved her more than ever.

They had held hands through the film, and she'd cuddled next to him in the car coming home.

He stopped once on the highway to kiss her.

The swim inflamed them both even more. They were in each other's arms as soon as the bedroom door was closed. During the middle years of their marriage, when she was busy with the children and he with wartime cases and then learning the craft of an appellate judge, his campaign to free his bride so that she could become a wanton had languished. Then, after a retreat with the Jesuits at Barrington, Tom realized that he had turned away from romance, a bad thing, especially for a medievalist.

After the retreat he discovered that Peg was at the height of her sexual desires, a breathtaking and head-spinning challenge.

Some retreat, he grinned ruefully.

She was, of course, still ashamed of her "animality" and doubtless pestered priests in the confessional for a reassurance that they could not give. Her shame did not, however, restrain her in their bedroom. Soon both their bodies were spent, but not satisfied.

After a long silence, she said, "Will they let him go back?"

She was thinking of Tim, their second son, a freshman at Notre Dame until he was suspended for smuggling liquor on campus.

"I think so. They usually give offenders one more chance. He did it for fun, not profit. Just an undergraduate prank."

"Why does he do such things?"

The judge sighed. He had heard too many cases in the Superior

Court before being appointed to the federal bench by President Roosevelt to deceive himself about Tim. The boy needed professional help, but did not seem to want to benefit from it.

"It's not easy to have a father who's a judge," he said guardedly.

"And Marge?" Nighttime was for lovemaking and worrying about children. "I never spoke to my mother the way she speaks to me."

"Things have changed since the war," he said lamely.

"I thought Maria would be a good influence on her."

"Thank God, she has friends like Maria," he agreed, knowing that it was Maria and Hugh who most worried his wife on this humid, passionate summer night. "That little Italian girl made a simple thing like swimming a sacrament, a revelation of God's grace. Very neat, very pointed, very simple. He did make the lake and the sky and the moon and us. Sometimes we Irish need to be reminded of the sacredness of such things."

"Sicilians are morally lax."

"Now, come on, you're as fond of the girl as everyone else."

"Of course, I like her. How can you not like her? I thought the swim was wonderful. But did you see how Hugh reacted to her? God forgive me for putting his vocation in such danger."

"If Hugh can't live in a world where there are young women like Maria and not lose his vocation, it seems to me that God doesn't want him all that much."

"I'm terribly worried about our responsibility," Peg insisted.

He stroked her thick black hair, in which a few streaks of handsome white had begun to appear. "All we can do is our best. God doesn't expect anything more."

"I hope you're right," his wife murmured anxiously, and the hand with the rosary began to caress his chest. Her lips pressed down on his. "I love you so much. I don't want to fail as the mother of your children."

Hugh still could not sleep. He gave it up as a bad job, pulled on slacks and a sweat shirt, and walked softly down the hall, out of the house, and down to the pier that jutted into Lake Geneva—a long, narrow, fjordlike lake carved out of the hills of southern Wisconsin by a glacier forty thousand years ago. Only the stars shared the early morning hours with him.

It had been said of him when he turned down the scholarship to

Michigan and went to the seminary that the vocation was his mother's, not his. But that did not seem fair either to his family or himself. Mom and Dad would be extremely happy, each in his own way, if he persevered to ordination. But they leaned over backward to grant him freedom in his decision. They were the ones who'd insisted that he go to Fenwick High School instead of the seminary after he had been caught necking with Flossie Mahoney in her basement. He had to "know his own mind," the judge had argued.

He could announce tomorrow that he was leaving the seminary and they would accept his decision, with a few tears from Mom, perhaps, but no recrimination.

Marry a girl like Maria? A wild thought under the starry skies.

They would accept her too. A good, sweet girl, his mother would say.

No, the vocation wasn't his mother's. Insofar as God worked through human beings, the vocation had to be attributed to the demanding religious faith in which he'd been raised, a faith that challenged him to do his best even, indeed especially, when it was difficult.

He thought of the problems when he had been in eighth grade, problems that led him to make up his mind that he had to be a priest. He had fought Marty Crawford in the schoolyard after Marty had called his mother a dirty name. The next week they'd lost to St. Kevin's in a football game because Father Shay, the priest from St. Kevin's, was also the ref and timekeeper and ended the game just before St. Ursula scored the winning touchdown. Hugh had told Father Shay that he was a cheater.

Then Marty was killed in an auto accident after he'd committed a mortal sin with a girl from the public school at Park Nine. At least everyone said they'd committed a mortal sin, and if they had, Marty went straight to hell.

Hugh felt responsible for Marty's death. If he hadn't beaten Marty so badly in the fight he would not have been reckless and stolen the car.

Then he'd kissed Flossie in the Mahoney's basement recreation room, and was taking off her blouse when Mrs. Mahoney caught them. He knew he was going to hell for all eternity, just like Marty. He was so angry at himself he didn't care.

All the problems came to a head at the retreat for the eighth-grade boys. The retreat master was Father Slawson, who used magic tricks and games as part of his instruction—dancing skeletons, exploding boxes, darkened rooms, pictures and diagrams of hell. He told the boys that they were cisterns of filth and that their dirty thoughts would lead them to an eternity of suffering in the deepest flames of hell.

"If you want to avoid hell," he said, "you must follow the call of God and become a priest. God gives everyone a call to the priesthood. He's as generous with his vocations as he is with the rain in the spring, the leaves in the fall, the snow in the winter. You can turn your back on a vocation, you can waste it, you can waste it away. But if you do, you will be consumed by the fires of hell for all eternity. If you wish to be happy forever with God and his angels and saints, you will flee this wicked world and become one of God's chosen priests."

On Friday night of the retreat week, Hugh sat in silence at the Donlons' supper table, pondering Father Slawson's grim words while Timmy, his freckled face twisted in its usual frown of complaint, protested against the fish.

"You should eat the fish even if you don't like it," Peggy told him. "Our Lord didn't want to die on the cross, but He did it anyway. The things that are hard to do are always the things that are best to do."

"Jesus didn't have to eat this fish." Tim pushed his red hair out of his eyes.

"But you do." The judge settled the matter as he would a sentence.

"Jesus could have found a lot easier way to save us from our sins." Peggy pushed her point. "He chose the terrible death of the cross to show us how much He loved us."

Hugh was puzzled. "You didn't marry Dad because it was the hardest thing to do, did you?"

The judge chuckled and Peggy blushed. "It's my purgatory on earth . . . no, seriously." She rested her hand on her husband's. "Your poor father is the one who's the saint for putting up with me. It's love that matters, the only thing that matters. When love says do something hard, then you do it. When love gives you a fine husband"—she smiled at Tom— "then you thank God for your good fortune."

"Can I have some more peas?" Margie, a pretty second grader with curly brown hair and wide brown eyes, interrupted on her favorite subject, food.

"What's for dessert?" asked Tim.

"No fish, no dessert," his mother said adamantly.

Tim looked as if he were going to cry, then remembered his mother's oft-repeated dictum "Donlons don't cry" and poked disconsolately at his fish.

That night Hugh decided he would certainly be a priest.

Older now, he knew that Father Slawson had exaggerated. Yet he also believed that to be an "alter Christus"—an Other Christ—was the most perfect thing a human being could do. It was a tough challenge. Responding to tough challenges made you a man, like his father.

So he would be a priest not because his mother and father wanted him to be a priest but because it was the most noble way of proving that he was a manly human being, brave enough and strong enough to give up appealing young women even if they set you on fire when they brushed against you in the waters of the lake.

You don't run away from them, Hugh told the skeptical stars, you resist the temptation.

Maria lay on the bed, hands clasped behind her head, listening to the crickets, the water lapping the shore, Marge's gentle breathing. Her friend had spilled out a story of passionate lovemaking after *Three Coins in a Fountain* and then quickly and easily fallen asleep. Marge would probably go all the way before the summer was over. Most likely without a twinge of guilt. How had such pious parents produced a daughter like Marge, who apparently had no morals, and a son like Tim, who was always in trouble for drinking or stealing or cheating?

And what was she doing as the guest of this convoluted Irish family, which had adopted her for the summer? She was, Peggy had insisted to Maria's mother, a good influence on Margie. Yet Maria's parents, whom she adored and who adored her, were dismayed by the invitation, because they feared their daughter would be moving into a situation that was way beyond her. On the other hand, like everyone else in St. Ursula's, they thought the Donlons were outranked only by the archangels, so they'd agreed.

Maria did not know what to think of the stern but gentle judge, who seemed to laugh whenever she spoke, and his gorgeous wife, who sometimes seemed to like Maria more than she did her own daughter. Uncertain how to act, Maria set out to charm them by her fun-loving, carefree manner. Beneath her laughter, however, there was a shrewd, calculating Sicilian mind, one that operated by feel, hunch, and occasional leaps of insight. She was not a rationalist like her Irish friends who made up plausible though self-deceiving explanations for the crazy things they did. Maria inched her way down the street of life, in the dark, taking only the chances that her instincts said were worth taking.

Marge was her best friend and Maria earned them the reputation of being the funniest girls in the class. Yet Maria knew that she was four or five years more grown-up than Marge.

There was a lot she could learn from the Donlons, her instincts told her, and maybe a little bit she could do for them. So she hid her bubble gum and listened carefully to the way the Donlons talked. She imitated their manners, not because she expected anything from them but because it seemed sensible to adjust herself to their life as long as she was their guest.

Hugh required more than adjustment, she realized. There was a frightening power in those eyes, a fire of barely concealed desire. When other men looked at her that way she felt dirty. When Hugh considered her as a woman . . . she shivered. She felt like a woman.

Was he really going to be a priest? Could a man become a priest and still ignite electric currents inside her?

Would not such a man make a terrible mistake if he tried to do without a woman?

Maria was a realist about her future. In a year she would be out of high school, working probably at the West End Bank, whose president was a customer of her father's. In another year or two she would be married, a prospect she didn't find especially appealing. She had almost no social life, despite Marge's attempts to push her into one. None of the boys she knew from a distance appealed to her, neither the rich kids from Fenwick who occasionally danced with her at Trinity mixers or the slick, sleek young men from the old neighborhood of whom her uncles and cousins spoke approvingly. They were not the kind of men with whom she would want to share a life or, she shuddered, a bedroom.

Hugh Donlon was different. He was throat-catchingly beautiful, six-one, broad shoulders, strong muscles, and with the graceful movements of the dancers she had seen in the movies. His thick black hair and pale skin, much like his mother's, and the sad eyes and quick smile reminded her of a preternaturally masculine angel.

"Shut up, heart," she whispered under her breath. "You'll wake up everyone in the house!"

She couldn't drive him out of her thoughts. He had been the towering hero of the neighborhood through the last years of grammar school and the four years at Fenwick. It was expected that he would go to Quigley Seminary, but his parents and Monsignor "Muggsy" Brannigan said he should have a normal adolescence and attend Fenwick, like the other boys from the parish. He'd done his best to keep a low profile. He'd refused to run for class office and stayed away from football and basketball because the judge was afraid too much success too young might "turn his head" and because his mother was afraid he would be hurt on the football field.

It didn't work. In his junior year he was elected class president by acclamation against his will and dragged out to football practice. As a senior he'd led the Friars through an up and down season to the city playoff at Soldiers Field against an awesomely powerful Austin High School team—a "West Side grudge match," it was called. Fenwick was outweighed, outcoached, and outplayed. Yet they had held Austin to a 6–0 lead for three quarters, the touchdown coming on a block of one of Hugh's many punts.

Maria remembered that game as if it had been the day before yesterday. A frantic sixth grader, she and her father watched the game from behind the goalpost. Some men who were sitting near them blamed Fenwick's coach for trying to beat Austin at their own game instead of "letting Donlon throw the ball." Maria hated the Fenwick coach with all her heart.

Then at the beginning of the fourth quarter, Hugh had to punt from his own goal line again. The men said it was time for a fake kick. If he broke beyond the Austin line, there would be no one to stop him. They also said that the Fenwick coach would never let him do it.

The ball was snapped and the Austin team swarmed in on Hugh

again, trying for another blocked punt. There was no time to kick the ball. As soon as he caught the snap, Hugh ran sharply to the right, dodged a massive Austin end, and took off down the sidelines. A hundred thousand people, most of them teen-agers, stormed to their feet, shouting encouragement or dismay. Maria couldn't see over the heads of the big people in front of her. Her last glimpse of the field was a golden jersey closing in on Hugh's streaking black. Her father, who knew how much she adored Hugh, boosted her to his shoulder, in time for her to see the black shirt cross the goal line.

Fenwick's kicker, who had such poor eyesight he could barely see the goalpost, kicked the extra point. Hugh, who had held for the kick, walked slowly off the field as the crowd shouted its approval. Fenwick's coach seemed displeased.

Maria hated him still more.

Fenwick won 7–6 and Kerry Regan, who was Hugh's steady, claimed that they went all the way that night. Maria did not believe it. Not Hugh.

He was offered athletic scholarships to Michigan and Harvard, but not to Notre Dame. Instead he went to the seminary and disappeared from sight.

But he'd never completely disappeared from Maria's thoughts. When she and Marge became close friends in their freshman year at Trinity, she bombarded her with questions about her brother who was going to be a priest. She knew other boys in the neighborhood who wanted to be priests, but they were not like Hugh. And she had never met anyone like the Donlons.

Yes, the Donlons were fascinating, passionate, and mysterious. And Hugh was the greatest of their mysteries.

Okay, do You *really* want him to be a priest?

If You don't, do You mind if I fall in love with him?

Again no answer. Maria gave up and went to sleep.

CHAPTER
THREE

1954

The next morning, in the clear light of another sizzling, humid day, Hugh felt foolish about his worries under the stars of the night before. Maria was, after all, a giggly teen-ager like his sister, beautiful, yes, in an understated way, but nothing to worry about. When it was decided that he was to take the two of them to the tennis courts, he did not object. At the courts Marge quickly abandoned them and sped off in Joe Delaney's Impala convertible—a plotted rendezvous, Hugh decided in disgust at his sister's flagrant violation of family rules about going steady.

He was left with Maria, a stunning vision in white halter and tennis shorts, borrowed from Marge.

Not all that understated.

Maria was graceful and quick on her feet, but no match for him, even though he spotted her thirty points a game. Yet she managed to win two games of the first seven, taking savage delight in beating him.

The day was ferociously hot and soon the sweat was pouring off both their bodies. Hugh removed his soaking shirt.

"Not fair," Maria shouted from the other side of the court, "trying to distract me. Afraid I'll beat you?"

"You're a fine one to talk about distractions," he yelled back.

She won the first point of their eighth game by returning his best serve, in a lucky mis-hit that sent her into fits of laughter. With her two-point handicap, she led forty-love, and Hugh had to struggle for each of the next four points because Maria, driven to a frenzy by the excitement of the final game, raced around the court like a dervish, making unconscious and impossible returns.

At set point, his first serve was long and he followed with a pow-der puff. Maria banged it into the net.

She threw her racket into the air and caught it. "You cheat, Irish, and if you dare jump over the net, I hope you fall on your face. I'm a poor loser."

"I think you're a great sport." He walked confidently to the net to shake her hand.

"Why didn't you give me three points . . . ?"

As their hands touched, time stood still for Hugh.

He leaned over the net and kissed her, his lips brushing her cheek, and then her waiting lips.

She was inexperienced and nervous, hardly ever kissed before. He put his arms around her and drew her head to his chest, sweat-ing young body against sweating young body. His hands felt the smooth skin of her back. Then he kissed her again, gently so as not to frighten her.

"Am I glad I didn't win!" she sighed contentedly.

You must look like an adoring little simp, Maria Angelica; you have no pride or dignity at all.

All right, I don't. I'm sorry, but he's gorgeous in his swimming trunks at the tiller of a sailing dory. On the water he seems so free and happy—not tied down to all those silly obligations that come from being a Donlon.

They had sailed for three hours in Hugh's trim little sailboat, the *Pegeen*. Maria had learned that the "sheet" was not the sail, but the rope that held the sail; that when he shouted "Ready about" she was supposed to loosen the jib sheet; and that when he shouted "Hard a lee" she was supposed to let it go and jump to the other side of the tiny craft and grab the other jib sheet, port or starboard, depending.

She knew she would never learn the difference between "port" and "starboard."

She fell over the side only once—when the boom hit her—and

thoroughly soaked her black Fenwick shirt (which she wore because he liked it) and white bermudas.

Hugh dragged her back into the boat and warned her sternly about watching the boom.

She insisted he'd never told her what the boom was and she laughed at his impatience. She also laughed every time he gave an order and promptly replied "Yes, sir" or "No, sir," as if she were a midshipman in *Mutiny on the Bounty.*

Then Hugh laughed with her and seemed to revel all the more in the freedom and joy of the *Pegeen* dancing on the waves.

"Why are you looking at me so oddly?" he asked, a faint flush on his face—at least his face seemed redder than the sun had made it.

"You've been looking at me oddly since I got my clothes wet," she replied.

"That's only admiration. . . ." His flush increased. "You're looking at me like . . . like a gambler, a countess in a gambling casino."

"All the Sicilian countesses are dead." She decided to tell the unvarnished truth. "I was admiring you . . . the way you seem so free and happy out here on the lake . . . kind of flowing along with the wind and the water and everything. I think right now you're the real Hugh Donlon."

He turned away, embarrassed, a second grader praised by his nun. Hugh Donlon shy and embarrassed. Wow, Maria.

"You see too much with those dancing blue eyes, young woman. You're right, though . . . the wind, the water, the sail, the tiller, my hand on the rope. . . ."

"Sheet. . . ."

"All right." He laughed delightedly. "I feel as if I'm part of God's creation out here, not pulling the world together but just fitting into place with the tiller and the sheet. You can laugh. I won't be mad."

And on shore you're trying to hold the whole world together. "I've already embarrassed you, so I won't embarrass you anymore, except by saying that you're beautiful when you're doing that."

He smiled, a gentle, modest smile, released the tiller, took her chin in his hand, kissed her gently, ran his hand lightly down her throat and over a Fenwick-covered breast, and recaptured the tiller—a smooth quick movement like that of a practiced dancer.

"Thank you, Maria." He sounded choked. "I'm glad you like me when I'm happy."

A legion of emotions raced through Maria's brain, all of them conspiring to make her light-headed. "I'll never settle for less," she said, and cursed herself for being a silly little fool. Silly lovesick little fool.

After Hugh skillfully brought the *Pegeen* into its slip on the other side of the pier from the diving board, he gave Maria a lesson in how canvas sails should be folded and packed. Hot, tired, and still light-headed, Maria was a bad pupil. The canvas slipped out of her hands and fell on the lawn.

"That's not the way to do it," he snapped. "Come on, Maria, you can do better."

Adoration turned to fury. Maria went into what her mother called "the Mount Aetna act."

"Don't you ever dare say anything like that to me again," she screamed at him. "I am not a summer camper, nor a slave girl, nor a kid in catechism class, nor a poor old nun in a sacristy, nor a housekeeper, nor an adoring Altar Society Woman. . . ."

Hugh collapsed on an old tree stump, laughing deliriously.

"What's so funny?" she demanded, hands jammed defiantly against her hips.

"Me." He grinned sheepishly. "If you're around me for long, Maria, you'll learn that I am a terrible dolt . . . the kind of dummy who spends a wonderful afternoon on a lake with a beautiful girl and then worries about the rules for folding canvas. I hope you'll forgive me. Irish conscience, I suppose. Now I've made you cry. . . ."

"You laugh at yourself often?" she said through the tears, her heart threatening to shatter for the sadness in his eyes.

"Not often enough. Why are you crying?"

"Because you're so wonderful." Maria turned away from him and ran up the lawn toward the house.

The judge stalked angrily out of the cottage as soon as Senator Joseph R. McCarthy appeared on their tiny TV screen. He could not stand the sight of the man. The Democrats would simply have to win the fall congressional elections and take away his committee chair.

He settled in a lounge chair in the shade of their huge oak tree at the foot of the pier and opened a book about late fourteenth-century French poetry. Maria, however, distracted him. Clad in a two-piece blue bathing suit, she was wrestling with Hugh at the other end of the pier. Lucky Hugh, to have such a gorgeous creature to throw into the lake. Young girls normally had little effect on Judge Donlon. Peg was more than enough woman for his life.

But it was a humid, sleepy day; he couldn't take his eyes off the little blond Sicilian, probably Norman or Germanic genes somewhere. And even if her father was a shoemaker, Manfredy was an aristocratic name. The girl had the elegance of a Dresden doll, the drive of a union organizer, and the quick intelligence of a high-priced lawyer for the defense—the kind the Mob employed.

He reproved himself for his ethnic prejudice.

Peg slipped by him, careful not to disturb his concentration on the medieval French—and also careful not to come too close. So great was the attraction between them this summer that they were afraid to touch one another in public.

The white strapless swimsuit with the broad red stripe from hip to opposite breast into which she had poured herself merited Maria's rapt appreciation.

Maria and Peg, he mused to himself, half asleep and half aroused. Such beautiful women. . . .

Hugh abandoned his combat with the little Sicilian and dragged his laughing mother toward the water.

For a moment Tom Donlon saw her nursing the boy in the apartment on Austin Boulevard. . . . He had told her of his "promise" to God after Tom Junior—or Tim, as he came to be called—was born. Peggy had not been impressed. "I dedicated Hugh to Our Lord the moment he stirred inside me," she said.

That had disturbed him. It laid a double burden on the child, and one Peg had imposed with too much innocence.

Marge (Margaret Junior) was the last of their children because there was a hysterectomy at the time of her birth, one the doctor thought necessary, although not as necessary as Tom had told his wife or the lurking Monsignor Clifton O'Meara, who thought the decision ought to be his. Three pregnancies and three miscarriages in seven years had not affected Peg's looks but had worked havoc with her uncertain reproductive system.

Tom regretted the need to deceive his wife. A Jesuit moralist from the seminary had assured him that the operation was justified. Peggy was too much of a child to be trusted with her own decisions in such crucial matters.

She was a wonderful wife, but she would never escape completely the damage done by Maude Curtin.

Hugh finally heaved her into the water, while Maria, who had withdrawn discreetly from the encounter, watched respectfully.

Would Maude Curtin's damage be visited on their own children? Tim and Marge certainly had their problems. And Hugh . . . mightn't he be better off if he left the seminary and took up with a girl like Maria?

At the edge of the pier, Hugh, tall, strong, and solidly muscled, momentarily appeared between the two women, one slender, the other voluptuous, one with short blond hair, the other with long black hair. The two women seemed to be fighting for him, one in the name of an overarching God, the other in the name of young love. Tom knew which one would win. He was not sure that she ought to win or that her victory would make her happy for very long.

There was conspiring at the end of the pier. Then the judge saw three attackers creeping toward him, a beautiful wife, a lovely girl, and his handsome son. Tom Donlon had never in his life been thrown into the lake. But, however much an affront such an attack was to the dignity of the federal judiciary, he'd come quietly.

Well, maybe a little struggle. For symbolic purposes. On a humid summer resort day, when two attractive women were tugging at you, symbols were quite important.

He carefully placed the French book under his chair. No reason to get it wet.

Maria was helping Peg set the table for supper, something she did routinely, without being asked, much to Marge's chagrin.

Marge and her mother had fought again earlier in the afternoon. Peg wondered whether it was "healthy" for Marge to see only Joe Delaney. There were so many other "nice boys" at Geneva this summer. "Can't you spend one night at home, and eat supper with us . . . ? Hugh's here for the first time this summer. And you have a guest. Don't you think you could help me prepare dinner occasionally?"

"You don't need me," Marge snapped. "Maria does all the housewife work. She likes it."

"Leave me out of your fights," Maria said quickly.

"You can't fight with my mother," Marge sulked. "She's too pious to fight. Just like Hugh. You'd think they were both priests."

"Don't say such wicked things," Peggy pleaded. "Why can't we have a little peace in this house? Why do you fight me all the time?"

"You bring it on yourself," Marge shouted, rushing out of the house in response to Joe Delaney's imperious horn.

Marge was spoiled. She fought ceaselessly with her parents, who loved her, and with Hugh, whom she worshiped as a big brother. She seemed to be hooked on fighting the way some men were hooked on drink.

When Marge staged her explosions, Maria slipped out of sight and hummed opera tunes to herself.

"You Italians are a happy, carefree people," Peggy said, remembering the mischief of tossing a fully clad judge of the Seventh Circuit into the waters of Lake Geneva.

"Not really." Maria interrupted the aria she'd been humming. "My father says we're a morose and fate-haunted people who try to pretend we're great lovers and singers and dancers."

"You don't pretend, Maria."

The girl had been puzzled the first day about the role of salad forks and horrified by the absence of wineglasses. She could not understand Peggy's grim opposition to "the creature." Still, she was a quick and discreet imitator. And could make fun of herself by joking about "potato forks, meat forks, vegetable forks, and, Peggy, *dessert* forks."

Peggy was "Mrs. Donlon" when others were around and "Peggy" privately. Instead of being offended, Peg was somehow flattered.

"That's because my mom and dad are really happy. We're exceptions, I think."

Back to the aria.

I like the poor thing. Why does she have to be a threat to Hugh's vocation? Why doesn't she go after Tim?

"Don't your parents want you to go to college? You're very smart; I'm sure you'd do well."

Maria considered, her expressive face in one of its rare interludes of thoughtfulness. "They'd be proud of me, I suppose, and they'd make any sacrifice. But I don't see the point. I can read books and listen to music without going to college."

Peggy had visited the shoemaker's shop to persuade Maria's mother to let her come to Lake Geneva. The mother was a very attractive but very shy woman in her midthirties who treated Peggy like royalty. It was a difficult conversation, because Paola spoke little English.

Yet she'd granted Peggy's request without the slightest loss of dignity.

"You'll probably marry quite young, then?"

Maria arranged the coffee cups. "Only if someone like the judge sweeps me off my feet."

They both laughed. "Brought it on myself," Peggy admitted.

Merciful heaven, I like her better than Marge. Such an appealing little body too. *Grandchildren.*

"Actually, I think I'll do what my father did and go to Italy to find myself a spouse. Someone handsome and quiet who will laugh at me all the time and do what I tell him."

"I think that few men would not want to."

Maria blushed. "Thank you," she said simply.

The girl was a threat to God's holy will.

Yet how could God object to someone so sweet?

"You look like you're angry at me." Dressed in a crisp white blouse and neatly pressed pink bermuda shorts, with a matching ribbon in her hair, Marge was leaving again with Joe Delaney, driving to Delevan for a dance. "Figure you're failing in your responsibilities to be a stabilizing influence on me?"

"You're a spoiled little bitch," Maria said bluntly.

"Okay, I've heard Hugh's lecture. Now I'll listen to yours."

"You adore Hugh, he's your wonderful big brother, that's what you've always told me."

It was dusk and the mosquitoes were beginning to bite, the fireflies to glow.

"You think I should drop Joe like the rest of them do." Her lower lip turned down in a childish pout.

"I think you should be nice to your family," Maria insisted, her own temper, normally as quiescent as a dormant volcano, sending up warning signals.

"You wouldn't if you were me. . . . Don't worry, my mother knows you're trying to stabilize me. Anyway, she likes you more than she does me."

Marge turned and ran toward the Delaney Cadillac, not permitting Maria a chance to blow.

So she walked over to the pier and cried instead . . . till the mosquitoes drove her into the house.

For a time, God, seminary, vocation, Father Meisterhorst, ceased to exist. Only Maria, Maria of the waiting lips and the submissive body. They kissed whenever they could, in the car, on the pier when no one was looking, in the water as he taught her to swim, outside the dance hall at the amusement pier in town, in the parlor of the cottage when they were alone, in the motorboat on the lake, in the back of the movie theater.

They ignored his parents and indeed everyone else in the adult world. They existed only for the sweet taste of each other's lips, the endearing touch of each other's hands, the warmth of each other's encircling arms.

The ritual dance of his high school years, in which young men and women fought a tug-of-war about where the line was to be drawn, was impossible with Maria. She drew no lines. He was the one who had to draw the line of tenderness and respect.

Then the seminary intruded itself, unannounced and unwanted.

They had watched *Three Coins in a Fountain* in rapt wonder, its sentimental romanticism matching their mood perfectly. He had caressed her leg lightly throughout the film and she had huddled in his arm as though her continued existence depended on his protection.

They had emerged from the theater into the humid night wrapped in a haze of dreamlike passion, she especially lovely in white bermuda shorts and a black Fenwick T-shirt that hung lightly against her breasts.

"Hello, Hugh." It was a chillingly familiar voice. "That wasn't the Rome I studied in, worse luck for me."

It was Father John Xavier Martin, a young professor of canon law from the seminary, one of the few diocesan priests on the mostly Jesuit faculty.

"Good evening, Father Xav." Hugh had stumbled over the

words, then quickly regained his balance. "Did you throw any coins in the Fontana Trevi?"

His arm was still around Maria. As deftly as he could, he slipped it away.

"Yeah," the young priest said disconsolately. "Hasn't worked so far."

"Uh, Father Martin, this is Maria Manfredy, a classmate of my sister, Marge."

"Hello, Maria." Father Martin pretended to notice her for the first time. "Happy to meet you. Did you go to Fenwick too?"

"I go to Trinity, Father, like Marge Donlon." The words came smoothly, just the right touch of respect for a priest in her voice. "We kind of cheer for Fenwick because there's nothing else around."

"That's the way life is." Father Martin took her in very carefully. "Nice to meet you, Maria . . . Have a good summer, Hugh."

He vanished into the summer night.

"Are you in trouble?" Maria was deadly pale in the glow of the street light.

"Nothing I can't talk my way out of if I have to," he said with more confidence than he felt.

Marge could hardly wait to get home and tell Maria about her triumph. Maria was the only one who understood her, the only one who cared, the only one who realized what a drag it was to be stuck with such dull, lifeless people as her parents.

She loved them, of course. They were wonderful people. But they lived by rules and regulations. They had no fun, no good times, no excitement. How had they managed to work up enough passion to conceive three children?

And Hugh, dear boy, was so pious, even though he didn't believe any of the stuff, not really. Tim was the only one in the family with any life and they were driving him to a head doctor.

No head doctor for Marge. She would split as soon as she could and sneak fun in the meantime.

Now that she was no longer a virgin, she thought triumphantly, there would be a lot more fun. Mom would be furious if she found out. What the hell did she think sexual organs were for?

Maria disapproved. But Maria understood. Indeed, when she

was preparing to go all the way with Joe Delaney she thought of it as a kind of travelogue she could celebrate with Maria.

Actually, it wasn't much. Joe was clumsy and crude. Unbutton the blouse, pull down the shorts, rip at the underwear, fondle me, get inside me, lay all over me like I was a water float, and then scream like a maniac. There's got to be more to it than that.

She had not particularly enjoyed her deflowering and now she hurt.

Well, it was done, anyhow. Out of the way. That's what counted.

Still, she'd make a big production out of it for Maria; give the pious little frump some thrills.

"See you tomorrow night?" Joe asked hungrily as she jumped out of the car.

"Maybe," she said curtly.

Maria, dressed in shorty pajamas, was sitting up in bed reading. She turned to Marge as she charged into the room, her face anguished by anxiety and love.

Marge fell into her arms and wept bitterly.

CHAPTER
FOUR

1954

Hugh's parents were painfully aware of the romance. He drove with them every morning to the eight o'clock Mass in the little church on the hills above Fontana and continued to receive Holy Communion, because, despite what Father Meisterhorst would say, he did not think he and Maria were sinning seriously. Then they would return to the cottage for breakfast before the two girls awoke. Dad would leave for the golf course, Mom would retreat to the gazebo converted into a studio for her watercolors, and he would sit in the parlor, read some passages from Abbot Marmion, without comprehending any of the words, and labor through a chapter of *The Lord of the Flies* before the girls appeared and the day began.

The judge and Peggy had spoken of their fears only once.

The morning after their meeting with Martin, on the way home from Mass, his father began tentatively, "Maria is a very lovely young woman."

"We feel responsible . . ." his mother said.

"Nothing to feel responsible about, Mom. Maria and I are having a good time together. Neither of us thinks it's going to last. I'll go back to Mundelein and she'll go back to Trinity. We'll both have pleasant memories for years to come. That's all."

The judge tried another tack as he brought the three-hole Buick to a halt in the driveway behind the cottage. "If you should decide to leave the seminary, Maria might be an ideal young woman to, uh . . . court. She and you seem to balance each other very nicely."

"We like her very much," his mother insisted. "We don't want to interfere with your decision or with God's will."

Hugh laughed easily. "It's not going to go that far. Can't I have a short summer romance without you thinking about grandchildren?"

Peg started to say something, then stopped.

Later that morning, after the judge had left for the golf course and his mother had retreated to the gazebo, Hugh sat in the parlor, waiting for the girls to come down for breakfast. As he reread the same page from Marmion for the third time, he reprimanded himself. It was not as easy as he'd pretended to his parents. He was in love with Maria. It was a passing summer love, no doubt, but also an exhilarating and disturbing love. He was breaking seminary rules, risking heartache for himself and for her, needlessly worrying his parents. He was both reckless and irresponsible. He couldn't stop.

He didn't want to stop.

Tim was more blunt than Mom and Dad. "Hey, does that Manfredy dish put out for you? Most Guinea girls do. I bet she's terrific!"

"She doesn't and we're just friends," Hugh replied hotly. As much as he liked Tim, or thought he did, he was offended by his incorrigible cynicism. In Tim's world nothing was straight. He conned professors at Notre Dame to give him an A or a B even though the con job took more time and effort than study. He lied to girls when it was as easy to tell them the truth. He cheated in tests even though he knew the answers without cheating. That was the way life was with Tim.

"Get it while you can, brother," Tim advised as they drove from the train stop at Williams Bay.

There was no point in arguing with Tim or being angry at him. "Go easy on the booze this weekend, will you?" Hugh said, changing the subject. "You know how Mom and Dad worry."

"I know." Tim sounded genuinely sorry. "I guess I do like it a little too much. But you gotta kill the pain of school. Once I escape from the damn classroom, I'll settle down."

Tim was the smartest of the three Donlons and, when he set his mind to it, the most charming. Only he didn't set his mind to it very often. He was too busy devising some new piece of kinkiness.

Girls thought Tim Donlon was cute—a thin little redhead with a freckle-drenched face and an appealing grin, he seemed to them to be a "perfect Irish leprechaun." His good humor, quick tongue, and ready wit confirmed the leprechaun image.

So he was much more successful with girls than were other Notre Dame freshmen with better looks and more athletic ability.

Tim for his part had learned how to get the most out of a young woman with the least effort. There were ways of necking and petting that gave a girl what she wanted and left her pretty much at his disposal.

Maria obviously liked him. She bantered with him more than she did with Hughie. Since she was probably putting out for Hugh, why not for him too?

It was a risk but that made it all the more fun.

So, driving over to the grocery in Fontana, he made his move. Poor Mom, I'm doing exactly what she wants, taking the girl's mind off Hugh.

She wasn't a bad kisser, either. Hugh had warmed her up nicely.

But then she struggled to escape from his arms, tears in those warm blue eyes.

You win some and you lose some.

"I wouldn't hurt you for the world, Maria," he said apologetically.

"I didn't say it wasn't nice." She rearranged her peasant blouse.

He laughed. "I like you, Maria, I really do." And that was the honest truth.

"Why are you always in trouble, Tim"—she was good at setting up defenses too—"stealing the chalice from the sacristy, taking the money from the parish carnival, getting caught with the beer at Notre Dame? What would you do with the chalice? And you don't need the money, do you? And I bet you didn't drink any of the beer."

"Not that beer, anyway." He laughed. "I don't know. But I can tell you what the head doctor says. He says I'm a thrill-seeker."

"Head doctor?" She seemed astonished that there was such a thing.

"Sure. If a Donlon has trouble, he goes first to the priest, then to the psychiatrist. You know the Bobs at Riverview? The most dangerous ride in the park? I ride them all day when I'm there. Nothing else is any fun."

"Do you *have* to?" she asked softly.

"No, not till I get on them. Then I can't get off."

"I don't understand." She sounded as if she were trying to grasp a theorem in math class.

"Remember the time I stole the chalice from the church over in Fontana? You know what I mean. I'm sure Marge told you all about it. I mean, they left it there in the sacristy, just asking for it to be stolen. And I jimmied the window one Sunday night and took it out. They didn't even notice the marks on the windowsill. Vanished into thin air." Timmy chuckled, remembering the expression on Monsignor Schultz's face.

"You *had* to take it?"

"I wanted it so bad I dreamed about it at nights, not because I would do anything with it and not because I needed it but because it was there to be taken. I would have been all right if I hadn't had to look at it on the altar during Mass. Then one Sunday it was too much. I had to have it, like riding the Bobs."

"Oh. . . . Did you feel good after you took it?"

"Kind of proud, for being so slick. But the real fun is actually doing it . . . and laughing at comic characters like old man Schultz. I was going to give it back. . . ."

"And then you were caught, much to your mother's distress."

"That's what the head doctor says."

"What?"

Tim glanced at her, at the opposite end of the front seat of the family Buick. God damn Hugh; why did he always have to get the best? Oh, well, that's the way it always was and always would be.

"The head doctor says I do it because my mother tells me not to."

"She never tells Hugh not to, does she?"

Too damn smart.

"I don't hurt anyone," he said.

Hugh and Maria were floating aimlessly on the Donlon Chris-Craft in the middle of the lake, under a ceiling of closely crowded stars, after watching Audrey Hepburn in *Roman Holiday*. They drove in the boat to Geneva town because it was more private and more romantic than a car, even if it did cause a faint lift of his mother's eyebrow when they walked down to the pier in the purple twilight.

After the movie, they visited the dance hall where Maria had sung "Buttons and Bows" for the cheering young people, and played at the pinball machines in the arcade on the amusement pier.

Now they were relaxing in the front seat of the boat, one of his arms around her shoulders, and the other at rest on her belly over the Fenwick T-shirt, which had become a kind of uniform, washed fastidiously every night before she went to bed.

"Wouldn't it be nice to float here forever?" he said contentedly.

"Marry me," she replied.

"Huh?" Hugh sat up, surprised, his hand retreating quickly from her stomach.

"I don't mean now." She was still passive in his arm. "I mean next year when I graduate from high school."

"You're too young to marry, Maria." A frigid terror crept into his veins despite the warmth of the night.

"I'll be as old as your mother was when she married the judge."

God, help me not to hurt her. "I can't imagine a better wife. . . ."

"I'm a great cook, and I'll be good in bed once I learn how, and I'll give you lots of cute babies and I'll be beautiful when I'm old like my mother is, and I'll learn to read books, and I won't embarrass you too much, and I'll love you always and I'll make you happy every day of your life."

"There would never be an unhappy day, or a dull one either." He edged out of their embrace. "But I'm going to be a priest, Maria."

"No, you're not," she said confidently. "You like women too much."

"We don't give up women because we don't like them, Maria." He shifted uneasily in the damp leather seat.

"Some men like women and can give them up. I guess it's a good idea. . . . You're not one of them, Hugh. You like us too much. You . . . you drink me in as if I were a cool glass of lemonade on a hot day."

"I don't mean to humiliate you." He laughed nervously.

"Who's humiliated? I love it. Any woman would. And you look

at every attractive woman that way. I saw you taking in that man's wife at the ice cream stand tonight. She was real old . . . at least thirty. . . . You won't be able to get along without one of us. I'll make the sacrifice." She laughed. "And be the one."

"You're wrong, Maria," he said slowly, wondering whence came her quick, sure insights.

"I'm right," she replied pleasantly. "The point is that you're in the seminary because of your family. If you had your own way, you'd be hunting for a wife."

"My family isn't forcing me." He retreated from her to the safety of the steering wheel of the Chris-Craft.

"They've persuaded you that you're free. They think you are. And you think you are. You're not, though. You know it will please the judge, especially if you're some kind of intellectual priest. And it will make Peg deliriously happy. And . . . now don't start this boat till I'm finished . . . and you'll satisfy the crazy Donlon notion that if something is hard, maybe impossible, then it has to be what God wants. And if it's something that's fun and will make you happy, then it has to be sinful."

"I have to start the motor, so we don't drift into Black Rock."

He turned over the engine and at slow speed pointed the boat back toward the middle of the lake, searching his heart for a response to her furious assault. I love you, Maria, even when you're angry. Especially when you're angry. "But if you're called to be a priest," he said finally, "you have to ask whether you dare turn down God's invitation. Happiness is irrelevant."

Maria exploded. "That's the worst thing I've ever heard in my life. I'm not as good a Catholic as you Donlons maybe, but I know God wants us to be happy. If you become a priest because you think you have to, Hugh, you're not doing what God wants."

"I am too," he snapped, trying to control his own anger.

"And it's not just the priesthood either." She jabbed his chest with an imperious finger. "Even if you weren't going to be a priest, you still wouldn't marry me. You'd be afraid I'd make you be Hugh Donlon on the sailboat, filled with joy and life . . . and love."

Hugh felt as if someone had opened a door inside him and let in a tiny sliver of light.

He slammed the door shut. "You're just being a romantic," he said, as something wonderful and terrifying faded away into the dark.

CHAPTER
FIVE

1954

One has to lose one's virginity sometime, Maria supposed. It might as well be with Hugh Donlon. He wouldn't hurt her, the way Joe Delaney had hurt poor Marge. Yet she was frightened as the red and white Buick bumped down the back road under a frowning gray sky. Clear-eyed about herself as always, Maria knew that her innocence and inexperience might make her act foolishly. She would keep her steady patter of wisecracks going till the last minute and then fall apart.

I hope you understand, God. I don't think You'll send me to hell. You do want me to love him, don't You?

The Lord had no comment.

A silly raspberry-picking expedition. "Len Mulloy has a couple of hundred acres of woods up there that they use for hunting. Even has a hunting lodge. He told us we could bootleg his raspberries."

All I want is that he love me a little longer.

And the worried look on poor Peg's face as they drove off. She knows lust when she sees it, that woman. We're rivals for you, my darling. She wants you for God and I want you for me.

Why can't I hate her?

And why do I love you so much?

There was no wind when they parked at the end of the twin ruts and hiked into the woods. But by the time their baskets were almost filled with the succulent red fruit and their fingers smeared with the juice, a stiff breeze was blowing through the tops of the trees and low clouds were scudding across the patches of sky above them. Maria shivered. It was turning cold.

"It's going to rain," she warned.

"No, it isn't, the weather forecast said the front wouldn't come through till tonight. Let's fill this last basket."

"All right, it's not going to rain. Heaven forbid that the forecast be wrong."

They plunged farther into the woods and filled the last bucket. A few raindrops were falling on their faces, then the drops turned into a torrent, quickly soaking them to the skin.

"It's not raining," she shouted over the wind. "Just a figment of my superstitious southern Italian imagination."

"Let's make a run for the hunting lodge," he shouted back in high good humor. "It's up this way, I think."

The rain fell in great billowing gray sheets; lightning darted across the sky and leaped occasionally into the woods. The wind howled through the treetops.

The rain was cold and Maria shivered as they dashed blindly about the woods, water streaming into their eyes and down their faces.

"Front's coming through tomorrow."

Breathless and battered, they stumbled into a clearing and, fruit baskets still banging against their legs, rushed across the open space to the door of the hunting lodge. Hugh fiddled with a number of keys and then threw the door open. Inside there were a couple of rustic couches and some old tables and chairs and a tattered rug thrown on the floor. The room smelled of mildew and disinfectant.

"You're soaking wet," Hugh said.

"Can't be. The front isn't coming till tonight."

He rummaged through a linen closet and found two beach towels. "Wrap this around yourself," he ordered, throwing her one. "I'll build a fire to warm us and dry out our clothes."

"Yes, master."

In the bathroom, Maria peeled off her clothes, and critically considered the young woman in the dark mirror. Almost as if you'd planned it this way, Maria Angelica. She folded the towel around herself and, appraising the short blond hair plastered down on her skull, ordered her heart to stop pounding. It refused to obey.

He's kidding himself about what will happen. I'm not.

So which one of us is worse? She took a deep breath and returned to the parlor.

A fire was already crackling in the fireplace. The room smelled of pitch and smoke, like a bonfire of autumn leaves. Clever boy scout, my man.

His towel tied at his waist, Hugh was making instant coffee on an ancient electric grill.

He handed her a cup. "I was wrong about the rain." He smiled apologetically.

"At least you provided a desert island with all the comforts of home."

He was thoughtful for a moment. Then his face turned quizzical, then hard and determined. Maria was frightened.

"What . . . ?" she said.

He stood up, took the coffee out of her hand, and lifted her to her feet, examining her as if she were a work of art he was about to bid on. His fingers touched the towel knotted under her shoulder and it dropped to the floor.

She didn't move, frozen in a mixture of fear, shame, and desire. He continued to examine her gravely, respectfully.

Then his fingers began to explore her face, as if the rest of her could wait until later, carefully examining her cheeks, chin, eyes, nose, lips, wet blond hair.

Maria gave herself to him.

His hands crept down her throat and neck and his lips followed where his fingers had prepared the way. Lightly he touched her shoulders, her back, her chest, and then with infinite delicacy her breasts, first one and then the other, encircling them as if they might break under the pressure of his touch.

"Oh, God, yes," Maria moaned as his lips relentlessly followed his fingers.

"Pretty, pretty," he murmured.

A languid peace suffused her flesh. All would be well. She would not fail.

They teetered on the brink. She waited expectantly to topple over the side with him.

Then, with a convulsive spasm, Hugh twisted away, fell on the rustic couch behind him, and buried his head in its pillows.

Maria stood above him, motionless as a statue, conscious of the firelight caressing the smooth contours of her body. Then she picked up the towel, wrapped it around herself once again, and sat on the edge of a chair across the room.

Hugh did not speak, did not move.

Maria waited.

"I'm sorry," he said at last in a choked voice.

"I'm not angry, nor hurt, nor humiliated, nor anything like that."

Surprisingly, she was not.

Another long wait. And Maria thought, all right, up there, You really taught me a lesson. Someday I'll thank You. But not now.

"The rainstorm we didn't have isn't here anymore," she said finally.

He didn't look up from the pillows. "Will you go down to the car and wait for me? I won't be long."

"Yes," Maria said softly. "I'll wait as long as you want."

Her clothes were still damp as she put them on in the bathroom. At the doorway of the lodge she paused. "I'm taking half the raspberries. Don't forget the rest."

Rain was still dripping from the trees as she trudged through the mud and water back down the path to the red and white Buick waiting, wet and indignant, at the end of the ruts. A typical summer storm, sudden, fierce, and over in an instant.

Hugh and his father drove Maria to the train station in Walworth on Sunday night to catch the Milwaukee Road to Chicago and the three rooms in the back of the shoemaker's shop on Division Street. Peggy was meeting with a committee planning the Lake Geneva Art Fair, Marge was having dinner at the Delaney house, and a sober Tim was at Notre Dame trying to arrange for his readmission.

Hugh was at the wheel of the lumbering Buick, his father next to him in the front seat. Maria was in the back, as vivacious as ever, entertaining them in the car with an account of a visit to the "old neighborhood"—where her life still had its emotional roots even though she lived on Division Street—by relatives from Sicily "via the University of Rome."

"My cousin Marco—he's the one from Rome—says to my uncle Geno, he says, 'Don Eugenio, what do you do for culture?'

"No one ever asks Geno this before. So he waves his hand and says, 'Marco, when you own three pizza parlors, who needs culture?'"

The judge didn't approve. "Culture's important, Maria."

"I know it is. That's why I listen to the opera every Saturday afternoon."

"What's your favorite opera, Maria?" the judge asked.

"*Rigoletto*," she said without hesitation. "It's so sad . . . but the poor girl got what she deserved, fooling around with dukes and important people like that."

They arrived at the railroad station.

The Walworth train stations on Sunday nights at the end of the summer were dismal places—husbands returning for a lonely week at the office, families sadly anticipating the end of vacation, older kids going back to jobs in the city and wondering why summers were better when they were fourteen, dust and dirt and the blinding sunlight of day's end, too much luggage, too many people, and the certainty that the train would be late, hot, and crowded.

Maria was wearing a light summer dress, two years old and a bit small. In shorts and slacks she could have passed for a countess. In a badly fitting dress she was a shoemaker's daughter.

They left the car, Hugh carrying her old-fashioned black suitcase. In it, he imagined, was the black Fenwick T-shirt.

"I want to say something to you, young woman." The judge was his most judicial.

"Yes, Your Honor?"

" I admire your loyalty to the old neighborhood and its culture, of which you make fun so lovingly. But the old neighborhood is changing, Maria. We're hiring law clerks from Taylor Street now . . . even one woman applicant this year who was better qualified than all the young men."

"Not a blonde, I hope."

The judge smiled his faint, quick smile. "It has not been my pleasure to meet the young woman. That's beside the point, Maria."

"I understand, Judge Donlon." The train whistle sounded only a few hundred yards away. "You don't want me to get lost between the old old neighborhood and the new old neighborhood . . . to say nothing of the new new neighborhood, where lots of kids growing up in the old old neighborhood will end up living . . . in River Forest." Her eyes filled with the tears she'd been fighting back during the ride.

"Precisely." The judge turned away so that he would not see them.

The yellow and green train huffed into the station and seemed to collapse with a weary sigh.

She embraced both of them, awarding each a fervent kiss on the cheek, clinging a little longer to Hugh. "Don't anyone say anything but good-bye or I'll be a weeper all the way to Chicago." Then she turned quickly and slipped into the crowd pushing toward the train.

"*Arriverderci,* Maria." The words fell softly from Hugh's lips.

On the step of the train she turned, smiled radiantly through her tears, and bid them farewell with a wave of the hand.

The countess again. The countess saying good-bye.

"For reasons I don't want to examine closely," the judge said in the Buick on the way back to Lake Geneva, "she reminds me of your mother at that age."

CHAPTER SIX

1954

Forgetting Maria after he returned to the seminary was much more difficult than Hugh had imagined. He raced through letters from home, hoping for news of her; he imagined the click of her heels on the empty sidewalks outside his window, although he had never seen her in high heels; he dreamed about her at night, fantasized about her through morning meditations, recalled her grin and her laughter during dull theology classes.

He would not, he could not, leave the seminary.

Sheer willpower, however, was not enough to exorcise the girl who followed him down the silent, dark corridors of the seminary residence hall.

In desperation, he turned to his friend Jack Howard. Their roles were now reversed. Hugh had helped Jack through a crisis in his vocation. Now it was Jack's turn. But the short, stocky young man was at a loss.

"It's beyond me, Hugh. Maybe you ought to leave."

"I can't do that. And I can't talk to Meisty or any of the Jebs. They'll report me to the rector and I'll be out on my buns."

"Pat Cleary talked to Xav Martin after you bailed him out of trouble last year, when the rector was going to expel him. He says that Xav is opposed to the whole system here, even if he pretends to go along. He says you can trust Xav to keep his mouth shut."

He had kept his mouth shut so far.

Hugh waited another week. At last the ghost of Maria was beginning to fade. Then he received two letters: a brisk businesslike note from the judge saying that Tim had been caught again with beer in his room and expelled, and one from Tim saying he was joining the Navy and protesting that he hadn't touched the beer but was only smuggling it into the dorm for others.

"The Navy is mostly my idea, Hughie. Mom thinks it will help. You know how the judge dislikes the military. I don't know, maybe it's a good idea to go away for a couple of years. It's not fair that I should be a problem for the rest of you."

Hugh pounded his desk in frustration. No, it wasn't a good idea at all. The Navy wouldn't help Tim. He needed professional assistance. He should never have stopped seeing his psychiatrist.

Fine lot of help I've been to him. More concerned with my own problems than with his. And my problems are mostly imaginary.

That night Hugh made an appointment with Father Martin.

Worried and nervous, he walked on tiptoes into the canon lawyer's room the next night at the end of the after-supper smoking period.

Father Martin waved his hand negligently. He was a lean, black Irishman, a canonical Tyrone Power. "Sit down, Hugh. What's on your mind?"

"The girl you didn't meet when we didn't encounter each other at a movie in Lake Geneva. She's on my mind all the time."

"What girl?" Martin raised his trim eyebrow.

Hugh leaned forward on the edge of his chair. The heat of early September had turned into a serene golden autumn, mellowing the red brick buildings and the vast green lawns of the seminary. The grass outside Father Martin's window seemed to be the same color as Maria's hair.

"The one in the Fenwick T-shirt."

"*That* one." Martin rolled his eyes. "Yes, I remember the T-shirt. I suppose she's worth talking about. Sit down and tell me about her."

Hugh did, at great length and in elaborate detail.

Xav Martin rubbed his cheek, which looked unshaven fifteen minutes after the razor had touched it. "Sounds like you're in love with her, or think you are. . . . Some of us are like that, Hugh. We go from one steamy romance to another. We're always in love. Mostly genes and hormones. It doesn't matter whether we're married or celibate. We're romantics. But the priest romantic doesn't have to jump into bed with his parishioners and the married romantic doesn't have to commit adultery with his secretary. If you're a romantic, life is more interesting and more difficult. Maria is probably the first of many, even if you should leave and marry her. You'll get used to it."

"What should I do?" Hugh pleaded.

"Right now? Nothing. The ghost will go away. Then you can make up your mind whether you want to be a priest."

"I do want to be a priest," Hugh said firmly.

Father Martin studied him intently.

"I do," Hugh insisted.

"Then you'll have to give up Maria."

"I know. . . ."

Hugh talked to Xavier Martin every week for the rest of the semester. Slowly Maria retreated from his consciousness. He did not see her the following summer; another Trinity girl replaced her as the "good influence" on Marge. The judge and Peg did not mention her name. Even Marge had seemed to forget her, although perhaps that was only a kindly pretense.

Maria remained only a memory etched in his brain, never to be completely erased.

CHAPTER SEVEN

1956

"It's for you and it's a boy," Paola yelled from the store, the location of their party-line phone.

Maria leaped up with such enthusiasm that her Introductory Accounting text flew across the room.

"Boys don't call me," she said breathlessly as she dived into the store and grabbed the phone from her smiling mother's hand. "Only one."

"Hello, Maria, I hope I'm not disturbing you."

Maria's heart did several flying turns and ended up in her throat. Hugh.

"Just going out," she lied.

Paola shook her head indulgently and slipped out of the store.

"I won't keep you a minute. . . ."

"I can spare a few." She grabbed one of her father's awls and held it up like a weapon. "How were the raspberries last summer?"

"Same old Maria." His nervous laugh suggested his heart was halfway up his throat too. Maria resolved to be nice. "I'd like to ask for some help."

Was he *leaving* the seminary? "I'll be serious," she promised.

"I'm flying to Las Vegas for part of the winter vacation. Marge is living there now, you know. I wonder if you have any ideas about how I can persuade her to go back to school. She did see you before she left San Francisco with the English dance director."

"When I saw her it was a Brazilian soccer player."

"Oh."

"My advice is don't," Maria said, rushing into the void. "Don't fly to Vegas. Don't try to persuade her to return to school. Don't do anything. She needs time away from the family. The more you folks lean on her, the longer that time will be."

"We love her, Maria."

"She loves you too; but she has to be free of that love for a while. It's the only way she'll ever grow up and leave the spoiled little girl behind."

How can I cry with you over the phone?

"That's harsh."

"Okay, it's harsh. It's also true."

"Maybe you're right. . . . How's the bank?"

"It survives."

"I'm glad to hear it. I hope you'll be able to attend my first Mass. . . ."

"Sure."

You need someone to make you laugh and make you cry, my darling Hugh. Why couldn't it be me?

She said good bye and hung up.

Hugh tried to distract himself from the memory of Maria's voice and the song in her laughter by absorbing every detail of the scenery below on the long flight from Midway Airport to Las Vegas. Calling her had been an impulsive mistake, undoing the hard-won independence of his years-long self-denial.

He hadn't wanted her advice about Marge. Rather, he'd wanted to talk to her, to hear her laughter, to revel in her vitality again.

Now he concentrated on the profligate beauty of the Grand Canyon, which curiously made him feel as if he were in church. He tried to put Maria out of his mind. For heaven's sake, he was only a few months away from the subdeaconate and a promise of perpetual celibacy. What had he been thinking?

The elder Donlons didn't travel much. Highway 12 to Lake Geneva had been enough for his father and mother. But now Tim was touring the world in the Navy, Marge had settled in Las Vegas with a lover, and he was spending half of his two-week winter vacation on a pagan fling in Las Vegas.

A winsome stewardess flirted with him outrageously during the flight, ignoring her other pasengers so she could sit on the armrest of the seat across the aisle from him and swing her lovely legs as she talked about the skiing at Vail, the shows in Vegas, and the surf at La Jolla.

A cute and lively little doll, with a neat figure and long brown hair, the sort of doll you would carry home to mother.

She broadly hinted that she would have time to see him during her two-day layover in Las Vegas.

Would she go to bed with him? Probably. She was looking for a husband. The celibate could not be sure what he was missing. What would it be like to carry this little doll into a bedroom?

After two quarters at Lone Mountain College in San Francisco, Marge had quit school and moved in with an English choreographer—the "English" calculated to be especially offensive to her parents. She refused to go home or to let her parents visit her, or even to talk more than a few minutes with them on the phone.

"I don't hate you," she wept bitterly on one occasion. "I love you terribly. That's why I can't talk to you."

The choreographer moved from San Francisco to Las Vegas, to direct a show at one of the casinos on the Strip. Marge went along as his "assistant," maintaining that she was learning to be a professional dance director, a claim her father said was so patently absurd as not to merit comment.

The judge still thought of Marge as the tousle-haired little girl who had climbed into his lap and stared worshipfully into his eyes. Angry and disgusted, he had wanted to give up on her. Peggy had rebuked him. "She's our daughter and we must stand by her. Maybe she'll change her mind. We must pray to God for her and try to understand where we failed."

Marge was torn between anger and eagerness as she waited at the airport with Larry and her friend Jean Hartmann for Hugh's plane to land.

Oddly enough, she missed Hugh the most. The big brother/little sister relationship had worked well for both of them, except when Hugh felt the urge to be pious. And even then, after delivering his sermons, he relaxed, forgot about them, and became her childhood hero again.

So she desperately wanted to see him.

On the other hand, she was furious with her parents for having sent him to lure her back, especially because she was lonely and more than a little afraid.

Damn it, why can't they leave me alone?

Larry was a dear but not terribly exciting after the first enthusiasms. There were times when he reminded her of her father.

Only he was not as good a choreographer, by a long shot, as her father was a judge. Larry was going nowhere and Marge did not intend to go nowhere with him.

"Why does your brother want to be a priest?" Jean asked.

"Beats me," Marge replied, not wanting to talk about it. "Mom's influence, I suppose; it's one way to keep your son for yourself."

Jean was a last-minute idea. She would distract Hugh from his mission and—who knows?—maybe he would fall for her. That would prevent him from wasting his life as a priest. Marge knew Jean was Hugh's kind of woman.

Like Maria.

Marge felt a pang of guilt. She'd lost touch with Maria. Had not answered any of her letters at Lone Mountain. Did not want to think about Maria's common sense. Or her love.

"Can one be a man and still be a priest?" Larry asked politely. "I should think it would be rather difficult."

"Wait and see," Marge said firmly.

The seat belt sign went on for the descent into Las Vegas. Hugh stuffed *The Man in the Gray Flannel Suit* into a duffel bag under the seat in front of him. Suburbia was another strange world—although perhaps more like the one in which he would work the year after next than Vegas would be.

All the more reason to find out what the Vegas world was like.

Or the world in which he would work if he turned down the Cardinal's offer of graduate study.

The white-haired, forgetful old man had called him into his red brick house on the lake across from the seminary on a weekend in early December. Seminary authorities, he'd said, spoke very highly of him. Most efficient sacristan in main chapel in years. Top-notch administrator. Didn't offend people. Advisers were telling him he should train a man in business administration. Didn't know whether it made much sense. Trusting in the Holy Spirit was better than newfangled planning ideas. Probably ought to give it a try. Send him to graduate school, Loyola or De Paul.

At first Hugh was exultant. He would put some order into the chaos of diocesan affairs. Then he hesitated. He wanted to be a parish priest, not a businessman in a Roman collar.

"I have to think about what such work might do to my prayer life," he'd said.

Understand the problem. Hard to pray in an office all day long.

Rumor had it that the job had been offered to Sean Cronin in the class ahead of him. Cronin was a moody, intense young man, son of a millionaire, with blond hair, hooded brown eyes. He kept his distance from most people, though he was well liked in his own class and close to Jimmy McGuire, who was one of the finest men in the seminary.

"No one told me anything about it," he'd replied curtly to Hugh's question. "Suit yourself. If you hate other human beings, it might be fun."

The "No Smoking" sign came on. Beneath him the desert was barren, like the life of a priest who was not happy.

Only one mention of Maria the last two years. On her midterm break from college—just before she'd quit—Marge had said that Maria liked her job at the bank. Hugh's heart had stood still. The sound of her name had hit him like an air hammer.

The weary Lockheed settled on the runway. His fellow passengers prepared to dash for the exit as soon as the plane stopped. In Vegas, apparently, you didn't waste a moment in your haste to get to the gaming tables.

"Have fun," the winsome cabin attendant said as he left.

"I'll try."

Tim Donlon strolled casually into the jeweler's shop. It was the most fashionable one he had yet visited, on Garden Road down the street from the Bank of China and a magnet for American and English tourists, who would marvel at how cheap Thai jade and silver were in Hong Kong.

He wore his full petty officer's uniform with radar technician's stripes and trim cap on such adventures. The cap hid his red hair. The uniform made him look honest and respectable.

The Navy was not as dull as Notre Dame. Tim enjoyed the ports his carrier visited in the Mediterranean, and later in the Pacific. But watching a radar screen for eight hours every day was a bore. The poker games when he was off duty were mildly exciting, even if his experience at the pinochle table on Mason Avenue made him so much better than most of his shipmates that there was little challenge in relieving them of their money. But not exciting enough.

He turned to theft and smuggling for excitement. The heady experience of lifting jewelry and carrying dope in the world's great ports was better than the sauce, even better than sex, although it was best when he mixed sex with it.

Some of the jewels he gave away to shipmates whose money he'd won or to women who amused him or to young American tourists on the street. Taking the forbidden article was more important than the money he might make from selling it.

The interior of the jeweler's shop was covered with thick red sound-absorbing carpet and the walls were hung with heavy orange drapes. The store was a cross between a cathouse and a funeral home.

He drifted to a glass counter where a young woman was showing jewels to an elderly American couple. Young women clerks were the easiest mark in every port in the world.

The girl was something special, classic Chinese beauty, slim, poised, with neatly coiffed hair, long lacquered nails, seductive little body, a vest-pocket dragon lady.

Her English was perfect, with a slight Irish accent—she was probably a convent-educated girl—more intelligent and sophisticated than her look-alikes in the cathouses on the other side of town.

"A present for your girl, sailor?" She smiled beguilingly.

"Something in jade and silver, miss." He talked like a redneck. "I hope it doesn't cost too much."

"We have all kinds of prices." She smiled again and removed a tray from the locked counter.

He searched for the piece he wanted to snatch—not too big; a large piece would be quickly missed. Ah, there it was, a pendant with exquisite carved jade; maybe fifteen hundred American dollars.

"How much is this, miss?" He pointed at a tasteless set of earrings. "I've only three hundred dollars to spend."

"Your girl can have a number of lovely things in that price range. May I suggest some possibilities?"

Now the trick was to wait till she was momentarily distracted, or to distract her himself.

CHAPTER
EIGHT

1956

Peg Donlon spent the cold blustery afternoon painting. She had not considered winter as a subject for watercolors before. Now she saw fire in the snow and sunlight. Fire, that was what people liked in her paintings; she was not a great artist, certainly, but her works sold consistently, making more money than she'd dreamed possible when Tom ordered her to go to the Art Institute, from which Maude Curtin had barred her on the strength of rumors it offered classes in Life Drawing.

The fire in her work was something new. She'd sold a half-dozen blazing paintings before she overheard someone discuss their "sexual content."

She replenished her brush and added a little blue to her sky. Most of her work was from memory or sketch.

Why did sex have to appear in everything . . . ? She hadn't even spoken the word before 1945.

She'd finally given up trying to talk to priests about her questions on sex. She used to confess impatience, distractions in prayer, unkind thoughts and words, and impure thoughts about her husband and other men and then add tentatively that she'd enjoyed too much pleasure in some of the actions involved in rendering the marriage debt. The priests would ask about birth control, then ask if the act was "completed in the proper way," then tell her that nothing else was sinful.

What if sexual relations were too intense, too pleasurable, too destructive of self-control? How did you ask a priest those things?

She tried to concentrate on her easel. Make the snow look thirsty for the sunlight.

Was she being punished for her animal pleasure by what was happening to her children? Would God punish Hugh by taking away his vocation because his mother enjoyed pleasure so much?

She put aside her paintbrush and reached for the comforting pearl rosary beads.

Marge was still angry at her brother. He was so goddamn smooth and personable. Larry, who was an atheist and prepared to dislike him intensely, was won over in two minutes. Jean Hartmann, a Missouri Synod Lutheran before she fled her Nebraska cow town, didn't want to meet him. By the time they were eating their steaks, his wide smile had thawed the Rhine Maiden too.

Marge had dished it out to Hugh as soon as he came off the plane and kissed her lightly on the forehead.

"I'm not going back, Hugh, not ever. I love all of you, but I won't live in that dull prison on North Mason. I don't believe in anything you believe in. I don't want any part of Church or God or rules. I want to be myself, to have fun, to love, to be free. Do you understand that? I won't listen to any sermons and I won't take any advice. I know what I'm doing and if you want to call it living in sin, that's your problem."

She realized as the torrent poured out how childish she sounded.

"I've come for the warm weather." He laughed. "And to tell you I love you."

The restaurant where they went for supper after he'd checked into his "respectable" motel a mile off Las Vegas Boulevard, was typical of the city—superb steaks, a juke box affirming that what Lola wants Lola gets, and slot machines clanking in the background. Beef and money, that's our Vegas.

Marge's plan was that Jean would take Hugh to the casinos after supper, show him the sights, and then end up at their show for the second performance. If Hugh objected to being turned loose with an unemployed Vegas chorus girl—available beef—he showed no sign of his displeasure.

He said with a boyish grin, "You must protect me from the card-sharps, Jean."

"The games are all honest, Hugh," she replied with her slow, dental-hygiene smile. "The players have to be protected only from themselves."

Jean was a bit too voluptuous and her hair a bit too white to be quite the all-American farmgirl. And she was too slender and too wholesome seeming to qualify as a German ice goddess. She was intelligent, lonely, and now terrified. She also couldn't get religion off her mind, though it was five years since she'd left her denominational college and run away to Vegas.

Hugh managed to take Marge aside for a few moments after they left the restaurant.

"I meant what I said about no pressure, kid, but I have to tell you I miss you."

The tears began to form, in the back of her head, it seemed.

"And I'd love to bring you home if you want or whenever you want. It has to be your choice, though. And any time I can help . . . now or later . . . I promise"—he winked—"no I-told-you-so's."

The tears came in torrents and she melted into his arms. He could have taken her back to the airport that moment.

But, instead, he went off with Jean to visit the casinos.

She knew she was being quite irrational. Most of her life was irrational. Nonetheless she was bitterly angry at him for not taking her back to the airport.

Hugh watched the blackjack dealer intently. The odds were a bit better than two-to-one that his down card was a nine or higher. With the eight card up he had seventeen points to Hugh's thirteen with three cards.

"Give me another," Hugh said in an artificially casual tone.

A three of hearts. The odds were still better than even that he would not go over twenty-one on the next card. He pushed the whole thousand dollars in chips into the center of the table. "Had a run of luck so far. May as well shoot the works."

Jean's fingers tightened on his arm, a disturbing but pleasant pressure. She didn't quite approve.

Five of diamonds.

"Twenty-one." He grinned merrily as he turned over his four of spades.

The dealer winced because he knew as well as Hugh did that only high cards remained in the deck. He dealt himself a queen of hearts.

"Never trust the deadly lady," Hugh said lightly. "Enough for me. Take the money and run, as my mother always said."

They cashed in their chips and left for the midnight show at Margie's casino.

"You took an awful chance," Jean said reprovingly, "with all that money."

"Not really. Those are the situations you dream about, a fifty-fifty chance after a night of luck."

"How did you know it was fifty-fifty?"

"I'll show you tomorrow. Incidentally, I've seen enough of the casinos. They scare me, these pale, unsmiling people in their vast mausoleums, all tied up in knots."

"I don't know what else to show you. . . . I don't want to be in the way."

"Why don't I take you to dinner tomorrow night and then we can see a movie and pick up Larry and Marge after their show. That is, if you have nothing else to do."

"Oh, no," Jean said bitterly, "I have nothing else to do."

The show was terrible, not obscene, not even vulgar, despite the scant garments on the chorus girls. Rather, it was dull. Larry didn't have much talent, a fact that Marge, smart little wench that she was, would soon figure out.

Las Vegas fascinated and repelled Hugh—pulsating, frantic, empty, hopeful, despairing, unsmiling, youthful, ancient. Purgatory and hell all rolled into one, with perhaps a touch of the excitement of paradise.

They congratulated Larry and Marge on the show. Hugh pleaded fatigue, promised he would go out with them the next night after the show, and went to look for a cab back to his motel.

"Tell them I love them when you report home," Marge yelled after him, "and that I'm staying here."

Hugh turned around and smiled affably. "I'll make my own reports."

"Disgusted by it all?" Jean asked in the cab.

"Not exactly. More bored. It isn't very good, is it? I mean, even as shows here go?"

"No, it's not. I'm promised the next opening in the chorus line, though, and I'll take it."

He walked with her from the cab to a shabby apartment on the very fringe of the desert. Paint was peeling from the outside wall, the sidewalk was cracked, and a garbage can had fallen across the outside stairway to the second floor. There was a faint and unpleasant smell, like a blocked toilet. Romantic Vegas.

"No pool? Why don't I pick you up tomorrow afternoon? I'll have a car then. You can swim at the motel with me and I'll prove I can count the deck."

"I'd like that." She extended a hand at the door of her apartment.

He took the hand and kissed her on the forehead, just as he'd kissed Marge. "See you."

The Chinese girl was good. She kept one eye on the tray and the other on the rest of the store. She'd learned the skills of a salesperson in a port city. You didn't trust anyone.

Tim pretended to ponder two purchases, a set of earrings worth about two hundred dollars and a bracelet that cost three hundred. He would return one of them to the tray and cup the pendant with the flying dragons in his hand with the same quick movement.

"I don't want to sound like money is the only thing, ma'am," he said in a broad Georgia drawl. "I think Cindy would like the earrings better, but I feel kind of cheap spending only two hundred dollars."

The girl laughed pleasantly. "She will be so glad to have her redhaired sailor back she won't mind how much you spend." The older woman who seemed to be the manager of the shop babbled impatiently in Chinese. The salesgirl answered, also impatiently, without taking her eyes off Tim.

"You Chinese folk certainly do notice red hair." Mistake to say that, bad mistake. It would reinforce her memory.

Again the impatient babble from Mrs. Manager.

Exasperated, the clerk turned away for an instant and spoke sharply to her boss. The older woman subsided into resentful silence.

Quickly Tim returned the bracelet and snatched the pendant.

Now was the moment of truth. "I'll follow your advice, miss, and take the earrings. They sure are pretty." He reached into his jacket pocket, dropped the pendant, and withdrew his wallet.

"Cindy will love her gift."

Gravely Tim handed her three fifty-dollar bills and five tens. The sales receipt was made out to CPO Marshall T. Sims of the destroyer *Evans Carlson*.

He thanked the girl for her helpfulness, complimented her on her courtesy, bowed politely to Mrs. Manager, and walked out the door and across the street, his heart pounding with suppressed excitement.

Halfway down the block toward the nineteenth-century Cathedral of St. John on Albert Road, he permitted himself the luxury of looking back.

Both the salesgirl and the manager were at the door of the shop, looking intently in his direction.

And a Hong Kong policeman was hurrying through the crowd to meet them.

CHAPTER
NINE

1956

In the darkness of a late winter afternoon, Tom Donlon stepped off the Austin Boulevard bus at Lemoyne Avenue with deliberate caution. The street was slippery, slush over ice. Not the time to spend a month in the hospital with a broken hip.

It was turning cold again; he shivered as he walked the short block to Mason Avenue and the oversize bungalow that Peggy had picked out just before Tim was born. She did not buy it herself, as she had bought the Packard. Yet it was clear that, even though he thought eight thousand dollars was a lot of money, Thomas Donlon had no real choice.

Many happy memories in that house. And sadness too. Tim in Asia someplace, writing rarely. Marge a rebel, living with an Englishman (he shuddered at the thought) in a gambling casino, and Hugh . . . the perhaps unwise bargain he'd made with God.

Dick Daley, the new mayor, had been blunt about it: If there was a Democratic administration in the next ten years, Tom Donlon was going to the Supreme Court. "Time we had someone from the great city of Chicago."

Tom doubted he would accept the appointment. The house on Mason Avenue was where he belonged. A house of deep love and anguished sorrows. . . .

What had they done wrong?

How many times had he asked that question?

But when he entered the house, after being careful not to slip on the steps of the front porch, he could think only of his wife.

"Peggy . . . ?"

The shower was running.

He walked rapidly to their bedroom in the rear of the house. Peg was all that remained as he faced old age and death.

And Peggy made life worth living.

"Isn't Jean gorgeous?" Marge asked, trying to avert another "it's your choice" conversation with her brother.

"Lovely girl. . . ." Hugh seemed uninterested. "Do you like Vegas?"

They were sitting in the parlor of her apartment. Hugh was properly impressed by its tasteful comfort. She prepared her own breakfast and his lunch—English muffins, fresh grapefruit, bacon, home-ground coffee. I'm a good cook too, big brother.

"What's the matter with it?" she asked defensively. Larry was still asleep. It had been a mistake not to wake him. She didn't want to face Hugh alone. "Sinful?"

"Unhappy. Dante would revel in it. Isn't unhappiness the worst of sins? No one smiles. The gambling is grimer than an Irish wake. The music is depressing, the shows are frantic, the people act like last-minute Christmas shoppers who don't believe in Christmas. It's a treadmill to nowhere."

"Lots of beautiful women." She tried to parry his attack by a counterattack.

"Right." He sighed. "I've seen more half-naked young women in the last twenty-four hours than I've seen in my whole life. But you know what? After the first hour it's a bore. At first I couldn't understand why the men didn't even notice the cocktail waitresses. Then I didn't notice them either. What's the point in being surrounded by voluptuous women if the place is so dismal you can hardly see them? Las Vegas is a frigid palace."

"I bet you'd like to lay Jean," Marge fired back.

Hugh laughed, stood up, and kissed her cheek. "You're wonderful, Marge," he said. "I love you."

Outside there was a cold wind and icy slush. Inside Thomas Donlon was enveloped in timeless warmth.

"I should put supper on," Peg murmured.

"It can wait." He stroked her back slowly.

"Are we abnormal, Tommy?"

"If you mean are there many men in St. Ursula who come home at five o'clock, drag their insincerely protesting spouse out of the shower, and make love before supper, the court will have to rule that we are not typical. Not abnormal though. Those other men don't have wives that are so pretty they can't keep their hands off them."

"We're emotional people." She rested her head against his chest. "Though we pretend to the world that we're not. Our children are emotional too, even Hugh. Remember Maria?"

"Speaking of Maria, I saw Mike Flaherty today on LaSalle Street, the president of West End Bank. Said they were quite pleased with her."

"Hugh was in love with her . . . so were you a little bit."

"So were we all."

"What if Hugh is too . . . too emotional to be a priest and marries someone who is not as nice as Maria. We froze her out, you know. What if it were God's will that Hugh marry Maria instead of becoming a priest?"

A typical Peggy scruple, convoluted as a Supreme Court opinion and, like many Supreme Court opinions, containing a valid point.

"We never told him we'd be happy to have her as a member of our family"—Peggy persisted in her scruple—"even if we would be happier if he became a priest. Could you have been a celibate, Tom?"

"What a time to ask a question like that, Margaret Mary Curtin Donlon. . . . Yes, I suppose I could have, if I were happy as a priest."

"I'm glad to know that," she sighed. "If you could have, then Hugh can."

Jean split the water of the motel pool with long, powerful strokes—Valkyrie as athlete. In love again, as Xav Martin had predicted? Well, not exactly.

Jean climbed out of the pool, wrapped a big towel around herself, and sat in the deck chair next to Hugh, breathing heavily. "The older you become the easier it is to get out of shape."

Nothing wrong with the shape as far as he could see; in a trim white bikini she was, despite her obvious physical strength, strangely vulnerable.

"Want to see the card trick?"

"Dying to."

She shrugged out of the towel and picked up the deck of cards lying on the poolside table. "What do I do?"

"Deal out twenty-six cards. Let me see each one and then put it on the pile facedown."

"I don't believe this and I don't know whether I'll believe it even if I see it, but here goes."

"You can go more quickly," he said as she showed him the cards. "I only need a glance. . . . All right, now pick them up and turn each one over from the bottom as I identify it. The first card is the nine of clubs. . . ."

He named each of the twenty-six cards.

"Gosh." She was awed.

"Now, I'll tell you the cards you're still holding, not, alas, in any order."

He didn't miss one of those either. For the last six he gave her the odds that each new card would be higher than a six.

Jean leaned back on the deck chair wide-eyed. "Amazing, you would make millions here. And you're going to be a priest?"

"Where the odds against success in any given case are astronomical."

"I suppose so." She rubbed suntan lotion on her long legs absently. Only a year or two older than he at most and already by the standards of this terrible place a has-been. He took the tube from her hand and rubbed the lotion on her back.

On the chorus line Jean would be just one more well-built dancer, indistinguishable from the others, an easily replaceable spare part. Only when a body became a person with fears and hopes did it invade his imagination and demand sympathy, affection, and desire.

"Tell me about it, Jean," he said quietly.

"About what?" She looked up quickly, too quickly.

He finished his businesslike work with the lotion. "You are up to your eyelids with worry, you've found a near-clergyman who is different from the pastors back home and enjoys being with you.

You want to tell him about it, but you're afraid." He gave her the tube. "Spill it."

First spilled the tears, accompanied by shoulder-racking sobs, such lovely shoulders. He resisted the urge to wrap his arm around them.

Then the story: honor student in high school, three years at a rigid denominational college, expelled for drinking, one drink and sick in the washroom; flight to Vegas in humiliation and rage, disowned by family, string of lovers, most of them cruel. Early success in chorus lines, aided by being in the right people's beds. Then the realization that she had little dancing and singing talent—Margie in a few years—unemployment, loneliness, chastity because she'd been hurt enough. The next choice, if she wanted to eat, was to become a call girl or go home and accept the role of scarlet woman.

My God, what do I say next? Pretend to be confident. "Enough for one afternoon, Jeanie. Put your clothes on. We'll eat a big steak, see *Smiles of a Summer Night*, and meet here at the parsonage tomorrow."

She wiped her nose with a tissue and smiled an all-American smile. "Parsonages can be anywhere, can't they?"

"I sure hope so."

That night when he kissed her on the forehead again, she leaned against him for a fraction of a second, not so much inviting or promising sex as yearning for support.

Dear God, help me to come up with something.

When he was trying to go to sleep, Hugh realized with a twinge of guilt that he had barely thought of his sister for the last eight hours. He had come to Vegas to salvage Marge, not to become involved with a terrified chorus girl.

Tim Donlon was scared. He ought to have stayed on his ship. Instead, he'd come ashore to sell the pendant, even though he didn't need the money. He offered it to a middle-aged American couple at the Star Ferry terminal. They almost bought it for a thousand dollars, a great bargain. The man was ready, but the wife was suspicious of what a "common sailor" would be doing with such an expensive piece.

So he'd walked back toward Government House, hoping to find

another such couple—prosperous but not minding a bit of crookedness.

He wandered near the shop where he'd snatched the piece. There were wealthy Americans on that street usually. And he was in dirty fatigues and looked like a different person. There was not much danger that he would be recognized.

Then he saw the pretty salesgirl only thirty yards behind him in the narrow, crowded street.

He hurried down Queen's Road, across Procession Street, and into the teeming Chinese district. His shadow kept doggedly behind him, almost running despite her spike heels. He dashed through the central marketplace and ducked into one of the tiny side lanes beyond it.

There was a razor-sharp switchblade in his back pocket, useful for threatening angry rednecks on the ship. Only twice in his adventures had it been necessary to open the blade and only one of those times had he actually cut anyone, a Corsican in an alley in Naples who was coming after him with a knife of his own—a quick slash from Tim and the surprised thug had dropped his blade and shouted in pain.

The woman was only a dozen yards behind him now, slipping through the crowd like an agile halfback. Alone, the crazy little fool.

He tried to lose her by dodging into a black passageway between two buildings; a few feet into it, the lights from the street offered only a dim glimmer. The crazy girl came after him.

He grabbed her, twisted her arm behind her back, and held the knife blade at her throat. "Make a sound and I'll kill you," he hissed.

If she'd cried out, he would have run like hell through the passageway, hoping that there was an opening at the other end.

"What's your name?" She was quaking against him. The power of life and death over her was unbearably sweet.

"Jane. Please, sailor . . . don't kill me."

He released her arm and, keeping the knife blade against her throat, fondled her gently. "Why did you chase me by yourself?"

"Manager woman blamed me, said she'd fire me. Don't kill me . . . I'll go to bed with you."

Everyone in Hong Kong had a price. He continued to caress her, reveling in his absolute control. He thought about hurting her, just a little.

"A nice offer, Jane, but I'll decline it. If you come after me again, I'll cut little pieces off your body for a couple of days, then you'll plead with me to let you die. Understand?"

He had to hold her so she wouldn't collapse. "I won't tell," she stammered.

He kissed the nape of her neck and dropped the chain of the pendant over her head. "You can figure out how to explain to the old dragon lady where you found this. If you want to be sliced up, turn your back before you're on Queen's Road."

In his bunk on the carrier, Tim savored the biggest kick yet. Restore a dead woman to life. Much more fun than screwing her.

Maybe that was how God got his kicks. You take something away, scare the hell out of them, and then give it back.

"Did you have summers like that?" Jean asked Hugh, handing him her tube of suntan cream.

He put aside *The Quiet American*, a book that deeply depressed him, and performed his cream-spreading responsibilities.

"You mean like *Smiles of a Summer Night*? Yes, one. And you?"

"Lots of them. Same guy every summer too."

"Is he married?"

"No, he claims he wants to marry me." She screwed the cover back on the tube. The cloudless desert sky was implacably blue above them.

"Henry Kincaid is his name, a classmate from the first grade on. Same church, same Sunday school, same high school and college. Nothing more than hugging and kissing, ever. We were dreadfully wholesome. Then they caught me in the washroom with liquor on my breath and he turned on me just like everyone else.

"He was a fundamentalist—we all were—but at Stanford Law School he changed. Now he's a successful lawyer in Los Angeles. Still a jock—ski, surf, backpack, the whole thing. Visits me every six months and politely asks me to forgive him and marry him."

"Redeeming the fallen woman?" Hugh asked.

"Oh, no, Henry's finished with self-righteousness. He wants me because he thinks he loves me. He's wrong, of course. I'm not the lawful-wife type anymore."

"Twenty years from now would he throw Vegas at you in an angry quarrel?"

The corner of her lip turned up in a curious smile. "More likely the other way around. I might tell him that I married him to avoid becoming a full-fledged hooker."

"Why not marry him, Jean?"

She sighed and pushed the long blond veil away from her face. "Sometimes I'm awfully close. I wouldn't have to work for the rest of my life. I could go back to school, have children. I'm mildly happy to see him when he comes over the mountains, mildly sorry when he goes back, and then I don't think of him for the next six months, except when I'm worried about how I'm going to pay the rent."

"Think about one thing for the next day or two. Or imagine one thing: What will it be like five years from now if you marry him?"

Her jaw tensed in Teutonic stubbornness. "I will not marry him, Hugh. . . ." Then the jaw relaxed and the half-smile returned. "I'll think about it, though, Pastor, if I can swim in your pool now."

He swam next to her, wondering about the various ways humans give themselves to each other. Because he would be a priest in another year and because she was frightened and lonely she had given him something much more intimate than her body. She had given him her trust.

Now what was he supposed to do with it?

Hugh was sipping a glass of sherry, something he'd learned to do despite Peggy's ban on drinking. Marge was gulping her second Scotch and water and Larry was at the theater fretting over his show.

"I'm surprised you found time to fit me into your schedule," she snapped irritably.

"And you'd complain as well if I was around too much," he replied bluntly. "No matter what I do, it's wrong. So this way I'm certainly not trying to deprive you of your freedom."

"You like Jean more than me. . . ."

Hugh laughed. She joined in.

"God, what a spoiled brat I am," she admitted.

"An unhappy spoiled brat. . . . Do you want to know what really annoys me about you?"

She didn't really. "I suppose so."

"Someday you're going to come home—on your own, you're too stubborn to do it any other way. Two months after that, you'll have bought back into everything you left behind and you'll never admit that there has been a change, much less that you were wrong."

"Goddamn bastard." She threw her Scotch at him, not the glass, because she didn't want to hurt him, only the precious brown liquid.

Still, they kissed affectionately when he left.

Was he right? No, of course not. She'd never go back.

Well, not for a long time.

Hugh woke up that night with imperious sexual longings. All those half-naked bodies had finally caught up with him. The licentiousness of Las Vegas had invaded his dreams, filled them with images of breasts and buttocks, and demanded that he find out what it was like to make love to a woman.

He threw on his clothes, bolted out the door of his room, and drove at seventy miles an hour across town to Jean's apartment, not altogether sure that he was not still dreaming.

Outside her door, parked in the car, and almost mindless with desire, he realized that he was awake.

He started the car, backed up to turn around, and drove slowly back to his motel.

What demons lurked in the desert darkness beyond the beam of his headlights? What beautiful, sensuous, enticing agents of hell?

How could they be so appealing and still be evil?

Such temptations would probably come often when he was a priest.

Every time a desirable woman trusted herself to him?

He licked his lips apprehensively. Not too many of them would live on the edge of the desert.

The next day Jean showed him Lake Meade and Hoover Dam. Not a word about her man in California. You can't force help on people if they don't want it.

Back at the pool she began very cautiously.

"I did the imagining I promised." She was sitting on a towel at his feet, clad today in a white one-piece swimming suit, her body slumped over pathetically.

"And?"

"Henry and I would have two, maybe three, well-behaved children. I'd be taking classes in voice or something of the sort. We'd belong to a country club. We wouldn't fight much, neither of us would be unfaithful, and we'd both be bored silly."

"You don't know that."

"There's no spark between us and never will be. He asks me to come back to California with him the way he'd ask me out for a Coke."

"Give me your hands, Jean." Punt formation on the goal line. "Both of them. Now, I'm going to presume a lot on a short friendship. You're still an innocent farmgirl, terribly guilty about her fall from grace. Your punishment will not be complete until you've degraded yourself so much that no one will want you." Her hands in his, she was like a medieval vassal, kneeling in front of a liege lord, a vassal smelling of suntan oil. "You don't want to be forgiven, Jean. That's why you won't forgive yourself."

She jerked her hands away furiously. "Leave me alone." She dashed into his room, emerged a few moments later fully clad in skirt and blouse, jumped into a cab at the door of the motel, and was gone.

Blocked kick.

Lesson for the future: Don't tell people the truth about themselves unless you're sure they're ready to hear it.

The next morning Hugh called his father. "He's not rich, Dad, and never will be. He does all right. He pays her a salary, probably more than she's worth. He's a kind man, probably better than she deserves."

A noncommittal grunt. Then, "How does she look?"

"Fine, more like Mom every day, taller and thinner maybe and with your hair, still . . ."

"I know, Hugh, I know. And the weather?"

"Dull, nothing but sun and clear blue sky."

His father chuckled, though clearly his heart wasn't in it.

After he'd hung up, Hugh considered the phone thoughtfully. Dangerous, potentially deadly instrument. He was going to meddle where he had no right to meddle. Part of being a priest. Follow your gut instincts.

He called information, then dialed the number he was given. "I'm Hugh Donlon, you've never heard of me, and you'd better listen to what I have to say."

The one at the other end listened. First astonishment, then, in rapid order, dismay, anger, outrage. At last a trace of amusement.

With a clear conscience, more or less, Hugh dove into the pool. It was up to God now.

Judge Donlon poured himself a cup of coffee and moved aside the tedious brief he'd been reviewing. Lawyers became more pedantic and obscure with each passing year. Hugh certainly sounded self-possessed. Very much in charge. Nearly twenty-four, the age of John of Austria at Lepanto, and Buckingham at Culloden Moor.

Peggy was right, even if she didn't quite comprehend the meaning of her instinct. There was no place in present-day Catholicism for any of the Donlon children. They were passionate activists who did not and could not hide their real nature as he and Peg did. The Church had found room for him and his wife because they carefully hid the violence of their love beneath a veneer of piety and convention that fooled everyone but their three children.

The veneer, the pose of angelic immunity to passion—that was what sent Tim to the Navy and Marge to Las Vegas.

What would it do to Hugh?

Could there possibly be a place in the priesthood, the dull, arid priesthood, for so turbulent a young man? How could he hide the restless energy and the relentless ambitions that even he himself did not perceive?

The judge sipped his coffee, black with no sugar. They had excluded the magic Maria too quickly. Could they bring her back? Did he and Peggy have the courage to talk to Hugh about her?

Hugh was to return to Chicago on a United DC-6 that Sunday morning. He'd left his Hertz Chevy at the in-town station. Margie picked him up there. First they would stop at the casino to see Larry and then pause at Jean's apartment. She'd called as Marge was leaving, pleading that they stop for just a minute.

He shrugged indifferently. "Plenty of time."

At Jean's house they encountered an unexpected scene. Hank Kincaid was there, not flustered as he usually was but determined. Jean was packing her clothes into two battered suitcases.

Hank was a hayseed—big, rawboned plainsman, support-your-local-sheriff-type, with bad eyes, rimless glasses, and a reedy voice.

But today his eyes were shining. He kissed Marge confidently—never did that before—and shook hands vigorously with Hugh.

"Glad to meet you, Father."

"I don't deserve the title quite yet," Hugh said modestly.

"What the hell is going on?" Marge demanded when she was able to corner Jean in the kitchen.

"He didn't ask this time. He insisted. I . . ." Happy tears were streaming down her cheeks. "I want to go with him now . . . we made love . . . I never . . . Marge." She hugged her friend. "He was wonderful."

Marge melted, temporarily, and congratulated her. Jean was happy and her happiness must be shared, however short-lived it was likely to be.

On the way to the airport, Marge vented her fury on Hugh. "Who gave you the right to play God?"

"Huh?" His innocence was not convincing.

"Do you realize what kind of hell you've condemned them to? What do you think they're going to be suffering in ten years?"

"I'm not responsible for what they do with their chance." His confidence had been shaken by her attack. "You're angry because Jean's going back to her past, as you know you're going to do someday."

"I'll never sell out," Marge screamed at him. "You treated her just like you treated Maria. Tease them and then run. That's my brother Hugh."

She swerved onto the shoulder and then recaptured control of the car.

"Don't kill us, you little fool."

"I can drive better than you can."

"You cannot."

They quarreled like sullen children but by the time they reached the airport Margie's temper had changed.

She patted Hugh's cheek affectionately. "You're not all that bad, Hughie." She redefined what they had witnessed at Jean's apartment—without the slightest twinge of guilt over the abrupt change. "Didn't you see the stars in their eyes? You gave them the push that they needed."

"I don't know. . . ."

"They're calling your flight. . . . Hughie, promise me something. Promise me you'll never forget how to laugh at yourself."

"I'll try. . . ."

They hugged again and he was gone.

The DC-6 staggered toward Chicago. The first part of the flight was smooth, but beyond the Rockies they encountered a massive weather front. One of the cabin attendants was sick.

Hugh put aside Edmund Wilson's disturbing book on the Dead Sea Scrolls. Wilson was anti-Catholic and anti-Christian, but the discoveries at the Wadi Qumran raised problems that worried Hugh. He'd paid little attention to the new theological currents that had swept up on the American shore from Europe and no attention at all to the new studies in sacred scripture. Classes in scripture at Mundelein were a time for mending socks and writing letters.

His restless imagination turned back to the scene in Jean's apartment.

It was easy to imagine what had happened. Hank insisted she come to California. She said no again. He said he'd take her by force if he had to. Surprised and probably not altogether displeased by his show of fire, she said he wouldn't dare. So he dared. Poor man, all the years of waiting.

There were stars in their eyes, were there not? Marge was right, he had not messed up their lives.

He prayed that he had done the right thing and then returned to his fantasy.

She resisted his affection at first, then passion and love broke through the barriers of fear and resentment and pain and despair.

Just as God had intended passion and love to cooperate.

Did he really want to give up such joy?

Could he give it up?

He thought of the cabin attendant on the flight out, then of Jean again.

How could he turn his back on such delights for the rest of his life?

Maria.

It was eleven o'clock when he arrived at Mason and Lemoyne tired and depressed. He reported to his parents when he reached their house that eventually Marge would bounce back and pretend that Las Vegas had never happened.

"Isn't there the risk she'll destroy herself first?" The judge looked older than his forty-nine years.

Too shrewd. Hugh threw up his hands in a gesture of helplessness.

"Where did we go wrong, Hugh?" his mother asked sadly.

"Where God went wrong." He was irritable and too tired to care. "He created human beings with freedom. You had children, a risky business for both you and God."

For a moment it seemed that they wanted to change the subject. He waited impatiently.

"I'm dead tired."

"Of course," said his father, with obvious relief. "Get some sleep."

"Poor dear." His mother hugged him and patted his cheek.

In bed Hugh wondered what his parents had been afraid to talk about.

The next day, Hugh sat in the tired old Buick on Madison Street across from the West End Bank. Although it was only one thirty, the clouds and falling snow made it seem like dusk. The lights in the bank window shone fitfully through the snowflakes and reminded him of Christmas decorations in the State Street stores, warm, appealing, but artificially gay.

He glanced at the *Sun-Times* on the seat next to him. Israel refused to withdraw from the Gaza Strip. Winter storm warning for tonight. Las Vegas light-years away. The big gentle snowflakes were melting as they touched the street. Soon, however, the snow would pile up again.

His excuse again was to seek Maria's advice about Marge. The foolish thoughts of the plane ride had been dismissed. He was motion sick, that was all.

He had bought new ice skates in the shopping center at Harlem and Lake. He was going home. He'd parked here for a moment's respite, a dangerous exercise.

No future, no point, no sense, no reason.

He turned on the ignition, eased the car backward, shifted the gear, and hesitated. What had she said? He couldn't live without a woman. Some men could, but he couldn't.

He shifted into first, inched forward, and then turned off the ignition.

The bank was bright and businesslike, only one woman at a teller's window. Not much trade on a February afternoon. His eyes roamed the desks for a blonde. He thought he saw her. The girl turned, as if hearing his thought; pretty, but not Maria.

"Can I help you, sir?" the guard asked politely.

"Is Maria here today?"

The crusty old man's lined face dissolved into a cheerful smile. "Maria is in school this afternoon, sir. She'll be back tomorrow morning."

"I see." Tomorrow morning would never come, not till after eternity. "No, no message."

The guard unbent a little more. "I suppose you know her, sir, so you'll understand my meaning when I say that it is a much less interesting bank when she's not here."

Outside the air was dense with big dancing snowflakes; now they were sticking to the pavement of Madison Street.

BOOK TWO

"Father forgive them, for they know not what they do."

CHAPTER

TEN

1964

"Father, may I ask you a personal question?"

A woman's cultivated voice, not from Chicago, not from Boston or New York either. Perhaps Philadelphia or Baltimore. The tone of intellectual respect sounded like what one would expect from a graduate of a Catholic women's college—Daughters of the Sacred Heart, perhaps Manhattanville.

"Surely." He was trapped in a sticky, airless confessional on a hot summer Saturday, just as he was trapped in St. Jarlath's parish and in the priesthood, which, despite the joys of ordination day, had not brought him the happiness he'd expected.

For seven years now he had fought a psychotic pastor. The battle was at best a draw. In the meantime, while he was stuck in a stagnant backwater, the Church had been going through the most dramatic change in its history.

In a way, it served him right. He had chosen the backwater. After his trip to Las Vegas, he had declined the cardinal's offer of business school training. Now the world had forgotten about him.

"It's a somewhat delicate matter.... I've hesitated ... you're such a sympathetic confessor...."

"I'll try to help."

"My husband and I engage in oral sex on some occasions. He says that it is not sinful—he is a devout Catholic, Father—and I don't know what to think. The sisters and priests in my college said that it was a terrible sin of perversion."

"Do you find it repellent?" Her question was asked with increasing frequency in the confessional. The sexual revolution was catching up even with well-educated, well-to-do Catholics.

"No, Father; at first, I was . . . a bit shocked, and then, frankly, found it quite enjoyable."

"The Church has always taught that a husband and wife may do anything to promote their love that is not repellent to either spouse, so long as the marriage act is properly completed. Is this a form of birth control for you and your husband?" The real sin, the only sin that mattered.

"Oh, no, Father, we have two children and we want more."

"Yet the seed is spilled when you make love this way?" Fall back on the biblical words; they're safe.

"In these matters, Father, as I'm sure you understand, the emotions are complicated. It's hard to sort out what one's intentions are. One wants to love one's husband with special intensity perhaps to make up for a cruel thing one has said. There are no conscious reflections on anything else."

"Do you think God would be angry at you for wanting to love your husband and heal wounds you had caused?"

"No, of course not. You've been very helpful, Father."

She was looking for the clear-cut ethical "yes" or "no" of the Moral Guidance college textbook. That he could not provide. Only she and her husband could make the moral decisions on such matters; yet they had been taught that the priest in the confessional could and indeed must make such moral choices for them.

He gave her absolution and sent her home to her husband, who probably didn't realize what a fortunate man he was.

Everything was changing, the questions people asked, the answers priests gave. Some priests were already hinting broadly in the confessional that there was a change on the way in birth control. His friend Jack Howard bluntly told his people to make up their own minds.

Hugh didn't see how there could be a change on the birth control question. Yet the spirit of change was in the air. Some priests thought that celibacy would be optional before the decade was over. Again, Hugh could not imagine that, any more than he could the altar being turned around to face the people, or the Mass being sung in English. Where would it all end?

Still, he had helped the woman and that was what a man became a priest to do. . . .

The thought brought with it one of the occasional experiences of joy that still made the priesthood worthwhile for him. They had not been so frequent lately, not as in the beginning.

The first Christmas at St. Jarlath's had been a time of exalted happiness. Sullivan was in Arizona for his "health." Kilbride was in the hospital. And Hugh was acting pastor, for all practical purposes. Pastor, his first year in the parish. He had conducted Midnight Mass with carols and flowers and bells ringing out across the snow, and felt the warmth of the people's support as he greeted them in the back of church.

That was the kind of joy of which the happiness of ordination was supposed to be a promise.

And how ecstatically happy he had been on that occasion too, the long-awaited, seemingly impossible goal finally a dazzling reality.

It had been a perfect clear blue day—filled with the resonance of possibility. When he was imparting his First Blessing, after the old cardinal ordained him, Peggy and the judge wept as they knelt in the radiant sunlight in front of the redbrick colonial-style main chapel. Even Tim briskly kissed his hand. Only Marge was absent—living in England, not even sending a note.

Three days later, on a postcard of Mount Vesuvius, he heard a voice from the past.

> *Dormant volcanoes remind me of you. Marriage a useful institution. First son a naval officer like his father. Salutes me every morning before breakfast. Crazy life, but I'm happy. Be a good priest. (Don't leave the sailboat.)*
>
> *Blessings, Maria!*

"Bless me, Father, because I have sinned." A lisping voice no more than seven years old interrupted his reverie about Maria. "I missed my morning prayers, I was disobedient sixteen times, and I committed adultery three times."

"You really should tell God good morning when you wake, shouldn't you?"

"Yes, Father."

"Sixteen times is a lot to be disobedient, isn't it?"

"My little sister is disobedient a lot more than that."

"Uh-huh. . . . Now, how did you commit adultery?"

"I called mother shit behind her back."

"That wasn't very nice."

"It was terrible, Father. I love Mommy, and I don't want to go to hell."

"God loves you too much to let you go to hell. That's a bad word, especially about your mommy. But God is like your mommy; he doesn't stay angry at you."

"Mommy would be awful mad if she knew I called her shit."

And Mommy would die of laughter if she were listening to this. Stay a comic angel, little guy.

"Well, we just won't tell her and we won't use that word about her again, okay?"

"Yes, Father."

Of such is the Kingdom of Heaven made? Well, sometimes.

"Father, I have a problem about my marriage." A man's voice this time, mature, successful, used to giving orders. What else in St. Jarlath's?

"I'll try to help."

"My wife and I were married outside the Church eighteen years ago. We have not received the sacraments since then. We tried for an annulment on the grounds that her first husband was insane at the time of the marriage. We couldn't find good enough proof, I guess, though the man has been in an asylum for twenty years. Now my wife's priest tells her that as long as she is convinced this first marriage was not valid because of her former husband's problem it is all right for us to return to the sacraments." A small laugh. "I keep up pretty much on the changes in the Church, Father; but I must have missed this one. Is it something new?"

"No, it's not new, sir. It's called the Internal Forum Solution. More use of it has been made recently. In an annulment case the Church merely decides whether the evidence is strong enough to say officially that the first marriage was invalid. Often, the evidence is too weak but the party involved is absolutely convinced in good faith that she or he is free to marry again because of the invalidity of the first marriage. The Church cannot officially so decree, but a confessor or an adviser can tell the person that his or her good faith seems sincere."

"Does that mean that my wife and I have been married all along?"

"Not in the eyes of the Church officially and publicly, but yes in the eyes of the Church privately and unofficially and, of course, in the eyes of God."

"I'll be damned. . . ."

"No, sir, that's what won't happen, not as long as you and your wife honestly believe that you were free to marry."

"Father, do you realize we have five kids, all in Catholic schools, and that tomorrow for the first time I'll be able to receive Communion with them?"

"Congratulations to all of you," Hugh said.

Some marriages worked, some didn't. Nine times out of ten a priest could tell on the wedding day whether it would work or not. It was the tenth one that threw you.

Maria has chosen well.

One radiant spring Sunday morning a year and half ago, after the nine o'clock Mass, a naval officer had approached him in the back of the church and extended a hand. "Lieutenant Commander Steven McLain, Father. I'm staying at the Admiral's house for the weekend."

Hugh detected a soft southern accent, Atlantic seaboard perhaps. "Welcome aboard, Commander," he replied, grasping his hand.

McLain was tall, about Hugh's height, but thinner, with a clear, handsome face, short brown hair and far-seeing eyes. Judging from his wings and campaign ribbons, he was a seasoned aviator. "I told my wife I'd be coming to Mass here today. She's still in Washington, and I'm on assignment to a shore base in the Far East. Just stopping over with my retired C.O. here. Maria said she doubted you'd remember her, but to extend her best wishes anyway."

"How long have you been married, Commander?" Hugh smiled.

"Six years, sir," he said, grinning complacently.

"If you've been married to that woman for six years, do you think it possible that anyone could ever forget her?"

The aviator beamed. "Actually, no, Father."

"Tell me more."

"We have two boys, five and four; we've had two terms of sea duty, one on a carrier off Vietnam, and a term just ending at the Pentagon. Maria has lived in Naples, San Diego, Tokyo, Honolulu, and Arlington, Virginia, and taken a good many courses in business administration all over the world."

"And now?"

The handsome face clouded. "I'm bound for shore duty at Cam-rahn Bay. She's going to live with her parents. The bank she used to work for has offered her a good position. Maria, as I'm sure you know, Father, is more than capable of taking care of herself—and the children. And she'll be much happier with her parents than in some naval port. Or with my folks in Charleston."

"Commander." Hugh shook the young officer's hand. "Anyone who married Maria would have to have taste. When you call her, please tell her that I think with you two it was mutual."

The commander smiled, enormously pleased by the compliment. "Pray for us, Father."

"Indeed I will."

A couple of times after that meeting, Hugh had fantasized about calling Maria. Images from the raspberry lodge danced in his head. But he decided not to. There was no reason to court trouble, and, besides, he genuinely liked her man.

Hugh shifted uneasily in the confessional. In the church, children's voices were singing the hauntingly sweet Gelineau psalms, music for an empty church on a stifling summer day. He peeked through the curtain. There was no one else in line.

Monsignor Sullivan, the pastor of St. Jarlath's, refused to believe that participated worship, much less worship in English, was coming. When it arrived, he said to Hugh, "You take care of the preparations, educate the people, that sort of thing."

After the first Sunday, Sullivan withdrew completely. "Hire a Vincentian or a Jesuit to take my Masses indefinitely. I'll have to read up on these things."

Monsignor Sullivan had not read a book in thirty years. He would say private Masses from now on, in Latin. "My doctor recommends it for health reasons," he told the people.

So Hugh had had to supervise the change in liturgical patterns that had existed for fifteen hundred years. Lloyd Kilbride, the other curate, was a drunk and could not be relied on even to find the church. The only resource in the parish to help Hugh was Sister Elizabeth Ann, an innocent and eager young nun, who was a few years out of college and a liturgical authority—which meant that she had attended two courses at the Summer Institute.

Two more courses on the Christian Worship than Hugh could claim.

"They sound wonderful, Sister," he said, standing at the rear of the sanctuary, which he had entered to encourage her last-minute liturgical preparations. "Sixth-grade girls learn more quickly than anyone else in the world."

"Thank you, Father." Sister Elizabeth, genuinely pleased, was blessed with long dark eyelashes, big brown eyes, and a sweet, open face that could become very lovely on such occasions. "We were just finishing. . . . Very nice, girls; be sure to be on time tomorrow. We want to teach your parents to sing with you."

The kids disappeared quickly; it was, after all, a sweltering August afternoon, and the pastor would not permit the use of air conditioning merely for confessions and choir practice.

"Shouldn't you be on vacation?" There was a flattering concern for him in her eyes.

"Father Kilbride is under the weather. The pastor's health prevents him from hearing confessions. And the Jesuits couldn't make it." He grinned. "Someone had to be here."

"So you came back from your vacation."

He nodded. Must be careful. Young nuns are prone to crushes on priests. "How was the Summer Institute?" he asked, changing the subject.

"It was wonderful." She lowered her eyes. "We learned about Karl Rahner's influence on Church music."

The great German theologian would have been horrified to be told that he'd influenced Church music in any way. "Maybe we could use him to direct our choir."

Sister Elizabeth Ann was a farmgirl from Iowa, possessed of the body of a model and the naiveté of a fourteen-year-old child. But she had a first-rate mind, and she had taken most of the courses required for a Master's in Theology. Despite her youthfulness, she had been a delegate to the Chapter that was reforming their Order. According to the other sisters at St. Jarlath's, Sister Elizabeth Ann had been one of the most influential delegates there.

"That one will be Mother General someday," said one of the old nuns in St. Jarlath's Convent, "or whatever they'll be calling it by then."

Jack Howard, who had attended the Summer Institute with Sister Elizabeth Ann, on the other hand, took a dyspeptic view of her and similar young nuns.

"They need a rigid and authoritarian Order, to have a Mother they can both love and hate. Now they're busy destroying their Mother. They won't have anything left to love or hate and they'll leave the day after they've won their final victory over her. Then they'll find some other love/hate object—some poor dumb, horny priest, I suppose."

"Not Elizabeth Ann," Hugh protested.

"Sweet and pretty and diffident, huh, Hugh? Keep a close eye on the set of that jaw and stay away from her."

Hugh didn't believe him, but maybe Jack was right about Sister. She could be tough if properly encouraged. She'd certainly done in Augustus Ambrose Aquinas Sullivan. She'd fought him with cool and collected intelligence and she'd won.

It had all begun when the sisters discarded the habit—the vestments their Order had worn for more than a century—and donned blue skirts, white blouses, and tiny blue veils. Some of the older nuns looked much less attractive and some of the younger ones emerged as very attractive indeed.

"That Elizabeth has great knockers," said Lloyd Kilbride at supper. "The studs in eighth grade will enjoy school a lot more than they used to."

When Lloyd was sober, he was vulgar; when he was drunk, he was obscene. That night he was halfway between.

"Can't have that sort of thing going on," Monsignor Sullivan mumbled inarticulately; he too was several sheets to the wind, a more recent habit for him than for Kilbride, who had been a lush since ordination.

The pastor had no idea who Sister Elizabeth Ann was; indeed he had no idea who any of the nuns were, as he avoided them as much as he avoided the schoolchildren. Sex, however, was one of his obsessions, and he was determined to drive it from his parish, much as St. Patrick drove the snakes from Ireland. No Christian Family groups and no Cana Conferences were tolerated in St. Jarlath's. The people should have better things to do than sit around and talk about sex.

Hugh had assumed that Sullivan would forget about Sister Elizabeth Ann, as he forgot about most other things that involved the parish.

However, the next week the old pastor happened into her classroom just as she was extolling the ethics of racial justice and the courage of Martin Luther King.

The pastor stormed out of the class, called the Mother General, and demanded that the "nigger lover" be removed from his parish.

A year or two earlier the miscreant would have been deported on the first train to the Mother House in Milwaukee. Gus Sullivan was used to winning his battles with nuns, whom he considered a form of life substantially inferior to his large German shepherd (named, appropriately, Adolph, or Dolphie for short). He would have won this fight too, if Sister had been less guileful and Hugh had not intervened.

Sister Elizabeth Ann had wept hysterically in Hugh's office. Finally Hugh had given in. He was, after all, in her camp.

"What am I supposed to do?" she sniffled.

"Fight the son of a bitch. You have more clout than I do. You're a member of the Chapter of your Order. Call the Mother General and demand that she support you. Tell her you'll go public if she doesn't. Turn the story over to the *National Catholic Reporter*."

She dried her tears, crumpled up the tissue, and looked at Hugh beseechingly. "Will you support me?"

He hesitated. "I'll talk to the Mother General if you want."

The next morning, Sister Baldwina, the Mother General, was on the phone. She did not sound like a pious and diffident old nun.

"We seem to have a problem, Father."

"Don't we all, Sister?"

"Is the man quite mad?"

"Try evil. He respects power, though."

"Aha . . . that sort. I know them well. What would you suggest?"

"Tell him Elizabeth Ann stays the school year or you withdraw all the sisters next week. He'll cave in."

"And at the end of the school year?"

"He's likely to forget it. He usually does. If not, renew the threat."

"Admirable, Father, admirable . . . we have high hopes for Sister Elizabeth . . . the kind of young woman who will see us through these troubled years. She is, however, so very young and so very fragile. I hope that we can protect Sister until she matures a little more."

"From men like Monsignor Sullivan? I may be some help in that regard. He's probably not her most serious problem though."

"Quite," said the Mother General, perhaps understanding more than Hugh meant.

Sister Elizabeth Ann listened closely to Father Donlon's homily, although not so closely as to forget about her sixth-grade class. If she took her eyes off them for a moment, the girls would squirm and giggle and perhaps offend the parishioners who were opposed to liturgical change.

Father Donlon was a good preacher, forceful and dramatic and very popular with the people. But theologically he was quite backward, and socially rather conservative. He needed a lot of "updating"—although there was nothing to criticize in this morning's homily.

"We must remember," he concluded, "that we do not earn God's forgiveness by our sorrow or by our reparation. God's love is a given. It's always there, waiting patiently for us. We need only turn to Him to receive it. He is pleased with our efforts but He is even more pleased with us. That's why He made us. You cannot earn God's love because He gave it to you before you started to earn it. No more than any love can be earned. Love is always given before the effort to win it or it will never be won."

The congregation shifted uneasily as he returned to the altar. Father Donlon, they were thinking, made it too easy. He was preaching strange new doctrines. There would be more phone calls of protest.

Sister sighed to herself as she prepared the choir for the offertory psalm. Father Donlon was not a happy man. Did he believe that God loved him?

Probably not.

He needed help, poor, lonely, confused priest.

And she wanted to help him.

There were only three calls to Hugh protesting his sermon, two anonymous and one from Professor Hines, who taught optics at Loyola and fancied himself an intellectual. The point in all the calls was the same—Hugh was a Protestant. God's love could too be earned. How dare he teach false doctrine and make people think the way to heaven was an easy one?

Hines promised that he would write a letter of protest to the chancery the next day, a promise made at least two Sunday afternoons every month.

"Tell them that I am preaching that First Grace is an unearned gift," Hugh said tartly.

"I certainly will," the professor replied.

"And then read the documents of the Council of Orange," Hugh slammed the phone down.

Last year he had been investigated by the chancery on orders from the Apostolic Delegate because someone had written a letter to the Pope complaining about his false doctrine.

It turned out that his offense was to read a gospel from the new Confraternity of Christian Doctrine New Testament translation— approved by the American Bishops, which referred to the "man, Jesus."

"That's a doctrine propounded by the Council of Ephesus, Father," he said to the chancery office investigator.

"We must be careful not to shock the laity," the bald bureaucrat had admonished him.

"Are you ordering me to retract and tell them that Jesus does not have a human nature?" he demanded. "And to repudiate the official translation of the American hierarchy?"

The canonist backed down quickly. And Xav Martin, by then the new rector at Mundelein, went to bat for him. The doddering old cardinal forgot about the Roman inquiry.

The phone rang again. "St. Jarlath's," he snapped. "Father Donlon."

"Hugh, there's going to be a marriage in our family. Your father is at Butterfield and I can't reach him. You're the first to know."

"Tim?" He wasn't going to marry that Maguire bitch, was he?

"Marge. She wants you to officiate, of course."

"Who's the groom?" he asked guardedly, conscious that his heart was beating rapidly. Dear God, protect Margie, she's still the little sister I adore.

"An English nobleman." His mother sounded as if she could hardly believe her own words.

"Oh, my God," Hugh replied. "What will Dad say?"

CHAPTER
ELEVEN

1964

His mother's call reached Tim Donlon in his bachelor apartment in Old Town just as he was preparing to make love to Estelle Maguire.

Estelle pouted over the delay.

"Doesn't that woman ever leave you alone?" she whined.

"It's not every day your sister announces her engagement to an English lord," he said mildly.

"It's time for you to marry too," Estelle replied.

She assumed they were going to march down the middle aisle soon. Nor was Tim opposed. He was almost thirty and he was tired of bachelorhood.

Estelle, moreover, was not a bad catch in his view—distracting in bed, fun at parties, a good beer drinker. But he'd become involved with her mostly because her father was rich. A wealthy real estate man on the fringes of the Organization, Larry Maguire had been convicted by a federal court on mail-fraud charges, a conviction sustained two-to-one on appeal, with his father casting the deciding vote. Maguire served six months and then was released on parole, coming home with a suntan.

Both Tim's parents regarded the Maguires with abhorrence; they were loud, vulgar, and corrupt. But they were also wealthy. Estelle was an architect with her own office and clientele, and although her designs were like haunted Gothic castles in a Charles Addams cartoon, her father's money and clout kept the money pouring in.

Not that Tim needed the money, really. Fresh out of the Navy, he'd bought himself a seat on the Board of Trade for $25,000 with his poker and smuggling earnings. He soon became a successful commodities trader notwithstanding a few scrapes with some of the fogies at the Exchange.

Tim loved every second of the Exchange. If you were caught once or twice, that went with the territory. It was like working all day in a gambling casino.

He no longer worked with the kids in the inner-city parishes, which he'd tried when he came out of the service. Whites were not wanted in those parishes anymore, and far be it from him to complain. So he turned to hospitals and routinely sent large checks every four months to Oak Park, where he was born, to St. Anne's, which was near his home parish, and to Mother Cabrini because, well, because that was where Maria had come into the world.

He no more understood his charity than he understood his gambling. Maria had said he was two different people. Well, maybe he was. But there was nothing to be done about it.

Estelle was only the most recent and persistent of his women. He'd often thought he should have gone after Maria in earnest when Hugh backed out. Why had he never tried?

Damn Hugh, anyway. Every time they saw each other, Hugh urged him to go back into therapy. Wasn't it obvious he wasn't the kind therapy helped?

So, after all, it was Estelle. Estelle was trying to get herself pregnant so he'd have to marry her. She didn't need to do that. He was prepared to marry her anyway. But if that was the way she wanted it, he was happy to oblige.

"I suppose you'll be going to the wedding," she said as he returned to the bed.

"If I'm invited." He rolled her over and swatted her ample rump.

Estelle laughed lasciviously.

He hit her again. Harder.

For a fleeting moment Tim Donlon realized how alone he was. And always would be.

o   o   o

Marge was more than amused to learn from her father, when he finally broke through the maze of the transatlantic phone net at one in the morning, British time, that he thought her intended was English.

Wait till they meet him, she said to herself when they'd finished talking. She laughed herself back to sleep.

Marge had traveled to London five years earlier and found herself a job at the Playboy Club in Park Lane. From there she'd graduated to a roulette table at Hugh Hefner's fashionable Clermont Club in Berkeley Square. There, in the flocked crimson, second-floor casino, and in very advanced décolletage, she had attracted almost as much attention as did the fortunes that rode on each spin of the wheel.

But she also saw that her time was running out. She finally knew how poor Jean Kincaid had felt. After a certain age, you're not much good to the Playboy empire, and there are a lot of lovely late-twenties hookers in the West End.

One night a great bear of a man appeared, a young fellow with long blond hair and a thick Irish brogue, and hung around her table, apparently enjoying more than his sizable winnings.

One of the younger girls later told Marge that he was Lord Kerry, an Anglo-Irish peer who had inherited a fortune in Dublin real estate and made a bigger one building towns in Nigeria.

Marge was surprised, because her best guess was that he was a couple of years younger than she and innocent of any wit.

He was waiting at the door when she left. She crisply told him she was not for sale and went back to her lonely apartment.

He was back the next night. "Only dinner, nothing else, solemn word."

So it was dinner and a handshake at the end—in the cabbage-smelling hallway of her second floor walk-up flat with a meter in which she inserted shillings when she wanted heat. He spoke in a rolling mumble that she barely understood: "Anglo-Irish. Church of Ireland, of course. Mother Catholic, though. Catholic myself. Bad show. Lose to everyone. Double outcast. No roots at all." Followed by a huge laugh and a giant, affectionate Irish grin.

Dinner again and another handshake. Marge decided that he was cute. And perhaps the most clever man she'd ever met.

After the third dinner she kissed him. He was flustered and unskilled.

"That won't do at all," she remonstrated. "Here, let me show you how."

He was much better after being instructed. She told him so.

"Learn quickly." He was hugely pleased with himself.

The next night he proposed. "Good Catholic gel. Good wife. Need one. Time to settle down. Hope you'll agree."

Marge was utterly astonished, and oddly moved. He was a lovely young man who had been taken in by a clever tongue and a sexy body.

"It won't work, Liam," she said at the door to her apartment. "I'm afraid I've not been a nice girl for the last couple of eons. Not exactly a hooker, mind you, but hardly the sweet Irish-American colleen you seem to think I am."

Liam Wentworth, Lord Kerry, took charge of her with a bear hug and demonstrated that he could speak perfectly grammatical English when it was necessary.

"My dear young woman, I know exactly who and what you are and even have a fairly good idea of the reasons you left your parents and acted so foolishly for several years. I intend to make you my wife regardless. I know who you are better than you do. Is that clear?"

He increased the pressure of his embrace, lifting her off the floor while his lips sought hers with vigorous determination.

Marge saw the life preserver that was being thrown. It was a comfortable, attractive, decent one, a life jacket you couldn't help but like. Instinctively she grabbed for it. And in the act of grabbing, like turned to love.

Hugh stood in the sanctuary of the nineteenth-century gray Gothic pile that was the Cathedral of His Gracious Lordship the Bishop of Kerry, as a fierce Irish rain pelted the stained-glass windows. A marriage two weeks after the engagement. His strange, fascinating brother-in-law wasted no time.

After he persuaded his mother that Kerry was in Ireland, as in the Kerry Dances ("Now, why didn't I think of that?"), and his father assured her that Liam was Norman Irish for Guillame ("Bill, my dear, nothing more than that"), Peggy was disposed to give her future son-in-law the benefit of the doubt ("If you're sure he's Catholic"). Liam won her over completely at first encounter.

"Know why the gel is so beautiful now. Doesn't hold a candle to her mother. Mind if I kiss you?"

Peggy didn't mind at all.

The transformation in Marge was breathtaking. Without the slightest admission that she'd been anything but a pious and devout Catholic all her life, she bought a white wedding dress worth a thousand dollars for the ceremony in the cathedral at Killarney.

Of course, Hugh would officiate. "Wouldn't have it any other way. Brother-in-law. Fine Yank. Cardinal can stand in the sanctuary."

Gus Sullivan had told Hugh he couldn't take time off for the wedding and Hugh had told Gus that if he wanted to complain to the administrator, now that the cardinal was dead, he could go right ahead and complain.

The Cardinal Primate of All Ireland (to be distinguished from the Archbishop of Dublin, not a cardinal and the primate only of Ireland, not All Ireland) and two visiting bishops, in addition to the Bishop of Kerry, waited in the sanctuary with Hugh, who had arrived only the night before the wedding and met only a couple of the members of the enormous wedding party.

The maid of honor was Liam's sister, a dreamy eighteen-year-old referred to as "the poet," who looked like a tragic heroine out of an Abbey Players film and drank John Jameson's like a lorry driver.

The first of the bride's attendants to come down the aisle, stunning in a light green dress and long blond hair, was not a poet. She was, rather, a disguised countess.

"Maria!" Hugh exclaimed as she devoutly genuflected to the altar, and, with a hint of mockery, to him.

"Late starter," she whispered, smiling.

His hands trembled through the ceremony and not because the evident nervousness of Liam and Marge infected him.

He tried not to look at Maria during his homily.

"Forgiveness is the essence of love. To love is to forgive, to forgive is to love. Liam and Margaret will have to forgive each other often during their years together. Each time they do they will grow in love and have a deeper awareness of God's forgiving love. They will teach one another how much God loves us. They will be sacraments of God's love for each other."

"Good show," mumbled Liam.

And later he added, "That was a fine homily, Hugh; someone like you should be preaching on TV."

None of the family could figure out the pattern according to which Liam spoke, sometimes in monosyllables and sometimes in sentences. In response to Hugh's question, Marge said that it made no difference to her at all.

Hugh was seated next to Maria at the main banquet table in the Great Southern Hotel in Killarney. Foolishly he wondered whether the renewal of their acquaintance would be awkward.

Marriage, motherhood, world travel, and business school had not changed Maria. She was still the sometime countess, sometime waitress.

In five seconds they were talking as if they had seen each other every Saturday for the last ten years.

"So we were in London on the way to Steve's new assignment— do you like him, Hugh? Isn't he a dear?—and I said I must look up my friend Margie, who is probably starving to death in some attic. And we find her with this massive Viking type, halberd and all, and she claims she's going to marry him in two days and can I be in the wedding party. Well, this Viking ordered his elves to stitch my threads together—don't you think the color of the gown matches my eyes, Hugh?—and here I am."

"And you're bound for Spain?"

"That's right. So the bank gives me a leave and I find somewhere else to take my last accounting course. Have you ever had any accounting? Priests ought to study accounting. Do you want to hear how I met Steven?"

"I don't have any choice, but, yes, I do."

The Donlons had been responsible for Steven in a way. If they hadn't hassled her about college, she wouldn't have gone to night school and therefore wouldn't have been offered a blind date for a summer dance in Lake Forest.

At Loyola she'd become a coffee-drinking companion of a girl from Manhattanville named Joan Cardin. Joan pleaded with her to attend the country club dance with a "nice Catholic Navy boy, quiet but cute."

Well, the boy was cute and had pretty eyes and not much to say, which was all right with her because, awed as she was by the country club, she was into more than her usual chatter.

He'd kissed her in the garden, which she assumed was part of country club routine. He was a healthy young male animal who wanted a woman. To her surprise, she discovered she was a healthy young female animal who wanted a man.

They'd laughed most of the rest of the evening. Then Maria dismissed him from her mind. Nice boy, good kisser, but nothing more.

Then letters and long-distance calls from Norfolk, Virginia, began pouring into the shoe repair store. She was spirited off to Charleston to meet mama and grandmama and a variety of sisters, brothers, cousins, uncles, and aunts, all of them more or less outrageous.

The McLains, it turned out, were Irish and Scotch and French, and part Indian (a fact of which they all were inordinately proud), and staunchly Catholic. They'd been polite and kind to her and hid their skepticism as well as they could. She'd countered by telling outlandish stories about her relatives in the Mafia. After two days, they realized she was pulling their legs and hailed her as one of the family.

She'd gone home quite certain she would postpone any decision for at least a year.

Six weeks later they were married at St. Ursula's, with Monsignor "Muggsy" Brannigan officiating.

"And that's the whole story." She smiled through her champagne glass at Hugh. "Are you impressed?"

"I'm glad you're happy, Maria," he said.

"Nice homily today." She ignored his cliché.

"Thank you." His face felt very hot.

"And you don't believe a word of it."

"I beg pardon?"

Her eyes were cool and calculating. "You figure that God forgives everyone but Donlons. For you folks there's a different set of rules. Well, maybe he even forgives Marge and poor Tim. But not Hugh Donlon; he has to earn God's love."

And she turned to the Bishop of Kerry, who was on the other side of her, and ignored Hugh for the rest of the meal.

"Are you angry with me?" he asked her after Liam's younger brother, Brendan, had proposed a toast in Gaelic.

"Exasperated." She touched his hand. "Hugh Thomas Donlon, there's as much goodness and power and love in you as there is water in Dingle Bay . . . well, I haven't seen Dingle Bay yet . . . all the love and trust in God you talked about in that beautiful homily." There were tears in her Rembrandt eyes. "And you've buried it under a mountain of rules. . . ."

"I should break the rules?" he said irritably.

"God help us if you did. You know what I mean, and it doesn't have anything to do with rules."

"I don't," he insisted.

"Do you still sail the *Pegeen*?" Another quick touch of her hand on his, this time a sign of hope.

He slammed the door shut again.

"It was too much of an expense. I sold it and bought a new set of golf clubs."

"How like a Donlon."

She turned from him just as she had on the lawn after she'd told him how beautiful he was.

After the bride and groom left, Maria took charge of the party, learning the step dances from the Irish cousins, singing with the bishop—an interminable ballad that pleaded with a certain Paddy Reilly to return to Ballyjamesduff—pouring champagne for everyone who wanted it, and even dancing in the rain that had poured down on Killarney all day.

Steve McLain, clearly adoring, asked Hugh, "Would you believe that the bishop asked her what county in Ireland her family was from and she told him County Palermo and the bishop thought she was kidding?"

"Like you, Steve, I'd believe anything about her."

The judge joined them a minute or two later. "Hugh," he said expansively, "do you have the feeling we may just have come in on a happy ending?"

"I told you it would work out."

"You did, indeed. But you didn't promise herself there as entertainment."

Herself, blond hair plastered to her head and dress plastered to her body, kissed Hugh on the cheek as she left. "Come see us in Spain."

"Please do," Steven urged him.

"I will," he lied.

On the Aer Lingus 707 back to Chicago, Tim told Hugh that there would be another wedding soon. Estelle was pregnant.

CHAPTER
TWELVE

1965

In the year after the two weddings, Sister Elizabeth Ann expanded her empire to include the teen-agers of the parish, a risky experiment, making her even more liable to Gus Sullivan's psychopathic wrath. One summer night Hugh checked in at the high club dance in the parish hall, half hoping to avert any trouble that the chief engineer could report to the vacationing monsignor.

Sister was the center of attention. There was no dancing, of course. The "high club" was in fact a drugstore corner moved inside. Lakeridge, the St. Jarlath's suburb, frowned on teen-age hangouts, so the kids who were too young to have cars hung out around the parish instead—that is, when Monsignor wasn't in town.

As they couldn't dance at the "dance," Elizabeth Ann had decided they ought to sing. At first the "nun with the guitar" had attracted only the girls, and only the freshman girls at that. But her singing was so pure and her laughter so appealing that by now everyone swarmed around her as soon as she walked into the parish hall. Even the senior boys showed up—perhaps, Hugh speculated, because they agreed with Lloyd Kilbride's appraisal of the nun's attractions.

Hugh, who enjoyed teen-agers and related well to them, felt somewhat rueful that he'd been abandoned for a pretty woman with a musical voice. But as he watched her lead the youthful chorus in "Cumbayah," he found himself fascinated to the point of transfixion by the rhythmic movements of her body, all the more compelling because she was quite unconscious of them.

A good thing Monsignor Sullivan wasn't about. Hugh thought of himself as a man almost unable to hate other human beings. Yet it was easy for him to hate Augustine Ambrose Aquinas Sullivan— Triple A to the rest of the diocese.

Gus Sullivan had been assigned to St. Jarlath's when the parish consisted of a handful of big homes along Sheridan Road facing the lake and a few blocks of servants' flats stretching toward the hinterland of northern Illinois. After the war, Lakeridge had expanded rapidly; the very wealthy on Sheridan Road were joined by the quite wealthy on the curving, treelined streets between the Northwestern tracks and the Eden's expressway: Corporation presidents were joined in church by brokers, doctors, lawyers, vice-presidents, and commodity traders.

In a few years the collections at St. Jarlath's quintupled and Gus Sullivan claimed credit for this success as a mark of his financial acumen, a judgment the Church officially validated by bestowing on him the monsignorial purple. Tireless in his scheming, even after receiving his purple, he'd expanded his network of cronies to include the most affluent people from the new neighborhoods and left the rest of the parish to his curates.

Unlike many of the old timers, who kept a careful watch on the activities of their young assistants, Sullivan didn't give a damn what Hugh did; he could have five mistresses on the side, as far as the pastor cared, so long as they didn't disturb his peace.

Monsignor Sullivan faced the world with a number of certainties.

Money was important. The church's steady income proved that he was a good pastor. Moreover, those parishioners who had the most money were the closest to God. Therefore, the pastor should be closest to them.

Authority was important. He possessed authority that he shared with the Pope and the cardinal. Therefore, he was right all the time because he could count on the Pope and the cardinal to back him up.

Sex was important—as the worst of all sins and the worst of all threats to the salvation of his people, especially those who were not as rich as his friends. Therefore, one must do all that one could to prevent any discussion of sex in the parish. "If they talk about it less, Father," he assured Hugh on one occasion, "they'll do it less."

Finally, his peace was important. Pastors had to be protected for those critical moments when they make the decisive choices that shape the future, like building a new twelve-room parochial school. That decision had been made in 1947. As far as Hugh could see, it was the last decision Sullivan had made and was about as risky as buying a dozen oranges. Nonetheless, Sullivan's peace and health had to be protected at all costs lest he be unprepared whenever another such crisis might arise.

Two conclusions followed from this final premise: first, that the pastor take as many vacations as possible to husband his resources—Palm Springs for the two months in the winter (usually during the troublesome season of Lent) and Eagle River for the two months in the summer (with his rich friends picking up the tab); and, second, that the curates do all of the work. This appealed to the pastor's sense of fairness. He did the thinking and they did the work.

Kilbride was useless, indeed worse, as Hugh had to cover up his drunkenness, an effort he felt was pointless but was still demanded by loyalty to the priesthood.

So Hugh did all the work.

Not that he minded work. He loved the work of the parish and was good at it. Sick calls early in the morning, the weary old faces smiling when he came into the bedroom; visits to grammar school classes to joke and laugh with the smart, bright-eyed kids; hospital calls to bring a little light to the anxious and depressed; counseling young people whose hopes could still be salvaged; instructing young couples before marriage and rejoicing in their discovery that the Church could be more than negative in its impact; reconciling older lovers who were tired and bored but still in love, even if they didn't know it; cheering for the grammar school football and volleyball teams and showing tall, taciturn teen-agers that he was still better at basketball than they were; instructing adults in the new, postconcilar Church, adults who were eager to understand and to act; helping business and professional men to think through the difficult ethical problems they faced in their work. Mass, sermons, anointing the dying, wakes, funerals—Hugh loved it all.

But the activity and the rewards were not enough to satisfy him.

He was restless, dissatisfied, often lonely. That should not be. He was working too hard, not praying enough, not controlling his fantasy life, nor his shamefully voyeuristic eyes. The women in the parish were mostly older than he, but he found them infuriatingly attractive in their aloof, well-groomed, artfully preserved, self-confident way.

Yet he no longer considered celibacy a serious problem in his life. When all was said and done, the most painful issue was not knowing where his own fault ended and Sullivan's began. Was Sullivan the problem or was there a deeper problem, inside himself?

He was a priest for life. And the answer now was not some other assignment but the one he had, St. Jarlath's, where he did all the work, bore all the responsibility, and had not the slightest authority to meet the responsibility with.

The last created constant problems. A typical St. Jarlath's cycle was for the pastor to order him to begin a new activity, such as a grammar school varsity sports program—usually because one of his wealthy cronies had complained that the "young priests aren't doing anything for the kids"—next, for him to succeed, because the organizational and economic resources of the parish assured that these programs were almost always successful, and then, as sure as the sun rose each morning over Lake Michigan, the eastern boundary of St. Jarlath's parish, the pastor would find one of his major premises violated—the project would cost too much money, or become a threat to authority, or involve sex, or disturb his peace.

It was Hugh's task to convey these definitive and arbitrary judgments to the parishioners and defend as best he could the mad pastor's whims. He did not miss the expressions of seething contempt in their eyes. Yet the theory of loyalty to a superior, "Christ's representative over you," that he had learned in the seminary demanded that he not criticize Gus to the people of the parish.

All he could say was that perhaps next year or the year after the program would be revived.

"After my kids are out of school," said the chairman of the St. Jarlath's Varsity Club at one of those times. "You've got no balls, Father; you're a hack; you're the dummy through which the monsignor speaks. A man like you would never make it in my world."

"We all have bosses, Mr. Ryan," he said, clenching his fists.

"I don't," Ryan sneered.

Ryan was right and Hugh knew it; he was a clerk, an errand boy, a flunky, a man permitted no hormones in a community where hormones counted enormously. Not to have a woman was perhaps understandable, but not to be his own man was inexcusable.

Moreover, not only was Sullivan arbitrary and unpredictable; he was insensitive and cruel. When an Army officer from the parish was killed in Vietnam and his wife and parents requested that a grammar school classmate who taught at Boston College say the Mass, Triple A said no. It was his iron rule that only parish priests officiate at weddings, funerals, and baptisms. Jesuits might be useful for Sunday help; they could not be counted on to say the proper things at funerals.

Hugh was deputed to convey the pastor's decision to the young widow. "Father Kilbride will say the Mass."

Father Kilbride did say the Mass. He was drunk. His sermon was an unintelligible babble and the idiot didn't even have in mind the right war.

"I'll never set foot in a Catholic church again," the widow said when Hugh apologized at the gravesite.

Another of Sullivan's decrees was that there would be no more mixed marriages in the parish—especially to Jews. Hugh was forced to tell young people who had lived their entire lives in St. Jarlath's to go to other parishes, unless, that is, they happened to be part of the pastor's clique, in which case the marriage was performed without challenge no matter how problematic it might be.

Gus Sullivan was a cruel and insensitive tyrant because any other approach to the world would have revealed him as an incompetent fool, and at some level in his armadillo personality he knew it. That was why he eventually went after Sister Elizabeth Ann, because he feared that if he didn't get her, she'd get him.

Most of the parishioners to whom Hugh talked complained bitterly about Gus. Some even wrote letters of protest to the chancery. Yet respect for the leader was so deeply ingrained in the Catholic people that there was not yet an organized campaign against him and no direct confrontations.

Moreover, much of the parish was quite content with old Gus. The monsignor, they would assert piously, had done such a wonderful job with St. Jarlath's, as if an orangutan could not have done as much.

"If there was a referendum," Lloyd Kilbride had said in one of his rare completely sober moments, "the bastard would win in a walk."

There were some parishioners who loyally supported Hugh, albeit Hugh was still less willing than they to do battle. Strongest in his support was Benedict Fowler, a millionaire commodities trader who had not penetrated the pastor's inner elite, although only because the pastor had not kept up on the distribution of wealth in the parish.

In his midforties, Fowler seemed the very stereoype of an Irish ward heeler—which is what his father had been. Big and gruff, with a genial grin, a gregarious tongue, and a cigar always clenched between his teeth, he worked a crowd the way Dick Daley did. When he moved laughingly into a group of people, they laughed too, unless, that is, they happened to notice that his hard brown eyes never did.

Ben had married somewhat late in life. Helen Fowler was at least ten years younger than he and, by almost unanimous agreement, was the most beautiful woman in the parish. "That ass is quite a piece of work," Father Kilbride had said appreciatively. A little less than average height, with soft honey-blond hair, a clear cream complexion, and a figure like a nineteenth-century odalisque, Helen was indeed something to look at.

Whenever she appeared at a meeting, with or without her husband, the men became attentive and the women restive. Unfortunately, "I think the young people deserve our support" was the most exalted intellectual contribution she seemed capable of making at parish committee meetings. The impassive mysterious face that hinted at secret insight appeared, in fact, to hide nothing at all. Although Ben seemed reasonably considerate and kind to her, he often acted as if he were unaware of her existence. And her daughter, Linda, a sullen but prematurely sexy and precociously intelligent child in her last year of grammar school, was quite frankly bored by her mother's interest in St. Jarlath School.

The spring after Helen first became involved, Hugh was invited to a giant garden party at the Fowlers', a sit-down dinner on a Sunday afternoon—five hundred guests under canopies, two orchestras, food from one of the finest French restaurants in Chicago. The silver sparkled, the linen gleamed, and the wine flowed. The bare-shouldered women chattered away while their mostly rotund men simply ogled.

"With what he made last week in soybeans," one guest remarked, "he won't even notice the cost of this bash."

Ben cornered Hugh after the roast beef had been served. He leaned over the table, genial grin and smelly Havana, quite at odds with the freshness of the day.

"How you doing, Padre? Glad you could come. Didn't invite the old man—don't want that so-and-so around here. How do you put up with him?"

"He's the pastor, Ben."

"Always loyal, huh? That's what I admire about you. Real Irish trooper." He coughed violently and wiped his mouth with his handkerchief. "Hey, look, this will all be over by eight o'clock. Some of the folks are coming back for a swim, about nine. Why don't you get your trunks and join us? See you then, Padre."

Ordinarily Hugh avoided intimate social gatherings with his parishioners. But he had missed his Thursday golf date with Jack Howard and Pat Cleary for two weeks running, and he needed the swim.

So he returned and found a group of four couples huddled in robes at poolside.

Only Helen Fowler was in the water, gliding with quiet, careful strokes. In the water she didn't seem the slightest bit awkward. Hugh dropped his towel on a chair and enthusiastically dove in beside her.

"Good evening, Father," she said softly.

"Good evening, Helen."

The subject of the conversation at the side of the pool was, as Hugh had feared, Monsignor Augustine Ambrose Aquinas Sullivan. Al Downs, a hip-shooting Loop trial lawyer, was just finishing the prosecution's case.

"What about it, Father?" Al leaned back complacently on his lounge chair. "Do we get a conviction?"

Helen climbed out of the pool and Hugh followed her, her statuesque charms disturbingly close. "I'm not a jury, Al," he said, sitting down, "and the Church doesn't try pastors."

"How can you put up with him, Father?" demanded a redhaired woman in her late thirties, the wife of a prominent doctor, who, as far as Hugh could tell, never said anything.

"If it keeps up much longer"—Al was closing in for a kill—"we'll have to send a formal protest to the new cardinal. Would you be on our side?"

"I don't think it'll do any good," Hugh said evasively. Helen leaned over him with a tall rum and tonic. Her scent lingered after her, teasing him with its sensual delight.

"You don't think the cardinal will force pastors to retire at seventy?" Ben waved his cigar. "Some of the boys down at the Exchange have heard that rumor."

Hugh felt increasingly uncomfortable. "I hope you buy or sell soybeans on better information than that."

There was general laughter; even Helen smiled faintly through the halo of cigarette smoke around her head.

Hugh stood up. "And now, if you'll excuse me, I think I'd better go back to work on tomorrow's homily." He turned to Helen and thanked her.

"You gotta come back, Father," Ben Fowler said as he left. "The pool's here; someone else should use it besides us."

The "dance" was breaking up and Sister Elizabeth Ann and her favorites were sweeping up the debris and picking up Coke bottles when Hugh returned to the school hall.

"A question came up at the Institute I'd like to discuss with you," Sister began at once, her eyes modestly lowered. "Some of the sisters say it's unjust for us not to be permitted to call priests by their first names. Do you agree with that?"

"In theory, I might, Sister. But in this parish we have enough trouble as it is without stirring up the pastor and the old timers because of something relatively unimportant."

"In private?" she asked.

"And run the risk of slipping in public?"

"You're right, of course." She smiled warmly.

"Thank you, Sister." He laughed and she laughed. Then he went into the rectory and she went across the yard toward the convent.

In his room he turned off the air conditioner and opened the window because he disliked the feeling of being closed in. He was trapped, sunk in the quicksands of St. Jarlath's, the way America seemed to be sinking in the quicksands of Vietnam.

He turned on the radio and then turned it off. "A Hard Day's Night" on every station. There was no TV in his room. He didn't feel like walking down the corridor of the empty building to the TV room. He should, as he'd said, work on tomorrow's sermon, still only half finished.

He picked up Robin Moore's *The Green Berets*, read a few pages, and tossed it aside. No sermon ideas there.

He dialed the first five numbers of the Fowlers' phone and then hung up.

He would have to talk to someone or he'd lose his mind.

He called the convent and asked for Sister Elizabeth Ann.

"Yes, Father," said the discreet voice, although he hadn't identified himself. Much too late to make this call.

"Calling about the liturgy, Sister."

Sister Elizabeth came on.

"Hi, Liz, this is Hugh. I'm sorry about being a prig on the first-name issue."

Her warm and joyous laughter eased his pain.

"You're impossible," she said affectionately.

CHAPTER
THIRTEEN

1965

Hugh and Sister Elizabeth Ann ate a long brunch after the ten-o'clock Mass, at which the sixth graders had sung "My Soul Is Thirsting for the Lord" with such gusto the congregation had spontaneously joined in. Many parishioners complimented Hugh in the back of the church; unfortunately other and more "important" ones clearly would have complained to the pastor had he not been in Eagle River.

It was an iron law of Catholic reform: Those who approved spoke to the curates; those who opposed complained to the pastor.

However, all triumphs, even small and temporary ones, were meant to be savored. So he and Liz were savoring theirs in the rectory kitchen.

They were the only ones in the rectory. The cook and housekeeper were personal servants to Monsignor Sullivan. When he went on vacation, they were furloughed with pay. Lloyd Kilbride had returned to Guest House, a treatment center for alcoholic priests. Hugh was expected to fend for himself.

Liz made bacon and eggs and thawed coffee cake from the freezer. Hugh liberated a bottle of the pastor's best sauterne from the private wine cellar, the key to which he'd copied a few years earlier. The pastor's wine, naturally, was purchased with parish funds, so it seemed only right, Hugh opined, that it be enjoyed by the curates as well as the pastor and his friends.

"To Gelineau and the sixth-grade psalmsters," he toasted.

"May they survive another year," Liz toasted back.

She was an extremely pretty woman, he realized, no makeup, simple skirt and blouse, simple smile, simple good looks. Sweet, fragile, lovely.

"I keep telling myself this place is an excellent opportunity to liberate souls in purgatory," he said grimly.

Liz colored faintly. "Oh, Father . . . I mean Hugh . . ." Redder yet, most becomingly so. "I hate to disillusion you. The souls in purgatory are *out*."

"Really? That's a loss. What do we tell kids in the dental chair when the drill begins . . . or people dying of cancer?"

He resented the loss of the souls in purgatory. They were useful for preaching and teaching about suffering.

"You tell both groups"—she smiled over her coffee cup—"that by spiritualizing their suffering, they do what Jesus did when he died on the cross; they purify themselves and absorb pain from others. That's sound psychological truth, you know, and it frees them from the burden of mythological stories about imaginary places like purgatory."

"Uh-huh, what about heaven?"

Liz shifted momentarily in her chair. As she did so, her breasts pressed against her freshly pressed blouse. In that instant of revelation, more devastating to Hugh than if the blouse had fallen away, he felt faith and virtue desert him.

She waved a hand and laughed. "We survive, perhaps immersed in the mind of God. That's not important. What is important is that we try to achieve as best we can the kingdom of God on earth by working for social justice."

He gulped the delicately sweet white wine, hoping it would distract him.

"Immersed in the mind of God, will I be me?" Lovely Liz and good white wine notwithstanding, Hugh was dismayed; his religion was being taken away from him.

And the wine made him more, not less, aware of her own delicate sweetness.

She smiled delightedly and filled his glass again. "Don't you think, *Father* Donlon, that that's a selfish concern. Are you willing to leave to God the way you survive?"

"I don't think so," he said somberly. "I want to be me."

Is this how a rapist feels before he assaults a woman? He quickly drained his glass and filled it again.

"I want to be what God wants," she said with the same piety that Sister Cunnegunda used to praise the devotion to the Sorrowful Mother. The substance of devout ideology might change, the style did not—simple ideas, phrased in terse phrases, and preached with intense conviction. Yet she did know more about what the Church was thinking these days than he did.

Later, in his room, Hugh decided he would have to ask Monsignor Martin, the new rector of the seminary, about Sister Elizabeth Ann's religion. What she had said had truly disturbed him, although the thought of Xav Martin mercifully had exorcised his temptation.

Xav would say, "Typical half-baked summer-school theology. Let me give you a list of books to read, Hugh, so you can immunize yourself against such drivel."

Unfortunately, there was no time at St. Jarlath's to read.

Hugh turned his attention to the two months accumulation of mail that was piled on his desk.

The mail was like a review test of his priesthood. First, requests for First Communion records: Some damn fools in the East were so obsessive they wouldn't marry parish young folks without proof of First Communion, a requirement that went far beyond the code of canon law. Second, marriage notices to record in the baptismal records. Third, checks for Mass stipends to be recorded, and fourth, corrections in the annual statement the parish sent on of a person's financial contribution. It was all secretarial work that he would have to do sometime before the school year started. The monsignor's secretary was too busy to take care of such matters.

There were occasional surprises: an advertisement for a series of books on the abnormal psychology of adolescence; a new sermon outline series; two new sets of Sunday missals with the latest liturgical changes; a revised hymnal with Vatican Council hymns, whatever they might be.

He shoved the pile away. None of it was worth a damn. He was

a failure. How many sermons, classes, lectures, instructions, programs, visits, conversations, conferences, meetings, phone calls . . .
and what did he have to show for it? Marge was going to produce
a child. And he had produced nothing at all except two months'
worth of sacramental records.

He pounded his tiny desk and watched the pile of mail slide off.

Wearily, he picked up the paper and envelopes and piled them
in a neat stack again.

There was one envelope he had not noticed. From "Kincaid" in
Manhattan Beach, California. They had moved.

Dear Hugh,

*I've been meaning to write you for a long time. The
pictures in the papers of Marge's wedding forced me to
renew my good intentions. As you must imagine, I had
a good laugh and a happy one over Marge's turning
respectable. I must say you predicted that long ago.*

*I finally went over to the priest's house and asked
Father Mihail, our priest, for your address. He wondered why I wanted to write to you and I told him a
little bit about what you did for us. He told me that
priests receive so little positive encouragement for good
work they've done that I ought to thank you.*

*I was surprised. I said I thought priests didn't get dis-
couraged. He laughed and said I had a lot to learn about
Catholicism yet, "and yourself with all that convert's
zeal too."*

*When Laura came we decided she had to be baptized.
We valued our Lutheran heritage but there didn't seem
to be any way to go back to it. We went over to the
priest's house and told Father Mihail that we'd never
been in a priest's house before and we'd never talked to
a full-fledged priest.*

*So he took our Laura in his arms—she's a very cute
little blond, much better looking than her mother—and
said he wasn't going to let her go and that if we wanted
to have her back we'd have to become Catholics too and,
sure, conversion nowadays meant that we would be
Catholics and Lutherans at the same time.*

So we became Catholics and think of ourselves as Lutherans and Catholics. We started thinking that way even before Pope John, who was a lot like Father Mihail. Laura has a little brother now and there's another one on the way, so you can see what good Catholics we've become.

All of which is a way of building up to you, Father Hugh. It didn't take me long to figure out why Hank had come across the mountains to carry me away like a captive princess. I was furious with you for about ten seconds and then I knew I'd love you for the rest of my life. It was the last chance for both of us. We never would have taken the chance unless you'd forced us to.

I was wrong about everything. Hank and I fight a lot and all my other predictions were wrong too. Well, not all of them. I do have my degree from UCLA and am in graduate school now.

Would you believe that Laura, poor thing, was born nine months to the day after Hank came over the mountains to drag me away?

Our love is not always easy. It is not supposed to be. But neither of us has any doubt about it. Nor do we doubt that we owe it all to you.

I'm sure you have better things to do than answer letters like this. But, please, do put us on your Christmas card list.

Love,
Jean

"Hey, honey, I forgot. Padre Hugh is coming over to swim in a couple of hours. Make him a sandwich and give him a beer, would you, sweetheart?"

"Of course."

She tingled with excitement. She thought Father Donlon was the most beautiful man she'd ever seen, and she was perfectly aware that he couldn't take his eyes off her. It would be nice to have him to herself for an hour or two on a sunny Sunday afternoon.

Helen was the product of a marriage that had broken up when she was three. During her grammar school and high school years she had lived at Maryville and then started to work as a typist in a

Loop law office. She worked there for five interesting years and became a competent and skillful legal secretary. She routinely fended off passes from men who wanted to use her, and longed for a man to marry. Unfortunately, the men she thought might want to marry found her dull after the first date.

She didn't think she was dull, only painfully shy. But it came to the same thing.

In recent years she had frequently looked back to the relative poverty of those working years with fondness. She knew she had been good at her work. When the partners in the firm raised her salary every six months and said she was the best legal secretary on LaSalle Street, she had glowed with happiness. She'd received few compliments in her years at Maryville and none that acknowledged her ability as well as her good looks.

Then Ben had appeared in the office and promptly asked for a date. He thought she was intelligent because she listened to him without interrupting. When he proposed, she'd asked herself, Why not?

She was fond of her husband. He was generous and kind if not always considerate. His sexual needs were minimal, which was all right with her. She kept a neat house, listened to his monologues, gave him a daughter who bitterly disliked her mother, and enjoyed the privileges and prerogatives of his wealth.

She was bored and starved for affection. Yet loyalty to her husband and a low level of sexual interest herself had made it easy for her to turn down the inevitable passes. For someone who looked like either an ex-model or a graduate of a rich girls' finishing school, propositions, usually crude, were as much part of daily life as were dawn and sunset.

When Father Hugh arrived, Helen waited for him at poolside in a new black bikini that most women her age wouldn't have dared wear even in the privacy of the bedroom. She was pleased by the quick widening of his eyes.

"Ben had to go to the airport for a sudden conference and Linda is with her friends. He said I should give you a drink and a sandwich."

Hugh swam a half mile in the pool, hardly noticing her as she waited patiently at the edge, legs curled underneath her.

Afterward he ate a roast beef sandwich and drank a bottle of Pepsi. While he ate, Helen smoked several cigarettes and watched him intently through large sunglasses. He was certainly gorgeous. What would it be like to kiss him?

What harm in finding out?

"A soybean conference?" he asked as he ate the sandwich.

She shrugged. "I suppose so. I don't understand his business very well."

They continued the small talk until at length he announced that he had to leave. He hardly looked as if he were running away.

She snubbed out her cigarette and sprayed her mouth with a tube from her purse. She kissed him on the lips as they walked through the vast sunken living room on their way to his car.

It was a long sweet kiss, longer and sweeter than she had expected.

"Good-bye, Father." She turned quickly so he could not see her face.

It was all she wanted. It had been enough.

Hugh had accepted Ben's invitation because he had experienced a terrible letdown after the high created by Jean's letter. He returned to the pool a half dozen more times in August, three of them times when Helen was there alone. Finally he did not wait to be invited but called and told her he was coming.

Whenever they were alone, they kissed, and the kissing became more passionate with every visit. The last time the kiss turned into a silent embrace on deep blue sofa cushions under a Motherwell collage. They clung to each other for minutes on end, a delirious, timeless experience like drowning in a sea of honey.

Moreover, she wanted nothing more, it seemed, than affection. There was no hint that she was willing to go further and indeed a strong hint in the opposite direction. When, almost automatically, his hands had begun to explore, she had slipped gracefully away from him.

He was shaken, nevertheless, when he encountered Linda Fowler as he was leaving the house, just as he had finished wiping her mother's lipstick off his face and jamming the telltale handkerchief into his Windbreaker pocket. The child smirked. Had she been watching? Did she know?

Probably not. Linda always smirked.

CHAPTER

FOURTEEN

1965

The *Pegeen* glided rapidly through the water, picking up speed; soon it was touching only the tops of the waves, like the old *Yankee Clipper* taking off from Flushing Bay.

Then they were airborne, spinning through the clouds in a glorious, dancing frenzy. The wind bit into his face and his naked chest, his long hair trailed behind him, and he was singing at the top of his lungs. His heart soared even higher than the whirling boat turned airplane.

Maria was working at the jib, laughing and singing with him.

No, not Maria. Helen.

He kissed her and began to tear at her clothes. The joy of flying through space turned to terror. He tried to pull back from her but couldn't.

The boat began to plummet toward the dismal waters below. He forced his way into her just before they hit the angry waves.

He awoke soaked in sweat. He could not remember the dream the next morning. He never could. But this wasn't the first time it had become a nightmare.

In his still groggy mind, he heard Maria's words at Killarney.

If you break one rule, you'll break them all.

Passionately kissing another man's wife. Why was he doing it? It made no sense.

Hugh spent the last weekend of the summer with his parents at the lake and returned to the parish firmly resolved to meditate fifteen minutes every day, do spiritual reading for ten minutes, and some other serious reading for fifteen minutes and to say the rosary and part of the Divine Office before he went to bed every night.

And to stay away from the Fowler house.

He was thoroughly ashamed of the flirtation, had confessed it humbly, and was determined that nothing like it would ever happen again.

At the rectory, the secretary told him that the pastor had been home for the weekend but was forced to leave on Sunday night by urgent business in San Diego. He'd left word that Hugh should make sure the boiler was repaired before the school year started and bids collected for resurfacing the parking lot.

Hugh threw the notes into the wastebasket in front of the secretary, punishing her because he could not punish Monsignor Sullivan, and went upstairs to unpack.

Then he walked over to the white stone convent to ask Sister Elizabeth Ann about the Sunday liturgy.

Sister Superior was away. The old nun who was the cook answered the door.

"Oh, Father, Sister isn't with us anymore. Monsignor was very upset about the hymns at the ten o'clock Mass yesterday. He called Mother Baldwina. Mother wasn't home, so Sister Gertrudis, our vicar general . . . er, vice-president, told Sister that she would have to return to the motherhouse and stay there till Mother came back. Sister was very unhappy, but she's a good, obedient, religious person, even if she is a little modern, so she went to the motherhouse last night. Mother won't be home till tomorrow."

Hugh put his golf clubs back into the trunk of his car, called Jack Howard, and pleaded with him to meet him at the course. He took out his fury on Bobolink Country Club and beat Jack by three strokes.

"I'll say one thing and one thing only," Jack said somberly. "Even though I'm not among that young woman's fans, I'm glad for her that she's escaped that hellhole. No, I'll say another thing. You get out of there too, just as quickly as you can. There's no kindly mother general to save you."

"I can't let the people down."

"They'd let you down at the drop of a hat. Most of them think Sullivan is not only sane, but lovable. Your image says that Hugh Donlon can beat everyone the way he beat Austin High School. The difference is that Austin wasn't a madman."

"I'll beat him," Hugh insisted.

"He'll destroy you. You can't beat a psychopath."

"Is that what he is?"

That was exactly what Mother Baldwina called monsignor the next morning.

"Even if I were here, dear Father, I would have made the same decision as my vice-president. I cannot permit Sister to suffer any more at the hands of that psychopath. Do you realize that he ordered the ushers forcibly to remove her from the sanctuary where she was directing the hymns? He didn't ask her to leave. He came in, saw her directing the music, and without a word to Sister instructed the ushers to drag her out by force. Sister was nearly hysterical when she finally got home to the motherhouse."

"She's so important to the parish, Mother," he said humbly.

"I realize that, dear Father, and she is also important to us. I will not have her humiliated again. The poor child is too fragile to be subjected to such treatment. I'm sorry for St. Jarlath's but my first duty is to protect Sister."

"Certainly." He tried to sound urbane. How could he explain that he would miss her terribly?

"I am also writing a detailed letter to the cardinal describing what happened and warning him that if there is any repetition all our sisters will leave on the first northwestern train."

"That won't make any difference."

"I hope you're wrong, Father. In any case, it is now out of your hands and mine and up to Cardinal McCarthy."

"Yes, Mother."

"You haven't asked about Sister's next assignment."

"No, Mother."

"Do you wish to know?"

Now, what in the hell was he supposed to make of that?

"I'm not about to run after her, Mother Baldwina, if that's what you think. It was not that kind of relationship."

"She admires you greatly."

"That's good of her, Mother; I repeat, it was not that kind of a relationship. I understand your concern, but you have the wrong man for that sort of thing."

The telephone was wet from his perspiring hand. He shifted it to the other.

A sigh. "My apologies, Father. These days one does not know. . . . In any event, I feel it best to send Sister back to full time university work so she can finish her degree program. She needs a vote of confidence from the Order."

"I'm glad there are some prudent religious leaders left in the Church."

"You are indeed a very clever young man with your tongue."

So the school year began without Sister Elizabeth Ann. Hugh tried to do the entire liturgy program by himself. His good intentions about reading and prayer vanished quickly. He was soon tired again. Nor were his spirits improved by the return of Lloyd Kilbride.

"Where's the nun with the big knockers?" were his first words to Hugh at supper the night he returned. "I hear she got the sack."

"The pastor raped her," snapped Hugh.

After supper there was a message that Ben Fowler had called. Hugh returned the call.

"Padre, Al Downs is having a meeting tonight about his favorite subject. At his house. He wanted me to ask you if you were interested in coming. No obligation."

"Are you going, Ben?"

A pause. "I think I have to."

"I'll be there."

It was a council of war—twenty people, fifteen more than Hugh had expected.

"It has to stop," Downs began. "If we have any integrity left, we've got to do something about him. I take it we're all agreed that dragging that poor young nun off the altar was the final act of lunacy?"

There was already a bill of particulars itemizing the cruelties and stupidities of Monsignor Sullivan for many years: widows and children insulted at funerals, young people driven out of the Church, parishioners humiliated, students summarily expelled from the school because the pastor did not think they were dressed modestly enough—especially girls whose physical development had begun early—programs arbitrarily terminated, unresponsiveness to parishioners' requests, frequent prolonged absences from the parish, signs recently of excessive drinking.

"What do you think, Padre?" asked Ben Fowler, cigar out of his mouth and pointing at the sheet of paper.

"A lot of it won't fly." Helen was not present. Why not? "He may well be within his canonical rights in his vacations. You should not make charges of alcoholism without better proof. He is also the pastor and can terminate programs whenever he wants. If you removed pastors for being unresponsive to their parishioners or driving young people out of the Church by authoritarianism, you'd have to fire half the pastors in the archdiocese. If I were you, I'd concentrate on the cruelties, particularly at the time of death. Also the persecution of grammar school girls for their sexual development. And you could make a good deal out of the public displays. He can terminate lecture programs if he wants, but to publicly insult a visiting priest who is on the seminary faculty is a bit of a scandal. And, of course, dragging the sister off the altar was quite improper, even though regulation of the parish liturgy is well within his authority."

"Anything else, Father?" Downs hunched forward like a cat moving in on a canary.

"Well, it's hard to say how the new cardinal will react to this sort of problem. He's been away at the Council a good deal and has not reshaped the diocese in his image yet. It's said that he's quite untraditional in some respects. Nevertheless, I would be very cautious, if I were you. Protest your respect for authority. Praise Monsignor Sullivan's many accomplishments—I'm sure you can think of some—and concentrate on the terrible harm being done to souls."

"Mail him the letter?" asked Downs.

Hugh thought for a moment. "No. Call Monsignor Cronin, the vice-chancellor for personnel, and ask for an appointment. Tell him what it's about and who will be coming. Cardinal Eammon McCarthy will apparently see anyone who asks for an appointment. Be courteous and respectful. But don't leave any doubt that you are deeply concerned."

"Anything else?" said the red-haired woman whose name he could never remember.

"Yes. It is critically important that you keep this plan secret. If Monsignor Sullivan finds out, he will make you the issue, not himself. He knows how to use power to protect himself."

"Thanks, Father." Ben beamed. "Glad to have you aboard."

The others crowded around to shake his hand.

Poor people. Even a craven priest on their side was better than none.

"If there's nothing else, I probably ought to be back in the rectory. No one else covering for sick calls."

Faker. The teen-ager in charge of the door and the phone, paid with money lifted from the collection, could find him with a quick phone call.

He was afraid to be too close to treason.

Helen was standing at the door of her Mercedes. "I came to pick Ben up."

Impulsively his lips brushed hers.

She quickly pulled away. "I think Linda has been spying on us. Ben is suspicious."

As he drove away, he thought he saw Benedict in the doorway. Might he have seen the kiss?

CHAPTER
FIFTEEN

1965

For the good of his soul Hugh decided to spend a few days at the retreat house at Mundelein. He would talk to Xav Martin, who always seemed to have the right answers in time of troubles. Hugh had avoided Monsignor Martin because he knew Xav would force the hard decision and the confessor at the monastery would not.

He locked the safe after Mass on Sunday, checked the Mass schedule for the week to make sure there were Jesuits and Vincentians coming to do the work that the parish clergy would not do, locked all the doors in the church, packed a small suitcase, and sat down for what he hoped would be a peaceful ham sandwich and Coke—his first meal since the cup of coffee at breakfast.

It was not to be peaceful. Sister Mariana, the new school principal, called and insisted that he come to the convent on a matter of "the utmost urgency."

Sister Mariana was a small thin woman with hard eyes and a harder voice. In her middle forties, she preached the new "collegiality" of power sharing in the Church, but ran her school with all the permissiveness of a German submarine captain on combat duty.

She did not like St. Jarlath's. The people had too much money and the children were spoiled. Nor did she like Hugh, who as the pastor's representative could overrule her decisions, a prerogative he rarely exercised but one that rankled nonetheless.

"I'm leaving in five minutes for a short retreat." Hugh glanced at his watch as he walked in the back door of the convent. "What's the problem?"

He stood in the corridor between the kitchen and the parlors, underneath ugly portraits of St. Pius X and St. Maria Goretti, making it clear that he had not come for a long talk.

"More trouble with your dear children from this wonderful parish of affluent Catholics. Serious trouble."

"What kind?"

"Sex." She said the forbidden word with unconcealed relish.

Hugh was not impressed. "What kind of sex?"

"Eighth-grade sex. There was a party at the Mintons' house last night. The Fowler child was apparently the leader. Mrs. Kennedy was on the phone to me this morning, demanding that we take action against her and the Minton child."

"Did they have intercourse, Sister?"

Sister Mariana was shocked and offended. "I'm sure they did not. Nevertheless, they went quite far. The Fowler girl was practically naked, according to Mrs. Kennedy."

Strip poker or some variant of it. Nothing changes. "Have you talked to anyone else?"

"All but the Fowlers. She is a very difficult child." Sister Mariana hesitated, realizing perhaps that she might be going too far.

"Sister, I'm leaving for Mundelein. I'll be back on Wednesday night. Till then you may want to discuss the matter with the pastor if he returns or with Father Kilbride. My position is that we are not in the business of policing the morals of the young people of the community when they are not on parish grounds. If Mrs. Kennedy has complaints against Linda Fowler, she should bring them to Mrs. Fowler and not to us. We cannot and will not expel children for what they do in private homes. I will have a chat with Linda and with her parents next week. Is that clear?"

"Yes, Father." The hatred in her eyes would have annihilated him if it could.

"Good, pray for me while I'm on retreat."

Fat chance.

Xav Martin, his hair turning silver and his dark eyes preoccupied by the tensions of transforming the seminary, listened patiently and sympathetically as Hugh poured out his story.

He remained silent when Hugh was finished.

"I guess I only see you when I'm in trouble." Hugh was flustered by the silence.

"No, that's all right." Xav crossed his legs and rubbed his jaw. "I'm here to help anytime you want me. . . . I can't help but wonder, Hugh"—he hesitated again—"why you have to do it all yourself. Can't God take care of a little bit of the work?"

"We're supposed to work as if everything depends on us," Hugh replied with a quote from seminary spirituality.

"Sure." Xav waved it away. "But you can't assume total responsibility for the people of St. Jarlath's. The woman is not the problem, as I'm sure you know. The problem is that you are too stubborn or too idealistic to give up a lost cause. Get out of St. Jarlath's before it destroys you."

"And Gus?"

"The new boss will retire him in a few months anyway."

"Somehow that doesn't seem . . ."

"Manly?" Xav's dark eyes flashed.

"Maybe I should make an appointment with Sean Cronin."

"Damn right you should."

Later he thought about it in the quiet of the ugly retreat house chapel.

In the last years at the seminary and the time since ordination he had kept his passions under rigid control, practicing the asceticism of denial he had been taught in the seminary. He had come to believe that sex was no longer a problem in his life. It was as if he'd built a great earthen dam to hold the torrents of sexual desire back. Then the touch of Helen's lips had excited a slight tremor; a tiny earthquake had sent a jagged crack across the face of the dam. Before he realized what had happened, the massive wall collapsed and, unwilling but powerless, he was swept along by the flood. Now the dam must be rebuilt from the ground up.

At St. Jarlath's that would be impossible.

He needed a parish with not quite so much work, more time to read and pray, and a long distance from Lakeridge and the Fowlers.

Dear God, he prayed wearily, thank You for helping me to see what I must do to continue to serve You as a priest. Forgive my pride. Help me to learn humility from the wonderful examples of that virtue You have given me in my parents. I want to be a priest.

Help me to persevere. Give me the strength to see that my refusal to admit defeat is weakness rather than strength. It is weakness of the spirit that has kept me at St. Jarlath's and made me prone to the weakness of the flesh.

It all seemed very neat.

The night Hugh returned to Chicago, Ben Fowler called him. "Could the wife and I come to see you tomorrow night? About this business with Linda?"

The man's voice sounded tired and discouraged. What were the costs of being a commodity millionaire? For the first time, Hugh had a hint that they could be very high.

"How about the day after? I'm tied up tomorrow." Sister Elizabeth had insisted he come to a lecture by a young Swiss theologian. "Okay, I'll be free at nine thirty." He searched his appointment book . . . six other appointments.

"How bad is it, Padre?"

"I don't think this incident itself was too bad, Ben. It's a warning signal, however, that Linda will need more supervision."

"I suppose you're right. Attractive women need supervision, don't they?"

The next morning Hugh drafted a one-paragraph note to Monsignor Cronin requesting an interview on the subject of a change of assignment. He signed the letter, put it in a St. Jarlath's envelope, and sealed the flap.

Now, when to mail it? Before or after the letter from the parishioners?

Wait till after their letter. Let them have the first shot. His interview might give the chancery an opportunity to ask what he thought about the situation.

Am I procrastinating? Nonsense, the letter is here on my desk, signed and sealed. I've made up my mind to mail it a week from Monday.

CHAPTER
SIXTEEN

1965

Hugh deliberated over whether to wear sports clothes or priestly garb for his dinner with Liz. The latter was safer and more appropriate. On the other hand, a Roman collar would be out of place at a lecture by the famous liberal Swiss theologian Hans Kung.

He was glad he'd chosen sports clothes when Liz embraced him and kissed him with rather more fervor than he thought advisable. And he was glad he'd chosen the rendezvous he had as he directed her toward their table in the Hungarian restaurant on Wabash Avenue, a more discreet place for this supper than one of his father's clubs. A priest kissed in the Chicago Club could cause the scandal of the century.

"Tell me everything about St. Jarlath's," she pleaded when they were seated.

She was dressed in skirt, blouse, and sweater, no veil—no sign, in fact, that she was a religious woman. Her face was slightly flushed with pleasure. A night out and intellectual stimulation too. Her bright-eyed zest made Hugh feel middle-aged.

"I'll begin with the scandal first." He told her about the eighth graders.

"Do you find her attractive, the mother, I mean? I suppose most men would." Her hand paused as she was buttering her fresh French bread.

"The goulash here is great, don't miss it . . . you mean Helen? She's certainly not unattractive. I'm not sure that she's very intelligent. . . ."

"She's socially useless." Liz dismissed Helen with a wave of her knife. "What does she do with her time? One child and help at home. She's a parasite, a whore; that's why the poor daughter is confused."

There was a nasty edge to Sister Liz tonight.

"I'd kind of feel sorry for her if that were true. . . . There's other news too. A letter is probably going to the cardinal this week about the pastor. The people, or some of them, are finally determined to have a change."

"Do you think it will work?"

"Not the first time, perhaps. The Church never acts against corruption or madness early enough. But it rarely waits till the bitter end either. The chancery will do something about St. Jarlath's at just the right time to offend the maximum number of people."

She laughed gaily and dug into the goulash. "Oh . . . this is good . . . you're a terrible cynic, Hugh."

"Now tell me about graduate school."

It was all that she had hoped for and more, she said—challenging teachers, stimulating fellow students, time to read books and write papers, an opportunity for personal development and self-fulfillment.

"What are you going to write your dissertation on?"

"I'm devoting my time to learning and developing myself, instead of doing that academic Mickey Mouse stuff."

"I though that dissertations were good training in self-discipline and skill."

She abruptly dismissed the thought. "Self-fulfillment is what matters these days, not self-discipline, Hugh; you know that." She sounded faintly disappointed in him. "Anyone can learn skills. . . . Now you tell me about yourself."

"Not much there. Well, that's not altogether true. I have a letter here in my wallet." He patted his jacket. "To the chancery, asking for a transfer from St. Jarlath's. I decided down at the Trappists' last week that I had to get out if I was going to survive. My emotions are mixed . . . guilt and relief."

A spasm of pain on her pretty face and a quick hand on his. "I know how hard that must be for you, Hugh. But it's right; I'm sure it's right. It will purify and spiritualize you."

"It will take a lot more than that to purify me," he laughed, liking and not liking her concern.

Sister Elizabeth paid little attention to Hans Küng's talk. She applauded for the charismatic young Swiss when everyone else did, and laughed and cheered when it seemed appropriate. Tonight would be considered an important and electrifying night, she was sure. It would be useful to be able to claim in the years ahead that one had been present at such a crucial historical event. But Hugh Donlon was more important to her than Hans Küng. Like most men, Hugh was insensitive and unperceptive. She supposed that it would take a long time to change that. His family was certainly a bad influence. He was also incorrigibly straight. He would not even kiss her good night at the end of the evening.

His theology was terribly old-fashioned. He thought that parishes like St. Jarlath's were important. He didn't realize that the local parishes would soon wither away in the New Church.

She sighed and joined the standing ovation for Küng in the great barn of McCormack place.

Honesty in the Church had been Küng's subject. Hugh Donlon needed to hear a lot of honesty, she thought. He needed to be told that he was not the knight in shining armor he thought he was. He needed to come into contact with his real self, his basic humanity, as she had done in graduate school.

He needed her help more than ever.

She introduced him to her friends from the Christ Commune as they left the hall. Hugh was ill-at-ease; he didn't want to be introduced to anyone on what seemed like a "date" with a nun.

Still, she was proud of him. He would straighten out in time. And she would take care of him.

Helen Fowler was terrified. She'd never seen Ben so mad. He was silent for several days about Linda's escapade and then erupted without warning at the supper table. It was her fault more than Linda's. She had only one child and all the money she needed. Couldn't she do anything right?

Helen was tongue-tied. "I try, Ben . . ." she stammered.

"Well, you don't try enough, you little nitwit."

Helen didn't try to defend herself. She was afraid that he would hit her.

"And you, you little tart, if you ever do anything like that again, I'll kill you, do you hear me, I'll kill you!"

Linda was terrified too. "I won't, Daddy. I won't do it again. I swear."

He slapped the girl twice across the face and she burst into hysterical sobs.

"Mommy makes love with Father Donlon and you don't hit her."

Ben hit Helen's face with a closed fist, sending her sprawling against one of the lacquered Chinese cabinets in their parlor.

"Whore!" he snarled.

"I didn't do anything wrong," she implored as she tried to control her sobs.

"Yeah? Well, let that be a warning to you not to."

"Nothing wrong at all," she pleaded.

"We'll see." His anger was spent and he half-believed her.

It was easy for Hans Kung to talk about honesty. He did not have to face Ben and Helen Fowler with the guilty knowledge that he had been too familiar with Helen. The conversation would be an exercise in dishonesty from the opening shot.

Hugh's efforts with Linda that afternoon had failed completely. The girl, tall for her age and on the way to being even more elegantly blond than her mother, opted for sulkiness rather than intelligence. The scandal over the Kennedy party was a bore to her. What was all the fuss about? Joannie Kennedy should have kept her big mouth shut. They hadn't done anything really wrong. Other people did worse things.

She seemed to Hugh to be amused by him. Was she really spying on them?

Then, at the door of the rectory office, she turned to him, suddenly a frightened little girl again. "Was it a terrible sin, Father Donlon?" she asked uncertainly. "Will I go to hell for it?"

"No, Linda." He tried to smile gently. "God loves you too much for that to happen. We grown-ups worry about how young people can hurt themselves terribly without realizing what they're doing."

"Yes, Father," she said docilely, as though she understood, which of course she did not.

After Linda left the rectory, Hugh was depressed. The girl had inherited her mother's beauty and her father's shrewdness. That ought to be enough to assure survival. Sadly, she had also acquired intelligence from some recessive gene, a gift that would probably push her into tragedy.

She would not only suffer, as beautiful and inexperienced young women unequipped with values must do. She would know she was suffering. And there was nothing he could do to help her.

His heart filled with love for her, the same kind of burning priestly love he had felt for the boy who'd called his mother shit. If only he could protect them all from the tragedies of life.

He sighed as he trudged up the terrazo stairs to his room. Priestly love, like all love, was powerless to shield children from the pains of experience. Still, a priest ought to be able to do something to help a child like Linda.

"As to the facts," he told her parents that evening, "it would appear that a number of the girls, including Linda, engaged in some necking and petting and may have taken off their blouses. No more and no less. They are not the first young women their age to engage in such activities out of boredom or curiosity or the need for affection."

"Geez, Padre." Ben's cigar dangled from his fingers. "I don't know what to think. Helen here says that the kid knows the score. I can't believe she's had enough instruction. . . ."

Hugh's hands, wet with perspiration, were shaking. There had been a two-word phone conversation with Helen before they came: "He knows."

He must keep Ben on the defensive. "A girl is much more likely to listen to what her father says about men than what her mother says, especially at her age."

"Me?" Ben was astonished. "Hey, Padre, when I come home from the Board of Trade I'm really beat. You ever been there? You know what it's like? I can't handle that sort of thing. That's the wife's job."

It wouldn't do any good, but Hugh was going to try. "Two things matter for a girl like Linda—what her father says to her and the relationship between her father and her mother. If her father is close and interested and if her parents' sexual relationship is warm and not exploitive, she learns far more than she would from all the explicit sex instruction we could possibly give her."

"Great, Padre, sure appreciate the help." Ben was on his feet, eager to escape from a situation he couldn't control.

"Hey, are you going to be at the meeting at Downs's house tomorrow night?"

"I suppose so."

"Great."

"Well, honey"—Ben stood back to let Helen out the door of the rectory—"we have to take the padre seriously. Gotta enjoy one another more, huh?"

He swatted her buttocks with his vast paw. He was deliberately hurting her in Hugh's presence and threatening to hurt her even more.

Helen turned crimson, not in anger so much as in shame.

In another era, Hugh thought as he went to his room, I would have killed him on the spot.

Ben said nothing to Helen on the way home. She knew he was furious. He must have sensed the chemistry between her and Hugh. She resigned herself to a savage beating. Maybe she even deserved it.

As soon as they were inside the house, he dragged her to their bedroom and beat her mercilessly. His rage was cool and controlled. He didn't strike her face, but he inflicted injuries that would hurt for many days. She wept but she didn't scream.

When he was finished, he threw her on the bed. "The next time I'll mess up your face and cut off your tits," he said. He was breathing heavily, choking on his rage, and on the phlegm from those terrible cigars.

Later he returned, beat her again, and then made brutal love to her.

"I'll fix that son of a bitch Donlon," he said when he was finished.

The final meeting of the protest committee, Hugh learned on Friday morning from Al Downs, had been stormy. Some people had lost their nerve. Two couples walked out, insisting they couldn't protest against a poor old man in bad health. Three others demanded a stronger letter, including a charge of faking bad health.

"I turned into a moderate, would you believe?" Al's laugh on the phone line reminded Hugh of the sound of hyenas in western movies. "We finally decided to go with the original letter. It'll be in the mail Monday."

Hugh was alarmed. "If those couples who walked out should go to Sullivan, you're finished."

"They won't. Ben Fowler put the fear of God in them. We're okay; you know, Father, it's a hell of a way to run a church."

"We're a long way from Galilee, Al. I suppose there's no way to avoid such situations as long as the Church is made up of human beings. We spend a lot of our time fighting one another."

"I'd hell of a lot sooner defend a murder rap than draft another letter to a cardinal, I can tell you that."

"Well, it's over now, Al, for better or for worse."

"It can't get any worse here, can it, Father?"

"I suppose not," Hugh replied.

He was wrong, it could get a lot worse.

As he was finishing the ten o'clock Mass on Sunday morning, Monsignor Sullivan, in full purple regalia, rochet, mozzetta, the whole works, appeared in the sanctuary like the Avenging Angel of the Apocalypse.

He knows, Hugh thought, feeling a big hole in the pit of his stomach.

"See that young priest," the monsignor thundered. "Get a good look at him because you'll never see him on the altar of this church again. He is a Judas priest, a traitor to your pastor and your parish, which have provided him a home for the last four years. . . ."

Three years off, Hugh thought, calmly drying the chalice.

"He and a tiny group of malcontents have organized a conspiracy to replace me, your beloved pastor who has served you generously and unselfishly for more than a quarter-century. Listen to the letter they're going to send to the cardinal tomorrow."

He had the letter, the whole thing. He read it with great gusto and parenthetical remarks of his own. "Promise to continue to cooperate, do they? Well, we don't need their cooperation, any more than we need this Judas priest, do we, my beloved people? We will get rid of them all, just like I'm going to get rid of this young punk. . . ."

Hugh finished Mass and calmly walked into the sacristy. As he was taking off his vestments, he heard Sullivan's final shot. "Mr. Guinan has the copy of a petition that has been assembled by a group of loyal parishioners in defense of their beloved and saintly pastor. Anyone who wants to sign it may. No obligation, of course. I'll be there in back of church to welcome your cooperation. Let's all band together against the Judases in our midst."

Hugh waited in the cool antiseptic sacristy with its pale stained-glass windows casting the kind of light you would expect in a hospital chapel.

"I took you into this parish and shared my people with you," the pastor rampaged as he entered. "You're a nothing. You have no rights other than those I give you. And you presume to challenge me with my own people. You are an ungrateful cad, Father Donlon; my people love me and will stand by me. They will drive you out of this parish and destroy your reputation, wherever you are assigned. You ought to leave the priesthood now, because I promise you that you will never have another happy day in it.

"How dare you presume to criticize and connive against a man who is God's appointed representative over you? Answer me, young man. Don't stand there with that self-satisfied smile on your face. . . ."

"I'm not smiling," Hugh said, choking back his rage. Gus Sullivan was indeed God's duly appointed representative. Did God appoint sociopaths to rule over parishes?

Hugh strode out of the sacristy and went to his room; he collected a few clothes, put them in a bag, tore up his letter to the chancery, got into his car, and drove home to Mason Avenue. His departure from St. Jarlath's would require some explaining to his parents.

On second thought, he would not need to offer any explanation. They would be overjoyed that he was out of the place.

Tuesday Sean Cronin called from the chancery. "I thought you'd be at home, Hugh. The boss would like to see you."

"I imagine so. When?"

Late that afternoon, Hugh was sitting in Cronin's office in the old-fashioned gray chancery building, with its high ceilings, dismal maroon carpets, and grotesque paintings of white-clad popes and red-clad hierarchs.

The vice-chancellor was nervous. He fidgeted with a paper-weight model of St. Peter's in Rome.

"Bad operation, Hugh. You never should have organized anything like that with such loose security. Now Sullivan has you on the defensive."

"I didn't organize it. They asked me how to write to the cardinal and I told them. I believe what we were taught at the seminary about loyalty and obedience."

Cronin rubbed his hand through thick blond hair. "Really? I didn't think anyone bought that stuff anymore. You didn't organize it? Well, I'm glad to hear that. I knew you would be much better at plotting. Still, you should have had enough sense not to trust that Fowler fellow. I hear that a lot of the other people want to boil him in oil."

"He'll keep."

Someday I'll smash that insect.

Then they were called into the cardinal's office. Hugh felt the touch of unease that high authority causes in priests. It was replaced with fury at the little sandy-haired man with the mild face and the thick glasses.

"I'll begin, Your Eminence, if you don't mind. . . ."

A quick little smile and a diffident hand gesture.

"I know that in the Church those who have authority can do no wrong and those who don't have it can do no right. So I'm fully prepared to be the scapegoat. Transfer me as you intend and retain Monsignor Sullivan as you intend. But spare me the hypocrisy. You know that the charges in the letter are mild compared to what you have in your files, and have had for years. You know that the man should have been removed long ago. Don't lecture me on the importance of loyalty or authority or respect for a sick old man."

The cardinal toyed with a ballpoint pen. "I quite agree, Father, that he should have been replaced long ago. In a month or two we will announce a retirement policy that will appeal to him, whether he wants it or not. I have been here briefly, as you know, and there are so many things. . . ." He dismissed his own problems with a minute movement of the pen. "I do not think of you as the disgraced curate and Monsignor as the betrayed pastor. . . ."

"He's still the winner and I'm the loser."

"Some will see it that way, Father. It is an unjust assessment. However, the world is unjust. Nevertheless, you are a man of great promise and abilities, Father Donlon. I would like to arrange an assignment for you that would do you honor, both because I do not want unjust judgments made about your new assignment and because I need your talents. . . ."

He paused, as though waiting for an answer.

"I need advisers with scholarly credentials, particularly in the areas that are important to the Church. I wonder if you would consider going to the university to obtain a degree in demography . . . the population issues the Church faces require expertise in this."

"I'll do it if I'm ordered to. Only if I'm ordered to."

The cardinal removed his glasses and began to polish them. "Perhaps when you're less angry."

"No!"

The cardinal sighed. "Very well. I hoped we could settle this more genially. You're . . . you have reason to be very angry, I suppose. . . . Monsignor Cronin, would you be good enough to make the arrangements?"

"I accept the order, Your Eminence." Hugh stood at the door. "I have no choice. Nevertheless, I consider the entire affair to be a violation of justice. I promise you that I will not forget it."

"We shall have no peace in the world, Father"—the cardinal readjusted his glasses—"as long as we refuse to forget violations of justice."

"I'm not looking for peace," Hugh said, then turned on his heel and walked out of the cardinal's office.

BOOK
THREE

"This day thou shalt be with me in paradise."

CHAPTER

SEVENTEEN

1968

"Is the boss around?" Professor Duncan Leo, a spare, trim young man with a blond mustache and transparent blue eyes peered into Hugh's cubbyhole in the Center for Research in Uniform Demography (CRUD). As the only man who had obtained tenure when Professor Talcott Kingsley Homans was out of the country, he was distinctly unwelcome at CRUD. Homans did not like to be reminded how his own summer promotion had been slipped by the Demography Department two decades earlier.

"Gone to Indonesia this morning and left me a batch of papers to correct." Hugh looked up from his calculator.

"So what else is new?" Duncan sat on the edge of the hard wooden chair that was the only concession to luxury in the cubbyhole CRUD had provided for Hugh. "Good news from Michigan; they've seen your dissertation draft and your article on village structure and agricultural productivity. They will offer you an appointment for next fall, tenure track, assistant professor at seventeen five, which is almost what I make, no requirement that the dissertation be accepted. They know that Talcott will make you sweat it out if he possibly can."

"It's certainly an attractive offer." Hugh hesitated. "I'll have to consider it; I feel I owe the Church in Chicago—"

"—nothing. You paid your dues by grinding out problems on

that machine for TKH and correcting his papers. Seriously, won't they let you go?"

"The cardinal said it was up to me."

"So, that settles it. Michigan is in no hurry. Let me know after Christmas and we'll initiate the process for a formal offer."

Duncan Leo bounced enthusiastically out of the cubbyhole.

Hugh pushed a stack of introductory demography exams under a pile of green-edged computer printouts. He was a good demographer, no doubt, with a nice fat offer from Michigan. They'd wanted him as a quarterback seventeen years ago and now they wanted him as something more important.

A first-rate demographer—and still a priest. Did it make any sense? Was he really a priest? Everyone thought he was—his family, Liz, the cardinal, the priests at St. Medard's, where he lived, the students and faculty in the department. The only one who had any doubts was he.

And he had shared those doubts with no one. Not even Liz, who was now his closest friend.

He said Mass every morning at St. Medard's, preached at two Masses on Sunday, wore clerical garb except when he was physically on the university campus (and black slacks there), went to the annual reunions of his seminary class, even played an occasional game of golf on Thursdays in the summer with Pat Cleary and Jack Howard. He would have spent his summer vacations with them too, if there had been time for summer vacations.

He was not a radical 1960s priest. He did not march on picket lines, did not sign petitions. And he'd stayed in his cubbyhole through the long summer week when Liz and the other members of the Christ Commune had confronted the Chicago police in front of the Conrad Hilton Hotel during the Democratic convention.

Liz was unhappy with his conservatism. His consciousness, he replied, laughing at her attractive anger, was unraisable.

Despite the closeness of his relationship with her, Hugh had kept some distance from the Christ Commune and its assorted group of priests, ex-priests, nuns, and ex-nuns, some of whom were married, some of whom were living together, some of whom were dating— a confusing example of Church reform run amok, he thought. He was skepical about couples engaged in "third way" relationships, the nongenital love affairs between priests and nuns that, they said, were neither "strictly celibate nor strictly noncelibate."

What the hell did that mean?

Yet he was careful not to ridicule the Commune itself, because Liz was part of it. Indeed, the only reason for hanging around there was to keep an eye on her.

Liz was having a hard time finding herself these days, especially since her return to the university after a two-year stint of high school teaching in Montana. They were very close now, the relationship more secure than ever because he kept his fantasies and desires under strict control. She was still sweetness and laughter, a lovely fund of joy and excitement, some of the time.

Yet there was an anger in her too, which he had barely noticed at St. Jarlath's, and a snappish impulse to intellectual arrogance. Both tendencies seemed to be especially strong when she was with the communards. Hugh was caught between an obligation to protect her and an obligation to respect her freedom. Hence he tolerated the Commune and waited for the return of her contagious smile as soon as they left the apartment building that the Commune occupied.

Supper there the other night had been typical.

Theo, a fat, balding priest from the Albertin Fathers (of whom Hugh had never heard), was lecturing on celibacy to the group as they ate.

"We historians are realists; we know that celibacy was imposed against the will of the clergy to prevent ecclesiastical property from passing into the hands of the children of priests. . . ."

"Was that a serious problem?" Hugh asked innocently.

"Of course, it was," Theo said, frowning in exasperation.

"Well, then, maybe it was a good solution."

"The point is that it is not a problem today."

"Might become one." Phony intellectuals like Theo were a pushover. He'd never finish a dissertation, never be a scholar.

"Anyway," Theo went on, "the spiritual arguments in favor of celibacy can easily be refuted by Marxist analysis. We are able to see correctly today that it is merely a technique for keeping the lower clergy in a subservient role. . . ."

"Jesus and St. Paul refuted by Marxist analysis?" Hugh asked in feigned dismay.

"Hugh, please," Liz said irritably.

Hugh remained loyally silent for the rest of the meal and even joined the long grace led thereafter by Jackie, a nun or an ex-nun, he couldn't remember which. She said the words of the Consecration of the Mass over the bread as part of her grace and distributed it to the rest of them, as though it were Holy Communion.

She also prayed for the destruction of the American imperialist aggressors in Vietnam.

Hugh consumed the make-believe Communion without a twinge of guilt. He did not pray for the destruction of the Americans in Vietnam, however. He would not pray for Steven McLain's destruction.

The archdiocese viewed Hugh as a voice of reason among a multitude of well-meaning crazies.

It was an image Hugh enjoyed.

Even his relationship with Liz was discreet. It was not a "third way" liaison by any means. Hugh's only mistake was to bring her for supper one Sunday to North Mason Avenue.

From the outset, Liz was defensive and insecure. The long periods of silence at the table embarrassed her, for, although Peggy appeared to be determined to be sweet with her, Liz sensed that Peggy was hostile underneath.

When Peggy responded to Liz's question about "what she did" with a brief description of her teacher's aid work at St. Ursula, on the other hand, Liz merely nodded in polite accompaniment. Hugh knew that she thought such volunteer work was "part of the problem."

Hugh rushed in. "She's a painter too."

"Oh, Hugh. They're just pretty watercolors, not *relevant* at all." Peggy said it with more irony than Hugh had imagined her capable of.

"I'd love to see them." Liz was as determined to be polite as Peggy was. She daintily cut her Yorkshire pudding.

So after dinner everyone went on a tour of Peggy's studio in the converted sleeping porch overlooking the backyard. Peggy was in what her husband called a "Monet mood" and the porch looked like a pastel children's nursery.

"How very interesting," Liz said guardedly.

Over coffee in the parlor, Peggy struck back. "And you're doing your dissertation in educational administration, my dear?"

"Theoretically," Liz said.

"I don't understand what you mean," Peggy pressed, sensing her defensiveness.

"Actually, I'm engaged in discovering myself."

"How very interesting. . . ."

All in all, Peggy won the match—the more experienced of the female cougars squabbling over the meat.

Bad chemistry between them, Hugh thought as he and Liz escaped the house on North Mason Avenue with enormous relief.

"The married parish priest has been more typical and more common in the history of Christianity than the celibate priest," Theo said at another supper.

"Besides," Jackie interrupted, "celibacy was originally based on the belief that sex was evil. If it is grounded on a false premise, then it has to be false, doesn't it? And those of us who are witness ing against celibacy by our life-style are bearing witness to the truth, as Jesus taught we should."

"Absolutely," Theo agreed.

Hugh was on the brink of pointing out Sister's logical fallacy when he heeded a warning look from Liz. Freedom of discussion was not one of the guiding principles of the Christ Commune. You could express any thought you wanted, so long as it was "correct." Alas, poor Hugh was almost always "incorrect."

What if there were to be a change in the vow of celibacy? he thought during a reverie in his cubicle. Had he been wrong all along? Had he sacrificed marriage for a historical mistake? If there was a change in the next ten years—and everyone in the Christ Commune was confident there would be—would it be too late for him?

To the world, Hugh was the sensible, loyal priest who kept his head in the midst of chaos, so sensible that he was able to resist the fads and fashions of the moment. He didn't even sign a petition to the Pope demanding reconsideration of the birth-control decision, although Liz refused to talk to him for a week.

He was much less obsessed by the Church than were the Christ Commune members. Although the disgrace and defeat at St. Jarlath's still rankled, he had learned that injustice and stupidity were as prevalent in the secular world as they were in the Church.

Liz and her Christ Commune colleagues were angry at the Church because it didn't live up to their faith. Hugh's problem was that he wasn't sure any religious faith was valid or necessary.

He spent most of his waking hours with men and women who didn't believe. Yet they were good and generous human beings. Unlike Professor Homans and some of the other exploiters of graduate students, they helped him in his work, were sympathetic to his early confusion, quietly supported him in his battles with Homans. Their questions about his religion were more curious than offensive.

How could such moral and intelligent men and women live without religion? Could a faith possibly be true that responded to none of their needs?

Having been raised in an environment in which faith was taken for granted, Hugh could not comprehend an environment in which nonbelieving was equally assumed. If he was right, then all these people were mistaken. But if they were right?

"You're a Catholic because you were raised a Catholic," Duncan Leo had said to him once, not as an objection but as a statement of fact. "I was raised a Unitarian. If I'd been raised a Catholic, I'd be like you."

The religion Hugh had inherited was as unconsidered as the language he used. He'd never examined his faith because it had never seemed to require examination.

Sometime he would have to resolve the God question, just as he would have to take a vacation, catch up on his theological and spiritual reading, and devote more time to prayer. But for the moment he had to concentrate on revising his dissertation and deciding whether to take the appointment at Michigan or to work for the cardinal.

"Is the world's best demographer still slaving away?"

It was Liz at the door, slim and lovely in a cloth coat, red scarf, and matching mittens; Liz, about whom he had erotic fantasies at night and whom he chastely admired when he was with her.

"The best has gone to Indonesia." He stood up and kissed her lightly on the cheek. "The second best has papers to correct."

"I thought you might walk home with me," she said, pretending to pout.

"I promised Jack and Pat I'd go to the *Messiah* with them tonight."

"The concert is Sunday." For Liz, the whole world was the university.

"At the University Chapel. We're going to Orchestra Hall for the Apollo Music Club."

She was lovely even when she pouted. How had he survived the last two years without her? Third way or not, it felt good to be important to a woman, especially one as gravely beautiful as Liz.

"So I'll take you on Sunday. No harm in hearing it twice."

"I'm not sure I'll be back by then. Mother wants to see me on Saturday. I'll have to drive all the way to Wisconsin." The pretended pout turned to a worried frown.

"Anything wrong?" Anxiety clutched at his throat too. "They promised you could finish your graduate work this time."

"Mother was very friendly and said she had good news to report." Her lip began to tremble. "Only I'm not sure we have the same definition of good news."

"I'll have lunch with you tomorrow." Hugh tried to reassure her. "I won't let her change her mind."

She rushed to him in gratitude. "Oh, Hugh. What a saint you are." She touched his cheek, then ardently embraced him.

He drew back, then drew her closer, impelled, despite himself, by a fundamental need to help.

Liz went limp in his arms, then pressed hard against him. Need, hunger, fear, combined into a desperate longing.

Their kisses were intimate, skillful, tender. They communicated their passion in the precise amounts needed by the other. Liz suddenly stiffened.

"What's wrong?"

A fantasy of the kind he didn't acknowledge raced through his fevered brain.

She relaxed and slipped away. "Worried about the trip to the motherhouse? Don't." She kissed him on the mouth. "See you tomorrow at noon."

Jack Howard and Pat Cleary were waiting for him in Orchestra Hall. As usual, Jack had obtained center-aisle seats.

"You look like hell, Hugh," he said. "Are you getting away at Christmas?"

"I don't think so. I've got to see Himself, a decision about next year."

Hugh told them about the Michigan job. They offered perfunctory congratulations.

"I can tell from your overjoyed expressions that you're dying for me to take it."

"There's room for you here in the archdiocese," Jack said mildly.

"At St. Jarlath's with Monsignor Sullivan?" Hugh was unable to hide his bitterness.

"That's not fair, Hugh," Jack remonstrated. "Gus is in retirement and so are all the other brats. Eammon's running a fine archdiocese. There's plenty of room for talented people here now."

The music began and hundreds of voices filled the red and ivory hall with joyous cadences celebrating the victory of the King of Kings over the forces of darkness.

It isn't that easy, Hugh thought. Too hard these days to tell what's light and what's darkness.

At intermission Hugh and Pat went to the lobby while Jack crossed the auditorium to speak to friends.

Still transported by the music, they watched the snowflakes falling lazily in the beams of the headlights on Michigan Avenue. Hugh felt a light kiss on his cheek.

"If it wasn't for that second glass of wine at dinner, I'd never have dared. Hugh, you know the commander. He's a full three-stripe commander now."

"Maria . . ."

"Don't look so astonished. I'm a big girl now. Home for the holidays"—she looked at her husband—"and maybe a little longer. . . . You look older, Hugh, but still as handsome as ever."

She turned to Pat. "I'm Maria McLain, Father. My old swain is too appalled by the deterioration of my appearance to observe the social amenities. This is my husband, Steven."

The commander shook hands with both of them, clearly delighted by his wife's social ease. "We've been at Glenview for a year and now I'm going back overseas," he said.

"You've been at Glenview, darling," Maria corrected. "I've been raising two hellions and getting an accounting degree." She turned to Hugh. "Is it celibacy or demography that's wearing you out? Don't answer me," she said without missing a beat. "How's the family?"

"They're fine," Hugh said shyly.

"How many kids?"

"Marge has two—two little daughters—and Tim has three. Mom and Dad are getting older but they seem to be all right."

Maria's face turned almost melancholy, transiently close to tears. "It's good to see you again, Hugh." The tears disappeared. "You see, there really is a Father Hugh Donlon. I tell my kids I knew this man who became a priest and they don't believe me. The young one says he wants to be a priest. Fortunately he hasn't reached the age of reason yet. . . ."

And so it went. A few bits of news exchanged, a few vain promises made to stay in touch, a lot of old memories inflamed and quickly extinguished, a couple of difficult, scaring, bittersweet, wonderful moments. Another firm handshake and an auld lang syne kiss. And she and her husband were lost in the crowd.

"My God," breathed Pat Cleary. "Who was that?"

"That was Maria, someone out of my past. . . ."

Maria of his dreams, countess, comic, clear-eyed waif, and now woman banker, alive and bigger than life, bigger even than his dreams. At the height of her physical attractiveness, somewhat more smoothly rounded and infinitely more sensual.

Oh, my lovely Maria, why did I ever lose you?

It was a foolish, romantic question, yet not even the soaring sopranos of George F. Handel could drive it out of his mind.

Maria's face was still warm and her heart was pounding when she and Steven returned to their seats. Hugh Donlon could still turn her into melting butter. She held her husband's hand. No point in trying to fool old Commander Steven.

He smiled at her and winked.

CHAPTER
EIGHTEEN

1968

On Saturday afternoon Hugh was scheduled to say Mass at the Christ Commune. A wan and red-eyed Liz kissed him quickly on the cheek when he came in. "Let's walk after dinner. It was terrible, simply terrible."

Her anguish distracted him from the holiday festivities at Mass. The reader wore a Santa Claus costume and the director of song a south-sea sarong, for which she lacked the figure. The bread of the Eucharist was brandied plum pudding and the wine was steaming wassail. Both were carried to the altar by priests wearing white placards around their necks, one reading, "Joseph, killed by American bombs," the other, "Mary, burned by American napalm." They offered prayers asking God to rain destruction on the Dow Chemical Company and urging the American people to overthrow Richard Nixon.

Hugh preached a sermon about the silent peace of the heart, the secret of the love in the cave at Bethlehem. "Only those who are at peace in their hearts," he told the Commune, "can bring peace to other hearts."

They'll climb all over me at dinner, he thought.

During the offertory there was a modern dance by women in leotards and men in swimming trunks. Hugh couldn't figure it out, save that it was about sex and Christmas.

Dinner was a vegetarian meal, in deference to the poor of the world. Bread and wine, banished from the altar, were served at the dinner table, along with fruit, a hot vegetable compote, and salad, the lettuce for which, having come from union fields, was not subject to the current boycott.

Jackie recited a long grace, reminding all present that Christianity embodied not peace but the sword.

Hugh didn't argue. He wanted to finish the meal as quickly as possible so that he and Liz could escape.

Finally they did.

Liz was crying as soon as they reached the foot of the stairs in the apartment building. Hugh let her cry as they walked down the snow-covered sidewalk in the brisk starlit winter night.

Where's Bethlehem now?

The tears slowly turned into spasms of sniffles.

"Bad?" They both walked on silently, feet crunching the newly fallen snow.

"It's all over. Mother is calling me home to be president of the college. I can do the dissertation in my spare time. Even come back for summer school. She has assigned me for the next six years. And no guarantee of anything after that. Hates to do it. For the good of the Order. The good of the Church. That kind of shit."

"I'm sorry," Hugh stammered.

"I don't want to spend the rest of my life playing nursemaid to late-adolescent females and creepy old nuns."

Then she clung to him and sobbed.

When the second onset of tears was over, she still held on to him, as if her existence depended on his support.

Then she pulled herself together, wiped the tears from her eyes, and leaned against him. "It was all so ruthless. I was just a thing to be used. None of them—the whole council was there with Mother—gave a damn about my wishes. I felt just exactly the way I did when those brutes dragged me from the altar at St. Jarlath's."

"Miserable bitches," Hugh muttered into her long soft hair.

The Church destroys its own.

Tim Donlon spend Christmas Eve in a cocktail lounge on Rush Street, sipping gin and getting quietly drunk.

He was more alone than ever.

The marriage wasn't working. Estelle was an old-fashioned Catholic who didn't believe in birth control. So after three children in four years, she'd ordered him out of her bed. And he'd gone, more or less quietly.

He had worked at the marriage, more than he thought he would. He didn't love Estelle, but he enjoyed the kids and it seemed worthwhile to him to try to hold the family together.

There would be more battles and more reconciliations. Estelle didn't believe in divorce either.

Not that divorce would help him.

The doctor said that character disorders like his could be controlled. A lot the doctor knew.

God knows he'd tried. He'd played it straight at the Exchange for two years and made a fortune. Then he'd grown bored and taken a few chances. He'd lost most of the money and was suspended again. Estelle had to use her own money to buy the kids Christmas presents.

And she absolutely refused to visit the Donlon house on Christmas Day.

"Creepy," she said. "No booze and that fat mother of yours looks down her nose at me like a dowager Chinese empress. We'll go to our house"—meaning her parents' house in Oak Brook, a grotesque Gothic pile she'd designed—"and that's that. You can stop by that old dump but I absolutely forbid you to take the kids."

Peggy was not fat. Indeed, Estelle outweighed her by twenty pounds and was jealous of her good looks.

Tim signaled for another drink. The fun had all run out.

And there weren't any hookers around on Christmas Eve.

Liz called Hugh at St. Medard's during the supper hour on Christmas Eve, between afternoon and evening confessions. "I'll be at the Midnight Mass. Most of the Commune has left already. Then I'm going up to St. Jarlath's for Christmas. That's right, darling. Only for the day though." She hesitated. "Could you come over here for breakfast after the Mass, just for an hour or so? It will be the only chance we'll have to celebrate Christmas."

"Sure."

The St. Medard's liturgy was excellent, well-prepared congregational singing and well-directed choir. The festive midnight service moved along with spirit and pomp. The gold vestments, the smell of evergreens, the banks of red poinsettia, stirring carols echoing in the heavy stone Romanesque vault—all brought back to Hugh memories of Christmases at St. Ursula's.

His sermon was strong and moving. "Bethlehem is light in darkness, love in hate, life in death, good in evil. Just as darkness will never put out the light of Bethlehem, so hate will never obliterate love, death will never destroy life, evil will never triumph over good.

"The light of Bethlehem has survived two thousand years of darkness. Nothing will ever put it out in the world. Only our own fears can extinguish it inside ourselves."

It was not enough, he said, to exult in the light of Bethlehem. We must make that light shine more brightly in the world. Bethlehem's was renewed by the light of patient and self-sacrificing love in all our lives. Therefore we must strive to love as fully every day as we do on Christmas Day. "Then the family of Bethlehem will be with us always."

After Mass there were more rituals, again evoking bittersweet memories of St. Ursula's—more carols, feet stamping on fresh snow, handshaking, and shouts of "Merry Christmas" in back of the church and then a weary, contented return to the rectory.

Hugh drank a Christmas toast with the pastor and shortly excused himself. "A breakfast with some priests from the university," he said.

His heart was beating rapidly as he climbed the steps to the Commune's apartment.

"A beautiful sermon, Hugh." Liz's smile shattered the cold and the darkness and her embrace suffused him with warmth and happiness.

He gave her a pair of jade earrings, which she unwrapped and put on with the delight of a high school girl.

"They're too good for me," she said, suddenly sad. She was especially beautiful that night, dressed in a light gray jersey dress, belted at the waist, that softly outlined her figure, her hair neatly done, face carefully made up, a sprig of holly at the open neck of the dress.

"You look lovely," he said, and he kissed her again, a slow, adoring kiss.

"There's nothing wrong with a feminist looking feminine if she does so to please herself," she said primly.

"It's all right, isn't it, if a man is pleased too?" He released her only slowly.

"I guess." She laughed and touched him on the chin. "So long as he doesn't think her femininity makes her inferior to him."

"God forbid."

Breakfast was elaborate, small steaks, homemade coffee cake, coffee brewed from freshly ground beans.

The vegetarian ideologues of the Christ Commune wouldn't approve at all, but Hugh decided not to mention them.

"Remember our first breakfast together?" she asked gaily as she filled his wineglass with a vintage red Rhone that the communards would not have appreciated either.

"Sure, the week before you were dragged from the altar."

"A lot of things have changed since then," she said softly, lighting her first cigarette of the day.

"Maybe for the better," he said. "Maybe if Michigan turns me down, you can hire me."

Her face fell. "I wish you hadn't said that, Hugh."

"Sorry; it was dumb."

She snubbed out her cigarette, knowing he didn't like her to smoke. "It's okay," she said at length. "I know you didn't mean to make fun of it."

The hours slipped past like minutes. Soon it was four in the morning.

Hugh realized he should be going, but didn't want to leave. Why couldn't it be the two of them, together for the rest of eternity?

He took her chin in his hand. "Very nice breakfast, ma'am."

Her eyes were troubled, her face grave. She was trying to control rough, painful emotions.

Hugh silently reassured himself that nothing was going to happen.

His hands caressed her face, her neck, her throat. They stopped, one hand on either side of her neck, her head drawn close, so he could inspect her face. He saw invitation and acceptance.

Why had he waited so long?

In her bedroom he kissed her and slowly opened the buttons of her dress. His hand slipped to the belt. He kissed her again. Her lips surrendered. She was his for whatever he wanted.

He eased the dress off her shoulders. She held it at her waist. He twisted it out of her hand and dropped it to the floor. Her underwear was delicate pearl-gray lace, matching her dress. Deftly, as if it were not the first time, he opened hooks, stretched elastic, peeled away her modest fingers, and removed the filmy garments.

His heart was pounding, his head giddy. He had not felt so free or so happy since his boyhood sailing on Lake Geneva. He would make her his own, become one with her the way he had once been one with the wind and the waves.

"Hugh, I love you," she breathed "You're so kind and good."

He quickly pulled off his own clothes. For a moment they stood clinging to each other, two terrified, naked animals, in a ritual older than the race. They knew they would go ahead. But first they would summon all the resources of their love.

Hugh wished he could think of something to say to break the tension. There were no words. His hands began to probe more fiercely.

No, not that way. She required the same delicate, experienced touch as the sails and the tiller of the *Pegeen*.

But his hands were unsteady, his lips uncertain, his movements fumbling and inept. So much beauty, so many places to touch for the first time . . . and no skills at touching them. He didn't know how to love a woman, and had only a few moments to learn.

"I don't want to hurt you," he groaned.

"You won't hurt me," she said, Liz tried to reassure him, though she was as uncertain as he.

The fierce demands of his ardor were too much for him. There was no time left to be tender. He eased her back onto the bed, struggling with all his might not to be abrupt. She sighed and moved awkwardly in his embrace. "Love me, Hugh," she pleaded.

Then he could endure no further delay. He parted her legs and, as gently as he could, invaded her, deflowered her, reveled in her flesh, and made her his mate.

Liz's maidenhood did not yield easily and her body did not explode in pleasure, as his did.

Still, she seemed blissfully happy in his arms. She kissed him repeatedly and assured him that it had been the happiest moment in her life, that it was the right, right thing for them, that at last they knew how much they loved.

Abruptly he looked at his watch. It was five o'clock. My God, he thought, I've got to get back.

"Again?" she asked, clinging to him, still naked as he left.

"Of course, again. Over the weekend."

He shouldn't leave her. But he had to. The priests at St. Medard's, the family later in the day. He had obligations. . . .

The *Pegeen* was floating in a soft, warm cloud high above the earth, its sails slack, its crew blissfully lolling in the stern. Maria was naked beside him, her face smeared with raspberry juice. He began to make love to her again.

She fought him. Their struggle tipped the boat to one side. It capsized and plunged out of the cloud and toward the earth, heading straight for the smoke- and fire-belching crater of a volcano.

Hugh struggled to regain control of the boat and still make love to his prisoner. Liz. No, Helen. No, Peggy.

No, it was Maria all along, laughing at him as she fought and changed appearances. He tried to explain about the volcano.

But it was too late.

He woke at eleven o'clock feeling both complacent and guilty.

Still half asleep, he remembered.

He had made love to a woman, he had successfully initiated a virgin. He was pleased and proud of his manhood. He would enjoy her again and again.

Then, as he emerged into full awareness, he felt enormous guilt. Mortal sin, sacrilege, violation of his priestly vows. He was a beast, an animal. "God in heaven, forgive me," he pleaded. "I'll never do it again."

CHAPTER
NINETEEN

1968–1969

The big bungalow at the corner of Lemoyne and Mason was beginning to show its age, along with the rest of the St. Ursula's neighborhood. Many of the parishioners had migrated to River Forest as black families moved into the south end of the parish. The decline of the neighborhood and the deterioration of his family home depressed Hugh. But even with the burden of Liz on his mind, he could hardly wait to be inside.

The Wentworths were already there. They had flown over from Shannon to spend three weeks. Liam was almost as much in love with his in-laws as he was with his wife. The two little girls, Fionna and Graine, aged two and three, were quiet, mysterious little creatures with elfin smiles and lovely eyes, promising the beauty of their mother and grandmother with a dash of the fey added to their personalities.

Tim wasn't there. He and Estelle had begged off again on the grounds they would be so busy with her large family that they "simply could not make it." Hugh discreetly asked no questions. Every year Tim was more of a burden. His drinking, his strange humor, and his scrapes with the Business Practices Committee at the Board of Trade caused constant worry to his mother and father.

But there was nothing anyone could do about poor Tim.

The four adults agreed that Hugh looked fine and fit, better than he had in years.

"Good skin color. Can tell a healthy man by his skin. Time you took it easy. Ireland."

That could mean he should come to Ireland or that was the way they lived there. Judging from what he'd read about Lord Kerry's involvement in oil exploration, Hugh was not sure he took it easy himself.

"The little girls think he's a doll. He looks so relaxed and happy," Marge agreed.

Both girls climbed into his lap and remained there contentedly until Christmas dinner was served.

At dinner Marge talked about her favorite subject, the Church. "Are many priests going to bed with women, Hugh? I think it's disgusting. I like the changes in the Church, but if I have to keep my promises to Liam, I don't see why they don't have to keep their promises to God."

"These are rough and uneven times, Marge. People do odd things before they straighten themselves out. My pastor at St. Jarlath's never laid a hand on a woman. But I don't think he was a very good priest."

"It must be very lonely for some of them, isn't it, Hugh?" Peggy said, pouring herself another drink of the claret Liam had brought with him. It was, she admitted, "rather tasty," appropriate for a holiday.

"Life is lonely for everyone, Mom. I suppose that loneliness is one of the reasons, and curiosity, desire, a willing woman, uncertainty about faith. . . ."

"I still think it's a disgrace," Marge insisted.

Disconcerted by Hugh's noncommittal response, they switched the conversation to his offer from Michigan.

"After all," Peggy observed serenely, "Ann Arbor is closer than Killarney."

"Not really, old girl," Lord Wentworth insisted. "Not really. Fly to O'Hare as quickly as you can drive from there. Surely, my dear. Have some more claret."

"Speaking of O'Hare"—Marge helped herself to a second serving of turkey stuffing—"did we tell you we saw Maria and Steven McLain at the airport? They were flying to Charleston to see his family before he goes back to Vietnam."

"Poor Maria," Peggy sympathized. "It's not fair that anyone should have to suffer that twice."

"He's going to command an air group," Judge Donlon said. "A dangerous job."

"I know she's worried sick, but she keeps her spirits up remarkably well." Marge shook her head in wonder. "Same old Maria. She pretended that Liam couldn't speak English and that I had to translate for him . . . said they saw you at the *Messiah* concert, Hugh."

"Same old Maria," he agreed cautiously.

"Hugh dated Maria for a while, Liam," Marge explained.

"Only for two weeks."

"Too long for that gel," Liam said, his eyes wide in appreciation. "One week or life."

They all laughed, even Hugh, whose stomach was knotted in pain, not from Christmas food, but from regret.

In her tiny room at St. Jarlath's convent, Liz tried to cry herself to sleep. The tears came and went but sleep did not follow them.

She was appalled by what they had done, ashamed, humiliated, and outraged. Hugh had deceived her, exploited her, practically raped her, in fact.

How dare he think he could use her in such a way? A receptacle to be enjoyed and thrown away. How dare he behave like such a bestial, such a gluttonous, middle-class pig?

She abruptly relented in a new outburst of tears. It wasn't true. He did care. And had tried to be gentle with her.

She recalled how beautiful he'd looked lying asleep in the bed beside her and how her rage had been transformed into sudden desire, how frightened she'd been, not for herself, but for him.

She loved him passionately, she had no doubt about that. But he had to be taught restraint so he would be able to love her appropriately in return.

Love, she must teach him, was not simply satisfying his sexual cravings.

Tom Donlon usually felt a letdown after festivities, and the more joyous the event, the greater the letdown. Despite Tim's absence, the Christmas dinner had been a great success. So now he was greatly depressed, lamenting the shortness of life, the fragility of its pleasures, the vanity of his hopes and ambitions.

He didn't regret for a moment his decision to decline LBJ's proffer of a Supreme Court seat, not even in light of the fact that Abe

Fortas, who was appointed in his place, might be forced to resign, giving President-elect Nixon a chance to fill the vacancy with a Republican.

He belonged here on Mason Avenue, not in Washington.

Yet this Christmas night he viewed his life as a failure.

He wanted to sleep, to shake off the gloom. When would Peggy finish her "quick cleanup" and join him?

At length she came into the bedroom dressed in her dark green Christmas nightgown and carrying a half-empty bottle of claret and two wine goblets.

"I'm tired, Peg; I don't want anything more to drink."

"Nonsense," she said primly. "You've been wanting the chance to make love to a tipsy wife since we were married. Here, drink up." She filled a glass and extended it to him. "Liam says you shouldn't empty the bottle." She considered it thoughtfully. "But then my palate is still untrained. Liam says that too." She giggled.

"Our children seemed well today." He was a little afraid of this wanton stranger.

She kissed him slowly, affectionately, then lasciviously. "Let's not talk about the children. We do that too often."

One of the straps of her gown slipped off her shoulder. Tom Donlon felt like a young man again.

"I suppose that wine makes you see things more clearly. Does it, Tommy? Or am I only imagining I see more clearly? Anyway, what I see tonight is that if I had spent less time worrying about the children and more time loving you, we all would be much happier."

Again her lips brushed his.

God bless Liam Wentworth and his claret.

The cardinal found time to see Hugh the day after Christmas.

"You look well, Father. Have you had some time off?"

Hugh shook his head. "Actually, the worst of the work is almost over. I should have the degree by spring or summer at the latest."

"I'm delighted to hear it. And my colleague in Detroit? Will he have a chance to avail himself of your occasional services?"

"That's why I came, Cardinal. The University of Michigan is making me a fine offer, as you know. I thought I'd tell you that while I must certainly be open to their offers and consider them seriously, I'm fairly certain that I want to stay here. . . . It's home, you see."

"Yes, you Chicagoans do value your city, not without reason, I might say." He touched his glasses, as he often did when hunting for the proper response. "I am not without some interest in your decision, as you may well imagine. And I do appreciate your telling me. Whatever your decision, you can count on my full blessing, for whatever it may be worth."

"Plenty." Hugh grinned.

It was a strange conversation to have right before going to an apartment to make love to a woman. Hugh wanted to explain his trip to Michigan. He also wanted to assure himself that, no matter how strong his doubts and no matter how much he would enjoy the things he was going to do with Liz, and no matter how much he would loathe himself for this lust after he left her, he was still a priest and would remain one.

Liz was still furious at him. Not only did he combine obnoxious masculine ego with clumsy lovemaking; he did not have the common human decency to call her the day after or the next or the next.

She also loved him with every angry cell in her body and wanted him back in her bed.

She had wanted what happened on Christmas, had expected it to happen, had prepared for it, and had dressed for it from the skin out. She would have been crushed and humiliated if he hadn't responded to her. Yet she still resented his imperious masculine triumph.

She was sitting at her typewriter, in jeans and a maroon university sweat shirt, working again on her dissertation when Hugh entered, smiling arrogantly.

"I'm going to make love to you all afternoon," he whispered into her ear.

"You are not," she said with little conviction in her voice.

"Yes, I am." His warm hands were already under her shirt, touching her cold flesh, one holding her so tight, she couldn't move, the other challenging, teasing, comforting. At first he was uncertain and awkward as he had been on Christmas morning; then, as he watched her eager reactions, he became more confident.

She heard, as though from a great distance, a voice inside her head, a voice both past and present. . . . He's seducing you. . . . Damn him, he's good at it. . . . You enjoy it, you shameless little slut. . . . Make him stop. . . . Oh, please, don't stop. . . . No, you must stop him. . . . Oh, God, no . . . too much pleasure . . .

He cuddled her, fondled her, rhythmically caressed her, laughing at her insincere protests.

Then her body discovered a rhythm of its own, independent of her wishes and her thoughts, demanding she give up to its movements and energies, insisting she merge with the raw powers and forces churning within her.

Her father's hands pawing her. No, not her father. Someone else.

A slow fuse lighted in her loins, the fire moving through her nervous system, then exploding, a mushroom cloud of pleasure, shudders, twists, contortions, groans of delight, and a writhing body—surely not her own—rose up to meet his, wanting only to become one with him.

A moment of blackness, then floods of peace and joy.

It was dark when he finally left. She lay limp and exhausted on her bed, a rumpled sheet carelessly pulled over her deeply satisfied body, her emotions a jumbled mess.

She was pleased, angry, and terrified. So this was what intimacy was like. Soon he would be able to do with her anything he liked. She was horrified, wanted to run away from him, wanted to run to him, didn't want him ever to touch her again, wanted him there touching her that very moment.

She was outraged. He was damnably pleased with himself. He knew he was a good lover, just as he was a good athlete. She hated his arrogance. She dreaded his dominance. But, above all, she wanted to be one with him.

She fell asleep happy, uncertain, confused. Her anger crept down into the subterranean regions of her soul and waited.

The reaction of the faculty and students at Michigan to Hugh's visit in early January was extremely flattering. Most of the senior faculty came to his lecture on village structure, and a large number of graduate students did too.

At supper with some of the faculty, the conversation ranged far and wide. They were impressed by Hugh's mastery of many of the key issues of international finance and delighted that he had found time to take courses in economics.

"One delicate matter that I suppose we have to raise, Father . . . " said the gray-haired dean. "I will be asked by others—up the line—if you will wear clerical garb in the classroom. You are perfectly within your rights to do so and if—"

"Forget it," Hugh said. "No problem. I don't think it worries anyone these days. They don't even wear clericals in the universities in Rome."

The dean sighed with relief.

"You are going to remain a priest?" asked an assistant professor tentatively.

"Sure," said Hugh. "Why not?"

On his way back to O'Hare from Detroit Metropolitan, he knew that he had impressed and charmed the Michigan faculty. They were a much more civilized and friendly bunch than his professors at the university. The Ann Arbor environment would be a pleasant one in which to work and intellectually exciting and stimulating.

It was tempting, more tempting than he'd expected. There would be time at Michigan to slow down, to read, to pray, to think out his religious problems, and to make the decisions he had to make.

The appointment would also be a natural end to the relationship with Liz, should the relationship last that long.

After his Mass the next morning, Hugh remained in church to pray. He should not be saying Mass without confessing his sins. Yet he'd made love in a different order of reality from that in which he said Mass. The body of Christ was one thing, the body of Sister Elizabeth Ann something else. God would not mind his saying Mass while he tried to straighten out his convictions and emotions.

Dear God, he prayed, I'm a mess. I don't know what I should do or what I want to do. Liz is a wonderful woman and I love her dearly, but neither of us wants marriage. I don't want to give her up, not yet anyway.

I know I should do what is most difficult. I should do what I am required to do, what I ought to do, what it is my obligation to do.

But what are my obligations now? How can I sort them out? What comes first?

It was all so easy when I was young—the seminary or Maria. It's not so easy anymore.

Help me, I pray.

The next day he sat at his desk in the cubbyhole at CRUD, working through the revision of his second chapter. TKH had not returned from Indonesia. Rather, he'd sent a cable: "Returning soon. Orientate students."

That meant "take my classes till I come back and be prepared to give them their final exams at the end of the quarter."

And it was snowing again.

He wanted Liz. The Christ Commune reassembled after the Christmas vacation. They would be tolerant of anything that went on in their circle of "absolute freedom to do your own thing," but they would not be silent about it.

Hugh drummed his pen on the page he was revising and called the hotel in Palm Desert where his parents and the Wentworths were vacationing.

Peggy answered. Wonderfully lovely place. Why hadn't they come every winter of their lives? Liam was a grace from heaven. No, I'm not drinking a lot of wine. Only a glass at meals, well sometimes two. Your father thinks it's funny too. Marge is really quite delightful. I think she still feels a little guilty about all those years. Yes, the heat is on in the house at Lake Geneva. This weekend? I'm so glad you finally are going to take a weekend off and relax. It's time you did.

Self-contempt and lust battled inside him as he hung up the phone. He knew he would hate himself even more after the weekend idyll. Fornication and sacrilege in his family's summer home . . . how low could he get?

He gave Liz five minutes to pack. "You'll only need a few things. The place is filled with clothes. Besides, I don't plan to let you be anything else but naked most of the weekend."

She didn't want to go, to put herself so completely at his disposal. But, afraid of a conflict, she packed a small bag and climbed into the car beside him.

At Lake Geneva, they walked in the snow and on the frozen

lake, lay by the blazing fire, drank wine from a bottle, ate roast beef, and talked. Mostly, however, they made love.

She gave up her attempts to isolate herself from her feelings. Instead, for two days she was nothing more than the sharp spasms of pleasure that racked her body and threatened to tear it delightfully apart.

She was viscerally terrified of his sexual dominance. But until Sunday afternoon she willed the terror not to interfere. He was using her as if she were a harem slave, and she was reveling in every minute of it. For this weekend, at least, she intended to live in paradise.

On Sunday afternoon the sky was a hard blue and the sun glared brightly off the ice. The temperature had fallen below zero the night before and a strong north wind was blowing. They paid but slight attention to the weather as, pleasantly exhausted, they lay in front of the fireplace, he with a blanket around his loins, she in one of his robes.

"Ready for some serious talk?" She rubbed his unshaven cheek with her hand.

Not terror, but common sense, she mentally insisted.

"If you say so." He kissed her lips.

"This has been wonderful. I wouldn't have believed such peace and happiness could exist. But, Hugh, these weekends of love can't go on forever. We both have responsibilities. We've committed ourselves to making the world a better place, bringing peace and justice to the oppressed, lifting the burdens of the poor, making the Church relevant again to the people of God. . . ."

"No room for us in all those grand designs?"

"Certainly . . . but we're not important, the purposes are."

"I want to be important," he insisted.

"You are important, Hugh. To me. . . ."

He rolled over and turned toward the fireplace. She wrapped her arms around him, lightly pressing against his back.

"You're the more realistic of the two of us, Liz; I'd rather not face that."

"We both must realize that this has to stop." Anger, buried through the weekend of delights, crawled up out of its underground cave. God, he was dumb. Did he think she would marry him?

"We both have our work, our obligations, our responsibilities."

She kissed his neck. If she could talk about responsibilities, her terror would go away.

"This is the last time?" He rolled over and drew the robe from her shoulders. She removed the blanket from his waist.

"Do we have any choice?" She snuggled close to him, confident now that her protective armor was returning to its place. She need no longer fear his power.

"No, I guess not. . . . All right, it ends tomorrow. But let's enjoy what's left of today."

On February tenth Hugh drafted a letter to the dean at Michigan telling him he regretfully was declining their generous offer. He sealed the letter and placed it on the hard chair at the door of his cubbyhole.

He had gone to confession in the busy marble sacrament factory at St. Peter's in the Loop. The young friar who heard his sins had been gentle and sympathetic.

"You must not be so disgusted with yourself, Father," he whispered softly. "You seem less willing to forgive yourself than God is."

"Thus adding pride to lust," Hugh said bitterly.

"Come, now," the young priest protested. "Some disgust is appropriate. But you have a purpose of amendment, you intend to end the relationship. You would do much better to atone by hard work instead of self-hatred."

Hugh restrained an urge to laugh at his own foolishness. "I'll try, Father."

"Which is all God expects of any of us."

Lifting the telephone receiver on his desk, he called Sean Cronin for an appointment with the cardinal.

As he hung up after the conversation with Cronin, Liz appeared at the door of the cubbyhole, her face stained with tears, handkerchief twisted in her hand. She seemed tired and sick.

She was due to leave for her new assignment at the end of the month. He'd miss her, but it would be the best thing in the world for her. Some administrative responsibility finally. Best thing for him too. He couldn't see her without wanting her.

"What's wrong? Second thoughts about the college? It's the best thing, Liz, it truly is. You'll love it by the end of the first term."

"Hugh," she sniffled, "I think I'm pregnant."

CHAPTER
TWENTY

1969

"Well, my dear, you have created a problem for yourself, haven't you?" Mother Baldwina, a vigorous, athletic nun in her middle fifties, was making a statement, not registering a complaint.

"Yes, Mother." Liz could hardly hear her own voice.

"Surely you must have anticipated this possibility?"

"I . . . I didn't think much about it . . . he should have. . . ."

"Come, now, Sister; we will not blame him here in this room. Doubtless he has his share of responsibility. Feminist ideology will not help us solve your problem, however."

"But he's so arrogant. . . . All men . . . "

"I will say this candidly, Sister. If you're pregnant the reason is that you wanted to be pregnant. I will not try to analyze what that reason might be. If you want to marry him, then I won't try to talk you out of it, though you do not talk like a woman in love."

"I do love him," she said stubbornly.

"Enough to spend the rest of your life with him? Think about that, Sister. It's a long time."

"I—I don't know. . . ."

"Matters can be arranged. You could take a leave. I will not recommend the cancellation of your appointment as president of our college. I think I can persuade the one or two board members to whom I must speak that the problem should be kept confidential. We are not going to force you out on your own, as we would have done only a few years ago, God forgive us."

Outside, through the Mother's windows, the fresh snow gleamed white and pure on the motherhouse grounds.

"I appreciate that, Mother." She dabbed at her eyes with a tissue. "I don't know what to do."

"Nor will I tell you, Sister." Mother's face was unreadable. "You must think it over yourself. You have some time to do so, not much but enough. I will support you whatever you do."

"Thank you, Mother," Liz said gratefully, barely sensing the rage she'd soon feel toward Mother Baldwina's presumption.

Xav Martin was more upset than Hugh had anticipated.

"Don't marry her, Hugh. I don't know the woman at all, but I know you shouldn't marry her."

"Why?" He leaned forward on the rector's chair—the same one he'd twisted on anxiously when he talked about Maria.

"You don't want to marry her. You've trapped yourself in your irrational sense of obligation. You'll crucify yourself if you marry her."

Hugh sat back in the chair. "I don't understand. . . ."

"You don't love her, Hugh, not one bit."

"I think I do, Xav," he said hotly.

"Then you're kidding yourself. Don't do it, Hugh; it won't be a happy marriage. Then there'll be other women. You won't be able to control yourself once you've gone off the deep end. The demons will drag you down into hell."

"Harsh words, Xav: demons, hell—do you mean them seriously?"

"I'm not talking about everlasting hellfire, Hugh." He waved off the suggestion with his usual quick gesture. "You know that. I'm talking about a man-made hell. Marry that woman and you'll take the first step on your own descent into hell."

"Maybe. . . ."

"Think about it, Hugh. And don't marry her because you feel responsible. There are other appropriate motivations for human behavior."

"Like what?" The words slipped out of Hugh's mouth before he realized how damning they were.

"Like survival."

"Do you want me to get an abortion?" Liz asked resentfully.

"No . . . don't be absurd; an abortion is out of the question."

"Why should it be out of the question? Most moral theologians today don't believe there is a human person for the first two weeks. A month, six weeks, isn't much longer."

"Do you want an abortion?" he asked wearily. It had been a long, convoluted, and acrimonious conversation in the office at St. Medard's, with boxes of collection envelopes piled in the corner and high, dirty walls looming around them in shocked silence, the only place where they could talk privately.

She hesitated before answering. It was a solution, heaven knows, however morally repugnant to them both.

Liz was bitterly angry. Men had the fun and women paid the price. Yes, the doctor was sure she was pregnant. No, of course, she had not done anything to prevent conception. No, she didn't want to marry. Yes, she would go away and have the child. No, she had no intention of staying in the Order.

He asked mildly if she hadn't thought she might conceive if she did nothing to prevent it.

She shouted furiously that he'd done nothing to prevent it either.

He took it for granted, still, that they would marry. It was the only thing for him to do. Liz knew that as well as he did. It was, he suspected, an altogether acceptable solution from her point of view. To be sure, she would need to work through her anger and outrage, draw from it the last measure of satisfaction, and then realistically face the future.

"Maybe an abortion is not a bad idea. It wouldn't be as terrible a sin as your forcing me into a marriage that neither of us wants."

He didn't blame her for bluffing. She was, after all, the victim more than he. Perhaps, nonetheless, it was a bluff that ought to be called.

"That's a decision that is entirely up to you," he said carefully. "I disapprove of it. I'm asking to marry you, I want to marry you, this . . . this event merely forces me to face what I wanted all along. . . ."

Did he? He didn't know. Michigan, a wife, a family . . .

"If you insist on having the child out of wedlock, I'll do whatever is needed. If you want an abortion, I won't cooperate, but I will grant you that it's your body and your choice."

"So I'm stuck with the mortal sin and you're home free?" She jumped up, grabbed her purse and gloves, and dashed from the room.

Hugh realized he must resign himself to not winning in the present crisis. Liz was upset and angry, struggling with her guilt. Her attitude would change.

But what if he were to dig in his heels. What if he took her at her word and refused to marry her? How often had he advised pregnant young women not to marry? Most marriages of that sort, he used to say serenely, were ill-advised. Was this one ill-advised? He knew he would despise himself if he dumped her. But maybe that was the best thing to do.

He dialed his father's private number in chambers. Could they meet tomorrow? No, not for lunch; he would prefer to see him in his office. Something important. Bad news? Not really.

Not much, Hugh thought as he hung up.

A considerable part of his life was being wiped out. There would be heartache and suffering for his family, reproach and recriminations from his friends, some explicit, most of it implied.

So be it.

He'd wasted a lot of time, seven years in the seminary, twelve years in the priesthood. He must begin to make up for lost time.

The judge listened quietly as Hugh talked, his face devoid of expression, his fingers toying with a paper clip. "You will forgive me, Hugh, for being the lawyer and asking a few questions?"

"That's a good way to begin, Dad."

"You're sure this child is yours . . .?"

"Quite sure."

"You are also sure that the young woman would not be better off having the child outside of wedlock?"

"She hasn't made up her mind, Dad. I have. I won't let down either her or our child."

"Indeed. Do you want to leave the priesthood?"

"That's the big one. And it's not easy to answer. Would I leave the priesthood now if Liz wasn't pregnant? Probably not. Would I leave eventually? I don't know. If I were a psychiatrist, I'd say that I did what I did because it would force me to leave."

"I see." His father delicately laid aside the paper clip. "Do you think becoming a priest in the first place was a mistake?"

"I wanted to be a priest, Dad. No one sold me on it. It . . . wasn't quite what I expected. I've never put it this way before, not even to myself . . . those years at St. Jarlath's were not very rewarding. If I hadn't had Monsignor Sullivan to fight, I might have been bored stiff."

"You will, I take it, seek a dispensation from your vows?"

"Yes, of course." He had thought that he wouldn't bother. It made no difference to him. But it would be important to his family.

"You wish me to speak to your mother before you do?"

"Whatever you think best."

The paper clip now was suspended between finger and thumb, like a life hesitating on the brink of extinction.

"I'm sure it would be advisable for me to discuss the matter with her. . . . Through the years one learns how to break bad news. As I'm sure you're aware, she will take it to be bad news."

"Yes."

The judge sighed softly. He looked very old. "I hardly need say, Hugh, that you are our son, and that we will stand by you. If you are making this choice, it is the right choice for you. You must be patient with our disappointment. . . . Do not misinterpret it."

The lump in Hugh's throat was so big he could not speak for a few seconds. "I knew I could count on you, Dad."

"Do you intend to continue your academic career? The appointment at Michigan?"

"That seems to be the wisest thing."

"You'll forgive me for raising an objection. If the work of the parish priest was not . . . ah . . . stimulating enough, do you think that college teaching will be?"

Hugh had not thought of that.

A sheepish Liz was waiting for him in his cubbyhole.

"I'm a terrible bitch," she said forlornly.

He touched her cheek. "No, you're not. You're under great strain, and sick every morning besides."

"Do you really want to marry such an awful woman?"

"Yes, certainly I do. There's nothing I want to do more."

She breathed deeply. "Do you think I seduced you so you would be forced to marry me?"

A dangerous mine field. "We've loved each other for a long time, Liz. We wanted to consummate that love. We knew what could happen . . . you no less than I and no more. . . ."

She frowned, puzzling over his response, searching perhaps for something more definitive. "I guess . . . I've tormented myself wondering. I'm not sure. I do love you. I do want to marry you. I know that."

He kissed her forehead. "That's all that matters. Let's not worry about sorting out the blame."

"Would you mind if Theo marries us? At the Commune?"

Yes, he would mind. Mom, Dad, maybe Tim, and Marge.

"I think it would be appropriate if we had something very quiet at the county clerk's office."

She was disappointed. If she insisted, he'd give in.

She didn't insist.

He wrote a new letter to the chairman at Michigan. He tentatively accepted the appointment, pending their formal offer at the end of March. It was not a binding commitment. Negotiation in the academic jungle was delicate and indirect until the ink was on the contract paper.

His father's question worried him. What was there for him to do that might be more exciting?

CHAPTER
TWENTY-ONE

1969

"Come on in, Hugh. Sit down." Sean Cronin was in an expansive mood. "Smoke if you want ... no, that's right, you don't smoke either. How you been?" Cronin put his feet up on the desk. "A strange time to be a priest, Hugh. The best of times, the worst of times. And it's hard to tell which is which. What's new in your life?"

"I'm resigning from the active ministry, Sean." He had been warned that Cronin was uptight on the subject of resignations and was prepared for an explosion.

If he had shoved a knife into the vice-chancellor's stomach, the pain on the man's face could not have been more intense. "Oh, God, Hugh, don't. . . ."

"I'm sorry, Sean."

"It will break the old man's heart. He was so pleased with your work."

"I have to do it."

"A year's leave of absence. . . . Take time off to think about it ... go to Michigan ... out West."

"I'm planning to marry, Sean. I've come for the forms for a dispensation."

The other priest nodded grimly, pulled open his desk, and took out a file of papers. "You'd better be prepared to say that at ordination you were not free to make a fully human choice and that you didn't understand completely what celibacy meant and that your salvation depends on entering a married life. . . . Are you prepared to swear to those things, Father?"

There was heavy irony in Cronin's voice, and bitter wrath.

"If that's what others swear to, then I suppose I can too."

Cronin nodded. "It's a game. I don't know . . . hell, send them in as soon as you can and I'll try to push them through. The Pope is erratic on these things, depending which way his conscience is swinging. When are you planning to be married?"

"In a few weeks."

"In a rush?" One of his eyebrows shot up.

"The young woman is pregnant, Monsignor."

"Yeah, I thought it was something like that." He shoved the papers to Hugh's edge of the desk with unconcealed contempt.

Hugh's anger finally erupted. Cronin was merely the perfect target for his own self-contempt. The vice-chancellor was a cold, ambitious bastard. Hugh grabbed the dispensation forms, tore them into shreds, and threw them at the dazed prelate. "Shove this stuff up your ass," he said.

As he rushed out into the corridor, wanting to get out of the creepy, clammy old building and never return, he heard Cronin's voice calling after him.

"I'll mail the forms to St. Médard's."

He turned. The monsignor was standing in his doorway, leaning against the doorframe, holding the torn documents, his shoulders slumped.

Hugh ran down the stairs and out into the street.

Thank God, he didn't have to see the cardinal.

In the thirty-six years of their marriage, Judge Tom Donlon and his wife had never quarreled so violently. For almost twenty-four hours, they had not said a word to each other. His confidence that he could "handle" Peg's passionate emotions was utterly spent.

God knew what would come of this confrontation—no other word was appropriate—with Hugh.

The son had sensed something was wrong the moment he entered the parlor and saw his mother, tight-lipped and white-faced, sitting rigidly upright on her "favorite" couch, the one on which she had repaired so many tattered pairs of socks.

"I'm sorry, Mom," he began miserably.

"You're a fool, Hugh, a terrible fool. Don't marry that woman; you'll regret it the rest of your life. Leave the priesthood if you must, become a professor if that's what you want, find youself a wife if you will be happier with one, but don't marry that self-righteous little bitch."

Hugh rocked back as if she had hit him with an iron pipe. "I love her, Mom."

"I doubt it. You lusted after her and she led you on. You don't love her."

"I'm sorry you feel that way, Mom. She's going to bear my child."

"So what?" said Peg harshly. "Would she be the first woman to bear a man's child out of wedlock?"

"We owe it to the child to give him . . . or her . . . a chance at a happy life."

"Your father says I should stand behind you. I do. Someone has to tell you the truth. And he won't. You are creating for yourself a life of unending misery."

"Peg," said the judge sharply, "that's enough."

"No, it isn't enough, Tom," she shot back. "I'm finished doing everything you want me to do. However late in the day, I'm declaring my independence. I can't stop you from marrying her, Hugh. If you want to be a martyr to her schemes and your weaknesses, go right ahead. But don't expect me to be at the wedding or treat her like a daughter-in-law. I can't do it, Hugh. I won't do it."

"Peg, I won't tolerate another word." The judge tried to face her down.

"I don't care what you won't tolerate," she cried, and she ran from the room.

"She'll get over it, son. The shock, you know. . . ."

"I don't think she will; she sounds like Xav Martin. . . ." Hugh stood in the middle of the parlor, his hands hanging powerlessly at his sides, looking as if he were a soldier deserted by his last comrade. "I'm sorry to have made trouble between you."

"It'll be all right in a few days," the judge said without much confidence. "You better go now."

Later, he tried to talk to Peg in her studio, where she was viciously dabbing paints on paper.

She refused to listen to him. "Get out and leave me alone."

He left, now angry as well as hurt and humiliated.

That night for the first time since they'd lived in the house, Tom Donlon did not sleep in the same bed as his wife. He moved into what had been Hugh's room, resigning himself regretfully to what might be for all practical purposes the end of their marriage.

And wondering if perhaps Peggy might not be right.

Hugh Donlon knelt in the darkened nave of St. Medard's Church and prayed as his father had told him he had prayed the night Hugh was born.

The vehemence of his mother's attack had seared him. Disappointment at his leaving the priesthood he had expected, but anger over Liz, especially such biting anger, was beyond his comprehension. She hardly knew the girl. One dinner on a Sunday afternoon was not enough to justify such harsh condemnation.

Dear God, if You are up there listening to me, what am I to do? I love Liz, I want her for my wife. I love my mother, I don't want to hurt her.

The answer was that a man must cleave to his wife.

Liz wasn't his wife yet. Maybe she ought not to be his wife. Maybe now was the time to jump ship while he still could. . . .

For one giddy moment, he made up his mind to follow Peggy's advice.

And experienced joy and relief.

But as he left the church to go to his basement bedroom and the third chapter of his dissertation, he knew that he could never abandon Liz.

"Good God," exclaimed Marge. "Hugh's getting married."

The rain was crashing against the windowpane and the mists were rushing by their house. A soft day in Ireland, indeed.

Liam looked up from his preprandial sherry. "Can't. He's a priest."

"He's marrying some ex-nun he's got pregnant."

"Most astonishing." Liam spilled half his glass of sherry.

"Mom and Dad had a terrible fight. They haven't talked to each other for a week. Can you imagine that, Liam?"

"Bad show."

"The marriage is in the county clerk's office next Monday. Only Dad and Tim and some other ex-nun are going."

Liam watched the mists swirl by, masking almost completely the waters of Dingle Bay and the Purple Mountain in the far distance.

"Is there anything we can do, my darling? Any way we can help? Should we fly over and try to bind up the wounds?"

Marge tapped the letter thoughtfully against her Sheraton desk.

"Right now the only thing for us to do is stay out of it and pray. . . ."

"I daresay you're right. Makes one feel helpless."

She walked over to him and laid her hand on his shoulder.

"I don't know what I would do without you, Liam."

"Too much credit. Bumbling oaf. Like all Anglo-Irish. Daft dolt."

She laughed and she cried and she clung to him as if she would never let go.

Later he called the judge and had a "word or two" with him.

Hugh and Liz fell from grace again, quite consciously and deliberately. He wanted desperately to make love. She was the one to suggest it, however.

"What difference do a few days make? And a legal ceremony?"

They checked into the Blackstone Hotel, a very proper old matron on Michigan Avenue that seemed to be holding up her skirts, lest they be muddied by the crowds of conventioneers down the street. They brought along two pieces of luggage, holding mostly books, and looked so much like a married couple that not an eyebrow was raised at the registration desk.

Their love was gentle, kind, and sweet. Hugh was proud of the speed with which he'd learned the little secrets of making love to Liz, the kisses she most enjoyed, the caresses that brought her the greatest pleasure, the most sensitive areas of her body, the mixture of gentleness and force that seemed to arouse her best, the points at which delay changed from delight to agony and at which sweet agony turned to unbearable need.

They ate supper in the hotel restaurant and returned for another session of tenderness. Then she knelt next to him in their bed, a picture of satisfied lust.

"Promise me one thing, please, my darling." She raised his hand to her lips.

Sleepily Hugh looked up at her.

"Don't let my moods come between us. You know how bad I can be. Don't let them ever keep us from loving each other the way we do tonight." She stroked his face lightly, as though he were a small child who needed the greatest delicacy of touch.

"Your moods aren't all that bad; we won't worry about them," he said.

She lay down beside him and reached across his chest. She pillowed his head against her full young breasts and contentedly he fell asleep.

Soon the difficulties would be behind them, she thought, and a new life would begin, one filled with innocence and promise.

The wedding was a five-minute affair. Liz wore a simple white dress under a cloth coat, and Hugh wore a navy blue suit. The county clerk was correct, too much the politician to hint at what he, a devout Irish Catholic, thought of a marriage between a nun and a priest.

Ex-Sister Jackie kissed everyone delightedly.

Tim was nervous and twitchy, his bloodshot eyes and lined face suggesting he didn't like what was happening. Strange that Tim should care.

The judge put a brave face on it all, congratulating the new Mr. and Mrs. Donlon and insisting the party have lunch with him in a private dining room he'd reserved at the Palmer House.

After the lunch, Hugh and Liz drove out to Lake Geneva for a three-day honeymoon. Both had to return to the university to finish their degrees. Liz's career as a college president had died aborning. She'd written a letter to Mother Baldwina, curtly ending her relationship with the Order.

That was that.

Their days at Lake Geneva were pleasant, despite the gray March weather. However, the blazing passion of the previous interlude there was not repeated. They were settling down into the serious routine of marriage, in which there would be little time or inclination for such luxurious escapades.

One afternoon Hugh walked around the shore of the lake, watching the ice melt. It had been a bitter cold winter and the cover of ice was thick. Even though there was water and slush on the surface, it would take weeks for the sunlight to break through the prison that held the blue waters of his youth.

And by then they'd be gone.

They ate dinner the last night in Geneva town and then walked out to the end of the sad, lonely pier, closed till the coming of summer.

"Strange place." Liz clung to his arm, gazing at the tawdry amusement arcade. "Did you have fun here when you were young?"

"It seemed so then. I was just a kid."

"Must have been a rendezvous for many a cheap encounter."

And one that was not so cheap.

Two weeks later, Liz awoke with a terrible pain in her stomach and blood all over the bed. Hugh rushed her to the emergency room at University Hospital. The young OB resident who was summoned examined her quickly and ordered her to surgery immediately.

Two hours later, he came out of the operating room.

"She's all right, Mr. Donlon," he said cheerfully. "Be sick for a few days and a little weak. Lost a lot of blood. We're giving her some transfusions. Nothing to worry about, though. Frequent enough in a first pregnancy."

"And our child?"

"There wasn't a child."

"No child?"

"No fetus, properly speaking. Just a ring of tissue cells with a hole as big as a pin. Nothing really, not after the first couple of weeks."

BOOK
FOUR

"My God, my God, why hast thou forsaken me?"

CHAPTER
TWENTY-TWO

1970

Every morning at five thirty Hugh Donlon rose carefully from the bed in his decrepit Hyde Park apartment, tiptoed quietly into the bathroom, so as not to wake Liz, who was pregnant again, and vomited.

He drank two cups of coffee in the dirty kitchen, looked over his records of the previous day's closings, slipped out of the apartment, and walked briskly to the 53rd Street train station to catch the first South Shore train to the Loop. On the brief ride he would glance at the headlines in the *Tribune*—American invasion of Cambodia, more student protests—and then turn to the financial pages.

His stomach was still tied in knots and would be until the end of the trading day. He ate his main meal of the day after two o'clock at one of the small restaurants off LaSalle Street where the runners and messengers and clerks who kept the Board of Trade working ate. He was not ready to join the other traders at such places as Trader's Inn till he won his spurs.

Liz left the apartment at noon for the parish in the south suburbs where she was director of religious education and did not return till eleven at night, long after Hugh had fallen into a deep but restless sleep, a dark and troubled oblivion from which he would often awaken in the morning darkness more exhausted than when he went to bed.

Hugh was a commodities trader instead of a college professor because of a conversation he'd had at the Faculty Club at the university shortly after his marriage.

His father, who'd proposed the lunch, said that Liam had called and that they together were prepared to stake him to a seat on the Chicago Board of Trade.

"Liam and I came to the same conclusion separately," the judge said. "We both think that you might be much happier if you followed Tim onto the CBT."

"Keep an eye on him?"

"Frankly, that would be one concern. Recently there has been a problem in deferred contracts, which fortunately did not lead to formal charges. I do think that your presence there would be helpful for him."

And so duty and family had won again, they and the old football-trained competitive instinct. If he wasn't going to be a priest any longer, he might as well make a splash. Too many years of denying that potential.

Liz had not been pleased with the change in his career plans when he told her about it in their tiny and rather dingy apartment in Hyde Park. She wanted to escape from Chicago and the influence of the Donlon family. She knew nothing of the Board of Trade and was wary of "capitalists." However, she saw the gleam in her husband's eye. She sulked for a day and then told him she felt a commodities trader's life was incompatible with marital happiness.

"I know from St. Jarlath's what kind of lives those men live. It's not healthy. Besides, we're beginning our marriage and you won't have time to work on it with me. A professor has more time for his wife and family than a trader."

"I'd be finished working at one thirty."

Liz sniffed disdainfully. "How many Ben Fowlers come home at one thirty?"

Hugh had been caught in the middle—his family wanted one career, his wife another. For a few moments he'd considered what he wanted and admitted to himself that he did not know.

No matter which choice he made, he would disappoint someone.

The marriage would require considerable effort if it were not to collapse. Liz's depression after her miscarriage had been intense.

She thought it was foolish to give up the $17,500 Michigan salary.

"How much money do these men make?" she asked.

"An experienced and skillful trader can easily clear a half million a year."

Liz didn't believe him.

The hours between 6:30 and 8:00 A.M. in the tiny office he shared with Tim were the best in the working day. Cut off from the rest of the world as surely as if he were in a monastery, Hugh prepared for combat, like an ambitious and hungry heavyweight boxer before a fight. Slowly the tension in his body turned from paralysis to creative energy. Like a gladiator readying himself for combat, like a quarterback before a playoff game, he went carefully through a routine of preparation, physical, mental, and moral, for the four and a half hours from eight forty to one twenty.

When the opening gong sounded, he was a new man. The anxiety and tension drained away to be replaced by an enormous surge of energy. He rushed onto the trading floor with the same disciplined enthusiasm that he had used to lead the Fenwick Friars onto the football field.

His colleagues already had him pegged as a "cool" operator who never winced under pressure. They had no notion of the terror with which he woke every morning, knowing that each day he would sink or swim on his own in the world's greatest game.

The Chicago Board of Trade was one of the last of the pure marketplaces in the world. Despite the mild regulation provided by the Commodities Exchange Authority of the Department of Agriculture, the "haggling" between buyers and sellers was more sustained and more frantic than it would have been in an Oriental bazaar where "real" objects were sold. In the trading pits no physical objects changed hands. The traders bought and sold "futures"— consignments of commodities that the traders never saw and never owned.

They spoke their own language, shouting fractions at one another and waving their hands to indicate whether they were selling or buying contracts, aided by hand signals that indicated the fraction of the trading price they were bidding or offering. Dressed in light, colored blazers, they swarmed around their "pit," one of the three-step platforms constructed on the trading floor. They scrawled sales contracts on small sheets of paper, which they dropped on the floor to be snatched by messengers and coordinated later in the day by the "Clearing Corporation," the self-policing and account-balancing organization that prevented the chaos of the trading floor from degenerating into anarchy.

Hugh was trading in silver, the least active of the commodities. New on the Board of Trade, silver contracts for the most part attracted speculators and brokers trying to avoid taxes legally by showing a loss at the end of one year and taking it all back as a capital gain the first week of the next.

He liked the silver pit. It was a place to learn the game in a relatively quiet way; silver, he was convinced, would develop into an attractive commodity as inflation rose and increased demand for the industrial uses of the metal put pressure on the world supply. Moreover, the fluctuations in silver were abrupt and dramatic and the game therefore exciting and demanding.

Exactly the kind of game for which Hugh was looking as a way to begin.

July silver was fluctuating around 160—a dollar sixty cents a troy ounce, or eight thousand dollars for a five-thousand-ounce contract. Because the margin requirement was only five percent, one could buy a silver contract for about four hundred dollars. A five-cent increase in the price would earn someone who had gone long, "bought" July silver the previous day, two hundred and fifty dollars on his investment or a sixty-three percent profit. If silver went up the ten-cent-per-ounce limit established by the Board, the contract purchaser would earn five hundred dollars, or a hundred and twenty-five percent profit.

On the other hand, if the price fell the limit (after which no more decline in price was permitted), the buyer would have his investment wiped out and would owe someone one hundred dollars. Moreover, if the price "locked down" at the opening of the following day and he was unable to sell his contract, he could lose six hundred dollars out of his pocket, in which hopefully there was some money left.

Moreover, in a bear market, the price would go "limit down" at the beginning of each day so that one would be stuck with a losing position for several days, losing more money each day and falling back on more of one's resources to meet the ever-increasing margin requirements.

If, instead of speculating with one contract, he was speculating with, say, one hundred contracts, he could make or lose more than fifty thousand dollars in a day or two. The unwary trader could be wiped out completely almost before he knew what happened. And it was easier to be wiped out than to make a fortune.

Commodities trading was popular with the speculator who liked to make big gains and was willing to run the risk of big losses precisely because of the "leverage" that the low margin requirements made possible. Now that the stock market was closely regulated by the government and dominated by the big institutional investors, such as pension funds, traders on the floor of the CBT were confidently predicting that the 1970s would be their decade.

And, Hugh Donlon told himself, his decade too.

"How's the wife doing?" Benedict Fowler greeted him with a broad grin as Hugh walked on the floor a few minutes before the opening gong. Ben traded in soybeans, soybean meal, and soybean oil, usually with a complex spread or "crush" involving all three commodities. He had shown Hugh the ropes in those pits, and occasionally when the silver market was even more quiet than usual, Hugh would join the mania in the soybean pit, just as he would join Tim at the frantic wheat pit. Because he was trading entirely for his own account, and not "with the deck," filling orders from brokers (who shied away from new men), he could go wherever he wanted.

"Pretty good; she's not sick as much as she was last week and the doctor says the danger of miscarriage is over now."

"She still working?"

"She'll finish out the school year," Hugh answered cautiously. He did not know when Liz would quit her job. When he'd asked, she'd refused to answer. It was her decision, she'd insisted, not his.

Ben apparently did not know that Hugh knew he was the one who'd warned Monsignor Sullivan about the parishioners' plot.

Hugh had abandoned his lust for revenge—or told himself he had—but he did not want Ben as a friend. Neither, however, did he want such a powerful trader as an enemy. So he kept up the pretense of camaraderie.

Still, it was none of Ben's business whether they needed Liz's income to live on, which Hugh suspected was the point of the question.

In fact, Hugh had made more than enough in his first year on the floor to survive without his wife's salary—no big killings yet, but no dramatic losses either.

Then the bell rang and Ben was pushing his hands to sell off a half-point from the previous day's closing.

The trading floor reminded Hugh, somewhat irreverently, of a parody of a solemn pontifical Mass. The traders in their multicolored jackets were the celebrants, the messengers and runners were acolytes, the huge windows looking out on LaSalle Street were the rose window, the quotation boards, some marked in chalk, some in computer-fed lights, were the stained-glass windows of the nave, and the choir stalls from which CBT officials, brokers, and commission house representatives watched and sent their messages were the choir lofts. The sometimes hysterical babble of the traders was plainsong rising in respectful worship of July silver and December wheat.

It was time for him to win a big one, to show the skeptics like Ben Fowler that an ex-priest could play the game with the best of them—no, better than the best of them. Hugh gave himself to his new vocation and to the service of his new deity with as much enthusiasm as he had to his old one.

His mother had taught him long ago that if you did something, you must do it well.

For a week silver had been fluctuating up and down with little reason. Something unusual was taking place, and as Hugh opened with a bid to acquire two more contracts, he resolved to be cautious. The Cambodian invasion should force the price of silver up and keep it up for a while. Yet on the last two days after rising the limit it had fallen back sharply to the opening price, the kind of market in which one could be cleaned out in a half minute if one were inattentive.

In the first half hour silver rose four and a half cents, a gain for Hugh of almost twenty-five hundred dollars on his ten-contract purchase.

The action in the silver pit then slowed down as quickly as it had flared. Who was buying all the silver and then selling it? Hugh violated his stern resolve to concentrate on nothing but silver and thought briefly of Liz.

The marriage was going through a period of "adjustment," or so he told himself. There was no reason to expect that he and Liz were immune to the ordinary processes of marital change.

There were moments of ecstatic contentment when they lay in each other's arms, exhausted and happy; or when on Sunday afternoons they sat peacefully next to each other in their apartment, reading and listening to music on the hi-fi and not talking because the emotions of love that bound them together made talking unnecessary.

But there'd been fewer such moments each passing month. Liz was not interested in his work. "I can't understand all that capitalist jargon," she would protest, "and I don't like gambling."

He knew there was no argument, practical or theoretical, against her ideology. After a few attempts to explain the social utility of futures trading he gave up.

He was forced, however, to listen to accounts of her work—the new techniques of religious education and particularly "salvation history," which sounded to him like one more obscure Belgian fad that satisfied the need of priests and nuns for the old certainties.

Children, he was sure, knew very little about history, did not understand the word "salvation," and were not particularly interested in the Old Testament.

He bit his tongue. Nor did he tell her that he was no longer interested in the internal fashions of the Catholic Church.

Liz, he realized, was still a nun, a married nun perhaps, but a nun, nevertheless. She would always be caught up in the clerical culture that he'd abandoned when he left the priesthood. Her friends would always be angry priests and nuns, and angry former priests and former nuns, who could not leave the clerical world behind.

When Hugh resigned from the priesthood, he'd left it; he wanted no part of the organized Church, and attended Mass on Sundays only to keep Liz happy. He did not return phone calls from priests, not even from Jack Howard.

If his wife wanted to continue to be part of the Church, that was her right. But strangely, she was much more angry at Catholicism, and her anger was fanned by the anger of her friends. They couldn't leave the Church and they couldn't stop hating it.

"You think I ought to forget about the Church, don't you, Hugh?" she had inquired one night, lying peacefully in his arms.

"You think I'm clinging to the past by associating with those people?"

"You have the right to do whatever you want," he said, and then, because the moments of tenderness were few and far between, he kissed her on the cheek. "I don't know whether all the anger helps, though."

She sighed peacefully. "I suppose a psychologist would say I'm working out anger I feel toward my parents."

"The Church has ruined enough of our lives." He felt a fierce need to defend this tense and haunted woman. He drew her closer, warm skin touching warm skin.

"Maybe I ought to see a shrink and get Catholicism out of my system." She held his head against her chest, as though she were afraid she'd lose him.

"That's up to you, darling."

But she had not seen a shrink, and Hugh suspected that she never would.

Her anger was like a cancer, slowly destroying her appealing sweetness. When talking about the children she was teaching and during their moments of love, she was the gentle sister of the past. Leaving the religious life should have removed her from the causes of much of her anger, but, instead, her break with the Order had made her more angry than ever.

Lately, especially during the sickness of early pregnancy, the anger seemed to be turning on him.

What could he do about that? What should he do?

They were questions he swept under the rug, to await his conquest of the Chicago Board of Trade.

At noon the silver pit came alive again in another buying wave. The price shot up five cents, wavered, and fell three. Hugh jumped in and bought four contracts of his own.

Almost at once there was another flood of purchase orders. The price rose to the limit.

He hesitated. He could pyramid his profits and buy more contracts at the end of the day when the price might fall a few points. Or he could take his eight-thousand-dollar profit and run.

Pigs lose, he told himself, and began to push his hands outward in an offer to sell at a point off the limit. His contracts were quickly snatched up, the price fell a point and a half, then rebounded back to the limit.

Then the price slumped again, down eight cents, back to where it was in early morning, then rallied a cent just as the bell rang.

"You stayed out of the final rush?" asked Ben Fowler.

"Got out at the limit."

"Smart man; you'll put us all out of business yet."

"I didn't sell short on the way down," he replied. "Might have doubled the haul."

"It takes time," said Ben sympathetically.

As Hugh walked off the floor, an elderly trader with white hair and a light blue jacket stopped him.

"Uh, Hugh, I have to catch a plane to Arizona and I'm not going to have time to go over to St. Pete's. Could you hear my confession?"

Hugh did not know how to respond to such a request. "I can do it legitimately only in a case of necessity," he said cautiously.

The other trader smiled. "Come on, Hugh; they can't take the power away from you. Besides, an airplane ride to Phoenix is serious danger as far as I'm concerned."

So in a quiet corner of the trading floor as the last of the traders straggled away to their lunch and their first drink, Hugh shrove the old man of sins of anger, impure thoughts, and drinking "too much, about twenty times."

So far Xav Martin's somber prophecy of "demons from hell" had not come true. He had left the priesthood, but the priesthood would not leave him.

"Saw you talking to Benedict the Manic," Tim said when Hugh joined him in the office. Tim never asked how he had done on the floor.

"Friendly chatter."

"Don't trust him." Tim's small eyes danced. "He's a bit of a fraud, you know, and he doesn't like you either. Ever make it with that gorgeous iceberg he's married to? Ben doesn't use her much; wants her around for show but doesn't want anyone else feeling up the merchandise."

"No, Tim, I haven't gone after Helen." Hugh considered he was telling only a half lie.

Tim shook his head. "Can't figure it, then. Anyway, he's got it in for you. Be careful."

"How do you know?" Hugh peeled off his coat, monsignorial red in color.

Tim stretched lazily. "Takes one to know one, maybe; I can feel it. . . . Anyway, there's a message here from someone named Cronin and Mom called to say that Maria Manfredy's husband—you remember her, don't you?—is missing in action in Nam . . . some kind of fly boy in the Navy."

"Yes, off a carrier."

"Well, maybe he's a prisoner." Tim wasn't very interested.

Hugh dialed the chancery office phone, trying for the moment to repress his sorrow for Maria's suffering. She was still working at the bank out on Madison Street. Poor woman.

"Cronin," said the vicar general of the Archdiocese of Chicago.

"Hugh Donlon. You called?"

"I've got good news. Well, I hope it's good news. Up to you, I guess. The dispensation came through. Paul the Sixth's conscience is working again. If you want—and I stress *want*—you can have a Church marriage. Jack Howard, I presume . . . "

Hugh hesitated. The dispensation meant nothing to him. Liz was his wife, no matter what the Church thought. Yet it would please his parents, and perhaps hers too.

"I'll talk to my wife, Sean," he said cautiously, emphasizing the word *wife*.

"Fine. There's a regulation about a private ceremony. You don't need to pay attention to that, if you don't want to. Family and friends, whoever you want."

"My wife is pregnant, Monsignor."

"Congratulations." Cronin was not flustered in the least. "Make a million or two at the Board of Trade, only don't leave it to the Church. Give me a ring."

Tim smiled beatifically. "Looks like another family crisis shaping up."

"Not my fault," said Hugh.

"Never mind fault," said Tim. "Sit back and enjoy."

Tim watched his brother's broad back as Hugh rushed out of the office. Always the boy scout.

Although Tim resented Hugh, he had resolved that the best way to live in his own isolated universe was to be cool, laid back, uninvolved. You seized the excitement when it came near you, but you did not go out of your way to find it.

A conflict with Hugh would require too much effort and there wouldn't be enough payoff. Tim despised the way his father and brother had muscled into the commodities racket with Marge's husband's money. He, God knows, could have found his own capital. Larry Maguire would have put it up and promised not to tell his daughter, Estelle. Now Hugh was the big Donlon on the floor.

Well, Tim would take life as it came. There were still plenty of women who found him attractive and a variety of thrills that did not require the risks of the trading floor. He and Estelle were in one of their reconciliations, seeing a priest counselor every week. Tim had learned from his various shrinks the answers to give, so both Estelle and Father Carmody thought he was making great progress.

Tim sighed and struggled to his feet. Time for the first drink of the afternoon.

Fowler was a barracuda. Hugh ought to be more worried about him. Tim would watch closely. The fight should be an interesting one—a barracuda and a boy scout.

There were some advantages in being alone. That way you could enjoy the battles between the other animals in the jungle without getting killed yourself.

CHAPTER
TWENTY-THREE

1970

Hugh assumed that Liz would not want to be bothered with the Church's blessing on their marriage. He was surprised by her reaction when he told her late that night.

"Of course, we'll do it," she said briskly. "In my role, it's important to be seen as one who is in a sacramental marriage."

"I think our marriage is sacramental enough," he said defensively.

"The waiting was unjust and the requirements are unjust," she said, unbuttoning her plain blouse. "Yet we shouldn't let that interfere with a public celebration of our union with each other in the Lord."

Some new party line among the religious-education crowd, he thought. A year ago she would have ridiculed the importance of the Church's blessing.

"All right, we'll have a celebration."

"Can we afford thirty or forty guests?"

"Of course, we can. . . ." Thirty or forty—her bearded priest friends and their nun mistresses, and the gays. What would his mother say, if she came this time?

Her skirt joined the blouse on the floor. Liz rarely picked things up. Even in drab white underwear—fancy lingerie was now a symbol of decadence and a concession to male chauvinism—Liz was delectable. Hugh enveloped her in his arms.

"Hugh, I'm so tired," she said weakly.

"So am I."

In a few minutes, however, she was as eager for love as he. Once they began, fatigue no longer seemed to interfere.

"Oh, Hugh," she sighed happily when they were through, "that was wonderful."

"You're what's wonderful," he said.

"Do you think we could make it fifty or sixty guests?" She snuggled closer to him.

"Whatever you want."

Hugh wondered what her thoughts had been when they were making love. Probably searching for an ideological cutting edge for her potential guest list. Women, he supposed, reacted differently.

Liz stayed awake after Hugh fell asleep. He could be quite sweet, she thought, tonight especially. But she was beginning to resent his constant sexual demands, particularly, as was increasingly the case, when she found them perfunctory. Why couldn't he love her for herself and not for her body.

Terror had been exorcised from their marriage, and with it most of the pleasure. She no longer feared his power over her and thus no longer especially felt the pleasure he could give. She was angry at him most of the time. How could anyone not be angry at his chauvinism and his false consciousness and his capitalist ambitions and his stupid family? He meant well, no doubt, but in the present state of the world that was not enough. Having ceased to confront the problems of social and sexual inequality, he was now part of the problem himself.

Their wedding might be a turning point. Liz believed in turning points—*kairoi*, as the Greeks called them—times when there were special opportunities. It had been such a turning point, during the retreat after her senior prom, that had led her to the religious life. And another, after the loss of their child—which was Hugh's fault for not listening to her fears about a miscarriage—that had made her decide to serve God by pursuing a career as a professional religious educator who would dedicate her life to raising the consciousness of young women.

As she fell asleep, she remembered the priest at the retreat, a wonderful old man, holy enough to be a saint, she'd thought then. He was the first person she'd dared tell about the things her father had done to her. He'd suggested the convent as a way she could find peace and forgiveness. But now she thought he had probably been a male chauvinist pig too.

"I'm not going to that wedding." Estelle looked up from the floor plans on which she was working. She was always working on plans. Usually the house was never built, for which Tim was deeply grateful.

"Suit yourself," he said. "I think it ought to be quite a show— her faggoty friends with my mom and dad, and Hugh playing Prince Valiant to everyone."

"I'll be visiting my mother in Florida." She returned her attention to the floor plans.

"First I've heard of it." Tim no longer found the game of bending Estelle to his wishes fun, save on the rare occasions when he wanted to make clear to everyone that he had the power to do so.

"She's a whore," Estelle said. "She seduced him."

"Probably did," Tim agreed philosophically. "Got herself pregnant so he had to marry her."

He watched with considerable pleasure the ring of red rise on the back of her fat neck.

The silver market continued to move erratically upward and Hugh continued to make substantial gains by sticking with a decisive choice made shortly after twelve o'clock. He had figured out the silver pit. If he could master a few other pits, then he would be ready to open his own firm and trade in his own name for everything from gold to plywood futures.

In the meantime, he wanted to make enough money to pay off Liam and his father by Saturday, the "wedding day"—and make a down payment on a decent house.

"Another great day?" Ben clapped him on the back as they walked off the trading floor.

"I guess so. I hate to make money on that Kent State shooting." Hugh's liberal conscience still bothered him.

"Can't be helped. Anyway, time the kids were taught a lesson."

He turned abruptly. "Stay away from the soybean pits till I make enough to retire. . . ."

Liz hardly heard Hugh when he confided to her his desire to buy her a house for a wedding present.

"Can't that wait till after Saturday, dear?" she pleaded in the saccharine tone of forced affection that he had grown to fear more than her anger. She was clearly living on her nerve ends.

"I thought you'd be happy to hear about it," he said.

"I am," she agreed carelessly, "but we have so much to do. Do you think you could call the caterer and tell him there'll be ten more? Sister Sophie is bringing all the sisters from Vandalia."

"Sister Sophie?"

"You remember her." She looked at him impatiently. "We were novices together."

"But the whole Order?"

"You begrudge me my few friends?" Her eyes were hard and resentful.

"Not at all," he responded easily. "Have as many guests as you want."

The ceremony would be in the combination school hall and church, made of concrete blocks and steal beams, in the South Holland parish where she worked. After Mass the church would be converted back into a hall for the wedding party—and for guests, most of them the clergy and ex-clergy that Liz cultivated and their dates.

Liz was celebrating her transition to the status of a "validly" married nun as if it were a triumph.

"Then please be helpful and make the phone call," she said, distracted by some other unfinished chore. "And after that, I have something else that needs to be done, if I can only remember what it is."

"A year ago you didn't want a Church validation," Hugh said.

"God damn it, Hugh, make the phone call and stop preaching."

She left the room, list in hand, mother superior on a rampage because no one else was as efficient as she.

Hugh made the phone call, as ordered.

Wednesday was a frantic day on the Exchange and Hugh was drawn taut as a high tension wire about to snap. His instincts told him that something was wrong. Someone was manipulating the price of silver, probably someone on the Comex in New York. He was making a large profit from guessing which way the price would bounce, yet he hesitated to risk too much on the wisdom of his guesses. He lacked the experience to understand who was playing with the silver market and why.

He wanted desperately to make a big profit so he could celebrate the Church's blessing of his union with Liz by paying off his debts and telling her they could buy the house.

"You Donlons always end on your feet." Maria considered her guests over the top of her beer mug. "Peggy becomes a painter whose work sells the day she opens her exhibits. And Marge finds a nobleperson who is quite nice even if he can't speak English and carries a pike all the time—and see, Margie, I've got the right weapon now. Irish pirates carry pikes, not halberds. The boys make tons of money in that gamblers den on LaSalle Street . . . and the judge turns down the Supreme Court and is celebrated on the cover of *Time*. Don't tell me it's just Donlon luck."

"You're doing all right yourself," Marge replied.

"Only because I heard about computers at the Pentagon when Steven was there and took a few courses."

She hoped her front wasn't wearing thin. Not a second passed in which she wasn't agonizing about Steven. He was alive—of that she was sure; his wingman had seen the parachute open—but the worry . . . the uncertainty . . . would she ever see him again? Pull yourself together, Maria Angelica. . . .

"They scare me," Peggy admitted. "I'm afraid they'll take over the world."

"Spoken like a true artist, darling. Don't worry. They're only smart adding machines. They're still dumb when they're not adding . . . rigid creatures . . . only cope with a yes or a no. Males, I think."

What did they want? Maria was confounded. Peggy had never once come in the bank, even to cash a check. Now she and Marge show up and are surprised to bump into the local computer whiz in the bank lobby telling off a software con man. Want to see how I'm holding up with Steve MIA? No, the Donlons aren't ghouls.

She'd brought them to Doc's for lunch because that's where she ate every day. Peggy didn't seem to mind the place, especially as they served beer and wine. The world sure was changing.

Marge's skirt was midthigh; the minis were shorter in Britain. Even Peggy had raised her hem to the knee.

I should have legs that good at her age.

At my age.

What's going on here?

"Hugh's being married day after tomorrow," Marge blurted. "I mean a real church wedding, with the Pope's permission."

"We thought you might want to come," Peggy said anxiously. "You were at Marge's wedding. . . ."

Warning lights went off and on in the back of Maria's head, bright red, Sicilian warning lights that said "Beware, Maria Angelica. . . ."

"Married?" she said.

"To the former nun."

"I think I might be out of place. . . ."

"You're a friend of the family," Marge said confidently.

"All the same . . . Oh, hell, darlings, in a way I'd love to. . . . But I don't know. . . ."

"We understand perfectly, my dear," Peg said.

Do you really? No, you don't. How can you when I don't?

In her office after lunch, Maria wished she'd ordered a third glass of beer.

Then she cried a little while. Not for herself. Not even for Hugh or his family.

Rather, for all the people in the world whose dreams didn't come true.

Peg was wearing a burgundy robe, lacy and low cut. She carried a tray with a bottle of unopened white wine and two glasses. She sat down across the desk. Tom pushed aside the manuscript on which he was working; Neirsteiner eiswein, he noted. Forty dollars a bottle.

He both welcomed and feared the conversation that was about to occur. She'd tried twice before to begin the reconciliation process. Hurt and in the mood to punish himself as well as her, he'd turned her away. Now he desperately wanted his wife back and didn't know how to begin.

She was making the start for him, and that gave her considerable moral superiority, which, to judge by the glint in her eye, she intended to use.

"I'm going to be here every night, Tommy, and in a different expensive gown. I don't think you will be able to resist me indefinitely."

"Oh?"

"It's gone on long enough," she said, ignoring his unpromising answer. "You know it and I know it. There are some things that have to be said first."

"Say them."

She folded her hands on the desk and leaned forward.

"I suppose that I've always done what you have wanted because I was so young when we married and because you are so much smarter than I am." She smiled ruefully. "I acted like a little fool. I'll go to the wedding—or whatever it is—even though I know it cuts off his last chance of escaping from her."

"You admit you were wrong?" He could not believe he was getting off so easily.

"Not for a moment. Hugh will regret the day he set eyes on her." Her own eyes flashed dangerously. "But you were right that I should have gone to that ceremony in City Hall." She paused and began to open the wine bottle. She was quite skillful at opening wine bottles these days. "I've already apologized to Hugh and to her. And I apologize to you."

"But—"

"But"—tears were forming in her eyes—"I'm not stupid and I'm not a little girl anymore. Never, never, Thomas Raymond Donlon, take for granted again that I'll go along with anything you say, simply because you say it."

He reached across the desk and began to caress her throat. She smiled at him the way she had smiled after Mass at Twin Lakes the first time they'd met.

Careful not to disturb the movements of his hand, she uncorked the wine bottle.

On the Thursday before the Church's official blessing of his marriage, Hugh Donlon was not thinking about the commodity market as he rode on the South Shore train from Hyde Park to the Loop.

He hardly noticed the serene blue of Lake Michigan and the soft green of Grant Park.

If there was no ceremony on Saturday, his marriage to Liz would not be valid in the eyes of the Church. He was committed to Liz for life, regardless of what the Church said or did. Yet there was a finality, a definitiveness, about the step that unnerved him.

After Saturday there would be no possibility of returning to the priesthood and no other loves in his life. He and Liz would be bound until death.

He wanted no other loves nor did he want to return to the priesthood. But there were too many undiscussed topics, too many subjects ruled off the agenda—the people with whom she associated, her contempt for his work, her refusal to leave the organized Church behind, her strident ideologies and shallow crusades.

The argument earlier in the week—if that's what it was—displayed a facet of her that he usually refused to acknowledge. She was sweet and lovely and often pliant in bed, yes, but she was also an angry and potentially domineering woman.

What was it Jack Howard had said? She needs a strong parent figure to blame for what goes wrong in her life; the Order was the old parent, her husband the new.

Jack was exaggerating, of course. Or was he?

Friday morning started quietly enough. The first contracts sold close to the previous day's closing price. Then, however, there was a brisk interlude of selling. It made no more sense than the locked-up close yesterday. The market stabilized at ten thirty, down five and a quarter cents, then at eleven fifteen it plunged again, limit down.

No sense at all—it's too low now; it's bound to soar.

He hesitated, trying to banish thoughts of Liz from his mind. You had to concentrate in this business, had to listen for every sound around the pit.

Then silver came off the limit, slowly at first, then quickly. By noon the loss was erased. Hugh cursed himself for his hesitancy. If he'd bought in at the low, he would already have the money to pay off Liam and his father.

He bought five hundred contracts, a hundred thousand dollars, almost all his equity. It was the biggest purchase he had ever attempted. The man across the pit was startled by the trade and watched him keenly as he jotted down the transaction on his card and stuffed it into his shirt pocket.

The man's expression turned to amazement and grudging respect as the silver quotations on the rapidly moving yellow band above the floor climbed, first a half point, then a point, then five points. At twelve forty-five, Hugh Donlon had made almost four hundred thousand dollars. He could have made more than that if he'd had the courage of his convictions and jumped in earlier.

Then the slide began, just as the price of silver went up, so it went down. Hugh watched in disbelief as panic selling exploded. The market was congested, investors were suddenly abandoning silver, no one was buying, the bulls were terrified, the bears were having a field day.

Hugh refused to panic. He would hang on, take a small profit, and then reclaim his gains next week.

Silver continued to fall, not pausing at the opening price. It plummeted like a stone thrown over the side of a boat.

Hugh felt as if he were a man frozen at the helm of the boat that was sinking. He ought to sell, quickly, before it was too late.

Yet he did not move. The price continued to fall until the bell rang at one twenty, ending the grain trading. It stirred him out of his reverie. Sell, yes, sell, while you still can.

It was too late. The silver market was locked down and no one was buying at that price.

His profits were wiped out and so was his investment equity.

Tomorrow the Church would bless the marriage of a penniless failure.

Tim was waiting for him in the office.

"Looks like you've had a rough day?"

"Cleaned out," Hugh said through clenched teeth. Tim knew; did everyone on the trading floor know too?

"Can you meet a margin call?" Tim stretched. "If not, you'll have to liquidate or the Clearing Corp. will do it for you."

"Just about. I won't have anything left. If we go limit down on Monday and I can't unload, I'll be finished."

"You shouldn't blame yourself. I warned you about Ben; he's been out to get you since you came on the floor. Maybe he'll leave you alone now that he's drawn some blood. Can't tell about Ben; maybe he'll want more blood."

Hugh slumped in his hardback chair. "What does Ben have to do with it?"

"I thought you knew." Tim's thin red eyebrows arched in surprise. "He and a couple of other guys have been buying and selling silver, shooting the market up and down like a roller coaster. They hedge everything in New York, of course; so they don't lose any money. Probably even make a few dollars on the arbitrage between here and Comex. But that wasn't the idea. Ben wanted to jiggle you off the rope. Start real gentlelike and then increase the motion till you were dangling and finally give it one sharp tug. Presto! Hughie falls into space."

"How did you know?"

Tim shrugged. "Heard some guys talking about it in the elevator. Rotten trick, they thought. Figured you'd get even with Ben eventually. I thought you'd caught on."

"I'll get even, all right," Hugh said, surprised at his vehemence. "Ben Fowler will regret the day he came on the trading floor by the time I'm finished with him."

"That's my boy," Tim said appreciatively.

And you better watch out too.

Hugh was only too well aware that he was at the mercy of misfits like his brother and bastards like Ben Fowler. All right, then, he vowed, he'd find power and plenty of it, more than he'd ever need.

And then Ben would pay in spades.

CHAPTER
TWENTY-FOUR

1970

Jack Howard presided over the brief wedding ceremony with dignity and taste. His few remarks about God's blessing on this couple who had given so much and who had so much to give set the right tone.

Unfortunately the tone ended as soon as Hugh and Liz turned away from the portable altar on the big, graceless auditorium stage. A group of women—they must have been nuns—whooped enthusiastically, as if their team had just won a basketball game. Liz, now about three months pregnant, had the sense not to wear white but she still acted like a blushing bride, hugging and kissing everyone without the slightest restraint.

Marge escaped with a brief bear hug, but Peggy was clutched for a full half-minute, while Liz assured her that everything would now be fine.

"Your idea, darling," Marge said, alluding to the disagreement they'd had before leaving Ireland. "Thank God Maria had more sense . . ."

"Tasteless little thing. Her family?"

"Oh, they wouldn't come; sacrilegious union or something like that. We're the ones who have to take the rap."

"Damn shame." That could mean it was a damn shame Liz's

family hadn't come, or that they thought the marriage was a sacrilege, or that the marriage was a damn shame.

Or all of the above.

"Too right," she agreed.

The beaded, bearded celebrants were finally persuaded to take their seats at the tables and Tim, reluctant and embarrassed, rose to propose a toast. "To my brother and sister-in-law"—Timmy raised his champagne glass—"may they have a long and happy marriage."

Before Hugh could get to his feet and attempt a reply, one of Liz's Commune brethren dashed to the head table and preempted him.

"I think we need more of a toast than that," he said. "This is an important event in Hugh's and Liz's life and I want to say some words about this event. First of all, we can't celebrate with an easy conscience while American soldiers are murdering innocent Vietnamese. So the first toast I offer is to the victory of the Vietcong and true freedom for all the Vietnamese people."

Cheers and shouts of "Ho, Ho, Ho Chi Minh!"

None of the Donlons drank the toast, not even Hugh. But Liz emptied her entire glass and extended it to the judge, who refilled it with a spasm of distaste.

"Then I want to drink to Father Hugh Donlon and his wife. Hugh is one of the best priests in the archdiocese. He's on a temporary leave of absence until the Church wakes up to the fact that it can no longer impose the archaic law of celibacy on its best priests. Hugh is a pioneer, a man who made a brave sacrifice to teach the Church a lesson; it won't be a useless sacrifice. Hugh, my boy, when enough other priests have the same courage as you do, the Vatican will have to bow to the will of the people and permit priests to marry. So I propose a toast to a married clergy and Hugh's speedy return to the active ministry."

More loud cheers. God, what a vulgar crowd, Marge thought. How many of them are still priests? Impossible to tell. Poor Jack Howard, the only one in a Roman collar.

Hugh sat ashen and silent next to Liz. She nudged him, but he didn't move. She whispered impatiently in his ear.

Slowly he rose to his feet. "Thanks, Tim; thanks, Charley, for the fine toasts. I simply want to drink to my wife."

There was polite applause.

Liz looked sullen and unhappy.

"Bad show," said Liam.

"Decidedly, darling," Marge agreed.

After the tables were cleared a three-piece orchestra arrived and the singing began. "We Shall Overcome" was the overture.

Then suddenly Liam jumped up and, snatching the violin from an astonished concertmaster, shouted at the top of his rich Celtic baritone, and with the brogue laid on thick, "Ah, sure'n I thought we should sing a few Irish tunes. First of all, one in honor of our brothers in Ulster. It's called the 'Old Orange Flute.' Sing along if you know the words."

Marge, who had heard Liam play only Bach partitas and sing in church, was amazed that he could dominate such an unlikely audience with songs in English, Gaelic, and Highland Scotch and wedding stories from all three cultures.

When he was finished the guests were exhausted and their voices hoarse. Quietly they straggled out. Only the Donlons and Jack Howard remained.

"Darling, I still don't believe it." Laughing, Marge kissed Liam on the cheek.

"Remarkable," said Jack Howard.

"Thank you very much, your lordship," said Liz, obviously tipsy.

"Cold winter nights in Ireland," said Liam, grinning like a giant leprechaun.

A few minutes later Liam cornered Hugh as he was getting into his Chevy; Liz was already asleep in the front seat.

"Good luck, that sort of thing."

"We're not going on a honeymoon, Liam, only back to the apartment. . . . I appreciate what you did. It saved Mom and Dad a terrible defeat. Liz's . . . our friends mean well. They just don't understand."

"Nothing. Heard about your trouble, the crook on the floor. Tim, you know. Bad show. Here's a loan, usual interest rates, stern accountant here. Pay me back when you can. I insist. That's all."

Hugh was left standing, an envelope in his hand, as Liam shambled across the church parking lot to his waiting wife and their rented Mercedes. I have to take it, don't I? It will save me on Monday. Another chance. God, do I need another chance.

The check was for one hundred thousand dollars.

"God bless you, Liam," Hugh mumbled through savagely clenched teeth. Damn right I'll pay it back. And I'll have so much power by then that I'll never have to depend on your charity again.

Nor anyone else's.

On Monday morning, Hugh was able to sell his silver contracts as soon as the market opened. The price was a cent and a half an ounce above Friday's close. He recovered some of his own money.

None of the money was his yet; he still had to prove himself, then to amass the power that would win him freedom from other people's help. It would be a long summer.

On a Sunday in July Ben Fowler invited Hugh and Liz to a lawn party at the Fowler beach house in Michigan. At first, Hugh decided not to attend, then he changed his mind. Let Ben think that he suspected nothing.

Liz agreed to accompany him, much to his surprise; she looked quite attractive in a maternity sundress and was charming through the afternoon. "Such an advantage for their children to have a place like this," she'd whispered to him, quite forgetting that it had been purchased by capitalist money.

"A swimming pool on the shore of the lake is a special advantage," he replied.

She missed his irony. "His wife certainly is lovely for a woman of her age, isn't she?"

Helen was climbing out of the pool, taut, solid, and sexy in a skintight black one-piece swimsuit. "For a woman of her age, yes."

"And her daughter is lovely; how old is she now?"

Linda was standing next to her mother, taller and more slender but just as sexy—two blond goddesses, on display to impress the world with Ben Fowler's success and power.

"Eighteen or so, I think. I'll get you a drink. Don't stay out in the sun too long."

"I'll go into the parlor; it has such a lovely view of the lake," Liz said wistfully.

"We'll have one of our own someday."

The Fowlers were standing at the informal bar, greeting their guests, Ben in gawdy Hawaiian shirt and swim trunks, sweat pouring down his face, and the two women in transparent cover-ups over their swimsuits.

"You look good, Hugh," Helen said coolly. "You seem a little thinner."

"What should I call you now, anyway?" Linda tossed her head to indicate the question was boring but she knew she had to say something. "Father isn't right anymore, is it?"

"Linda." Helen was stunned. "Please, don't be so bold."

"Hugh's fine," he said easily.

"Your wife is very pretty," Helen volunteered. "I never noticed that when she was a nun. I suppose one wouldn't."

"And she doesn't wear nunny clothes either," Linda agreed. "So many nuns could use a course in a charm school after they leave the convent."

"Liz is very happy these days."

"How are you, pal?" Ben's big fleshy hand grabbed Hugh's shoulder. "Glad you could make it. The little woman looks fine, though she won't be little much longer, huh? Great, great . . . and with your profits it won't be long before you have a house like this."

"Next year," Hugh said. He picked up his drink and walked away, feeling quite ashamed of himself. Were his preposterous fantasies about Helen and Linda the beginning of Xav Martin's descent into hell?

"Thought you'd never come, we're both dying of thirst," Liz said when he entered the parlor with her gin and tonic.

"Sorry, I was distracted."

"No problem; I was enjoying the view of the lake." Since the wedding ceremony debacle, Liz had been on her best behavior. She'd stopped working and was attending the Pastoral Institute at Loyola only two mornings a week.

Hugh crossed Helen's path once more during the party. She was serving potato salad at the buffet and he was filling plates for himself and Liz. There was a moment when no one was near enough to hear what was said.

"I'm sorry about St. Jarlath's," she said quickly under her breath. "It was my fault. I'm terribly sorry."

"It didn't matter. Don't worry about it," he said, just as quickly, and shifted a plate from one hand to the other.

When he made love to a willing and eager Liz that night, it was Helen's bland face and compact body that invaded his imagination.

The next week there was another attempt to jiggle him off the rope at the Exchange, as if Ben knew of his lustful thoughts. Hugh was ready this time, made his own hedges on the Comex in New York, and cleared a neat profit working the arbitrage between the two exchanges. Ben wasn't so fortunate.

"I hear he got a minor bloody nose on a silver arbitrage thing," said Tim at the end of the trading day.

"Did he really?"

"Maybe the rope jiggling is over."

"I doubt it." Ben wanted him off the floor and would not be content till he was beaten into the ground and forced to give up in disgrace.

"We'll see."

"We sure will, Tim."

That night Henry and Jean Kincaid phoned. One of Henry's clients was involved in complex litigation in Chicago. Jean and Henry came to the city occasionally and took Hugh to supper at the crowded Cape Cod Room at the Drake. Liz had never found the time to join him at these pleasant meals.

Their third child, a five-year-old boy, had been injured by a hit and run driver. He was in a coma. The doctors were not too hopeful.

"We called for your prayers," Jean said.

"I'm not a priest anymore," he replied ruefully.

"Of course, you are, Father Hugh," Henry insisted.

"You always will be for us," Jean said. "You know that, Hugh. . . . Laura wants to say hello."

"When are you going to come see us, Uncle Hugh?"

How old was Laura? Twelve? Thirteen?

"I won't recognize a grown-up thirteen-year-old."

"Fourteen," she corrected him. "Yes, you will. I look just like my mother. . . . Maybe if you come now you could give Johnny a special blessing to make him well again."

Catholic schooling had prevailed over Lutheran ancestry. The child believed in blessings, even from renegade priests.

"I'll say a special prayer for him here, Laura, and I'll see you people by Christmas."

"Anyone I know?" Liz asked as he hung up.

"Old friends, voices from the past." He told her again about the Kincaids, and about the injury to their child.

"How horrible . . . the poor family . . . but, you see, Hugh, once a priest always a priest for those you help."

"Perhaps for others, Liz. Not for me. I've left that role behind."

"Maybe it won't leave you behind."

Two weeks later Hugh shared lunch with Jack Howard at the Sign of the Trader, a crowded noisy restaurant on the first floor of the Exchange.

"You seem to be thriving on the excitement."

"All my life, Jack . . . hey, more roast beef? It's good, isn't it? Nothing elaborate for your wealthy Irish traders, just the best quality meat. Where was I? Oh, yeah, all my life I've made it on someone else's name. Judge Donlon's son, Father Donlon the priest, now I have to make it on my own, build up my own power. I love it."

Jack moved aside his plate. "No, no more wine. I have to drive back to the West Side. These are strange times in the Church, Hugh." His comment did not seem to follow from what Hugh had said. Perhaps it was an attempt to explain why he had not followed Hugh out of the priesthood. "You can accomplish a lot if you know how to work within the system. In St. Mark's, for example, the old monsignor never heard of a budget or a financial plan, never even made an annual report. Now there's a parish finance committee headed by a woman banker and we're the best organized parish in the diocese. It's all on computer tapes and disks and she has the old man eating out of her hand."

Hugh's heart did a little dance. "Oh? What's her name?"

Maria's pilgrimage had brought her to the new, new neighborhood, just as his father had thought it might.

"Maria McLain. Her husband's a Navy pilot missing in Vietnam. A classy, classy woman. Why? Do you know her?"

"Not really. She went to school with Marge." Hugh felt an onrush of pride. "Give her my best and tell her I'm praying for her husband."

Hugh made enough money during the summer to take a vacation the last two weeks of August. He would rather have stayed on the job and continued the slow repair of his fortunes from the havoc that Ben had worked, but he and Liz needed the time together. She'd agreed to the vacation cheerfully and suggested they drive to Iowa to visit her family.

"Maybe next year when we have a grandchild to please them," he'd said. "It might be a little awkward now. Besides, we need some time together."

"We could see them and still have time together."

"It wouldn't work out, Liz."

"All right," she relented. "I suppose you know best."

Their love was renewed on the trip. The future looked hopeful again. Ben Fowler and his family were bad memories from a past that was no longer important.

Liz seemed to agree. She held him close as they watched the sunrise over the Atlantic from a small hotel on the Maine coast, listened to the drum fire of the surf, and breathed the healing salt air.

"Not much sleep."

"I don't see how you can love a woman who's so fat."

"It's easy."

"It certainly seems that way." She coughed.

"Every marriage has its ups and downs," he quoted from his Cana Conference talk. "We must have sense enough in the middle of the downs to know that we should go away together and straighten things out."

"You're so busy with your job and next year we'll both be busy with Brian. . . ."

He patted the forthcoming offspring—around Christmastime it would appear. "My work will ease up in a year or so when I make my big breakthrough on the Board. Then I'll have afternoons free. I'll be home by two thirty, under your feet all the time."

"I'll love that. I should continue my own career, you know."

"That's up to you. I agree with you feminists that a father should know his children." He agreed in theory, at any rate, though he was not sure that a mother was wise to have a career, at least while the children were young.

"Otherwise I'm just a sex object, good only for lovemaking and bearing children."

"You're not an object, Liz, and never will be, whether you have a career or not."

"You don't want me to have a career?" She tightened up in his arms.

"Of course, I do. You know that. But a career won't provide you with any more dignity or worth as a person than you already have, which is plenty."

"I don't like that." She remained tense. "If you must prove yourself at that terrible place, why can't I prove myself?"

"That's different."

"How?" She tried to pull away from him.

He recaptured her gently. "I'm only trying to prove I can do that kind of work. My worth as a man doesn't depend on it."

He didn't quite believe that.

"All right, then." She relaxed. "So long as you see it that way, then I can do my kind of work too."

"I couldn't agree more."

He didn't quite believe that either.

The trip was a success and they returned confident about the future of their marriage. However, Hugh still felt niggling little doubts. Liz wasn't like his mother or Marge or any of the other women he knew. The others he could watch and study and understand. Their reactions were predictable. Even the unpredictable Maria was not mysterious, only illusive.

Liz's reactions depended on her mood, and her moods were erratic and patternless. They seemed to be shaped not by the world outside but rather by her inner world, a world frequently distracted by distant drums.

On the way home, Liz brooded on that conversation. Hugh would never change. It was not even his fault. His mother's false consciousness had been pounded into him at such an early age that he couldn't overcome it. He might make all the right sounds, but he was still an incorrigible chauvinist. He would not help her to raise the children. And he didn't think her career was as important as his—it was a hobby, like collecting stamps or being a candy striper at the hospital.

Liz vowed that she would show him. She would be a successful mother and a successful careerperson. And he would fail as a father and as a trader. Then he would come to her seeking her forgiveness.

That was the only way he would ever learn.

In late November, Jean Kincaid phoned again. Johnny was dead. Could Hugh spend a few days with them in Manhattan Beach? They desperately needed someone to talk to. The new priest in their parish wasn't much help.

Hugh didn't want to leave Chicago. His slow climb back up the ladder to success was progressing. He couldn't afford to miss a day at the Exchange. Besides, he didn't want to be forced back into the priest role he had given up. Moreover, the baby was due in only a month.

But he could not refuse Jean and Henry and grief-stricken Laura. In a way they were all that was left of his parish. And, he realized intuitively, it was only the remnants of his parish that had prevented the descent into hell that Xav Martin had predicted.

"I think it's a terrible imposition." Liz was querulous in the final month of her pregnancy. "You hardly knew the little boy. And what if our baby comes?"

"You're only five minutes from Billings Hospital."

"What if it's the middle of the night?"

"And I'm only five hours from O'Hare. Didn't the doctor say that the baby would be on time or even late?"

"A lot he knows."

"I have to go to them, Liz; it's an obligation from my past."

"And I'm an obligation in the present. Is she better-looking than I am?"

"That has nothing to do with it."

"Oh, all right, go ahead if you have to. But stay in touch."

He promised he would. It was the first separation since their marriage.

He looked forward to it eagerly.

CHAPTER
TWENTY-FIVE

1970

Hugh flew out of O'Hare on Friday morning, planning to return on Monday morning, thus missing only two days on the Board. The only plane on which he could find a reservation stopped at Denver. Another hour would have to be wasted.

The weather forecast called for clear, cold weather all the way to the Pacific mountains, then high clouds into Los Angeles. As the DC-8 winged its way westward, he looked down at the brown fields with snow lacing, like frosting on a pound cake. Tim's winter wheat, food for the world, Hugh thought as they turned south for the approach to Denver. Then he saw an ominous line of black hanging across the northwest horizon and inching slowly in their direction.

He watched it with detached interest. It disappeared behind the Rockies as the plane settled onto Stapleton Field.

He decided not to leave the plane. As the baggage trucks pulled up to the plane like eager puppies seeking nourishment from their mother, a vague notion, floating hazily in his mind, began to take shape.

It was supposed to be a bumper crop of winter wheat. Tim insisted that no one in his right mind would buy wheat with a big harvest staring him in the face.

He walked up to the flight deck.

"Bit of weather on the other side of the mountains, Captain?"

The pilot, a grizzled veteran with a dazzling smile, said "Is there ever. Don't worry, though. We'll be out of here long before it hits. There's going to be a lot of snow from here to Chicago by tomorrow night."

"I imagine. A big one, huh?"

"You bet. Came up all of a sudden. The weather people haven't caught on to it yet. It'll take them another hour."

Calmly Hugh strolled off the plane, walked through the jetway, and went out to the lobby. He found only one unoccupied phone booth. The phone in it was not working. Patiently, he waited, watching the Denver passengers checking in for his flight.

Finally, an elderly woman tottered away from one of the booths. The phone at the office was busy.

He cursed mildly and called again.

Still busy.

Boarding for his flight was announced. He phoned once more. Tim answered. "Tim Donlon."

"Hugh . . ."

"Hi . . . nothing in the market; silver is down a few cents."

"What's the weather like?" He tried to restrain his excitement.

"Cold but sunny, supposed to warm up over the weekend. Why?"

"I want to buy two million bushels of December wheat at the market."

"You're crazy . . , that's all the money you have."

"I have to catch a plane." He would not tell Tim about the storm; the news would spread all over the floor in a half hour if he did. "Do it, Tim, and if you're smart, buy some yourself."

"What stop loss?"

"There isn't going to be any loss. We'll let it ride till Tuesday when I come back. I have to run."

As the plane lifted out of Stapleton, Hugh was reassured by the weather front. It was much closer now and darkly evil, like a deadly infection sweeping toward the wheat fields.

Tim was the bear of the family, selling short and profiting from bad news. No one really liked a bear. A bull went long, investing in good news. Or so they told themselves.

The snow storm was good news for the market. December wheat

would run sky high. It would lock up for three days, making Hugh almost a millionaire.

Yet it was bad news for the farmers and the hungry of the world. He would become rich because of a natural disaster.

Yet if it were not for the commodity exchanges, the disaster would be even worse. The loss for the farmers had already been absorbed by the speculators, who, in the tried and true apologia for the Board, were said to take the risk out of farming as a price they paid for the opportunity to speculate.

The speculators would pay for the storm. They would be the losers. Other speculators, that is. Hugh Donlon would be the winner because he had seen the meaning in a huge low-pressure ridge over the Rockies.

And with victory would come power and freedom.

He hoped that Ben Fowler was short December wheat.

Hugh made another phone call as soon as they touched down in Los Angeles.

"I did it," Tim said. "I even bought some myself. Both at the low. I wouldn't be surprised if it locks down on Monday. You could lose your shirt."

"Not on your life. There's a granddaddy of a winter storm on its way."

"No trace of it on LaSalle Street. Let me look out the window. . . . My God." His voice was suddenly as hushed as if he were praying. "The sky outside is dark gray. I should have bought more for myself."

"You haven't seen anything yet."

The Kincaids were badly shaken, mother, father, two teen-age children—Laura and her brother Pete—and a sweet little blond three-year-old named Tillie, short for Mathilda.

Laura, a tall slender blond plainswoman like her mother, was the hardest hit by her brother's death. "If only I'd watched for the traffic," she said softly and solemnly.

"Stop that, Laura," Hugh ordered sharply, the automatic response of a priest to a potentially hysterical adolescent. "God wanted Johnny home. It's not your fault."

"I know, Uncle Hugh. But I miss him so much. Would you say Mass for us? It was so terrible at the church."

"A birth control sermon," said Jean, who was even more handsome than Hugh had remembered her from the last dinner at the Cape Cod Room. "The new pastor is an Old Country Irishman without much feeling for anyone. Trust in God. Sure we trust in God, but that doesn't mean we don't hurt."

"Do say Mass for us," Henry pleaded. "Laura borrowed the vestments from her high school. We need to have a funeral ceremony at which we can grieve."

"I'm not supposed to say Mass anymore," Hugh objected.

"Please, Uncle Hugh," Laura implored.

So with his congregation gathered around the table in the kitchen overlooking the Pacific, Hugh Donlon said Mass for the first time since he'd resigned from the active ministry, with the surging blue waves of the ocean, framed in a picture window, serving as the altar-piece. He preached feelingly of Johnny Kincaid, now a spiritual and human giant in the life that awaits us all. He wasn't sure he believed any of it, but his congregation believed, and that perhaps was enough.

All the Kincaids wept.

At supper, however, their vitality returned. Even the lovely Laura laughed.

Later in the evening, Hugh phoned Liz, guilty that he had not called before.

"I thought you'd never call," she complained.

"Weather delay," he excused himself. "What's it like there?"

"It's snowing, an inch on the ground already. Hugh, what if the baby comes tonight? You won't be able to get home."

"Planes fly in snowstorms. Why? Any signs?"

"No," she admitted reluctantly. "And I don't want you flying in a snowstorm. What would we do without you?"

"Nothing will happen, Liz. Don't worry. I'll call you first thing in the morning."

Hugh lay awake in his bed in the guest room for hours, listening to the Pacific surf and brooding on the terrible misfortune that had befallen his friends. He had wanted to use his life to bring happiness and comfort to others. But somehow it hadn't worked out that way. The passionate love that periodically surged within him was damned up like a raw mountain stream, which, because of ingenious human intervention, could not rush madly to the sea. The priesthood hadn't freed him to love. Neither had marriage. So he would make a fortune on a tragic winter storm.

Something had gone wrong with his ability to love, to bring others happiness and himself joy. The pounding surf of his emotions had been reduced to a quiet murmur—or sometimes a nasty whine.

The plane was vectored to the north of O'Hare on Monday afternoon. Hugh caught a quick glimpse of the red brick buildings of the seminary. I'm a rich and powerful man now, Monsignor Xav, he said to himself. We'll see whether anyone dares to try to drag me down into hell.

The snow was plowed into enormous piles on the side of the runways, the sky was clear and hard and the sun bright, but there was no water on the runway to indicate that melting had begun.

He phoned the office.

"Locked up," said Tim without waiting to hear who it was.

"Only the beginning. I hope Ben was short."

"Like everyone else."

Good. He would pay off his father and Liam, and buy a new house for his wife and son.

And then he'd settle with Benedict Fowler.

Now he was one of the big guys.

And on his way to being the biggest.

CHAPTER
TWENTY-SIX

1972

"May I see you after the session, Mr. Donlon?" It was one of the runners. Her pretty gray eyes were worried. "It's a . . . uh . . . something private."

Hugh didn't have time for her.

He'd abandoned his heavy investment in silver at the end of 1971, at the time his daughter Lise was born; he was convinced that the 1970s silver boom would not start till after the presidential election and after the conclusion of some kind of peace in Vietnam.

To his surprise, silver had shot up in January and was now selling at two dollars and sixty-eight cents an ounce, almost a dollar higher than when he and his Managed Accounts pulled out. Some of his select group of clients for whom he had recently begun to work were muttering unhappily.

It was a mistake, one of a large number in the past three years. Now he was successful enough and powerful enough to admit that mistakes were part of the game, even big ones.

By the end of March, he suspected, silver would fall below two dollars and twenty cents. Then he would jump in and bring his clients with him. The roller coaster would ride up to almost three dollars by the end of May and then he would slip out and wait for the next upswing.

He had no time to play priest counselor to a pregnant teen-ager, and he had seen the worried eyes often enough to know what the problem was. She probably wanted a priest, even an unfrocked priest, to approve of an abortion.

"Of course, Kathy; my office after the gong?"

Why had he said that? Still the superstition that the tattered remains of the priesthood would protect him from Xav Martin's prediction, a prophecy that he now thought of as a curse?

The girl had nodded solemnly. "Thank you very much, Mr. Donlon."

What was her last name? Something Polish? Clear fresh face, native intelligence, lots of self-possession. Probably would survive. Damn, he should remember her last name. He prided himself on knowing the last names of all the kids on the floor, as he had in the days when he was running the High Club.

Now he'd be late for his date with Helen at the harbor. She'd wait. She always did.

Tim drifted by the silver pit after the one-fifteen bell ended the grain markets.

"Still sitting tight? My brother the bull acting like a bear? I thought the unsettled world economy made metals the real thing? What about the Russian winter wheat fiasco?"

"Just wait."

Hugh Donlon was now a successful man with a large home in Kenilworth, a number of wealthy private accounts, and the respect due a trader with uncanny instincts and iron nerve.

He was not, however, satisfied. He was weary of the narrowness of floor trading. He still reveled in the intense thrills of a turbulent market; but he wanted something more, grander thrills and more challenging excitement.

He had become a thrill addict like Tim. Maybe worse than Tim.

That was probably part of Xav Martin's hell.

Why couldn't he drive Xav's warning from his mind?

Anyway, he wanted his own commission house and the opportunity to manage other people's money as well as his own, to throw the dice for others as well as himself and to throw them in many different games simultaneously.

But in the meantime there was Kathy and her abortion.

"Well, Kath?" He put on his kindliest face as his imagination routinely peeled off her clothes. Nice young body. Cute breasts, trim thighs.

Women are easier to dominate when you strip them, even mentally. They sense that you've done it and that they've lost a little of their independence.

She sat on the edge of the chair, a sixth-grader called to the principal's office for throwing snowballs.

"I'm pregnant, Mr. Donlon." The words and the tears came in torrents. "My parents want me to go away to have the baby. Joe and I want to get married; Joe, he's my boyfriend, doesn't have a job; he's still in school; and he came back from the service at Christmastime; and his family is against the marriage too. And you're so kind and friendly I thought you might advise us what to do."

"You're not thinking of an abortion?" The priest replaced the collector of women. His imagination respectfully put her clothes back on.

"Oh, no." Her eyes were wide in horror. "I mean, you always think of something like that, but I couldn't do it. I have to give the little thing a chance to live. I love Joe; we've been best friends since grammar school; and we were planning to be married in three years when he graduates."

The automatic calculus a priest makes in such a case changed. The indicators were positive—they'd known each other a long time, same religious and cultural background, eventual plans to marry. . . . Nowak, that was her last name, probably short for Nowakowski.

"Eighteen is too young to marry. . . ." What would Peggy say about that.

"I know, Mr. Donlon. . . ."

"Age is important, but it doesn't guarantee maturity necessarily. Would Joe come and see me with you?"

"Oh, yes. Our parish priest is old-fashioned. He yells at us and won't listen. Says we're terrible sinners. We know that, Mr. Donlon. We don't want to sin anymore."

"We're all terrible sinners, Kathy. But God must like us because he made so many of us."

A minute later Hugh left a grateful and happy Kathy Nowak and walked under the implacable sun across the Loop and through the crowded park to Burnham Harbor and his own sin, an offense for which he felt no guilt at all, nor fear of the wrath of a problematic God.

Financial success had created an overpowering sexual hunger in him, as if the pressures of lust that had built up through the years of celibacy had finally broken through the red line on the safety gauge and exploded. In the morning he reveled in the thrill of conquest on the trading floor and in the afternoon, as often as possible, he luxuriated in the embrace of a woman.

His marriage was floundering. Liz had become pregnant again within three months after the birth of Brian—her choice, not his— and was now totally preoccupied with her two children.

She was obsessed by an obligation to care for the children even when they didn't need care. The two babies, nervous kids to begin with, it seemed, had reacted anxiously to their mother's anxieties and quickly learned to manipulate her. Liz smothered them with attention.

They were raising two little monsters—spoiled, neurotic children. His dutiful attempts to come home early to assist Liz were swept aside with ridicule; Lise was forcibly pulled from his arms and he was told that he was spoiling the child by giving her too much affection and holding her the wrong way besides.

He gave up, hoping that at a later stage in their life he might have a chance to reclaim them.

Even before Lise's birth, Liz's interest in sex had fallen "limit down" to zero. His amorous advances were rejected with "how dare you?" anger or "how could you?" tears.

At the same time, he'd become a skilled and sensitive connoisseur of women, like the collectors of vintage French wines. A woman was a puzzle to be solved, a mystery to be explored, a prize to be won. You explored a woman's whims and weaknesses, you studied her reactions, you flattered her vanities, you deluged her with gifts, eventually you explored her body, discovering its pleasure points and its pain points. You rewarded her, you punished her, you pleasured her, plundered her, you delighted her, and you teased and caressed her.

You understood that the best way to keep her under your control until the next time you wanted her was to make the last experience as rewarding as possible for her.

And when all else failed, you took possession of her by winning her sympathy.

Not that women were merely bodies to be enjoyed. They were endlessly intriguing subjects for investigation and understanding, so like you and so different. Even a Helen Fowler, who seemed at first to be bland and uninteresting, could be forced to reveal herself and emerge as a complex, indeed fascinating, human being.

A woman's psychological self-revelation was pure delight, far more enjoyable than her physical undressing. Self-disclosure bound her closely to you, as long as you wanted her to be bound. She became a more valuable trophy in your collection after you had invaded her deepest secrets.

As a collector's item, a woman existed for you.

Judge Donlon spotted Maria at the beginning of his lecture. The Chicago Association of Financial Planners had grown sufficiently liberal in the last few years to admit a few women members and even to allow them to attend meetings in the prestigious, if somewhat dull, oak-paneled University Club. The women bankers, however, were not usually strikingly attractive blondes. Nor did the typical woman member wear a red dress that skated close to the boundary of sexiness and then skated triumphantly away.

"It is not for a judge to say, of course, since, despite the propensity of some of my colleagues to be instant experts on all subjects, the law will be of little direct, positive help to planners. Yet the law came from small communities and perhaps in reflecting on the origins of the law in such communities you may discover insights that will be useful in your work."

Maria's expressive face said, "Come on, Your Honor, don't be humble; you know what we drones should be doing."

Ah, Maria, how could we have lost you?

"Great talk, Your Honor." She kissed him generously, despite a few raised eyebrows from her stuffy male colleagues.

"Your husband?" he asked gently.

"We saw a picture of him on TV with that bitch Jane Fonda. So he's alive." Maria was in command of her grief, neither hiding it nor giving in to it. "The McLains are old hands at POW camps. Great-Great-Granddaddy Alexander Bonaparte McLain was in Andersonville during the War Between the States."

"Andersonville was a Confederate prison, my dear."

"I know; the McLains are from South Carolina but one line of the family supported the Union. You should hear them talk about Mr. Lincoln. You expect this guy with a beard to come around the corner. . . . My man will get out alive and well and cultivated and charming. . . . And how's your family? Herself rejoicing in the grandkids?"

"The Wentworths are pure joy, if I may say so. We don't see them as often as we'd like."

"And Tim?"

"It is no secret that we are not close to Tim's family. His wife and Mrs. Donlon will never get along."

"She designs weird homes. I'd like one of her summer palaces for the fun of it. . . ." There was a slight pause. "And Hugh?"

"I candidly do not know, my dear; he's successful. It seems to me that he has yet to find the happiness he's seeking."

"He will someday, Judge Donlon; don't doubt that for a moment."

"I hope you're right, my dear. I truly hope you're right."

She kissed him again. "That's for Peggy. Tell her to keep painting up a storm. I loved her last exhibition."

Joe Marshal was at the most an inch taller than Kathy and looked even younger than she, a very polite and very worried choir boy. If only one could take charge of their marriage—for they would surely marry if he did not tell them not to—and protect them from all the mistakes.

"You were in computer work for the Army, Joe?"

"Yes, sir. Never got out of Washington for the whole first year. Simulations mostly. Lot of graph and chart work."

"Oh?" Hugh picked up the latest copy of *Commodity Perspectives*. "What would you make of this chart?"

Joe glanced at it quickly. "I'd say that you should always sell May wheat by February."

"You never heard that before?"

"No, sir. Kathy and I haven't had time to talk about her work. It seems interesting though."

Hugh rapidly flipped the pages. Joe's comments on soybeans, pork bellies, and plywood were as quick, as definitive, and as correct as his comments on wheat.

"Why do you folks only have two-dimensional charts, Mr. Donlon?" He frowned, trying to puzzle it out. "You could learn a lot more from three dimensions, build weather in, for example. I don't know anything about it, of course. . . ."

Hugh realized that he had stumbled onto someone who was likely to be a charting genius, and indispensable to the firm he hoped to start.

"Kathy?" He spoke slowly. "Would you mind if your husband went to work making charts for me part-time while he finishes school?"

"Mr. Donlon, you're wonderful!"

"If our baby is a boy, we'll call him Hugh," Joe declared, dazed by relief and happiness.

"Don't you dare," Hugh laughed.

The two happy young people left his office hand in hand, as though they were leaving a rectory.

And Hugh sat slumped at his desk for a long time.

CHAPTER
TWENTY-SEVEN

1972

In April silver fell back to its 1971 levels and speculators lost interest. Hugh learned from a phone call to Zurich that Europeans were buying silver in New York and shipping it across the Atlantic. However, the purchases were not being made on the Exchanges. Hence the low rate of activity and the sideways movement of silver prices in the market.

It was still a potential bull market, waiting for momentum. His instincts about the upswing in silver as a hedge against inflation were correct. He'd missed the last surge because he had mistaken the timing, not the basic trend.

Still, he did not jump back into the market. He would wait patiently until the time seemed right. It was impatience that had hurt him the last time around.

Silver hung for three weeks, till late April, hesitating between two dollars and ten cents and two dollars and twenty cents.

At the end of the third week, with the price at two dollars and eight cents, Hugh bought a hundred contracts for himself and his clients, a lot of money for all concerned. However, if he was right and there was a quick run-up and they could sell off at the top, his reputation as a sage would be made and the Donlon company would be on its way.

"Did you jump in today?" asked Tim in the office, now a bigger and more plush suite with separate rooms for each of the brothers and their private secretaries and a cubbyhole for Joe Marshal.

"Finally."

"Thought you would. It's going to be a quiet summer in everything else. The Russian grain projections are optimistic. No fortunes this year."

"Don't count on it."

Tim shrugged cheerfully. "I know better now than to argue with your instincts. . . . Hey, you know we have to do something about this Ben Fowler one of these days. He's never going to let up on us unless we do."

"What now?" Tim might be telling the truth and, then again, he might not.

"He's trying to block our membership in the Clearing Corp., although everyone knows we have enough money to get in. And he's after me about playing some games with deferred contracts, as though that's the kind of thing I'm into."

If the new firm was to be successful, its reputation must be above reproach. That might be difficult with Tim aboard.

"Can he make any of it stick?"

"I don't think so." Tim slyly ducked the question and glanced at Joe Marshal's work sheets. "Hey, that looks pretty; next thing you'll be moving a computer into the office here."

Joe had created a three-dimensional chart that looked like a mountain range. "Soybeans with a month of bad weather," he observed. "Look, Mr. Donlon, if you have a month of rain, soybeans sell at thirteen dollars."

"Never happen," Tim said flatly.

"We'll have to wait for the month of rain." Hugh looked at the chart. "Sure would be a disaster for Benedict the Badman, wouldn't it?"

Tim considered the chart more carefully. "I may hire me some Sioux to do a rain dance."

Hugh smiled shrewdly.

May was a fantastic month for silver. The price soared from two dollars and eight cents to two dollars and sixty-five cents. On the Friday before the Memorial Day weekend, Hugh decided that it was time for him and his clients to get out. They had made the money that his bad timing had prevented them from making earlier in the year. His mistake was canceled. He had won again and won big.

At home Liz was withdrawn and fretful. Lise, usually a healthy little girl despite her mother's excessive care, was running a slight temperature. Liz was worried that there might be no pediatrician available over the long weekend.

So she listened with little interest as he recapped the day's trading in silver.

"I don't know what you're going to do with all that money," she said. She cradled the unhappy child in her arms while her son tugged at her skirt for his rightful share of attention.

"We could use some of it to make a down payment on that house at the Lake Shore you've been wanting." It was the grand surprise he had been hoarding in hopes that it would make her smile again and give him a chance to break through the wall between them.

"I never said I wanted such a house. I don't know where you come up with such absurd ideas, Hugh. You know very well how dangerous beach houses are for children. Just the other day two children drowned on the Jersey coast."

"We would be very careful."

"How could I keep up a house over there and this terrible big place too and go to the Pastoral Institute during the summer?"

"I didn't know you were planning to go to the Institute." It was the first he had heard of it.

"Of course, I am. Or don't you want me to take interest in my own professional development? You want me to spend all my time around here with these children?"

She rocked Lise too brusquely and the child wailed again.

He clenched his hands. My God, he thought, is there nothing I can do right?

"I want you to do whatever you want to do." He tried to keep his voice even. "Certainly you can go to the Pastoral Institute. I thought you had your heart set on a place across the lake near the Fowlers'."

"Certainly not. . . . Now, Brian, can't you see I'm taking care of Lise? You've had your share of time."

Hugh tried to take Brian into his own arms, but the youngster was having no part of it. He wailed for his mother as soon as Hugh picked him up.

"How many times do I have to tell you not to give in to the child that way? Put him down. I'll take care of him."

Brian rushed to his mother's arms and sniffled into silence.

"If Lise is better, might we go house hunting tomorrow morning, nothing definite . . . just look around?"

Liz was horrified. "In Memorial Day traffic? Do you want us all killed?"

"I meant in midmorning when the traffic is light."

"You can go if you want," she said in a martyr's voice. "I'll stay home with the children."

He would accept her last clear and positive signals and look for a home on the Michigan shore.

Liz was thirty-one and, despite her current slovenliness, a beautiful and gifted woman still, with a long and productive life ahead of her—if she could break out of her present malaise.

Was there anything he could do to salvage their marriage? He longed for the sweet and vulnerable young woman to whom he'd first made love in the Hyde Park apartment only a few years before.

Perhaps she was descending into a hell of her own, in a solitary confinement in which there was no room for him or anyone else.

A hell like his.

Liz was upset with herself after Hugh left. Yes, of course, she wanted the house at the lake. Then why hadn't she said yes?

Because Hugh so infuriated her with his money and success and the arrogance that money and success had given him that she couldn't resist the opportunity to put him down.

That was wrong. Their relationship was not properly synchronized. When she wanted to be friend and lover he was not home. And when he tried to pull the marriage together she was not in the mood to humor him.

Partly because he was so insufferably superior and condescending.

And mostly because when they were synchronized, her fears of his power over her returned to threaten her with the loss of her personhood if she lowered all her defenses.

She should have known it would be this way. She could have been a college president probably and a nationally known leader of the movement if he had not seduced her out of the religious life.

If only she'd understood what men were like then.

Not all men were as bad as Hugh. His brother, Tim, for example, was sensitive and sympathetic. And married to that terribly fat woman. Tim knew how to make a woman happy.

She tingled at the memory. Nothing shameful had happened. It was merely an affectionate exchange on a warm April evening. Tim wasn't a beast. Sex was not what he wanted. Merely friendship and understanding.

And none of the other Donlons would give it to him.

There were several superb lakeside homes for sale. Hugh hesitated about his decision. His sentimental memories of Lake Geneva were powerful. Yet Lake Geneva was too crowded. Maybe it was part of the past, just as was the house on Mason Avenue, now that his parents had sold it and moved into a lakefront condominium.

The old new neighborhood was no more. His parents were virtually the last to leave St. Ursula.

He would make an offer on a house next week. It would be a good investment no matter who won the presidential election— Nixon or McGovern—or what happened to the silver market.

When he drove past the Fowler place, he saw a silver Porsche parked in the driveway. Linda was there.

He parked his Mercedes behind the Porsche and rang the bell.

Linda was struggling unsuccessfully into the halter of a bikini as she opened the door. "Oh, hi, Hugh. The folks are in Naples . . . hey, can you tie this for me? I came running . . . thanks . . . Naples, Florida, that is. Come on in. I'll make you a drink."

She was a tall girl with blond hair that fell to her incredibly narrow waist. Her face was the same model's mask that her mother's wore. Although she had lost the bored sultriness of her early teens, there was still an invitation in her provocative posture, somehow a wholesome invitation.

He stepped inside.

"No, don't bother with the drink. I thought I'd take a chance . . ."

"Really, come on and stay a few minutes anyway. I'm not doing anything but catching rays. What will it be? Gin and tonic? Scotch?"

It was early afternoon but he asked for a Scotch. She smelled of suntan oil and sweat.

He drank two Scotches and she matched him. They talked of her problems at school and of her plans to study modern dance after graduation. She was an intelligent young woman, and very much interested in his opinion. She even took notes about books he recommended, after searching fretfully in the parlor for pencil and paper.

"I really should be going. . . ." He rose to leave.

"A last one for the road," she pleaded. "I'll make some coffee and sandwiches too. It's creepy here all alone."

He followed her into the kitchen, where the remains of her breakfast were scattered in the sink.

He stood behind her, put his arms around her waist, and began to kiss her back. It tasted of suntan oil. She was passive, neither resisting nor cooperating, as though she were trying to make up her mind.

He recalled the priestly love he'd once felt for her, his concern to protect her from suffering. He forced himself to release her, freeing her rapidly moving rib cage from his embrace.

She took his hands and pressed them to her firm flesh. "I really want you. I really like you."

After Mass the next morning, on the way out of church, he and Liz met Pat Cleary, assigned to the parish in the new transfers. Pat greeted them warmly. He had finished his Ph.D. in psychology and his twinkling brown eyes and friendly freckled Irish face radiated even more sympathy and understanding than in the seminary, when he had been considered the class "Going My Way" priest.

"I'll be looking forward to working with you both." He looked at Hugh. "It will be like old times."

"That will be exciting, Pat; it really will. Of course, I've got a lot of commitments and responsibilities just now. . . ."

CHAPTER
TWENTY-EIGHT

1972

The fall and winter of 1972 were so hectic on the Board of Trade that Hugh barely noticed Richard Nixon's re-election and the beginning of the Watergate investigation. The soybean crop was the largest on record and the wise traders went short, expecting prices to plummet. Then Joe Marshal's three-dimensional model became prophetic: It rained every day in September. Soybeans rotted in the fields.

The Humboldt current then changed its course, imperceptibly, carrying the anchovy schools away from the coasts where they were harvested.

The result of these two quirks of nature was a worldwide shortage of cooking oil. The prices of all three commodities took off.

There was also a worldwide shortage of wheat. The Russian harvest had been a disaster, and Russia moved quickly to purchase American wheat before the news was out. Shrewd traders, the Russians visited the various American grain export firms—Continental, Bunge, Cargill—and bought them out at basement prices, keeping secret each purchase while negotiating for the others.

The Nixon administration, pathetically eager for farm votes, quietly accepted these deals, which in effect forced American consumers to subsidize the mistakes of socialist agriculture.

At the same time, the price of silver took off, its erratic ascent made even more unstable by the volatility of the grain markets.

Seats on the Board of Trade, which had sold for thirty-five thousand dollars only a few years earlier now cost more than a hundred thousand dollars. Wealthy families, perceiving that commodities trading had become a rich man's game, bought them for troublesome sons; the old apprenticeship relations between traders and clerks and runners broke down. Marijuana and cocaine were added to the commodities that could be bought in the building, although no one suggested a futures market in them.

Hugh Donlon was a tower of strength in the days and weeks of panic in September. The more turbulent the market and the more money at stake, the more relaxed he became.

He'd studied Joe's chart carefully, and after the first three days of rain in September, he'd bought one million bushels of soybeans.

"Your friend Ben Fowler finally liquidated his soybean position today," Tim said on an afternoon late in September when the rain was still falling. "Do you think Joe's charts are like voodoo dolls? What if we hint to Ben that we put a curse on him?"

"What did he quit at?" Now was the time to finish off Ben Fowler, make him a lesson to anyone who would dare cross Hugh Donlon.

"Three dollars and ninety-five cents." Tim sounded as if he were personally responsible for the rain that had caused the run-up. "He went short at three forty."

Hugh made a note on his chart and glanced at his watch. "Two million bushels . . . one million-dollar loss. Even for Ben that'll be a lot."

Tim uncrossed his legs and crossed them again. His tiny, hard eyes were bloodshot. "A lot more than that; I suspect that like many of the other old timers, he had a couple of accounts in other people's names. He could go down six mil."

Hugh tapped his ballpoint pen thoughtfully. "Can Ben take that?"

"Not for long; he's probably hoping to bounce back, but if this rain keeps up . . ." He looked out the window. The curtains of water, opaque drapes shutting out the light, were so thick you could barely see LaSalle Street. " . . . and it looks like it will, he won't do it in soybeans."

"How will he meet his calls . . .?" Hugh clenched his fists. "Will he start dipping?"

"Into client funds? Probably. He's done it before and got away with it. A few others have too, although it's a dangerous business. What if the CEA should come in with a random audit?" Tim was watching Hugh narrowly, as he often did these days, afraid of his brother's rampaging hunger to destroy Ben Fowler.

"Not segregating client funds is the mortal sin here."

"If you're caught," Tim said. "No way of knowing for sure whether he's doing it."

"I bet I can find out."

Sex had been unimportant to Helen Fowler at the beginning of her affair with Hugh; her years in the orphanage had taught her to contain her emotions lest she get hurt. She had faked pleasure with him as she had with Ben and for the same reason—in her affection-starved life physical contact with a man was more important than pleasure.

Then Hugh had invaded the inner citadels of her body and soul and captured her completely. There were no secrets there, no place to hide, no last barrier to throw up to protect herself. With Hugh, she was thereafter always naked, always open to pain.

And unspeakably happy.

Their love affair would end someday, she knew, and life would go on to something else. Even now she saw him less often than she had in the past. Still, she would enjoy the romance for as long as it lasted and remember the sweet paralysis that possessed her whenever she heard his voice or saw his face or felt the touch of his hand.

She continued to love her husband as she always had, a quiet, passive love with little conflict and only occasional passion. Ben entered her body as if he were performing a duty, not so much to her as to his own image, the same way he entered a golf club a few Saturdays during the summer months, even though he no longer enjoyed the game and played badly.

In bed and out, he'd been a more gentle husband since his outburst at the time of the St. Jarlath's battle. He hadn't apologized for the beatings, but he hadn't repeated them either. Lavish care and generosity were Ben's rhetoric of apology and he inundated her with gifts as if he were courting her all over again.

She forgave him, telling herself that perhaps she deserved her punishment. They were fond of each other in a desultory way, like colleagues in a law office who worked at opposite desks on different legal matters. It wasn't Ben's fault that sex was a low priority in his life. So it once had been in hers and so it would surely be again. Conjugal affection with one man, passion with another—so, she supposed, did every adultress justify her sin.

She was lying in Hugh's arms in the apartment he had rented for their meetings on the near North Side, the second floor of an elegant old two-story flat with high ceilings and long corridors. It was furnished with late-nineteenth-century antiques to match the style of the building itself—Hugh was obsessed with furniture and his impossible wife refused to share his interest. Outside the rain was still beating against the windows. Helen was exhausted and content.

"Do you have any positions in the soybean market?" he asked as they lay contentedly together.

"Not real ones; Ben has some in my name, of course; he always does that. It's his money, though."

"A lot . . . ?"

"Two million . . . two million something . . . I don't know. . . ."

"Is he worried like the rest of us?"

"Who . . . you mean Ben? I don't think so. He says he may have to dip . . . whatever that means. It's done all the time, though, so there's nothing to worry about."

Then he loved her again, overwhelming her with sweetness.

After Helen left, Hugh changed the sheets on the bed and remade it the way he was taught to make a bed in the seminary. He waited in the apartment for two hours, reading *The Wall Street Journal* and *The New York Times* from the past several days. Then a key turned in the door.

It was Linda, wet from the rain and glorious in her excitement over the literature courses she was taking at Hugh's suggestion. He was father, mentor, confidant, and lover to this superb young woman, who idolized and adored him.

Whereas her mother was a passive lover, Linda was athletic and aggressive, not exactly the challenge Hugh needed after an hour of love earlier in the afternoon.

The rain had stopped when Hugh entered his home in Kenilworth. Liz was reading a religious book by someone named Henri Nouwen.

She seemed uninterested in both the fact and the time of his return.

"Good book?"

"Hmm . . . "

"It was another humdinger at the Board today."

"Was it?" She flipped a page.

"Ben Fowler is in deep trouble."

"Serves him right. He's a capitalist pig." All conversational subjects now seemed to demand quick and decisive moral judgments from Liz.

"He might be indicted."

She looked up for the first time from her book. "Hugh," she said, "I've told you that this is the only time I have during the day to myself. Can't you grant me a little privacy and peace?"

"Sure," he said contritely. "Sorry to interrupt."

"He's dipping all right," said Hugh Donlon, "and don't ask me how I know. I know, that's all."

"I won't ask," Tim replied. Either the wife or the daughter or both. You scare the hell out of me, brother, dear. Most of the animals in our jungle don't have to hate the way you do.

They were in the office suite before the beginning of the trading day. Outside, light, perhaps even sunlight, threatened to break through the rain clouds that hovered over LaSalle Street.

"How do we do it?" Hugh was frowning.

"Simple. I make a phone call to a friend over at the CEA and drop a hint in the course of conversation . . . subtle enough so they have to think about it and not so subtle that they miss the point. They'll ruminate through the day and probably tomorrow morning show up in Fowler and Company offices with their adding machines. Tomorrow afternoon you'll receive an urgent call from the Business Practices Committee to attend a confidential meeting."

"Brutal."

"That's what we want, isn't it?"

"That's what we want."

Hugh picked up the cards with his own positions on them, shoved them into his shirt pocket, and strode from the office.

"You'd do the same thing to me if I got in the way, wouldn't you?" Tim said to the empty room.

The elderly trader squirmed uncomfortably, adjusting his yellow trading jacket. "It isn't as if Ben's the first one to do it. He's been with us a long time. He may be able to straighten himself out. Hell, which of us wouldn't be grateful for a second chance someday?"

The Business Practices Committee was meeting informally in a windowless room just off the Board of Trade Library. All they knew officially was that there was an audit underway of Fowler and Company. Unofficially they knew the whole story and were preparing a reaction for press and public.

"Sure, Mike," said a younger trader. "We all like second chances. But not when the public is watching the Board as closely as it is now. We're making a lot of money here—well, some of us are"—he corrected himself with a grin; a couple of members of the committee were disastrously short in wheat or soybeans—"and the public and the press are sniffing for scandal. Congress doesn't think that CEA is up to policing us as it is."

Hugh had remained silent till this point in the discussion.

"We don't have any choice. A year's suspension is the least we can do. I don't think we should destroy him though."

"He'll have to liquidate his company to pay off the clients. How will the man live for a year?" protested the elderly trader. "My God, he has a wife and a family."

"Maybe someone can buy out the company and keep Ben on as a junior partner," suggested the younger trader, scratching his head thoughtfully. "Save face for everyone, and leave Ben a little capital and a chance to trade through the firm."

"Who'd do that?" snorted the old man. "Someone would have to love the exchange a hell of a lot to take on Ben."

"There's basically nothing wrong with Ben's organization, a little old-fashioned, not up to computer technology and that sort of thing. Yet it's a good base, especially with a new and energetic management. . . . Hugh, stop me if I'm out of order. . . . I've been hearing that you and Tim might want to open a medium-size commission house. Would his kind of deal appeal to you?"

Hugh hesitated. He didn't want to seem too eager. "I'd have to think about that. It's a funny thing, you know. Ben's firm is about the right size . . . this is not the ideal time . . . still, if there's no other way and Ben is willing . . . I'd not want to let anyone down. The Board has been very good to me in the last three years."

It was just the right note: aware of the possibilities, not eager to sacrifice, and willing to take the chances for the common good.

The meeting broke up with everyone feeling that it had found a solution to the Ben Fowler problem.

"Tell Ben to see me" were Hugh's last words.

He hoped the other members of the committee hadn't seen him licking his lips.

"You hinted you'd buy the SOB out?" Tim asked his brother in disbelief the next morning. "That's wild, Hugh, wild! I wouldn't have come up with anything that good, myself."

"It solves a lot of problems, Tim."

"Fowler and Donlon." Tim savored the name on his lips.

"Donlon, Fowler, and Donlon," Hugh corrected with a broad grin.

"Which Donlon is first?" Tim asked curiously, wondering how Hugh would handle that.

"Whichever one happens to be talking."

"Hot shit," said Tim. "We're going to have one hell of a good time."

The two Donlons went to Ben's office to settle the details. Tim assumed that his brother would be gracious and sympathetic. That's the way things were done in the club. You didn't kick a man when he was down.

"I'm not sure we can do it, Ben," Hugh began unceremoniously.

A muscle under Ben's eye twitched. His face was the color of his green trader's jacket. "My God, Hugh, you must be able to do it . . . I thought we had an agreement. You're the senior partner. . . ."

Hugh shook his head sadly. "Hard times, Ben, hard times; I can't justify the risk of my capital. You're in deeper than I thought. All those accounts in Helen's name. And Linda's."

"I'll go under, maybe to jail." Ben laid his cold cigar in an ashtray in the shape of a cabin cruiser, his hand trembling so violently that the cigar rolled off like a porpoise thrown back into the ocean. "Think of my family. . . ."

"You should have thought of them when you started dipping."

"Please," Ben slobbered, "I'll do anything. I don't want to go to jail."

"That's not likely to happen; when was the last time they sent a trader to jail? You should be able to make good on your contracts." Hugh stood up, ready to leave Ben's opulent suite of offices.

"I can't make good. I'm finished. God in heaven, Hugh. Don't do this to me."

Tears were running down his ugly face.

Hugh shrugged. "Make me an offer."

Ben coughed. "Why don't I—" Then a spasm of coughing.

"I don't have all day." Hugh moved toward the door.

"Full control. . . ." Ben choked out the words.

"All right. You've got yourself a deal. Work out the details with our lawyers. Today."

"What was the name of that priest at St. Jarlath's?" Tim asked as they rode down the elevator to their own offices.

"Gus Sullivan. Why?"

"Are you going after him now?"

There was an odd light in Hugh's eyes. Disappointment.

"I can't. He's dead."

CHAPTER
TWENTY-NINE

1973

On a Sunday evening in January Hugh and Liz were watching the late TV news. The children were in bed and Liz was trying to read the new Hans Küng book on papal infallibility, a subject that seemed to Hugh to be as remote from his world as a planet in another galaxy.

Suddenly Maria was on the screen.

"What is the first thing you are going to do when Captain McLain comes home, Mrs. McLain?" asked the reporter.

Maria, trim and happy in a blue knit dress that matched her eyes, was standing between two neat and handsome kids in their early teens, with a three-year-old child in her arms.

"First thing I'll make my own original lasagna recipe and then I'll eat at least half of it."

"Is that the captain's favorite dish, Mrs. McLain?"

Mock surprise. "Gosh, I don't know. It's my favorite dish, though, and I'm going to celebrate. Right, guys?"

"Right!" shouted the teen-agers, obviously enjoying the limelight as much as their mother.

"That woman ought to be ashamed," snapped Liz, "making an exhibition of herself and her family over a war criminal. She should be confessing her family's guilt instead of planning a celebration."

"Maybe she doesn't think he's a war criminal."

"Of course, he's a war criminal. He's killed innocent children. Doesn't that make him a criminal?"

Hugh thought of the tall, gentle naval officer he had met many years before.

"Maybe he thinks he was protecting innocent children from the Vietcong."

"Romantic sentimentalism. The Vietcong are the People. They don't kill innocent women and children but only enemies of the People and then only when they have to."

Hugh gave up the argument.

Tom and Peg Donlon saw the news program about the POWs' families.

"Don't think about it, Peggy," he said firmly. "It was not God's will."

"Can you imagine Hugh living such a frantic, pointless life with Maria his wife instead of Liz?"

"No," he said, "I can't." There wouldn't be any love affairs with a wife like Maria.

Not twice at any rate.

"It was not to be, I suppose. I don't enjoy the thought of explaining to God my part in it. I was so convinced he had a vocation . . . what a fool. . . ."

"Don't be harsh on yourself, Peg. Maybe he did have a vocation. Maybe he did all the good God wanted as a priest and is now doing good at the Board of Trade."

Peggy did not reply.

Hugh celebrated his fortieth birthday by taking his father to lunch at the Trader's Inn, across from the Board of Trade. The formal party woud be at his parents' condo on Sunday.

"Liz will be able to come?" his father asked anxiously. "The Wentworths are flying in from Ireland the night before."

Like everyone else, the judge was in awe of Hugh. He chose his words very carefully, so as not to touch his son's hairtrigger temper.

"Yes, Mom said they were. It'll be great to see them again. I imagine I won't recognize the kids. Marge sure lucked out, didn't she?"

I wanted my *enemies* to be afraid of me, not my family.

"Oh, yes." His father wiped his lips discreetly with a napkin. "And Liz will be at the party Sunday?"

"I think so, if Brian and Lise are all right. We've had a bad winter of colds and flu. You know how seriously she takes her responsibilities as a mother."

There was a pause. His father cleared his throat as if he were preparing to deliver an opinion from the bench.

"I was daydreaming as I came down here in the cab. You were born on Good Friday in 1933; the banks were beginning to reopen; we were singing "Happy Days Are Here Again," though to be more precise we were really whistling it in the dark. Roosevelt's voice was magic on the radio. Hitler had come to power in Germany. If anyone had told me that day, when my only concerns were your health and your mother's survival, the events that would transpire in these four decades, I would have thought them mad."

"Did you have any plans for me that first day? I mean after you knew that Mom would be all right?"

His father hesitated ever so slightly. "No . . . none at all."

So I was programmed for the priesthood from the start.

After lunch they rode up to the coolly modern new offices of Donlon, Fowler, and Donlon.

A surprise party was awaiting him. The judge had distracted him at lunch while his mother arranged the cake and champagne and supervised the hanging of the bunting and the balloons in their new offices.

Hugh's new employees, friends from the floor, a few relatives, and a lot of the runners and clerks sang a lusty "Happy Birthday" when he and the judge walked in.

His mother stood next to Kathy Marshal while he cut the cake. Kathy was slim and starry-eyed, and glowing after the birth of little Joseph Hugh.

Liz was not present. She had been invited, but of course, Hugh told himself, she'd turned it down, damning the whole enterprise as "irrelevant."

Poor old Ben wandered around like a lost sheep, out of place now in what until only a few days before had been his suite. It wouldn't be long before he went to Florida to stay, it appeared.

Ben Fowler's head on a platter—that's my fortieth birthday

present, Hugh mused. And Ben Fowler's wife on a king-size bed. He looked at Helen and then at her daughter. You had to admit it, he thought—they both had class.

After Hugh's family and friends had gone, one of the younger traders offered Hugh a sniff of coke.

He left for the apartment and his rendezvous with Helen in a glorious daze.

Her cry of pain shocked him out of his daze. He pulled away from her, his potency gone, his whole body quaking as though he had been seized by sudden high fever.

"I'm sorry, Helen, my God, I'm sorry . . . the damn cocaine . . ." he moaned, horrified at the rivulet of blood running down her breast. "I didn't mean to hurt you."

Helen put her arm around his waist and caressed him maternally. "You're a violent man, Hugh," she said sadly. "A woman who loves you knows she runs the risk. . . ."

"Forgive me," he pleaded.

She laughed cheerfully. "Of course, I forgive you."

For forty years he had believed that men should protect women, the way his father had protected Peggy. And now he had celebrated his fortieth birthday by inflicting pain on a woman. And for all his shock and dismay, he'd enjoyed it.

Gently and carefully she reawakened his passion and they made tender, affectionate love. He caressed and soothed her, assuring her that he never would hurt her again. Then he covered her violated body with kisses as she purred complacently.

Yet as he rode home on the train that evening he knew that Monsignor Martin's demons must be celebrating.

Exultation in his power to hurt her and heal her tasted like rare white wine. Some of the items in his collection were designed to be hurt and then to be healed so they could be hurt again.

He shivered.

Like silver on a day of the bears, he was locked down.

At the bottom of the pit.

When the housekeeper brought word to the supper table that the visitor was Hugh Donlon, Pat Cleary left the table and went to the rectory parlor.

Hugh poured out his story.

"You always were one for the spectacular, weren't you, Hugh?" Pat said when Hugh had finished the long story of the love affairs of the last two years.

"Or the grotesque."

Pat sighed. "What do you think would happen to the adultery rate if the Church announced that it was only a venial sin?"

Hugh was startled. "I imagine it would hardly change at all."

"Right, sin morality doesn't work. I'm not saying you haven't sinned. You'll understand, however, only when you find what you're looking for."

"Which is . . . ?" he asked.

Pat Cleary seemed surprised. "God . . . who else?"

CHAPTER THIRTY

1973

From June to August of 1973 the price of silver was frozen by government edict. Hugh was restless and bored. The exquisite joy of revenge had faded quickly. Ben Fowler was an unimportant nuisance, hardly worth the trouble. And there were no new enemies to humiliate.

He lost Linda, who told him bluntly, "I like you a lot, Hugh, but I have a boyfriend at school who wants to marry me and he's old-fashioned. He says we should try to be chaste till we're married. If I can't sleep with him, I shouldn't sleep with you."

She called him several times a month to ask advice on courses and papers and to share her excited and sometimes intelligent literary insights. He was no longer a lover to his enemy's daughter; only a mentor, a tamed dirty old man.

So old in fact that his memories of what she was like in bed were quickly reduced to a single word—exhausting.

Exhibit closed because of costly upkeep.

He dreamed often that he was trading in a new pit, not in silver or soybeans, but in ice, something very Dante's seventh circle—a pit formed by loneliness and fear and hatred.

He wanted to escape from the pit before he was frozen into it—ascend back through hell. But he was not yet ready to pay the price.

He came home early one evening to find a forceful Polish-American matron who would not admit him to the house. She was the baby-sitter, hired for two evenings and three days a week. "Missus" said nothing about anyone coming home. His children confirmed his identity, somewhat reluctantly, before she called the police.

"Missus" had joined a Winnetka consciousness-raising group. "I'm sick of being an unpaid day-care center for you. I'm not going to do it anymore."

With a severe short haircut and a trim brown very businesslike suit, Liz looked like a double agent of the KGB.

"I'm delighted that you've found interests outside the house, Liz," Hugh said. "We have the money for all the help you need. I hope the group works out for you."

"Men think we're supposed to spend our lives with diapers, fevers, running noses, and temper tantrums. It's time we confronted them with their own obligations to child rearing."

Impulsively Hugh tried an idea he'd been mulling over a long time. "Do you think we might also go into family therapy? There are some things in our own relationship that we might be able to straighten out."

She blew up. "I show the first signs of independence since we've been married and you want to drag me off to a shrink to force me back into line."

She stormed out of the parlor, leaving Hugh to drive the baby-sitter to her bus.

Despite the hectic pace of the market, Hugh would sneak home early several afternoons a week to play with his children while they were in charge of the baby-sitter. Mostly he told them stories like the ones he told the kids at St. Jarlath's. Maxie the Mad Monk and his friends Erik the Anchorite, Warren the Weird War Lord, and Winnie the Wicked Witch, were reborn. Brian loved the stories and so did Lise when he learned how to adjust them to her age.

Liz caught him one afternoon and exploded that he was interfering with their naps. The baby-sitter was fired and replaced by a new one who made sure the children were protected from their father.

Hugh felt guilty. Maybe he was keeping them from their needed rest. And maybe Liz was right that the stories were scaring them.

So he withdrew, somewhat shamefaced, from one more failure with his children.

Liz was afraid of Hugh that summer, not of the power over her that pleasure and intimacy might give him, but of the unsuppressed rage hiding behind his phony protests of concern and support. Instead of his usual clumsy and hypocritical attempts to take the kids away from her, he now frightened Brian with ridiculous and terrifying stories. Brian and Lise not only disliked him, which made sense; they were afraid of him too.

He's losing his mind, she thought. How else to explain his crazy notion that we need marriage counseling.

There's nothing wrong with me. He knows that. He's the one who needs help. He should see the shrink.

The consciousness-raising group and her new career at St. Rock's were an escape from his anger. In a year or two, when she was in full possession of her own self, there would still be time for her to save him.

Hugh went to dinner at the Marshals' new home. Liz had declined to accompany him because the invitation was "trivial."

Joe and Kathy lived in the small upper story of a brick two-flat a block off Milwaukee Avenue in Jefferson Park, impeccably neat and spotlessly clean, if already overcrowded with furniture.

The sleeping baby was proudly presented, a pleasant-faced replica of his father. He nestled quietly in Hugh's arms, more at ease there than were his own children.

"Nothing wakes him up, Mr. Donlon," Joe said. "You don't have to whisper. I think he has the nerves of a trader."

"We want you to baptize Joe Hughie, Mr. Donlon," Kathy said as she put his coffee cup in front of him after dinner. "You're our priest and we want you to be his priest."

There was a sharp and determined tilt to her ample jaw and an appealing plea in her gray eyes.

"Please. . . ."

"I can't do it, Kathy. I'm not an active priest anymore."

"Kathyrn," her husband said gently, "we ought to respect Mr. Donlon's feelings."

"Of course. . . . I'm sorry. I'm being selfish."

The next day at the end of the trading session, Hugh's secretary said that a Monsignor Martin wanted to see him.

Monsignor Martin was the last man in the world he wanted to see.

Looking out the windows of the boardroom, he saw Xav Martin, white-haired and dapper, the perfect, neatly groomed, collegial postconciliar pastor. After serving as a wise and flexible rector at Mundelein through a tumultuous transition to the new Order, Xav had been recently rewarded with the pastorate of St. Mark's. He was Jack Howard's new boss.

"Happy, Hugh?"

"Happy enough." He was also the pastor of Maria's parish. Would he remember her from the movie at Lake Geneva a decade and a half and more ago? Would he say anything about her?

"Certainly successful enough. More challenge here than in the priesthood?"

Should he tell Xav that his prophecy had come true? Perhaps now was the time to begin his climb out of hell.

"A certain kind of challenge. You never will be able to accept any of your students' leaving the priesthood, will you, Xav?"

The handsome priest sighed. "I know it's old-fashioned of me, but no, not really. If you did it, Hugh, it was the right thing for you, I don't question that. Yet . . . somehow . . . it's not . . . it's odd your not being in the active ministry. I can't quite adjust to you trading in pork bellies and T bills."

Xav apparently didn't remember his prediction. He too was uneasy in the presence of the great man. *My God, what have I done?*

"And silver, don't forget the silver. . . ."

"I don't."

"More change than you ever expected when you smuggled in the uncut paperbound books of the French theologians in the old days?" Hugh tried to conjure up nostalgic memories.

The monsignor wanted no part of nostalgia.

"Maybe . . . well, that's not why I barged in here without an appointment. The word is that you don't answer phone calls from priests, so Sean told me to turn up on your doorstep without a warning."

"Sean? What does our new auxiliary bishop want of me?"

Xav Martin turned nervously in his chair, crossing and uncrossing carefully creased tailor-made legs. "He's setting up a board of financial advisers to make recommendations about diocesan investment. He wants to know if you'd accept an appointment on that board."

Would Maria be on such a board? Would she be afraid of him too? No, of course, she wouldn't be on it; she would have left the bank and moved away to be with her husband again.

"An ex-priest? What's the matter with Cronin?"

"He says you're the best commodity man of your generation. The silver king."

"Tell him thanks but no thanks. I have not forgiven the Catholic Church for St. Jarlath's and I never will."

Xav Martin was obviously relieved to be off the hook. "May I tell him that you'll consider the request again in a few years?"

"Fine, if that satisfies him."

There was sadness in Monsignor Martin's black eyes as he said good-bye. Perhaps he and the bishop and Jack Howard had huddled about the Donlon problem. They wanted to help.

But Hugh was not ready to accept help.

From the Church or anyone else.

CHAPTER
THIRTY-ONE

1973

On the feast of Yom Kippur Anwar Sadat's armies poured across the Suez Canal without warning. The unprepared Israeli defenders were overwhelmed. Simultaneously, Syrian tanks pushed almost to the rim of the Golan and threatened for thirty-six hours to swarm down into the plains of Galilee. Israel rallied and pushed her enemies back. The Syrian tanks were smashed and an Egyptian army was trapped in the Sinai.

Sadat was able to claim victory, and the Arab oil-producing states imposed an embargo on the United States. OPEC, a Venezuelan cabinet minister's pipedream, suddenly emerged as the most dangerous cartel in human history and the price of petroleum soared.

President Nixon was ill-equipped to deal with these national and international crises because the net of the various Watergate investigations was slowly tightening around his presidency.

On the Board of Trade the Yom Kippur War, the oil embargo, and the long lines at the gas stations created a sensation almost as dramatic as did the soybean crises of the previous year.

Silver began a rise that was to peak at six dollars by the end of the year; gold, grain, government paper all became hot items. As usual, bad news for others meant good news on the exchange. Fortunes were made, unmade, and then made again in the space of a few riotous weeks.

Hugh Donlon amassed more money than he would have dreamed possible. There were no other goals in his life. He gave up his collection of women. He cut himself off from family and friends as best he could.

He enjoyed feeling sorry for himself in his aloneness.

By the end of October he had more client accounts than he wanted. Ben Fowler, restless and unhappy because he was barred from the floor, continued to pace the boardroom of Donlon et al—as the firm was now called—like a father awaiting the birth of a child, his face now permanently gray, his green jacket now permanently dirty, and his cough sounding like a ruler rasping against a blackboard.

One day at the end of October, Hugh was to have lunch with his mother and inspect the watercolors she'd done during her two-month stay with Marge and Liam in the west of Ireland.

Hugh suggested Crickets in the refurbished Tremont Hotel on Chestnut Street. Although it was an insufferably pretentious place, it was far from the bustle of LaSalle Street, which overwhelmed her, and fairly convenient to the new condo on the lake.

Lunch with Peggy, glowing and happy after her trip to Ireland, was blessedly cheerful. There was at least one woman left in the world with whom he could relax.

Her watercolors were a misty green, the Ireland of dreams and visions and gentle ghosts.

Yet Peggy would not have been Peggy if she hadn't provided one short interlude of worry. Hugh explained to her how he had made more money in the previous three weeks than his father, who was reasonably well paid, would make in ten years.

"Do you do anything dishonest, Hugh?" she asked when he was finished.

"No," he said promptly. "Some traders come close to the edge of the law and a few wander over the edge. I don't even come close; I was raised by a strict judge and a conscientious Irish mother . . ."

Peg knew something was wrong and wanted to help. How could he explain that his problem did not fit into her clear-cut moral categories.

" . . . who worries too much?" She leaned across the table and kissed him.

"I'm okay, Mom. I'm not breaking any commandments on the trading floor."

"A good Irish mother always worries." Peggy winked at him, something she'd never done before, and toasted him with the expensive Burgundy he'd bought at her suggestion.

Hugh had kept his resolution to avoid Helen till Christmastime, shaken as he was by Pat Cleary's suggestion that his urge to hurt her might be in some way connected with unacknowledged anger toward his mother, of whom Helen reminded him physically.

On Christmas Eve in early afternoon, she phoned him at home, for the first time. "Ben's at Old Orchard doing some last-minute shopping. Could you come over for an hour or so?" No mention of the weeks during which he had not said a word to her.

He told Liz, who was correcting papers, that he'd be out doing some last-minute shopping.

"Suit yourself," she said indifferently.

He parked the car two blocks away from the house and walked the remaining distance, his feet crunching on the newly fallen snow, his face stinging from the winter wind blowing off the lake, his heart beating rapidly.

Helen was clad in jeans and a sweat shirt, her hair was disordered and she wore no makeup. Her forty-four years showed, but they made her somehow even more desirable. Her lips were warm and soft.

"You're a disease, Hugh," she said. His hands slipped underneath her shirt, touching her breasts lightly. She winced with pleasure. "I don't ever want to be cured. . . . Not here: Ben or Linda might come. There's a room in the basement."

She led the way to the basement. The pine-paneled bedroom was steeped in a pungent North Woods smell. It was next to their elaborate recreation room filled with pinball machines and a pool table. Next to the furnace as well, the room was as hot as a summer beach.

Soon both their bodies were covered with sweat.

Hugh loved her slowly, in a mood of half-sad, half-sweet nostalgia, a mood that seemed to match her own. Their slippery bodies combined easily and naturally and remained joined, as though glued, long after their passions were spent.

When they were finished, Helen curled up at the end of the bed, her sweat shirt protectively at her loins, and lit a cigarette.

"That was different, Hugh," she said thoughtfully, her eyes examining his face in a mixture of curiosity and bewilderment.

"Was it?"

She exhaled smoke. "Christmas spirit?"

"Would you believe me if I said love?"

She smiled affectionately, a mother who has caught her son in a harmless lie. She touched his chest gently. "You're terribly vulnerable, Hugh." She leaned toward him, her breasts brushing his chest. "But you don't love me enough to let me live with you where you hurt."

A moment of delicious fear; a woman living with you where you hurt.

"Ben will be home soon," he said wearily.

Reluctantly she snubbed out her cigarette, dried herself with her sweat shirt, and pulled on her panties and slacks, routine movements of such natural and unself-conscious grace that he was almost hypnotized by their rhythm.

"Something wrong?" she asked lightly as she fastened her black bra.

"You still wouldn't believe me," he said sadly. "I don't blame you."

She kissed him briefly. "But it's nice of you to say it. . . . Come on, get dressed. I have some presents to wrap."

He pulled himself together for a return to the surface and followed her as she led the way up the stairs, sweat shirt folded over her arm.

At the top of the stairs she pulled the sweat shirt over her head and pushed the door open.

Hugh would later tell himself that a sweat shirt donned a moment too late and a hint of black lace caused the tragedy, but he knew better.

She screamed as if she'd been stabbed.

Ben Fowler stood next to the Christmas tree, cigar in hand, his face a purple mask of triumph. He raised the cigar hand to identify the adulterers to the world, his lips moving as the accusing words jammed his mouth.

But no words came out. A spasm of coughing, accompanied by an ugly retching rumble, seized him and twisted his body into a parody of orgasmic delight. The mask on his face turned dull white and then darker purple.

He stumbled forward, swayed to regain his balance, then toppled sideways to the floor, knocking down the Christmas tree as he fell.

Hugh pushed around her. Fowler's body was spread-eagled under the tree and surrounded by Christmas gifts. His face was decorated with evergreen and tinsel and his accusing right hand, still brandishing the cigar, had scattered the pieces of the Christmas crèche and smashed to bits the manger and the little figure within it.

Ben Fowler hung between life and death in the Intensive Care Unit of Evanston Hospital till the first week of January and then slowly returned to the ranks of the living.

The doctor said that if Helen had not come downstairs to answer the door when Hugh Donlon rang to leave Christmas presents, Fowler would surely have died.

"You've taken everything away from him, haven't you, Hugh?" Helen said to him as they waited in the hospital corridor on New Year's Day. "His wife, his daughter, his business, maybe even his life? You play for keeps, don't you?"

She looked haggard, old. Her shoulders were slumped despondently and her voice wavered near hysteria.

"Oh, yes, I know about Linda. She told me on Christmas Day. She doesn't know about me. You made your Playboy fantasy come true, didn't you? Was it good?"

"That's not altogether fair," he pleaded.

"When have you been fair?" she fired back at him. "You never gave a damn about me. I was a means of wreaking your terrible revenge."

The look of death on Ben Fowler's face and the trail of spittle on his chin were scorched into Hugh's brain, a fierce warning of his own mortality. He hadn't thought to give Ben absolution. He wasn't a priest at the side of a sick man. Rather, he was just a guilty lover who had escaped again.

"You wouldn't hurt her physically again, but you didn't mind hurting her psychologically?" Pat Cleary said, once more dragged away from his supper table.

"Neither one of us had any illusions."

"Bologna, not to use more scatological language.... Tell me, Hugh, have there been any times in your life when you felt free of all these burdens you carry around and that force you into behavior that hurts you and others?"

"Burdens?"

"You know what I mean," Pat said imperiously.

"Well, when I used to sail on the *Pegeen* at Lake Geneva ... Sometimes it was almost like a religious experience."

"And you sold the boat? Typical. Any memories of it?"

"Some dreams occasionally," he said cautiously, thinking that he had never before been fully aware of the *Pegeen* dreams in his waking hours. "They're good some of the time; nightmares other times...."

"Always had those moments of peace when you were sailing along?"

The tone of Pat's voice said that he assumed the answer would be yes. Hugh would prove him wrong.

"A couple of times with Maria."

Pat jumped from his chair. "That woman we met at the concert? Were you in love with her too?"

"Summer infatuation," he murmured, wishing he hadn't mentioned her ... and that Pat hadn't remembered the meeting.

"And she loved you too. Why?"

"I don't know." He was lying. He remembered her saying that he was beautiful as if the words had been spoken only yesterday.

"You're a lousy liar. Why did you give her up?"

"Because I had a vocation ... thought I had a vocation."

Cleary leaned over the desk till his face was only a few inches away. "Even if you hadn't been in the seminary, you'd have run from that one. She was a threat to everything you think you are...."

He saw or felt the sweet, scary light that sometimes was associated with memories of Maria.

"You're wrong, Pat," he insisted, slamming a door shut again.

Pat slumped back into his chair. "You're full of shit, Hugh."

"I'm sorry," he sighed.

"Tell that to the Old Fella," Pat said, apparently in no mood to continue.

"He's not listening to me ... maybe not to anyone."

"I'm not interested in your theological problems, Hugh. My guess is that you're finished with your era of keeping women at bay by killing them with kindness and pleasure."

"I hope so," he said fervently.

"Maybe, but women are only human. In the next phase, I think you're going to cut yourself off from everyone, man, woman, and child—everyone."

"Why would I do that?" Hugh felt his stomach lurch.

"Because you're still running," Cleary said, shaking his head. "Down the nights and down the years."

CHAPTER
THIRTY-TWO

1974

"You and Liz," Pat Cleary said as he sank his putt on the fourteenth green, "should go away on a long vacation. Someplace in the South Pacific . . . and start over again."

"It won't help the basic problems." Hugh missed his putt by an inch. Damn, he was out of condition.

His sins had stopped. The monster within was tamed, temporarily. He was faithful to his wife, forgiving of his enemies, considerate to his friends, devoted to his parents.

He was trying to spend more time with his children, though Liz insisted that he made them nervous.

"Who's talking about basic problems?" Pat removed his orange golf hat, wiped his brown hair, and put the hat back on. "It'll give you a new lease on life, away from the kids, the firm, the family, the memories of the past. Isn't that enough?"

Hugh realized that there were two ways of looking at his life and it all depended on the point of view.

To an outsider it would seem that Hugh had every reason to be happy. The new firm was a huge success. Hugh and Les Rosenthal, cautious allies because they were too smart to be enemies, were the most powerful men at the exchange. And Hugh was now nationally famous as well. As a highly respected member of the Trilateral Commission, he'd been asked by the State Department to represent the United States at a GATT meeting in Bangkok, and was often in Washington on consultation. In short, he'd achieved everything he wanted when he first rode on the South Shore Railroad with a knot in his stomach and lust in his heart to do battle with the trading floor.

His wife was attractive-looking and his children seemingly well-behaved. What more could a man want out of life?

But it was all a sham.

The marriage had settled down into a grim containment. The anger was over and so was the hope. Liz's contract at St. Rock's was not renewed, because of conflicts with both the pastor and the parents. She dropped out of the consciousness group. The army of mothers' helpers and baby-sitters remained, although the personnel constantly changed because Liz fought with them so frequently—which, he supposed, was much better than her fighting with him.

Hugh no longer knew what she did during the day, except that in the summer she went with the children to the Lake Shore house. Ironically, she and Helen had become fast friends, part of a group of matrons who sipped more than enough martinis in late afternoon and early evening on the lakeside verandas of their homes.

He and Liz made love occasionally, sometimes at her behest. At those times, he tried to make the union of bodies memorable, faintly hoping that some new flame might be kindled.

But his skills as a lover had deserted him. The results were mildly satisfying for both of them, but did not begin to approach the ecstasy out of which a new love might emerge. Like everything else in their marriage, their sex life had settled into a routine of modest expectations and modest involvements.

"You think that if Liz and I go away together we will fall in love again? We might just as well fight."

"Either would be an improvement."

"We need family therapy, not a vacation." He dubbed his drive.

"A vacation could be a first step." Pat's drive was perfect, 250 yards right down the center of the fairway.

"Liz won't be interested."

After the golf game Hugh found Liz and Helen, both slightly tipsy from the martini pitcher on the table in front of them, lolling on the porch of the Donlon house overlooking Lake Michigan.

Helen's greeting kiss was light and sisterly, as though there were no history of passion between them.

Her mouth smelled faintly of vermouth. "Looks like you lost again," she said, faintly amused. "I was just showing Liz the pictures of Linda's baby. Looks like her father, I think."

Hugh agreed as he kissed his wife. No difference at all between the two kisses. Hesitantly, he offered Pat's suggestion about the need for a long vacation from his job.

"Wonderful idea." Liz was ecstatic. "I was telling Helen this afternoon—wasn't I, darling?—that I need to get away from everything, I know just the place—Corfu. The books say that late September is the best time of the year to go to Greece."

She'd been reading books about a vacation.

So Hugh found that he was going to Corfu, after a stop in London, and that once more he had misunderstood his wife's moods.

They spent a week in New York before flying to London. It was the best week of their marriage since their summer trip to New England years before. Liz was Elizabeth Ann again, happy, wide-eyed, enthusiastic, affectionate. The skyline of the Big Apple blotted out all the anger of the years. Pat Cleary was right. You could begin again.

They were walking down Fifth Avenue after lunch at the Four Seasons. Hugh stopped, took Liz's arms in his hands, and said, "You don't mind a profession of love on Fifth Avenue, do you?"

Her pretty blue eyes sparkled. "I'd enjoy every second of it."

"There've been good times and bad times, Liz; a week like this cancels out a lot of bad times."

He realized he'd said the same thing in Maine. Déjà vu?

"Let's say a prayer in St. Patrick's," Liz said. "God won't mind our hugging in there."

So they climbed the steps to the great gray Gothic monument. Inside, Liz was a demure, mystical nun again, kneeling erectly with head bowed, in deep communion with the Deity.

God was out to lunch for Hugh. After Ben's heart attack, he'd tried to pray. The words came easily enough, but no one seemed to be listening. It was as if God had tired of waiting for Hugh Donlon to rediscover Him and was busy on other matters when the affluent Mr. Donlon came to call.

So it was in St. Patrick's too.

"Help me, help her, please, dear God, help us. Forgive me for running out on You in the priesthood. I tried. I'm still trying. So far, my best hasn't been good enough. Give me the strength and the courage to do better."

That night after the theater, Liz insisted they call his parents to tell them how well the vacation was going.

"If the rest of the trip is like New York," Liz bubbled to an astonished Peggy, "we might stay away for a year."

The rest of the trip was not like New York. Their reborn and revitalized marriage was done in by the jet lag. As soon as they checked into the Grosvenor House, Liz collapsed into bed with a migraine and announced that she was tired of traveling.

Hugh pleaded for a few days grace to give the lag time to work out of her system. Liz replied that she didn't like the London rain, the way the English talked, or the condescension of the hotel help, and that the sooner they escaped from London the better.

Marge and Liam flew over from Shannon for dinner in the gracious old dining room of the Connaught. Liz refused to stir from her bed.

"Too bad the gel is under the weather," Liam clucked sympathetically as he destroyed a large hunk of Yorkshire pudding. "Fine food at this place."

"When are you going to live for yourself and not for others?" Marge demanded

"We all should live for others, unless we want to have selfish and narrow lives," Hugh replied, conscious that Marge seemed to draw from him the same pious clichés that grated at Lake Geneva when she was chasing Joe Delaney.

"You became a priest for Mom, so you could take care of God, and a trader for Dad, so you could take care of Tim, and a husband for Liz, so you could take care of her baby. I don't think you wanted to do any of those things."

"Strong words." Liam drained his glass of claret. "It's Hugh's life."

"I know it's his life, darling; that's my point. Hugh's living other people's commitments, not his own. And besides"—she turned to her brother—"you once promised me, Hugh, that you would never forget how to laugh at yourself. When was the last time you did that?"

Hugh couldn't remember.

The next day he visited the London Metals Exchange. Dressed in bowlers and morning suits, LME traders worked for only five-minute "rings," or "fixings," each morning and afternoon. Not unreasonably, they assumed they could do what Americans did in the final minute of a session without the rest of the session. They also were burdened with much less exchange regulation. There were no limits to the positions a trader might take and no limits to the rise and fall of daily prices.

"Why are you so relaxed about regulations?" Hugh asked one trader.

"Actually, old chap, we think you Americans are rather uptight about limits and that sort of thing. Do you think it might be your puritanism?"

"Not among the Irish. They've never been puritanical about money, only sex."

"I shouldn't have thought the Irish would have the temperament for successful trading."

"There's one man from a family of Irish policemen who made more than twenty million dollars in a month."

"Really? I shouldn't imagine that he managed to save much of it."

"Practically all of it," Hugh said. "Invested it in natural gas reserves."

They attended a black-tie dinner in Hugh's honor at the Grosvenor House that night. Liz, in an off-the-shoulder blue net gown, was convincingly beautiful. Her jet lag forgotten, she was the center of attention and appeared to delight in it. She made small talk with the traders and their wives, and many of the men frankly admitted they envied Hugh such a lovely and intelligent wife.

When it came to commodities, however, the London men were given to understatement in the same way that Chicago traders were given to overstatement. Their opinion seemed to be that the metal markets would go up if they didn't go down. Or possibly the other way around.

They didn't know any more about it than Hugh did, even though they sounded far more sophisticated and experienced. The tones of bullshit were different around the world, but the message was the same. We Chicago Irish are better at it than anyone else, Hugh thought, because we can do it in any language.

"I don't see how you can stand conversation as dull as that," Liz complained as she sank into bed. "Can there be any subject more boring than precious metals?"

"It's a matter of perspective, Liz; they'd find religious education dull."

"I don't make you go to religious education meetings," she sniffed.

He'd wanted to embrace her and recapture the magic of the Big Apple. But tonight, clearly, was not the night to try.

Corfu might be his last chance.

·

CHAPTER THIRTY-THREE

1974

Corfu was the subtropical paradise Liz had promised it would be, an island covered with silvery olive trees, stately cypresses, and sturdy evergreens. Multicolored pastel mountain towns perched precariously on verdant hillsides; steep cliffs, crystal-clear blue lagoons, the glass-smooth waters of the Ionian Sea, and the gentle surf of the Adriatic made Corfu seem precisely the right place for Ulysses to wash ashore as, according to local legend, he did, for his rendezvous with the white-armed (as she called herself) Nausikaa.

The Corfu Hilton was in the hamlet of Kanoni, a few miles south of Corfu town on a peninsula overlooking one shining white Greek Orthodox monastery at its end and another on an island in the sea beyond. The sun rose over the mountains of Albania in the morning, hovered over the placid Ionian during the day, and sank contentedly behind the mountains of the island in the evening, changing the olive trees from silver to gold. Hugh felt as if he were in paradise.

Liz, on the other hand, complained bitterly about the noise from the nearby airport and about the slovenly service of the Corfiote staff at the hotel, who were very pleasant but somewhat indifferent to the demands of their mostly American and German patrons.

Hugh reveled in the warm waters of the Ionian and marveled at the caïques with their high stern rudders that lazily sliced the waves off their beach.

Liz complained about the uncomfortable beds and the pebbles and rocks on the beach.

Yet the soothing charms of this magic island were not entirely lost on her either. One day they drove across the island to Paleo-kastritsa, the seven lagoons of which the nineteenth-century British governor was so fond that he built the best highway on the island in order that he and his native wife could ride there frequently. Liz was enthralled by the beauty and mystery of the Adriatic, as precious and timeless, it seemed to her, as a piece of ancient Egyptian lapis lazuli. "I wish I could stay there till the end of time," she said.

Indeed, Corfu brought out to the point of caricature the ambiguities in her tormented soul. One moment she was sweet, affectionate, and wide-eyed with wonder, and the next the inflexible ideologue, ethnocentric and judgmental, contemptuous of the slovenliness of the Corfiote people and the squalor of their cheap concrete tourist hotels.

Hugh wanted to help her. Yet, unable to help himself, he did not know how to help his wife, save with the mixture of patience and kindness, duty and responsibility, that had characterized their whole marriage and that patently did not work.

The morning after their trip across the island, Hugh awoke as the sky was turning gray. Liz, in a thin nightgown, stood at the open door to their balcony, watching the quiet Ionian.

He slipped out of bed and put his arm around her. Her upper arms and shoulders were covered with goose bumps, though it was not cold.

"Do you want a robe?" he asked softly.

She shook her head in a negative response. Then he saw the tears falling softly down her face.

"I don't know what demons are fighting inside of you," he said cautiously. "I want to help if I can."

She leaned her head against his shoulder. "If only you could."

"Can you give them a name?"

Again the negative shake of the head and now silent sobs.

"Can I do anything?"

No response.

"Will you come back to bed and let me keep you warm?"

She nodded agreement and leaned on him for support as she walked back toward the bed.

"Do you want me to make love to you or just hold you tight?"

"Just hold me."

After Hugh slipped out of the room to take the bus into town to shop for souvenirs and gifts for the children, Liz showered, put on her bathrobe, and ordered breakfast on the balcony. As she peeled an orange and watched the water skiers cavort on the Ionian Sea, she resolved again to organize her life. Hugh was trying hard to save the trip. But, finally, he could not give up his male chauvinism. She and the children were not human beings; they were burdens, responsibilities, obligations. Whatever he did for them was what he was obliged to do. Even the trip had been an obligation, a responsibility imposed by a well-meaning Pat Cleary.

That was the way Hugh was. If something wasn't an obligation, he couldn't do it.

Instead of a personality, he was a collection of obligations.

He needed her help more than she needed his.

What good did it do for a woman to be on the receiving end of tenderness when she realized that the tenderness was someone's fulfillment of a rule?

Maybe he got some points for trying. But not for realism. She was the more realistic of the two.

She knew that their efforts would always be a waste of time.

With a guilty conscience and a sense of his own incompetency, Hugh rode into Corfu town on the public bus, which lurched from Kanoni to the esplanade at the edge of the harbor every half hour.

Cream-colored buildings, tiny domed churches, arched balconies, narrow streets, stairway sidewalks, pushing crowds, noisy tourists, handsome men, and not-so-handsome women—Corfu town was part Greek and part Italian, revealing both its Greek ethnic origins and its Venetian history. Hugh walked up and down the side streets, dodging three-wheeled vans and small cars and absorbing, as though he were a native sponge, the color and the noise and the intensity of the people and their community. As the lagoons and hills of the Adriatic side were heaven for his wife, the crowds of Corfu town were Elysium for him.

Then he saw a woman examining a Corfu T-shirt on a stand at the entrance to a souvenir shop—red outline of the island with "CORFU" emblazoned in half-foot-high letters. She tossed it aside, obviously perceiving that it wouldn't last one cycle in the automatic washer.

She was dressed in black jeans and a black T-shirt with white trim on the sleeves. Her blond hair was tied in a careless knot on the top of her head.

He followed her down the street as, with a subtle mixture of rowdiness and grace, she slipped through the crowds of Corfu town.

He approached her from behind and looked over her shoulder.

"Maria," he said in disbelief.

"I wondered how long you were going to follow me before you made up your mind whether to run or talk." She turned around and embraced him. "I'm glad you didn't run. Now, to answer your questions in order of importance, Steven and I are staying at the Agios Gordis on the other side of the island, he has a meeting at the embassy in Athens day after tomorrow and, yes, we will be delighted to have dinner with you and your wife—Liz, isn't it?— tonight at the Corfu Palace."

"Would you have let me run?" Reluctantly he let her slip from his arms.

"You saw me first and followed me," she said, directing him with a shove toward the esplanade, which loomed invitingly at the end of the street. "Then you stood behind me and debated, as if I were blind and couldn't see your reflection in the shop window. Anyway, I'll buy you lunch . . . what have you been doing lately . . . since Walworth, Wisconsin, I mean? And don't tell me about making money . . . I know about *that*, though I must say I never quite pictured you in the silver pit."

"Are you as nervous as I am?" he asked.

"Aha, an interesting way to cover up awkwardness. No, I'm not nervous at all. My purse turns wet in my hand this way whenever handsome men follow me down the streets of Levantine towns . . . you like that? Levantine . . . not bad for an illiterate accountant?" She pulled Hugh into a chair at one of the sidewalk restaurants facing the water and deftly summoned a waiter.

"Lunch is on me," she said. "I'm a full-fledged fighting feminist and a bank vice-president on leave, but you can pick up the tab for dinner. Now, seriously, without self-pity and undue modesty, tell me what you've been doing since 1954."

So he and Maria sparred and laughed and talked and reminisced and forgave but did not forget for a lunch that lasted two hours.

As they were about to rise from the table, Maria touched his hand. "I've had some pain and a lot of happiness since Lake Geneva. I hope you've been happy too."

"And happy to see you again," he said gallantly.

On the way back to Kanoni, his heart sang. The past had returned to the present, an old friendship was reborn, and some ghosts were exorcised.

Liz didn't seem to mind meeting strangers for dinner. "It will be nice to talk to another American couple. Who is this woman? I never heard you mention her."

"A classmate of Marge's. From the old neighborhood."

Which was true, though hardly the whole truth.

Liz dressed for dinner in a green chiffon evening dress. As always, Hugh was astonished by how quickly she could change from dowdy to chic when the will to impress was upon her.

She was so striking that Maria, herself more than presentable in a white cotton dress and carrying a matching jacket, nodded approval when they were introduced.

Captain McLain's hair was as white as Maria's dress and his eyes were tense. He was, however, as quietly charming as ever.

"Do you like it on the other side of the island?" Hugh asked as they were seated at table on the terrace of the Corfu Palace overlooking the harbor and its glittering lights.

"My husband says it reminds him of the sea islands off South Carolina, which is the highest compliment a McLain can pay. But isn't this nice?"

"The sand is lovely and the surf's mesmerizing," Steve said softly. "Not much for water skiing, though, I'm afraid."

"Not like the other side, I'll tell you." Maria was running on as she did when she was nervous. "A block away from our hotel the women go topless . . . they'd be drawn and quartered in Spain. Not here, though. You're overdressed if you wear more than a G-string."

"I'm glad I'm over here," Liz said primly as, equally nervous, she took a deep draft of her vodka martini.

Maria tried to put her down gently. "Hugh's father said once that people used to swim naked in the Middle Ages. . . ."

"False consciousness," Liz snapped, emptying her drink.

Maria seemed momentarily confused. "Well, I guess one woman's consciousness is another woman's poison," she said.

Good God, Liz, Hugh thought, you don't have to be afraid of her. She wants to like you. Give it a chance.

Liz wasn't about to give it a chance. She drank another martini and chased it with two quick glasses of Greek wine before the lamb was served.

"Are you going to Vietnam?" she suddenly asked Steven.

"Not exactly," he replied. "I'll be on a helicopter platform ship that's standing by to remove personnel from Saigon if the war turns bad, as it probably will."

"You've been there before?" Liz's fingers tightened on her wineglass.

"Yes, twice."

"What did you do?"

"Flew a Phantom," he replied.

"You're a war criminal, in other words." Liz was clearly drunk.

"Some might think so."

Maria bowed her head—no wisecrack, no anger, no fight. A side of her Hugh had never known.

"You killed innocent women and children."

"I hope not. I did my best not to." Steven remained calm, self-possessed, unthreatened.

"Everyone on our side is a war criminal."

He hesitated. It was an old argument, one he knew he couldn't win.

"The military didn't start the war, ma'am. Liberal political leaders did. We advised against the war and we fought it under the most difficult conditions, so as not to harm innocent people. I'm not sure that it's a just war. I'm not sure that it's an unjust one either. But I am sure of one thing. The Vietcong have not spared anyone—military or civilian—whom they perceived to be an obstacle to their aims."

"American propaganda."

Maria was tracing a line on the tablecloth with the handle of a teaspoon, no sign of emotion on her face.

"I think that's enough, Liz," Hugh said.

"You're just as bad as the rest. A mindless apologist." She grabbed the wine bottle and refilled her glass.

She said no more, however, and the meal wound down in awkward monosyllables. They managed a friendly parting, but that was all.

"You once loved him very much?" Steven said as he drove the rented car carefully over the mountains to the Adriatic coast.

"Teen-age crush. Threatened?"

He patted her knee and quickly returned his hand to the steering wheel. "Would be kind of silly, wouldn't it, Maria?"

"I suppose." She put her arm around him. "If I met one of *your* teen-age sweethearts, I'd be insanely jealous."

"No," he said calmly. "But you would feel constrained to act as if you were."

Maria laughed. "You know me too well. . . . Poor Liz, I feel as sorry for her as I do for Hugh."

"A very disturbed woman. She was a nun?"

"So I understand. He should never have left the priesthood."

"Maybe he shouldn't have been a priest in the first place."

Steven was so damn fair.

"Then I'd be in the Corfu Hilton tonight." She kissed his neck, confident that a good jet pilot wouldn't be distracted by such minor affection, even on a dark mountain road in Corfu.

Dear God, she prayed, protect my Steven for me.

And while you're at it, if you have time, protect poor Hugh too.

CHAPTER
THIRTY-FOUR

1974

A book clutched under one arm, a vast beach towel draped around her neck, an outsize purse slung over her shoulder, Maria walked north on the Agios Gordis beach, looking for a secluded dune. She'd wanted to fly to Athens with Steven, but he sensibly had argued that he wouldn't be with her even at night during the two-day gathering at the embassy.

And she would be safer on crime-free Corfu than in Athens.

She found a break between two dunes, spread her towel, and, sitting down, emptied the various suntan locations from her purse. She stood by her defense of topless beaches, but wanted privacy for her daring nonetheless.

Maria was proud of her durable attractiveness and not at all displeased that men still admired her. If they wanted to look at her bare breasts under the deep blue sky, even that was fine.

But only from a distance, you understand.

She shed her skirt and T-shirt, annointed herself with oil, put her sailor's cap on her head, and curled up with a copy of *Computer Programming for Bankers* to see whether the competition was catching up. As she rested the book on her belly, she wagered with herself that she was the only half-naked woman on the beach reading that book.

She thought about the dinner with the Donlons the previous night. Weird.

The last time she'd seen Hugh had been at Orchestra Hall. He'd still been a priest then, and he'd thrown her for a tailspin in a ten-minute conversation. Same tailspin phenomenon again. Always would love him, she guessed. Too bad polygamy was out of fashion.

She laughed at herself. It was demanding enough being married to one passionate lover without comtemplating another.

Her marriage had been transformed since Steven had left for his second tour in Vietnam. During the long months of uncertainty before she knew he was alive and then through the months after that, she'd endured pain she couldn't have imagined before. And she'd kept up her spirits too, not out of virtue, God knew, but out of necessity. Either she smiled or she'd crack.

It was a different Steven who'd come home from the POW camp. The Navy had warned them that they'd find their husbands and sons changed. But she hadn't believed it. Not her Steven.

Her Steven most of all. The patriotic camp leader they'd tortured but couldn't break had returned hoarding all his anger at the enemy and at the American government for getting involved in a stupid war and at the protesters who hadn't understood a thing about it and at the press for turning the men who had to fight into villains and at Maria for not being with him in the POW camp and at his sons for growing up while he was gone.

She didn't know what to do. Her man's simple depths had been twisted and bent. How could she remake him?

Only two gifts could she offer—laughter and love. No anger in return, no long discussion, no self-defense. She wouldn't fight with him. She wouldn't let him fight with her. She simply laughed and sang and tried to find him again.

And she didn't quit, even though the first six months were even worse than the time he'd been MIA. Then one day she came back to their apartment in Alexandria to find a long letter of apology: He had been heartless and cruel, punishing her and the children because of what the Vietnamese had done to him. He was a monster, permanently damaged goods, not to be endured. Surely the Church would grant her an annulment. He would be at the Mayflower until he could move into BOQ.

She drove into Washington against the flow of the rush-hour

traffic, stormed up to his room, dragged, pushed, and kicked him out the door and down the hall and into the elevator to the station wagon, which she had abandoned, engine running, in the charge of the doorman. If he ever did anything like that again, she would personally break his neck. Now, drive this around the block while I go back and pay the bill.

It was the turning point, as Steven, poor man, probably sensed it would be. He laughed on the ride home and laughed again when they made love, after she'd disposed of the baby-sitter. The worst was over. Maria's act still worked.

She thereby became the moral leader in the marriage. He refused to reassume the role, preferring to bask in the glow of her tough grace. The family was cemented together by Kenny, the dream child of their reunion, a little doll for an aging mom to play with, a wonder for his father to watch with fascination for hours and a punk for Fast Eddie to protect fiercely.

Their marriage became both deeper and more relaxed. The ups and downs were less dramatic and the course more smooth. She would never be as good a person as Steven, but now that was all right. She didn't have to be.

Now he was returning to Vietnam for the third time. He could have asked for a different assignment and no one would have complained. He didn't plan to stay in the Navy indefinitely. After he made admiral, he'd retire. And he didn't have to do a third tour to make admiral.

This time, her superstitious Sicilian fatalism told her, you will say good-bye to him and never see him again on earth.

She found a tissue in her purse and dried her eyes. Her heart was breaking and she couldn't even share the pain.

Why did their love have to be tested again?

Angry at herself now, she brushed her anxiety aside and focused her attention on her book again.

The surf washed up in gentle rollers, staining the beach each time it came. A pleasant breeze stirred the blue air. The tart smell of brine teased her nostrils and made her sleepy. She dozed off a couple of times.

"Good book?" she heard Hugh say.

Her half-sleep ended abruptly. What a fool she'd been not to have expected him. You're in trouble, Maria Angelica. She pulled on the T-shirt and sat up. "Just happened by, huh?"

"I walked away from your hotel, not toward it; actually, we'd both planned to come over here today. But Liz is under the weather . . . and I thought the rule here was anything goes."

"Not with people from the old neighborhood."

"May I sit down?"

"I don't own the beach."

"I want to apologize."

"Not your fault." Oh, God, what a mess.

"Accept my apology anyway. Last night was an off night. It's not always that way. Forgive?"

"Of course. Now, if you give me five minutes to finish this chapter, you can buy me lunch at that pink restaurant down the beach."

"You'll have to pay. I left my wallet in the car. I told you I wasn't looking for you. I'll owe you two when we get back to Chicago."

"We won't be lunching together in Chicago, Hugh, and you know that as well as I do."

Firm, self-disciplined, realistic; that's our Maria Angelica.

"You're right, I suppose."

She pretended to plow through the program designs at the end of Chapter Three, knowing she would have to go over them all again.

"Okay, I have the answer to our problem of cashing bad checks . . . don't take them in the first place. Here, you can carry the book and the towel. I'll handle the luggage."

Lunch was fun at first. The roast lamb was no tougher than usual and the vegetables were spicy and mysterious. And Hugh told scandalous stories about the commodities business while she laughed and mostly forgot the tired lines in his face and the sadness in his eyes.

"I try, Maria." He rested his head in his hands. "God knows, if there is a God, I've tried everything. There's nothing that seems to work. . . ."

She refilled his glass with wine.

"And the kids?" Maria didn't want to know more about Hugh Donlon's suffering. Yet she couldn't stop her catechism.

Hugh shifted guiltily on his chair, playing with a tiny piece of driftwood, unable to look her in the eye. "They're her children, Maria; she's cut them off from me. They don't like me and I can't get through to them."

"That's nonsense, Hugh," she said briskly. "You're their father. Of course, you can get through to them—if you want to."

He clenched his fist. "From the very beginning, Maria, I've done everything I could, absolutely everything. I don't know what more I can do."

Maria exploded. "How like a Donlon! Do! Do! Do! Why not just try *being* for a change?"

"I don't know what you're talking about." He sounded angry. Too bad for him.

"I don't think you love her, Hugh. I don't think you ever loved her. You married her because it was the right thing to do. You go through the motions of loving her because that's what you should do. You try to be close to the kids because that's what a father is expected to do—like the judge did with you. Maybe it wouldn't have worked anyway. But you didn't give it a chance. You were too busy keeping all your goddamn rules ever to *be* anything for her or the kids, much less to be a lover for her. Don't come crying to me. . . ."

"I'm not crying to you," he said hotly.

She touched his hand. "I'm sorry. I didn't mean to shout. Here, have some more wine; it substitutes for purgatory. But, Hugh, my wonderful teen-age dreamboat, why don't you forget all your obligations to them, especially the kids, and try to just plain love them?"

Maria signaled the waiter for another bottle of wine. Careful, Maria Angelica, it may taste terrible but it contains as much alcohol as good wine.

"Maybe you're right."

But he didn't understand. Maybe he never would. She'd preached the same sermon on an old sailing dory twenty years ago. He hadn't understood it then and he doesn't understand it now.

They walked back to her dune, peace and quiet restored.

Hugh closed his eyes and stretched out in the sun.

"I've made pretty much a mess of my life," he said.

Maria hugged her book under her chin, as if to protect herself from his sadness.

"Should you have stayed in the priesthood?"

"I don't know. I wasn't happy as a priest. Then I tried marriage and fatherhood, money and power. They didn't help much either. Neither did some intense sexual experiences."

"I heard about them," Maria said indignantly.

He looked up at her and smiled ruefully. "I can't tell you how much I regret them. I don't know whether I still believe in sin, but I'm sorrier for them than for anything else, except letting the kids down, I guess."

His voice broke.

"The problem isn't sex, is it, Hugh? Not with Liz and not with the others either. . . ."

"No," he agreed sadly, "not really. Power, fear, male ego, you name it. . . ."

The surf lapped at the edge of the beach. Two half-naked girls ran out of the water. Hugh didn't even notice them.

There wasn't a damn thing Maria could do; and she shouldn't try or she'd be in as much trouble as he.

Still, the wine and the sun and the excitement of being with Hugh made her light-headed and reckless.

"Want to swim before you go back?" She pulled off the T-shirt. Wet T-shirts were worse than nothing at all, she reasoned, and, besides, he'd seen her before. She laughed as she rushed into the surf.

He charged into the water behind her. They dove into a wave, rode it to the beach, and then dove again. Wind and water seemed to clear the wine from her brain. She felt free and relaxed. There was, after all, nothing to worry about. They were merely old friends frolicking together on a gorgeous Mediterranean beach.

Says you, Maria Angelica.

A big roller knocked her over and the undertow, gentle and safe, tugged her after it. Hugh helped her to her feet.

"Look at the caïque . . . isn't that a beautiful sail?"

Hugh forced his eyes away from her to the boat. "Lovely. . . ."

"It reminds me of the *Pegeen*." Then an arm around him, her face against his chest. "Oh, God, Hugh, I have to say it. Despite the bad things that have happened and the ugly chains you've tied around yourself, there's as much beauty in you as there was that day. You can still be happy. . . ."

He touched her face, and then her throat, as he'd done so long ago. "Thank you, Maria," he said, repeating the words from the past.

"A glass of lemonade again, Hugh. We've been here before."

"A much more attractive glass now, if I may say so."

"You'd better say so, even if it isn't true. . . . Enough water for one day?" She slipped away from him, alarmed by the ease with which she'd precipitated such tense emotion. A quip, a laugh, and then you walk back to the dune, as steadily as you can.

In the lee of the dune, she reclined on the towel and reached for her T-shirt. He took it out of her hand and touched her hair lightly with his fingers.

Too early with the compliments, Maria Angelica, now you have big problems.

The other hand on her stomach, so tender and gentle; their lips moving toward each other, hers as eagerly as his; then their bodies pressing together, her nipples hard against his chest; his hand moving down her flank to her thigh, her body busy preparing itself.

Dear God, help.

Sweet-tasting fire.

It's my turn to end it.

She wrenched away from him and leaned on the sand, her back to him as his was once to her.

"Go away, Hugh," she said in a low voice. "I never want to see you again."

She heard his soft footsteps vanish down the beach.

She pounded the sand.

Then the tears came.

Liz was waiting for him on the balcony of their suite at the Hilton, two empty Pepsi cans and an ashtray full of cigarette butts beside her.

She reached out a hand to take his as he sat opposite her. The sleeve of her nylon robe slipped back. Did she want him to reassure her with lovemaking? There was no desire left in him, nor would there be for a long time.

So this is what despair is like, he thought.

BOOK
FIVE

"It is finished."

CHAPTER
THIRTY-FIVE

1979

A call to prayer floated above the morning mist rising from the majestically moving river. On the balcony of the ambassador's house, it was still pleasantly cool. In a few hours heat would prostrate the entire city.

For the moment, Hugh Donlon, the Ambassador of the United States of America to the People's Democratic Republic of the Upper River, ignored the smells and imagined that the minarets and the gleaming buildings, the river and the jungle on the other side, the slowly moving dugouts and the graceful people in them, were all parts of a romance from the Arabian Nights.

In such, however, there would have been no trucks with Uzi-brandishing national police, no rotting concrete soccer stadium, no KGB antennae monitoring his pillow talk with his wife—such as it was—and, of course, no United States Embassy.

He pulled his thin kimono tighter, if only so the KGB binoculars wouldn't discover that he was fifteen pounds overweight. Being an ambassador was very much like being an associate pastor: your freedom of action was strictly limited and both your enemies and your friends spied on you. Royce, his first secretary, a career foreign service officer who had hoped to be named ambassador himself, was just as surely reporting on him to the State Department as was the KGB resident down the street reporting on him to the Kremlin.

Hugh had accepted President Carter's appointment because he thought a term of public service, motivated by generosity if not idealism, might be a way of atoning for his greed. While he shared none of the illusions of his wife and her radical Catholic friends about the Third World, he did hope that he could contribute in some way to preserving order in East Africa while facilitating moderate change.

His training as a demographer, his doctoral dissertation, and the investments he'd made during the Russian wheat run-up had turned him into an acknowledged expert on certain aspects of international agriculture. To be sure, the universities were filled with men who knew more, but they didn't have his money or his power in the business community.

He was one of the first Americans to speak out against rapid modernization and in favor of labor-intensive agriculture for the developing nations. This was a country where labor-intensive agriculture had worked for centuries. Perhaps such a successful economy could be sustained instead of being modernized out of existence.

He would do what he could, for the good of both nations. He would expiate.

But expiation, like contrition, does not set one free. He was still frozen in the pit that Dante described as the seventh circle of hell.

The prayer call lingered in his ear as he walked back into his bedroom. How long since he'd prayed? How long since he'd been to church? Was he restless because he still hungered for God, as Pat Cleary would say? Probably.

Maybe there would be some forgiveness for him, if he could persuade the American government that the secret of aiding a lesser developed country was to strengthen the village structure that was the core of the native culture.

The Principal Leader, himself the product of an up-country village, was terrified of the village people. Should they ever lose their superstitious fear of him as a magically powerful chief, he would end up floating in the river, his body horribly mutilated, as had his four predecessors.

Liz was still asleep, her face relaxed and attractive. Hugh

thought reflexively of sex and then abandoned the idea. It wasn't important anymore. Liz could be constrained to make love when his needs were compelling; indeed, as he had slowly discovered, she enjoyed being forced into it. But neither any longer cherished the other.

Liz could have been a good ambassador's wife, he thought. But in the event she'd been a failure. Ideology had stood between her and any slightest sympathy for either nation and her demoralization had begun to show in her clothes and appearance.

She had formed a close relationship with the Papal Nuncio, a fat Italian who loved to expostulate on papal politics. The Nuncio apparently was not enamored of John Paul, an opinion shared by Liz, who thought the Pope was a reactionary and a chauvinist. The Nuncio's objections came from the right, not the left, but as long as Liz could keep informed about Episcopal appointments in the States—all of which displeased her—she felt she was still in touch with "the life of the Church," as she called it.

Her complaints were increasingly shrill. In America she had sung the praises of the Third World. Here, she ridiculed the inefficiency of the local people. She was appalled at the plight of women in the country, but treated the embassy servants with utter disdain. She denounced racism on the one hand and deplored the toilet habits of the natives on the other.

She should have complained just as bitterly if he'd turned down the ambassadorial appointment, or if he'd tried to leave her and the children at home. It was in Liz's nature to complain, it had now become clear. And so, it seemed, was it in the nature of her children, who were, even at eight and seven, chronic malcontents. Hugh remembered how close he'd been to his father when he was their age. He felt guilty that he did not have the same kind of relationship with Brian. Yet it was quite impossible to be close to a child whom Liz had already made an inveterate whiner.

So he dealt with his family the only way he could—with a mixture of tolerance and authoritarianism. It worked, or it worked well enough. No joy, but only occasional pain.

One of the most painful incidents of the last several years had occurred when he took Brian and Lise and the three Wentworth children to the circus, haunted by Maria's charge that he would be close to the children if he wanted to be close to them. The three little micks were wide-eyed and well-behaved. His own two were restless and unpleasant, complaining about the uncomfortable benches in the tattered old International Amphitheater, fighting with one another, stuffing themselves with food and drink and then complaining of stomachaches and refusing to enjoy the fun of the circus.

Liz, he reflected, was no longer the obstacle. Her protection and his indifference in the early years had built walls that would never break. Maria was right that he might have done better when the children were small. She did not realize, however, that once you were frozen into your mistakes, there was no way out of them.

Brian wanted to see the tigers up close. The little girls were not interested. Seamus Wentworth—the husky, green-eyed Wentworth heir—was game for anything. So he left Fionna in charge of the younger girls during the intermission and led the two boys behind the stands to the tiger cage.

The smell of the animals, the taste of cotton candy, and the feel of the sawdust under his feet reminded him of his own childhood circus adventures.

The two boys watched the sleek and sleepy striped animals with awe.

"Big bugger," murmured Seamus.

As though she were offended, a female tiger snarled in protest and leaped at the side of her cage.

Both boys jumped, badly frightened.

Seamus grabbed Hugh's arm in pure terror. Hugh put his hand on Brian's shoulder to reassure him.

Brian twisted away. "I don't need your help," he said.

They walked back to their seats. Fionna, black eyes dancing, had to tell about what the clown said about her Irish brogue.

Hugh barely heard her.

Oddly he was still a priest to many of his embassy colleagues; a Marine guard asked him to hear his confession the day before yesterday, and a young woman foreign service officer—much more able than most—who was deeply involved with a local intellectual, sought his advice a week before. She would get over her dark-skinned lover, hopefully before he ended up in one of the Principal Leader's jails.

All very middle-aged, gray, and gloomy. But he could still enjoy the embassy Cadillac and the salute of the Marine guards and an occasional trip upriver as temporary respites from what Fred Allen, his father's favorite comedian in the old days of radio, called the treadmill to oblivion.

His business was another thing; there, he had no control at all.

Moreover, the latest commodity news from America was disturbing. Bunker Hunt and his family and Arab friends were playing games with silver. Fifteen dollars a troy ounce was too high a price for silver, yet if Bunker and his associates were really building a corner, the price could run up much higher. Hugh felt a faint stir of excitement.

Tim was probably making the most of it, overreaching himself with some kinky scheme that was seventy-five percent sensible and twenty-five percent mindless. In the last letter Hugh received from his mother, she told him about the monstrosity of a house Tim was building in Oakland Beach. He was even planning to build an indoor swimming pool. Since the funds came from his silver speculation, Tim dubbed it his "silver-plated pool." Peggy called it "Tim's folly." So it would always be with Tim.

Hugh had stopped trading before testifying at his Senate confirmation hearing and had liquidated all his positions and turned over his assets to a blind trust. So Tim's bizarre schemes wouldn't cost him a penny, though they might ruin the firm.

Well, he would not intervene. It wouldn't be ethical and no good ever came of his intervening with Tim anyway.

"Why didn't you close the door?" Liz opened her eyes. "You know what it's like trying to cool this place off once it gets hot. I don't know why the government can't provide embassies with air conditioning that works."

CHAPTER
THIRTY-SIX

1979

Maria McLain strode briskly down LaSalle Street, enjoying both the crisp October air and the admiring glances of the men who passed her. Her expensive clothes and confident walk said that she was a stunning woman who was a success in the business world.

She put enough time and work into her face, body, and clothes to justify a little vanity, one of the simple joys in life in which you ought to take pleasure as long as you could, she thought.

The visit to her lawyer's office had been a dreary affair, a tryst with mortality in which she'd worked out the provisions of her will to take care of her sons should anything happen to her while they were still young.

"Since you've become a bank president are you too good to notice a hack commodities trader?"

She squinted at the man. "Too vain to wear my glasses, Timmy Donlon." She laughed at herself. "It's great to see you. How's the family? How's the silver market these exciting days? And how's the ambassador?"

"Family's fine. Folks are in Ireland. Silver is more fun than popcorn and from the ambassador I don't hear. How does it feel to be the youngest woman bank president in Cook County?"

She and Tim had met occasionally at meetings and financial community parties. She still enjoyed his wit, though his bloodshot eyes and disheveled clothes and the stories of his marital troubles that everyone in town had heard made her feel bad.

"It feels good, Tim, to tell you the truth. Tell me about Bunker Hunt's silver."

A slow, dark gleam appeared in Tim's bloodshot eyes.

"The Hunts are smart people. They've sewed up Bache and have the Jarecki brothers worried sick. They bought themselves twelve thousand contracts without pushing the price up beyond twelve dollars. They used just about every commission house in the world, ours included, and kept the secret. Now they're going to sit back and watch the price double, maybe triple before they get out."

"Seven or eight billion dollars?"

"Right. You want in?"

"My bank isn't going to play with the Hunts. They're clever, Tim, but from what I hear they're not too bright. They should sell at twenty five an ounce. You watch, though. They'll hold on. Bears and bulls don't lose; pigs do."

Tim shoved his hands into the pockets of his suit. He probably hadn't been home last night.

"They'll change their position at thirty. So the smart traders will sell short when the price hits twenty-two or so. By March it will be down to ten, where it belongs. The bears will make a killing."

Most investors, even the shrewd traders on the floor of the CBT, Maria knew, were bulls. They loved a bull market and hated a bear market even when they made money on it. They went short with guilty consciences, as though it were somehow un-American to profit from an economic decline, particularly a spectacular one. Hugh Donlon, from what she'd heard, was a classic bull, though one who knew when to quit.

His brother was just the opposite. Tim loved the dark thrill of profiting from bad news. Temperamentally, he was the ideal bear, but probably too greedy to make as much from his temperamental skills as he should.

"What if they hang on after that? People don't become billionaires by quitting early."

Tim winked. "That's not what Hugh says. Anyway, the CBT and the Comex won't let them do it. They'll push the margin rates up so high the Hunt crowd will have to sell before thirty-five dollars an ounce. Want just one contract, I mean personally?"

Maria shook her head. "I put my cash, such as it is, in money market notes. Got a couple of kids to educate."

"The oldest boy's at the Citadel, I understand. That's nice. Like his father."

Maria winced, as she almost always did whenever Steven was mentioned. It had been five years since the helicopter had disappeared in a ball of flame during the evacuation of Saigon, but Maria still had nightmares about the crash she'd seen on the TV screen the next night.

"That's right. He likes it there, just as his father did. And, Tim, promise me that if you're into this silver thing, you've got a hedge."

Tim's grin broadened. "I always have a hedge, Maria, always. I wouldn't make a big investment unless I had something stored away to protect me if the market goes the other way. You know that."

Maria was chilled despite the October sunshine. Tim Donlon had been a little kooky all his life. Now the dark light in his eyes as he discussed the silver market was the glow of a lunatic wizard on the edge of being consumed by his own mad magic.

"Don't get hurt," she said lightly.

"When have I been hurt?" he responded just as lightly.

"And Hugh?" she asked.

"Oh, he's not in it at all. He put everything in blind trust. No conflict of interest. Probably didn't have to do that. You know Hugh, though. Keep all the rules. And then break them all. I know you like him, Maria, but Hugh is nothing but rules. Some kept and some broken."

Maria finished her day in the Loop with a visit to the woman's athletic club, which was, as she put it, her downtown swimming hole. She thought about the will and about Steven as she put on her tank suit and dove into the pool. Then with the strong discipline that she had developed over her emotional life since Steven's death, she chased such morbid imaginings away; life now was for her children. Another husband? Maybe. So far no one compared to Steven, who had been the rising and setting sun of her life for a decade and a half.

Tim was a little shark swimming in a sea of big sharks. The Hunt clan were outsiders, rich bumpkins from Texas who wore ready-made suits, took taxis instead of limousines, and stayed at the Palmer House when they were in Chicago instead of the Whitehall. They were, nonetheless, the biggest commodities speculators in America.

She switched from the crawl to a backstroke that was supposed to be good for stomach muscles.

She was savvy enough in the ways of the world to imagine the rest of the silver scenario. The Hunts wanted a corner; they didn't figure to own all the silver in the world, but they might control two thirds of it. Then those who sold short, like the powerful Moccata Metals and Englehart Metals companies would be forced to buy silver from the Hunts at enormous losses.

If they were smart, the Hunts would bail out long before that, but while they were rich and determined and even smart in a single-minded fashion, they weren't sophisticated enough to know that the financial powers-that-be wouldn't let them get away with it. The exchanges would force up the margin requirements, the Hunts would suddenly need a lot of money, the silver market would fall, and the government would have to step in to constrain some banks to bail the Hunts out, with big loans probably to their oil company. The establishment would first punish the Hunts, then save them. Salvation would come not because of love, but out of fear that a silver panic might spread to the other commodities and then to the stock market and then to the whole elaborate and shaky financial structure of the country.

Tim was counting on the Hunts to take the money and run, as he would, as any sophisticated speculator would.

The powers would protect the big sharks because they belonged to the club. They wouldn't salvage a small shark like Tim, who didn't belong to the club.

She climbed out of the pool, her fifty laps finished, and shivered under a towel. The Hunts were rogue sharks, the big-time sharks who were part of the pack. Tim was a small and unimportant shark. Guess who would be eaten alive.

She shivered again, though the shower was steaming hot. Then there was Corfu.

She had made a terrible fool out of herself.

No sense, Maria Angelica, in dwelling on the fact that you're a fool where Hugh Donlon's concerned. You've known that since you were sixteen.

Mary, Mother of God—she turned to prayer as she often did under a shower—don't let any of the Donlons be caught among the sharks.

Judge Donlon put aside the galleys of his manuscript on mysticism and law in the Middle Ages. The proofreader from Cornell University Press had missed three typos in the first hundred pages. Before he became a "senior judge"—semiretired but still serving on an occasional panel—he'd paid little attention to the typing mistakes of secretaries. Now that he was working on his pride and joy, however, he demanded perfection. Foolish old man.

Peggy was discussing her next exhibit with Father Waldek Bronowski, the young art expert of the archdiocese.

"They're wonderful watercolors, Mrs. Donlon," said the round-faced, pudgy priest, "exuding vitality and erotic tension—beautiful bodies elegantly constrained—and your paradoxical soft pastel colors add to the grace of the scenes."

"I only hope they're not sinful, Waldek," she murmured as she filled his sherry glass again. Peg served sherry in her house now, and called young priests by their first names.

The priest laughed softly—everything he did was soft and civilized. "Those who wish to see obscenity can buy *Playboy* or *Penthouse*. Those who come to admire your work will be impressed rather with the purity of the human form."

"I don't know where those pictures came from." Peg put on her glasses to consider them more carefully and more skeptically.

Waldek waved his hands as if he were bestowing a papal blessing. "They come from your own grace-filled and God-filled experience of flesh, Mrs. Donlon. Where does any artist's vision of the body come from? These do you great honor."

Tom Donlon kept a straight face with considerable difficulty. The young priest was confirming Peg's worst fears, telling her that her own sexuality was unveiled in the tense and ecstatic colors and then adding that they revealed high virtue. Finally she had found a priest who answered her anxious questions, and he didn't even know that she was asking them.

At sixty-four, Peg was so handsome that when she entered a

dining room men and women turned to admire her. Tom loved her as much as ever, maybe more. And their sex life, openly celebrated now in her paintings, was more pleasurable than it had ever been.

Peggy had stood the test of time and change, heartbreak, and a revolutionary Church better than most people in her generation. She still carried the pearl rosaries, but she also distributed Holy Communion at Mass.

The terrible wrenching pain she and Tom had inflicted on each other at the time of Hugh's wedding was not forgotten, but it was not mentioned either. Never once did Peg hint at "I told you so" on the subject of Liz.

Peggy would always feel that the hostility of her two daughters-in-law and the absence of affection from her sons' children was a punishment from God. "Punishment theology is hard to give up; it seems so accurate," Waldek had said earlier. The Wentworth children, on the other hand, adored her and visited often, but it was a long way from Killarney to Chicago. Even that physical distance seemed sometimes a punishment.

Nevertheless, Peggy was willing to exhibit the misty thighs and buttocks, arms and legs, breasts and throats, that populated her watercolors. God might still punish her, but He might be even more angry if she continued to hide them. He would object, as Father Waldek had once delicately hinted, to her concealing the talents He had given her.

". . . so I cannot speak for the cardinal's schedule." The priest smiled faintly. "Not even his appointment secretary can do that. But you may be sure that he will visit the gallery and if it is possible he will attend the opening."

"The poor, dear man; he has such a busy schedule," Peg protested.

"He likes you, Mrs. Donlon," the priest said dryly.

"I can't imagine why," the judge said, no longer able to contain his laughter.

"I really can't either," Peg agreed, laughing and blushing together.

"Three more years to our golden wedding anniversary, Father," the judge said, not all that irrelevantly, as the priest was leaving.

Peggy put her arms around him and pressed against him a

moment later. The feel of her pleased him as much now as when he'd held her first in back of the Red Barn at Twin Lakes.

"We don't deserve such happiness," she said through her tears.

"Let's enjoy it just the same."

She quivered in his embrace. "Oh, Tommy, I have the most terrible feeling. . . ."

"What?" He buried his face in her hair, hardly listening.

"I've felt for days that something terrible is about to happen."

"Nothing terrible is going to happen, Peg, not as long as we have each other." In the darkest corner of his soul, however, Tom Donlon was afraid she was right.

CHAPTER
THIRTY-SEVEN

1979

"So you're going short in silver? Risky. Does Hugh know?" Benedict Fowler frowned unpleasantly.

"Suppose I give you an answer to that question? Suppose I say that, yes, he's on the phone every day? Suppose I say that I'm really investing his money because he can't do it himself while he's working for the government?"

Ben pondered the flashing lights of the quotation board outside Tim's office. "You're not serious, of course." His skin was brown but he didn't look healthy. Suntan couldn't hide his pallor any more than makeup hid the whiteness of a corpse.

Tim waved his hand negligently. Silver was up another half-dollar an ounce. The boardroom outside his office was humming with frantic activity. "Not much," he said.

Fowler nodded heavily. "I see."

The Principal Leader reminded Hugh of his brother. Same small, skinny body, same fixed grin, same squinting eyes, same love of the tricky and the risky. Crazier than Tim, surely, and infinitely more dangerous, but basically the same kind of person.

The black man fondled the machete with which he was reputed to mutilate his enemies. "It is most regretable that the local police force has found reason to establish roadblocks near the village of mir Hassun," he said, his eyes dreamy. Was he on drugs too? Probably. From the Russians or the Chinese.

"I'm sure they have their reasons, Exalted One," Hugh said. "Yet we are interested in that village, as you know. It seemed to be the place where our joint plan of labor-intensive agriculture was most likely to succeed, an outcome that would please us all."

The leader waved his knife and smiled. "This year labor-intensive, next year tractors again. What does it matter, Mr. Ambassador? It is only important that our peoples resist communism together."

Probably a more realistic view of American foreign policy than I have, Hugh thought grimly. "We are also concerned about our personnel at mir Hassun. We haven't been able to communicate with them for a week."

"The lovely Miss Kincaid?" The caresses on the knife became more tender.

Hugh nodded. Laura Kincaid was a Peace Corps volunteer in the country to which he'd been assigned. The agonized phone call yesterday from Hank and Jean still haunted him.

"There is nothing to worry about." The Leader laid aside his knife. "Miss Kincaid is well. This is a civilized country. The police will lift the roadblocks in a day or two. Then she can return." He rose from his chair, slowly and majestically, like a rich tribal chieftain rising from an ivory throne, to indicate that the audience was over.

Hugh left only slightly reassured. He was learning, as the staff at Tehran had discovered, that serving the United States abroad could be dicey, especially if revolution was in the air. He wished he was back in Chicago, trading in the silver pit again.

Tim leaned back comfortably in his vast chair. The market had paused briefly at twenty-two. Outside the snow was falling. LaSalle Street had assumed its somewhat cynical pre-Christmas glow. Between then and the first of the year, silver would shoot up again, perhaps a dollar a day. Right after the first of the year, the Hunts would unload, and by March or even February the price would be back to less than fifteen dollars. The directors of the Board of Trade were already muttering that the Board was more important than Bunker Hunt and that margin requirements would have to be raised. Les Rosenthal, the chairman of the CBT, was smarter and tougher than the Hunt clan. He'd force them to end the run-up.

So now was the time to make his own move.

He walked out of the office to the desk of Norma Austin, a vice-president of the firm and his principle assistant and occasional mistress.

"Get on the horn to our best floor contact, Norma. For my own personal account . . . a hundred contracts for April silver, spread between twenty-one fifty an ounce and twenty-three fifty."

The tall, stylish brunette gasped. "That's almost four million dollars, Mr. Donlon."

He was Mr. Donlon everywhere but in bed.

Tim smiled happily. "Shoot the works."

"Buy a hundred contracts." She dutifully made a note as Tim turned away.

"No." He smiled beatifically. "Sell!"

Maria McLain walked through the chic Near North Side Gallery on Oak Street just off Rush as if she were in the cathedral at High Mass. Peggy Donlon was a special woman, of that Maria had always been certain; but these paintings were superb.

God, I'm the age she was when I visited them at Lake Geneva, she thought.

Maria usually avoided the elder Donlons even though they moved in the same circles. She saw them occasionally at Butterfield after she finally caved in and bought a membership in the club— mostly to see her parents beam with pleasure when they walked across the dining room like a distinguished duke and duchess entering the new palace of their daughter the empress.

She was still ambivalent about the Donlons, loving their power and charm, and not trusting the chaos she saw in their lives. Moreover, she didn't want to be reminded of Hugh. Maria had loved only two men in her life. One was dead, God rest him, and the other was married to a bitch and a fool.

Her lips tightened in anger and then she laughed at herself. Loneliness often made her think of the two weeks at Lake Geneva, a magic memory in her life, before the world became complicated.

Was it possible to recapture any of that youthful joy of first love?

Of course, it wasn't. You're a grown-up, Maria Angelica. She must drive Hugh Donlon from her bloodstream. It was time for her to marry again. Five years of widowhood were enough. Yet as she'd told her son Eddie when he said the same thing, you marry not because you need a husband, nor even because you want one, but because you can't do without this particular man.

No such man had come along, though there'd been no dearth of contenders. Maybe he never would.

What if Hugh Donlon should seek an annulment of his marriage to Liz? Would she be interested?

Damn right. And you ought not even to think about such things.

She did just the same.

Peggy was talking to a tall, very handsome middle-aged priest, in front of a picture that reminded Maria of herself.

She took Ed's arm and dragged him toward the painting.

Ed pulled on her sleeve as Maria zeroed in on it.

"Mother, I don't think . . . "

"It isn't me, Ed. I never was that good-looking."

"I don't . . . "

"Peggy Curtin Donlon, that picture reminds me of a girl I knew a long time ago. It's sinful and shameful."

Peggy embraced her with grateful tears. "Maria, darling, I'm so glad you could come. We hardly ever see you. The picture isn't anyone. Father Waldek says I paint out of memories. I'm sure I have a memory of you, but I didn't intend . . . "

"I'll buy it," Maria said enthusiastically. "And tell everyone that it's me even if it isn't."

"Perhaps I should draw from live models," Peggy said thoughtfully. "Tommy will tell you that I was the one who wanted to see the Sally Rand show at the World's Fair. . . ."

"I really love it. . . ."

"How wonderful, Maria, but I insist it be a gift."

Maria started to protest and then abandoned the idea. There was no way to get the best of Peggy. "Peg, this is my son, Eddie."

"You look just like your grandfather," Peg said, "and that's a compliment, young man. . . . I suppose you both know Cardinal Cronin?"

"I do," Ed said sheepishly.

Maria felt her face grow warm. "How do you do, Your Eminence? I didn't expect . . . "

Sean Cronin was indeed a charmer. "I do think the picture looks like you, Mrs. McLain. And if you call me Your Eminence again, your son's career in the seminary is finished."

For once, Maria found herself without words.

CHAPTER
THIRTY-EIGHT

1980

Christmas was over. It was early January and Laura Kincaid's team was still isolated up-country. There'd been one letter just before Christmas, a hasty handwritten note saying they were safe and would be out soon.

At least Henry and Jean knew that their adored Laura was still alive.

The ambassador and his family were eating dinner. Lise was complaining that Brian had hit her, and Brian was complaining that the teacher at the embassy school was mean. And Liz was complaining that the Nuncio would no longer talk to her because of an argument about abortion—he was shocked that a devout Catholic mother would approve of murder.

Royce came into the dining room after his usual discreet knock.

"The Interior Minister called to say that if we send a boat upriver tomorrow we can bring back the team from mir Hassun. It must leave tomorrow morning, however, and you must lead it. Sounds odd to me."

"Royce, we're dealing with a madman; of course, I'll lead it." The people up there were his responsibility. "See that it's organized."

On Friday, January 11, at one thirty-five, April silver closed at thirty-four and a half. In India precious heirlooms were being melted. In New York thieves were bringing their loot directly to silver markets. In Chicago silverware was being sold briskly at second-hand stores. Dentists were even removing silver fillings and replacing them with acrylic.

The greedy Hunts were killing themselves. Unfortunately, Tim thought, they are killing me too.

"You don't have enough of your own funds to cover for the Clearing Corporation on Monday morning." Norma was pale and frightened. Tim was getting tired of her, though now was hardly the time to end the relationship. "At eight thirty tomorrow morning Continental Bank will tell them, and we are in very hot water."

"No problem." There really wasn't a problem because Tim still had plenty of hedges. "Transfer the funds from the segregated accounts."

"Customer money?"

"We'll be all right by this time Monday. But don't tell anyone else."

Norma hesitated and then with a faint shrug turned to her computer terminal to make the transfer.

Tim Donlon was happy that Hugh was in the peaceful tropics.

The jungle smelled of sweet flowers and rotting bodies. Hugh, Liz—who'd insisted on coming along—the third secretary, an innocuous and useless young man from a teachers college in Arkansas, two drivers, and the five-person team from mir Hassun bumped down rutted tracks toward the relative safety of the river, tracks that once had led to silver mines, long since abandoned, beyond mir Hassun.

The team was battered and nervous after six weeks of isolation and three elaborately staged mock executions. The "rebels' forces" had wiped out their new farms, terrorized the villagers who'd cooperated with them, and kept the team in fear every day of its captivity, without, however, doing it any physical harm. Everson, the team leader, was worn out with fever and Laura Kincaid, the youngest member, was now the de facto leader. Thin and tired, but still beautiful, Laura had greeted the rescue party with the confidence of a warrior queen.

Birds squawked in protest and animals stirred restlessly as they wound their way tortuously toward the river. In another year the forest would obliterate the trail completely. There would be no more village agricultural experiments at mir Hassun; the message from the Principal Leader was loud and clear.

"Were the rebel soldiers from the Leader's army?" Hugh asked Laura, who sat next to him in the jeep.

"Battle fatigues and a different color beret," she said, shaking her head wearily. "And they had Russian guns. But they were working for him. Otherwise we'd be dead."

Hugh relaxed a little. If the Leader was indulging in a little game with his American allies, then they were safe in the jungle. The group that was playing hide and seek on the track behind them was following them as protection to make sure the drama came to its prescribed end.

After several more turns they finally reached the river, and found their launch still securely tied up at the decaying pier.

Thank God.

As they piled out of their jeeps and hurried toward the launch, an old truck lurched down the track and stopped right behind them. A dozen dark-skinned soldiers armed with rifles and machine pistols poured out of the truck and swarmed all around them.

The Principal Leader had written a different scenario, after all.

One of the troopers jabbed Hugh in the stomach and another hit him over the head with the butt of his rifle. As Hugh staggered backward, he smelled the alcohol. He thought of all the things that had been done to white captives, especially white women captives, in this part of the world by drunken soldiers.

And for the first time in his life he was numb with fear.

First the soldiers beat the men and then they tied them to trees. Then they went after the women, holding both of them at bayonet point against a tree until all the troopers were ready. The noncom in charge then barked an order in a dialect Hugh didn't understand, whereupon several of the men tore off Liz's and Laura's clothes. Fabric that would not tear was cut away with the bayonets. Naked and terrified, the two women were pushed from soldier to soldier, slapped, fondled, pinched, and squeezed. When they tried to resist, they were beaten, but just enough to intimidate them into passivity again. Dark fingers pawed at white flesh, amusing themselves, taking their time, stretching out their own pleasure and the women's pain and humiliation as long as they could. Torture as foreplay, it seemed.

Hugh watched as in a nightmare. So this was Liz's Third World. He hoped she was happy with it.

On January 18, after the silver pit at the CBT had closed, Tim Donlon sat at his desk as if he were frozen there. Silver had closed at forty dollars and fifty cents an ounce, an eighteen dollar run-up since his sale a month ago, an increase of ninety thousand dollars a contract. Those who had bought at that price had made a huge profit; those who had gone short had suffered a gigantic loss.

Tim was one of the losers—more than nine million dollars. There was no money left. The Clearing Corporation would make the call the next morning. He would not be able to meet it. By nine thirty, nervous auditors would be all over them, fearing a scandal that could rock the venerable CBT to its foundations. They would discover that he'd used customers' money to cover almost five million dollars. Before noon they would have a floor broker liquidate his contracts and the firm would be wiped out. Donlon, Fowler, and Donlon would be no more. The clients would have his hide and Hugh would return home to put his personal resources into paying off the debts.

"One more day, just one more day and the market will break," he'd said disconsolately to Norma.

"Can't you get money from your wife?"

"Are you kidding? We've tied up a fortune in the new house. Even the doorknobs are gold-plated—or silver-plated anyway." He laughed to himself as if he'd just said something terribly witty. He was weary of Norma, but he would need her in the days ahead, especially if the Commodity Futures Trading Commission started talking indictment. They usually were satisfied with a suspension if the cusomters got their money back, but you never could be certain.

Tim was frightened. He'd thought about activating his final hedge, an elegant and ironic protection against this disaster. But there hadn't been enough money in the hedge to cover the margin calls. It would be eaten up in a few days and he would have nothing left.

What if something were to happen to him? Tim considered for a moment. How would Hugh prove his noninvolvement?

He spun to his typewriter and began to put down a statement.

I, Timothy Donlon, do hereby attest that my brother, Hugh Donlon, at no time intervened in the activities of our investment firm during his term as ambassador, that he never discussed our silver contracts with me during that time, that it was not his money with which I purchased half of those contracts, and that he never advised me to unsegregate clients' funds to meet our calls at that time. I also attest that I persuaded Benedict Fowler and Norma Austin of precisely the opposite of this. I do not apologize to anyone.

Nonetheless, I am writing this affidavit, which Norma Austin will notarize, in case anything should happen to me while investigations are still in progress. I will not disclose here the whereabouts of my final hedge against the current silver market, as I intend to use that for my own honorable retirement.

The "rebels" enjoyed their game with the two women, a game that by the standards of native soldiery was almost gentle. Liz screamed hysterically as they pawed and jabbed her; Laura gritted her teeth and yelled only when she was being hurt.

The worst of their torments had not begun. And might not. Hugh remained detached and skeptical. The beating administered to the men in the party had been perfunctory. The women were being degraded and humiliated but not seriously injured. Hugh returned to his first explanation: It was a show enacted by the Leader, a disgusting trick.

Or they might die. He did not want to die, although he wasn't quite sure why. His life was such a waste—failed priest, failed husband, failed father, failed human being. Would God forgive him? Was there a God? He'd tried to do his best . . . Maria had faulted him for that. Do, do, do, she'd said. What else was there?

The noncom gave another order.

Hugh searched deep within himself for the courage and the strength to do something. He should be able to react. Passive fatalism, detached despair—that was not Hugh Donlon. He found nothing.

Dear God, save us.

The two women were stretched on the ground, their hands and

feet held by troopers, bayonet points at their throats. The noncom swaggered over and stood above them, as if trying to decide which one he would enjoy first.

He pointed at Liz. The soldiers holding her feet jerked them apart. The noncom unfastened his ammunition belt, lowered his pants, and knelt between her legs. Liz screamed and tried to twist away. The bayonet pricked her throat. Blood streaked down her neck.

Another soldier knelt in front of Laura.

"Give me absolution, Hugh, please," she screamed.

An odd time to think about God. God? There was no God. How could there be a God?

"Please," she screamed again.

A soldier hit her breasts with his rifle butt.

Hugh said the words. "I absolve you of your sins, in the name of the Father and of the Son and of the Holy Spirit." Another soldier hit him in the stomach. He vomited.

Then the Principal Leader's gendarmes arrived in a high-powered launch, precisely, Hugh realized, at the prearranged moment.

Hugh was ashamed of his terror and despair. He should have known better.

The smart, handsome young captain of the gendarmes told him that the "rebel" prisoners would be executed. He gestured to his lieutenant, and the bound prisoners were marched away into the jungle, guarded by two powerful gendarmes brandishing deadly Uzis. Laura and Everson and the boy from Arkansas were vomiting. Liz lay unconscious in the embassy launch.

"Let me see them die," Hugh said. "They tortured my wife. I want to see them die."

"We prevented rape," the officer said defensively. "It is not permitted to watch executions of rebels."

As they moved out in the launch, they heard bloodcurdling screams from the jungle and then the light death rattle of the Uzis. Then silence.

"The men who hurt and humiliated you have been hurt in their turn," the captain announced solemnly. "They have died as dogs deserve to die. In the name of the Principal Leader, I apologize to you."

"Bullshit," Hugh said, confident that the rebels were marching back to their homes to playact another day. "Let us see the bodies."

"It is not permitted to see the bodies," said the captain.

A charade, a cunning game arranged by a madman who thought he was God. The Exalted One had arranged a scenario that entertained him, won praises for his police, and sent a powerful message to the American government. There was no reality in the story. It was just a horror film for a few terrified whites.

CHAPTER THIRTY-NINE

1980

Harold Marks, the official who covered Donlon, Fowler, and Donlon for the Commodity Futures Trading Commission, arrived at Tim's office shortly after the auditors. Outside, in the boardroom, panic had not yet begun; the brokers and researchers, the secretaries and the wire room operators, the clerks and messengers, had yet to comprehend what was happening and what it meant to them.

"This is James McConnell of the United States Attorney's office, Mr. Donlon," Marks said with quiet deference, "and these are Special Agents Scott and Harrison of the Federal Bureau of Investigation."

"Come in, gentlemen," Tim said cordially. "Can I get anyone some coffee?"

McConnell was a lean, hard man with thin hair, piercing brown eyes, and a Dakota twang. "You may want to have your attorney present, Mr. Donlon, even at this preliminary stage," he said.

"Mr. Gallagher is on the way over," Tim said cheerfully. "I regret all of this, of course, but I can assure you the partnership will make good all client losses promptly."

"Then why wasn't the partnership money used to meet the calls?" sniffed Marks.

"Communication problem," Tim said airily. "As you know, my brother is an ambassador and is no longer active in the firm. He advised me to proceed in this fashion if a serious situation developed and he would cover for it. He preferred to remain in the background with his positions while serving abroad."

"You were trading with your brother's money and acting on his advice?" McConnell's voice was even softer.

Tim was delighted by his power. "I can't comment on that."

"And he agreed to the use of clients' funds to meet the clearing house calls?"

"Or that either," Tim said.

"He called you from the embassy?"

"Of course not," Tim said, as if such a suggestion was an insult to Hugh's intelligence. "I don't know where he called from."

"Very interesting. I suppose there were no witnesses to these arrangements."

"I don't see what difference it makes, do you, Mr. Marks? The money's going to be paid back as soon as we reach my brother. He's up some river in darkest Africa."

"He may also be up a creek," Marks said through tight lips.

"So there were no witnesses?" McConnell probed.

"Well, if it comes to that, sure there were," said Tim, eager to be helpful and cooperative, "though I don't know what's the big deal. Mr. Benedict Fowler, a former partner, attended the luncheon at which he worked out the arrangement before Hugh went abroad. He also talked with him on the phone the last time he was in here. And Mrs. Norma Austin, our vice-president, has participated in most of our phone conversations. I still don't see what's the problem."

"The problem, Mr. Donlon"—McConnell sounded like the sheriff giving orders for a hanging—"is that an employee of the federal government seems to have participated in the theft of five million dollars—at least—of clients' money, in addition to perhaps violating conflict-of-interest laws. Even if the money is returned, the law has been violated. There are silver mines in that country, if I recall correctly. You may not realize it, Mr. Donlon, but the United States government does not approve of the violation of its laws, especially by its own employees."

Poor Hugh, Tim thought. He would get one with a poker up his ass.

Hugh and Laura were sitting in the ambassador's office. The young woman had recovered from her ordeal with remarkable speed, but Hugh's stomach and shoulder were still sore, reminders that the Principal Leader played hardball when he was in the mood for games.

"We'll miss you here," Hugh said, "but I certainly am thankful you're going. You'll have some time at home to make up your mind whether you want to keep on earning a living in upriver villages."

"I've made up my mind," she said promptly, her unblemished face smiling radiantly.

"A lucky man?" The radiance could only mean love.

"A lucky someone. I pretty much made up my mind two months ago. I decided definitely up in the village when they were holding us prisoner. It's important to me, Hugh, that you understand." She smiled again. "And I want you to know that what happened day before yesterday didn't affect my decision."

"I'm glad I'm important, Laura, but who's the lucky someone?"

"God."

"Who?"

"I'm joining the Poor Clare's. The monastery's in Chicago, so I'll be close to your family. They're more liberal now about visitors. I hope you'll visit me sometimes."

Outside the ambassador's window the mighty river flowed on unastonished.

"Why?" was all he could say.

"Why any love, Hugh? Since I was tiny I've known that someone loved me and wanted me specially. I don't know why He does. I'm perfectly happy in the world. I'm not running, I assure you. He doesn't insist. He doesn't even push. He just waits. He won't love me any less if I say no. Only I don't want to say no." She kissed him on the forehead, the way he'd once kissed her mother.

When she left, he felt very old.

The United States Attorney for the Northern District of Illinois considered James McConnell with distaste that he hoped he didn't conceal.

"I don't see it, Jimmy. We've never pushed one of these CFTC things to a grand jury before. The people over at the Board of Trade have their own rules and their own games. Clients get their money back and the government doesn't waste money on a trial. Maybe there's grounds for civil suits, but I can't see a criminal indictment."

"Five million dollars was stolen, sir. That's not a small matter."

"Was it really stolen, Jimmy? A change in a computer record for a few days with the knowledge that one way or another there was the money to change it back? Only a technicality."

"And a government official?"

"Your two witnesses are not all that reliable. The Austin woman was getting herself banged by that creep Tim Donlon. And I hear Ben Fowler has grudges to settle with Hugh Donlon. A good defense lawyer would tear them apart on the stand."

"It might not come to that. If there's substance to Fowler's allegations, then Hugh Donlon will have to plea-bargain for probation. We get a conviction without ever worrying about a jury."

The U.S. Attorney had used the strategy himself on more than one occasion, but never with quite so thin a case. "A lot of taxpayers' money to improve our record."

"And to send a warning to those people over at the CBT that they have to respect other people's money, even if their father is a federal judge."

So that was it. Old Judge Donlon had written a scathing opinion about one of the cases McConnell had messed up. The U.S. Attorney made a mental note to get rid of the man as soon as he could and to make some discreet remarks in the Bar Association dining room.

"We'll see what Washington says." He ended the conversation.

Jimmy McConnell didn't give up easily. He called a reporter at the *Star Herald* that afternoon. The next morning Chicago woke to characteristically distorted and dishonest headlines that announced, "Diplomat Involved in Ten Million Dollar Silver Fraud."

Royce burst into Hugh's office, unable to conceal his elation. "The Secretary is on the phone . . . he wants to talk to you at once."

Hugh was impressed neither by the Secretary's importance nor by his ability. He took his time walking to the phone.

"Donlon," he said.

"I want your resignation today," the cabinet officer said curtly.

"Any special reason?" Hugh felt a tug of fear. Something was terribly wrong. A scandal about the upriver mess?

"I think you know already, Ambassador."

"I don't," Hugh said. "I serve at the pleasure of the President, and am ready to cease serving whenever it's his pleasure; but if you want me out of here, you're going to have to tell me why."

"Because you've just been accused of stealing ten million dollars, that's why," the Secretary said triumphantly.

CHAPTER
FORTY

1980

Hugh sat in Buck Phelan's inner office, waiting for his lawyer to return from the final conference with the U.S. Attorney, who was clearly embarrassed by the situation one of his assistants and the press had created. If Buck read the signs correctly, then everything would be over in a few days. Hugh could then try to pick up the pieces of his life and career.

Liam Wentworth, who was a mountain of support with money, advice, encouragement, and affection during the crisis, had strongly urged against plea-bargaining. "You'll kill them in court, old chap," he had bellowed. "They don't have a case. Hire yourself another solicitor; Phelan is too slick by half. You deserve to be exonerated for all our sakes."

But the fighting spirit and spontaneous resourcefulness that had appeared in past crises failed to appear this time. Hugh stood paralyzed on the goal line with the football in his hands, able neither to punt nor run.

Mir Hassun again.

So he watched his own downfall as if it were an old black-and-white film on late-night TV. He could not expose his family to the horrors of a trial with Tim testifying against him, and Tim had already accepted a grant of immunity, guessing perhaps that the threat of his testimony would force Hugh to plea-bargain. Tim probably rationalized that in this way no one would be hurt or at least no one would go to jail. Hugh's parents aged before his eyes. The judge immediately resigned from the federal bench, on which he had served with honor and distinction for more than forty years. Peggy put aside her paintbrush and sat by the window of their lakefront condo, staring at the gray waters, searching in the drab mysteries of Lake Michigan for consolation that God could not or would not give.

He would win a trial. But what difference did six months probation make? Like the Principal Leader, McConnell had devised a scenario that pretended to be real but was only dramatic fiction.

Marge agreed with Hugh. "He's right, you know, Liam; the old folks couldn't take a public performance by Tim."

"Time he didn't get away with it."

"Maybe you're right," she said sadly, "but it's too late to change now. We've protected Tim all our lives. This is the last time."

"Damn right," Liam said, wishing perhaps for the old days when traitors were driven out of the hill fort with the wolf hounds howling after them.

Hugh liquidated virtually all of his assets and restored the customers' money. There might be some civil suits about profits lost, but the commodity business was so unpredictable that they could be settled easily out of court. Only the home in Kenilworth was safe; it was registered in Liz's name.

Liz seemed to be considering him much as she would be considering a strange form of insect life she'd found in their room in the embassy. Of all those around him, only Liz might believe Tim's story to be true.

The grand jury believed Tim, however, and returned a quick indictment on fourteen counts of violation of the CFTC act and of fraud. Hugh was arraigned before Judge Arnold Crawford and pleaded not guilty. A further hearing was set for the end of March when the plea might be changed, a light sentence of probation imposed, and the matter forgotten.

He would never forget the shame: His picture on the front page of the paper, a man charged with stealing the money of trusting clients; the reporters and the TV cameras in front of his house every morning; the loud angry questions from the reporters; the suspicious and disdainful expressions on the faces of people on the street. He was an accused criminal and, as far as they were concerned, certainly guilty.

"Ex-Priest Charged in Multi-Million Dollar Theft," said the *National Catholic Reporter.*

Shame was like a virus. Even though it was a foreign substance that invaded your system, it became part of you and aggravated the infection caused by your own guilt and self-hatred. Would to God that he could die before that next courtroom appearance.

Buck Phelan, a slick little man who, despite his success as a political lawyer, reminded Hugh of the kind of attorney who hangs around Traffic Court fixing tickets, rushed into his office, breathless and beaming.

"We cut it, Hughie boy, it's all set. The U.S. Attorney hasn't liked this prosecution from day one. All we need is a nolo contendere plea. They'll settle for a fine and a few months probation. By the first of April you'll be a free man without a care or a worry in the world."

"What about Crawford? He's had a grudge against me for a long time. I pushed his brother around in a schoolyard fight back in the forties. Shouldn't we ask him to disqualify himself? Will he go along?"

"I mentioned that problem to our friend over in the federal building. It's informal, as these things have to be, of course, but Arnie swears that he doesn't even remember the fight and hardly remembers his brother. He says the bargain strikes him as being reasonable and just."

"I guess that's it, then." Hugh was uneasy. It was dishonorable to confess even nolo contendere to something when you were innocent.

"Cheer up, man," said the genial Buck. "Call your family and tell them the good news."

Tim at first had taken refuge with Norma Austin in his grotesque new home at Oakland Beach, complete with sauna bath and indoor swimming pool. But his intuition was to dump Norma and leave Chicago as soon as Hugh's sentence was imposed. Tim had thrown himself on Liz's mercy, easily convincing her that Hugh had been planning to make him take the rap for something Hugh himself had done.

It all seemed altogether plausible to Liz, as Hugh had not made the slightest effort to exonerate himself. A week after they returned to Chicago, she took the children and moved out.

On his way to be sentenced, in a courtroom in the Dirksen Federal Building in which his father had often sat, Hugh walked down Dearborn Street, savoring the beauties of his native city—the Daley Plaza with its Picasso sculpture and a Miro across the street, the Bank Plaza with its Chagall, and the Federal Plaza, just ahead of him now, with his favorite piece of Chicago outdoor art, the red "flamingo" mobile of Alexander Calder. Dearborn Street was the most interesting street in the world. Too bad he'd never found the time to enjoy it. Too busy working LaSalle Street instead.

Judge Arnold Crawford accepted the change of plea to nolo contendere without comment. "Mr. District Attorney, do you have any recommendations about sentencing?"

The U.S. Attorney spoke himself, not trusting McConnell to carry off the deal. "Your Honor, our office feels that there must be a fine as a warning to others who might consider violating the Commodity Futures Trading Act and we also feel that some kind of probationary sentence, six months to a year, would be appropriate. The defendant is not a hardened criminal, the money that was misused has been repaid, his distance from the country in what was actually brave government service at the time of the crime is certainly a mitigating factor. We feel that the disgrace that he has suffered is a sufficient punishment and deterrent to similar crimes."

Crawford tapped his pen lightly on the bench in front of him. The reporters in the courtroom leaned forward eagerly, the court's dramatic pause giving them hope that there might be more of a story here than the reported plea-bargain deal.

"I normally respect the opinion of the U.S. Attorney's office," the judge said sternly, "but in the present case, I feel I must respectfully disagree.

"Hugh Thomas Donlon, you are a man of great talents and achievements. You have been well endowed both by nature and by your family background. You have served effectively in several different professions. But I am of the opinion, sir, that you have never learned the meaning of self-restraint or integrity. You have always taken it for granted that you can possess anything or anyone you wanted, by whatever means, legal when convenient, illegal when necessary. To suspend your sentence in a federal correctional institution would be to make a mockery of justice. It would tell the young people of this judicial district that a man from the right family and with the right friends can violate the law with impunity." The judge's gray eyes were shining with the triumph of revenge. "I therefore sentence you to eighteen months in the Federal Correctional Institution at Lexington, Kentucky, and urge you to spend however many of those months you actually serve reflecting on the models of humility that were held up to you for imitation during your years of preparation for the priesthood."

That day at one thirty, trading in April silver ended at fifteen dollars eighty cents an ounce, and trading in June silver at twenty-two dollars, twenty cents an ounce. The great "Bunker Hunt" silver run-up was over.

The next morning the *Tribune* carried a headline on its third page, "Marxists Take Over African Government." The story reported that the mutilated body of the Principal Leader had been found floating in a dugout ten miles downstream from the capital city.

CHAPTER
FORTY-ONE

1980

The Federal Correctional Institution at Lexington, Kentucky, was, as Pete McQueen, Hugh's new lawyer, put it, a jail for those the government knew it ought not to lock away and a place where all the modern penal techniques worked because they were unnecessary.

"The prisoners they send here," McQueen told Hugh, "are guilty of crimes they will never commit again. The place isn't bad enough to deter anyone from committing a similar offense. Society doesn't profit from their being in prison, the taxpayers lose money on it, and certainly the convicts don't benefit. A term here represents the ultimate victory of the prosecuting attorney over the attorney for the defense. It's vengeance, pure and simple. Even if you were guilty, ten months here would not be a constructive way of repaying your debt to society."

The list of items Hugh could bring revealed the contradictions inherent in the prison—two sports jackets, a tennis racket, a swimming suit, one ring, one watch, two bed sheets, one billfold, two ties . . . not quite the paraphernalia for a country club, but not the sort of things one is usually told to bring to prison.

Yet, even with time off for good behavior, Lexington, a foreboding red brick former narcotics sanatorium, would be Hugh's home for ten months.

It was, in many ways, not nearly as bad as the Catholic seminary of the 1950s. There was more freedom of movement, less censorship of mail, and no attempt at thought control. Moreover, inmates were rewarded with periodic home leaves for keeping the rules, a reward the seminary had never offered.

Hugh was "processed" through a battery of psychological tests, an interview with a staff psychologist, and an introductory conference with a "social adviser"—the title sounded like that of a dorm mother in a women's college; apparently "social worker" was thought to be an offensive phrase—who monitored his problems much more gently than had Father Meisterhorst.

His "social adviser" was a wispy twenty-five-year-old woman from Georgia named Marilyn Henderson. Her lank blond hair hung around her plain face in shanks.

"I've noticed, Mr. Donlon, that you are working in the laundry. With your skills you could serve on the library staff, or in the computational center, or teach courses. We have a social science program here."

"I like it in the laundry," Hugh replied; it was exhausting work but an excellent substitute for thought, and better than teaching a course on "Coming to Terms with Yourself."

"I've also noticed that you have not asked for another appointment with the psychological staff."

"Is that obligatory? Is it part of the good behavior for which I receive time off?"

"Of course not." She pushed the hair out of her eyes, a useless nervous gesture. "The psychologist reports that, aside from a normal depressive reaction, you are in better mental health than most of the admittees he sees."

"What's normal depression, Ms. Henderson?"

"The sort of depression that men and women who are not institutionalized feel under severe stress."

"I see."

"I've also noticed that you say you expect no visitors. We feel that visitors are an important part of our program. The family is subjected to minimum supervision and there is no harassment or . . . humiliation."

"I think it would be better for me to see my family during the home furlough if I'm granted one. My attorney may come occasionally."

"It's entirely your decision. And you must remember, Mr. Donlon"—she was quoting from a textbook now—"that we on the staff make no judgments about a person's legal or moral standing. Those matters have been decided by other agencies. We are here to help. As you realize, the supervision is minimal. There are no bars. You can even walk out. A minimum security facility such as this is predicated on the assumption that it is to the perceived self-interest of the inmates to monitor their own behavior. Hence, staff members like myself are really here to facilitate your development during the time you are with us. You must think of me as someone who is at your service instead of the other way around."

"I quite understand that, Ms. Henderson."

Hugh didn't feel a victim of the system. Nor did he ever protest his innocence in prison. Nor did he explain why he hadn't contested the indictment in the first place. Before he came to Lexington, he'd depersonalized himself, established a wall between his emotions and the facts of his life.

There was nothing left that merited enthusiasm or commitment, not Church, not government, not business, not even his family. Life in Lexington was only slightly more pointless than life outside.

Yet he was still, oddly, a priest. He gave an occasional absolution to a nervous or scrupulous inmate and counseled several who, like himself, were having severe, if understandable, marital problems. The second week he was in the facility he administered the last rites to a heart attack victim while the chaplain was away on his day off. Ms. Henderson somewhat dubiously found him the key for the sacred oils. The man recovered and the chaplain was anxious lest the ecclesiastical authorities discover that Hugh had dispensed the sacrament. Contemptuously, Hugh cited the relevant canon from the code and offered to write a letter to the archbishop.

Hard work in the laundry, hard exercise in the recreation yard, careful dieting, exhausted sleep at night—these were Hugh's therapies. He lost weight and regained his physical strength. He avoided books and amused himself with summer reruns on TV.

And tried to pretend that the virus of shame was not becoming worse each passing day.

McQueen visited him on a blistering day at the end of August.

"Your mother and father are fine . . . I'm sure you hear from them. The Kerrys or the Wentworths . . . never know what to call them . . . are spending the summer at Lake Geneva with your parents. Hauntingly attractive kids, like characters from an Irish saga. Your parents are holding up well."

Hugh hardly thought of his parents and not at all of Lake Geneva. "I'm glad."

"No luck on the reduction of sentence, I'm afraid. The people at Justice admit there's been a mistake—nice choice of words, huh?— but it has not escaped your attention that Mr. Carter is running for reelection. They don't want it to look like they're taking care of one of their own."

Pete McQueen was a feisty brown-haired young South Side Irishman who looked and acted like a successful lightweight boxer. If he'd been Hugh's attorney at the beginning, Hugh might be at Lake Geneva too. Not that it made much difference.

"Have you heard from your wife?" McQueen acted like a man who'd jumped off a cliff and wondered whether it was a mistake.

"No . . . not a word. Why?"

"She's filing for divorce. Her attorney is one of the toughest divorce lawyers in the city. She wants everything you have, Hugh, and a substantial chunk of the rest of your life."

"Charges?"

"Cruelty, adultery, desertion, the works. It could be messy if we contest it."

"Nolo contendere seems to be my routine plea, doesn't it? She can have everything there is. See that she gets a proportion of my income instead of a dollar figure."

Pete looked up from his notebook, frowning. "Why do that, Hugh? You're going to make a lot of money when you're released. Let her go into court when she wants more."

"Suppose I find a job as a teacher in a junior college somewhere in the sticks, or in the inner city?"

"You wouldn't make such a choice, would you?" His fighter's face showed dismay.

"Do it," Hugh said with more firmness than he'd displayed in months, "and do it all as quietly as possible. I don't want to cause the family any more embarrassment."

"Do you ever think of yourself, Hugh?" He closed the notebook.

"How else do you think I ended up here?"

"I'm not your priest . . . I'm sorry . . . I forgot . . ."

"No problem." It was the first time he'd felt a smile in a long time. "Even priests can have priests."

Two weeks later Ms. Henderson informed Hugh that there was an "extraordinary visitor" waiting for him.

Oh, God, he thought to himself, not Liz.

"Do I have to see this person?" he asked as she led him away from the laundry.

"Not if you don't want to. His name"—she glanced at the file card in her hand—"is Mr. Cronin."

The cardinal was wearing a white open-neck shirt, gray slacks, and a black Windbreaker—an incognito of tailor-made casuals chosen by a determined sister-in-law who was also a U.S. senator.

With no preliminaries other than a firm handshake, the cardinal began talking about the U.S. senator. "I've asked my sister-in-law Nora to work on the Justice Department. A bunch of phonies. They say there's been an injustice but they can't do anything about it in an election year. You were framed, weren't you?" The hoods retracted from his probing brown eyes.

"That's what every con says."

"I'm not interested in every con. I'm interested in one of the priests of my diocese."

"I'm an ex-priest. I don't have to answer questions from a bishop."

Sean leaned back in his easy chair and laughed. "Oh, you'll always be a priest, Hugh, till the day you die. Theologically, of course, but personally too. You say Mass here?"

"Lord, no. I administered the last rites when the chaplain was away and he almost had a stroke."

"I'll have a word with him before I leave. If an inactive priest occasionally says Mass privately, I'm not going to send him off to the dungeons of the Holy Office. Now answer my question."

"I had no knowledge of anything that was done at Donlon, Fowler, and Donlon during the silver run-up. Tim lied, Fowler lied, Norma Austin lied. Judge Crawford lied when he agreed to a plea-bargain and then used his power to settle an old family feud. I'm guilty of a lot of things in my wasted life, Cardinal, but not of any of the crimes for which I'm here."

"Sean." The cardinal grimaced. "Okay, I wanted to make sure that my judgment was right. Your wife really leaving you?"

"Yes."

"Bitch."

"Maybe I've given her reason."

The cardinal ignored that. "You know about the new annulment rules? We could get you an annulment in short order."

"I've broken one promise in my life. I don't want to break another."

"Let God punish you if he wants. Don't punish yourself."

Hugh understood. "You want me back in the priesthood?"

"You're a priest now, Hugh. Just inactive."

"After all I've done, you want me back in the active ministry?" He exhaled a long breath of astonishment.

"As I tell my Polish friend over on the fifth floor of the Vatican, we let the first pope back in, we can let anyone back in . . . and Peter had a wife too."

"Sean, I'm deeply moved. . . ." And he was. For the first time in months genuine emotions tugged at him—humility, gratitude, perhaps even a touch of hope.

"Forget that," the cardinal said as he rose from the chair. "I must be in the big city for a Confirmation at seven thirty. It's an open offer, Hugh. And I'll be back."

CHAPTER
FORTY-TWO

1980

On a Sunday afternoon in the middle of November Marilyn Henderson appeared at the door of the recreation room, where Hugh was agonizing through another disaster by the Chicago Bears. She motioned to him.

It was unusual for her to be working on Sunday and even more unusual for her to be near the rec room.

He followed her into the corridor, noting as he always did how much he expected the smell of disinfectant in what had been a hospital corridor.

"I'm afraid I have bad news, Mr. Donlon. . . ."

Oh, God, not Mom or Dad.

"Your father called from Chicago. There's been an airplane crash in Puerto Rico, a plane flying from St. Maarten to San Juan crashed on landing in a rainstorm. Your brother, Timothy, and his wife and two of their children were on it. I'm afraid we don't know yet which children. You might want to pack some clothes. A furlough authorization will come through shortly."

"Oh," Hugh said dully, realizing how relieved he was that it was Tim and not his parents. Selfish, selfish, selfish. Poor doomed Tim.

"You'll want to go home for the wake and funeral?" she asked uneasily.

Some of his old graciousness toward women returned. Poor kid, she was trying hard. "Certainly, Ms. Henderson, I appreciate your concern very much, particularly on Sunday afternoon, when I'm sure you'd rather be with your family."

His smile had its usual effect on a woman. She blushed and smiled radiantly in return. "My husband is watching the football game, so he didn't mind." When she laughed she was not unattractive. Making life difficult for her was one more sin.

She drove him to the airport in Louisville so he could catch the last Sunday plane to Chicago.

Jack Howard, balding and heavy but with the old infectious grin, was waiting for him at O'Hare.

The grin didn't last long. "Your dad asked me to pick you up, Hugh. They're having a hard time sorting things out. You heard the news?"

"Timmy and Estelle and two of the kids?"

"Then you haven't heard the latest news. . . . I—I guess I have to be the one to tell you." Jack was sweating profusely; he wiped his face with a handkerchief. "Estelle is alive and so are her kids. She's raising hell about the error. . . ."

"But my social adviser . . . said that it was Mr. and Mrs. Timothy Donlon who were missing in the crash. It was Timmy?"

Jack nodded miserably.

"Then who were the woman and children?"

Jack gulped. "Your wife and your two kids."

Maria didn't want to go to the wake, but her two older sons insisted, as did her parents. "The Irish expect it," her father said simply.

The judge and Peggy would be happy to see her. Marge's reaction was hard to predict. She didn't want to think about Hugh.

He was a stranger, a man she never knew, only a faint reflection of a boy she was mad about a quarter of a century ago, a dream stored in the back of her imagination, a fantasy for nights when she was lonely and drank an extra glass of wine.

Still.

Still, what, Maria Angelica?

Still, I'm going to the wake and see what happens.

She almost lost her nerve in the parking lot of the North Shore Funeral Home.

"I'm not going in with all those people," she insisted.

"Well, we're going in, whether you do or not. Right, Steve?" Eddie was as feisty as his mom and as darkly handsome a Taylor Street entrepreneur as his grandfather.

The taller brother, so much like his father, said softly, "No question."

"Stay close to me," Maria entreated.

At the door they met the redoubtable Monsignor Muggsy Brannigan, who bragged that he'd shot his age twice last summer, eighty-two, and broke into the seventies once. "These two galoots yours, Maria? Bet they went to Fenwick."

She introduced her two sons, told Monsignor Muggsy where they were going to college, and added, "And Kenny, the youngest, is in school at St. Mark's. He's the only one in the family who looks like me."

Muggsy's eyes, weak and covered by thick glasses, danced with fun. "She still chew bubble gum, guys?"

Ed pulled a package from his pocket. "Makes me carry it for her."

"Real proud of you, Maria," said the genial old man. "Keep it up . . . and pray for that crowd in there. They need it."

Inside, there were three groups of mourners arrayed in different positions near the four sealed caskets.

On the far right were Liz's family, big, hard-bodied, quiet people from Iowa—old parents, brothers and sisters, nieces and nephews, awkward, silent, grim-faced. There was no line waiting for them and only a few people from the other two lines bothered to speak with them. Neither Chicago nor Irish; they didn't belong. At the center was Estelle, red-faced, fat, bitter, surrounded by her mother and father and children, pointedly ignoring the Donlons and loudly complaining about the funeral arrangements.

Then there were the Donlons on the left—the judge, shaken and bemused; Peggy, pale and drawn; Marge, weeping and lovely; and Hugh, lean now and silver-haired.

"Will they bury them from church?" she whispered to Ed as they waited in line.

"Why not? Oh, you mean the public sin thing? Maybe the local pastor, who's a nerd, will wonder about it. He'll call Sean and get his orders and that will be that."

"Is that what you call the cardinal?" she said disapprovingly.

"Why not? That's his name, isn't it? Everyone calls him Sean—seminarians not quite to his face yet, though he probably couldn't care less. Anyway, if the Apostle John showed up, we wouldn't call him Cardinal Ben Zebedee, would we?"

"I never knew his middle name was Ben."

Peg and Tom barely recognized Maria or the boys. Only when she turned to Marge did Peg realize who they were.

Marge was more forthcoming. "Wonderful of you to come. It's easiest on me; I have Liam and the kids."

Lord Kerry's massive, slow smile made Maria feel warm. The two girls who were with them were fey, lovely creatures who favored her own sons with warm greetings that went beyond courtesy. She would have to warn the boys to avoid Irish colleens.

"Poor Hugh," she said awkwardly. "His whole family. . . ."

Marge sighed. "I think it will be a relief for him to be able to return to the priesthood . . . a blessing in disguise."

Maria had not considered that possibility and she didn't like it a bit.

"Maria . . ." he said, holding her hand. Oh, God, she thought, such pain in those wonderful blue eyes.

"I'm sorry, Hugh."

"It all comes to an end eventually." He seemed spaced out, the smile not empty but otherworldly. What were they doing to him in prison?

There was no Hugh Donlon left, an empty man, hollow, drained of all life and vitality.

More than prison.

He'd been in a prison all his life. The Donlon family prison. A splendid, comfortable, well-intentioned prison. But one that destroyed you just the same. And you couldn't help loving the jailors.

"My son Steve and my son Ed." She introduced the boys.

"You go to the Citadel like your father?" A routine, automatic question. Recited from a memorized script.

"Yes, sir. Family tradition."

"Wonderful, keep it up. And Ed?"

Oh, oh, never thought of that.

"Niles College. I'm going to be a priest."

Hugh was shaken. "Jean and Hank's daughter is becoming a

Poor Clare. It all swings around . . . I'm sorry, another family. I'm confused. Good luck to you."

"We'll pray," Maria said helplessly as they edged away.

In the parking lot Maria and her sons met the cardinal, Bishop McGuire, his red-haired, genial second-in-command, the cardinal's tall, striking sister-in-law, Senator Nora Cronin, and her husband, Roy Hurley, the handsome sports announcer. The cardinal performed introductions all around.

The senator knew Steven, who had escorted her daughter Noreen to a number of Washington dances.

"He doesn't tell me about his social life," Maria laughed. "Lucky Steve."

"Lucky Noreen," the senator corrected her.

"Ed, Steve, can you spare me your mother for a moment?" asked the cardinal.

"Sure, Cardinal," the two boys said in unison.

They stepped away from the cardinal's limousine.

"You were once close to him, weren't you, Mrs. McLain?"

"A long time ago, teen-age." Maria was taken aback.

"Forgive me for having asked questions about you and the Donlons. I had a kind of hunch."

"Oh?"

"Maria, I hope you don't mind my using your first name, because I'm going to insist that you call me Sean. Now, shall we leave the future in God's hands and concentrate on getting Hugh out of that hellhole down south? I pried the truth out of him: He didn't know a thing. Tim, God be good to the poor man, lied. Ben Fowler and the Austin woman lied too. So did Judge Crawford, who promised a plea bargain and then reneged."

"I didn't think about any of those things," she admitted. "I knew he hadn't done anything wrong. That was enough."

"Find me the evidence and Nora will take care of the rest." The cardinal's eyes gleamed with a mad light of battle, an Irish freebooter from long ago, one of the wild geese of song.

"Why me?"

Sean Cronin smiled enthusiastically. "I don't know anyone else who cares about him and is smart enough to get him out of jail."

o   o   o

Wearily, as if she had not slept in months, Peg Donlon opened the door of her apartment. She had seen Liz's family off on the plane to Iowa, a dour group departing sullenly, not even pretending to graciousness. Estelle and her family had at least gone through the motions of courtesy, though with enough of an edge to let Peg know they were condescending.

Peg had lost a child too, but that didn't seem important to any of them.

Her stomach was upset—too much hasty eating during the past week. And there was probably not a single Tums in the apartment.

There was a package inside the front door. The people from reception must have brought it up.

She lifted it to the hallway table. Not too heavy but it strained her left shoulder, which had been bothering her for the past few days. Getting old. Sometimes she didn't feel old at all. Now she felt ancient.

She opened the package. How wonderful. The first copies of Tom's book from Cornell. She must try to read it again, though she had no idea what Tom was talking about. She hoped that the academic reviewers would be kind.

What a lovely print of the Chartres rose window on the cover. Maybe after Christmas she and Tom could travel. It would be a cold, lonely Christmas this year.

She laid Tom's book reverently on the coffee table and stood back to admire it.

Then the pain struck, the worst pain she had ever known, an elephant stomping on her chest.

I'm having a heart attack, she thought as she collapsed to the floor. I'm going to die. Poor Tom. I always thought he'd be the first to go. Where is my rosary?

Hugh was poking around his house, preparing to return to Lexington. Marilyn Henderson had offered to extend his furlough, but he'd told her he would prefer time at Christmas.

Actually, he would be happy to be back in Lexington, just as sometimes during the long summer vacations from the seminary he had missed the order and the blessed tedium of its routine. At Lexington there would be no memories.

In the small desk she'd used for her paperwork he found Liz's mementos, a little stack of precious keepsakes that survived after thirty-nine years of life: high school yearbooks, a dry, pressed prom corsage, report cards, love letters from a boy at Iowa State who had manfully accepted her decision to be a "bride of Christ," even congratulations on her marriage.

Vocations, he thought, were different matters these days. Young people like Laura Kincaid had a much clearer idea of what they were doing.

And the young man who was going to be a priest . . . who was he? Hugh had met him at the wake. Ed something or other. Handsome, dark-skinned lad, with a brilliant smile and flashing black eyes.

Ed McLain . . . Maria's son? Maria's son a priest?

He shook his head. Strange.

He went back to Liz's mementos: a prize-winning term paper, seeing signs of grace in Graham Greene, not bad actually; graduation picture; invitation to her profession, picture at her sister's wedding, lovely in the maid of honor's dress; another picture, in a white bridal gown on the day of her own commitment as a bride of Christ—how corny that sounded only a decade and a half later—a letter from the provincial reluctantly approving her plea to attend graduate school. Dispensation from her vows; wedding pictures, baptism pictures of Brian, not of Lise—too busy to take pictures then.

Hugh thought of the early weeks, the first time early Christmas morning, the Sunday afternoon after that, the weekend at Lake Geneva. Bright and promising moments.

How little remains of your hopes and dreams after you are gone, a few perishable records that after ten years would interest no one.

Most poignant of all, Hugh found a first draft of her letter seeking admission to the Order. An eighteen-year-old child who was filled with bright, intelligent youthful ideals—serve God and my fellow human beings with all my heart and to the best of my ability. Dedicate my life to bringing more love and kindness into the world, work for our Lord and his Church. The only way I will ever be happy. Not worthy of a vocation but inspired by the Holy Ghost—he was still a ghost then—to respond to a wonderful gift.

Hugh shoved the papers aside.

How long had she loved Tim? Had she become silent and withdrawn when the scandal broke because she was on Tim's side?

It didn't matter. He'd failed her and their children. Now they were all dead. The grief inside him was so deep he couldn't experience it, face it, discharge it.

He would finish his life frozen and emotionless, like the blue waters of Lake Geneva imprisoned in winter ice.

He picked up from the bed on which he'd been piling the keepsakes the latest school pictures of Brian and Lise—taken at the embassy school by a Marine photographer. Lise would have grown into a beautiful woman. Brian was well-coordinated but not interested in sports. . . .

He wanted with all his soul to grieve for them. Flesh of my flesh, bone of my bone. He remembered the few times that he had played with them. There had been beginnings . . . nothing came of them. His fault . . . ? Liz's? What did it matter?

He remembered other children, the little boy who had committed adultery by saying "shit" to his mother. He had been good with kids in those days.

Brian and Lise would still be dead, even if he had been close to them.

Yet, so much waste. . . .

I do love you, my lost children. Forgive me, you harmless little ones. I failed you. I don't even understand why I failed you, but I did. If there is a place where we can undo our mistakes, I will love you there. Give me another chance.

He sat on the edge of the bed, burying his head in the crook of his arm. Still the tears would not come.

I who was loved so much by my mother and father did not pass love on.

"What's his problem?" Ed McLain asked, watching Hugh Donlon stare grimly at the TV cameras as he walked away from the gravesite of his wife and children.

Maria looked up from her terminal, on which she was pretending to work. What would her sons feel about her having a romance with a man involved in a public scandal? And a former priest? "Same as the whole family. The mother—you met her—wasn't she ravishing?"

"Sure was," Ed said appreciatively, "for a woman her age."

The McLains' living room was furnished with stark modern Scandinavian teak and thick burgundy leather cushions, sufficiently unlikely to boggle most visitors' minds. "Norman background" was her usual explanation.

"We won't discuss women's ages tonight," she warned him. "She's a wonderful woman, full of energy and warmth. The kids all fell in love with her, unsurprisingly enough. But neither she nor the kids ever figured out how to cope with her sex appeal."

Ed was into psychology, so Maria, who'd read a few books herself, tried to speak his language.

"Lingering over rites of passage, such as giving up the nipple?"

"Eddie, that's the dirtiest thing I've ever heard."

"Sorry, Mom." He smiled his Valentino smile. "Call it introjection if you like."

"And that's even worse," she added.

"Are you implying"—he paid no attention to her protest—"that boys who get tied up in intimate relationships with sexy mothers will have troubled lives?"

"If they haven't learned," Maria shot back at him, "that mother's love doesn't have to be earned by pleasing her and if mother isn't up front about her sex appeal, yes."

"You in love with Donlon?" Eddie asked.

So there was the question, out in the open where it belonged. How did a younger son of a widow react when his mother might be falling in love? What did Ed's books tell him about that?

"I was once and I might be again," she said cautiously.

She didn't want to admit to Ed or anyone else that she'd evaluated every man she'd met in the last five years against two models, Steven McLain and Hugh Donlon, and so far no one had passed the test.

"You'll make an impulsive decision, like you always do?"

"Not impulsive, instinctive," Maria said defensively. "And my instincts have served me pretty well all my life. Do you object?"

"Me?" Ed asked in some surprise. "Gosh, no, Mom. I trust your instincts as much as you do. He seems to be a good guy. Tough enough to put up with you when you're in one of your bitchy Sicilian moods."

"Are you sure?"

"Why would I disapprove?" The young man was puzzled. "I don't claim veto rights over your affairs. Anyway, if any woman can straighten him out, it'd be you."

"Oh, Eddie." She rolled up her magazine and smacked the palm of her hand. "Say a prayer for a superannuated teen-ager, will you?"

Eddie got up and, crossing the room, lightly kissed her on the forehead. "Sure will," he said.

Hugh began to pack his clothes. Everyone seemed to assume that now that he was free of his family he would return to the priesthood. Marge was explicit about it. "You never would have resigned unless Liz had got herself pregnant. I don't say you shouldn't have left, but now you're free to return. It will make Mom and Dad so happy."

Jack Howard, Bishop Jimmy McGuire, even that strange Polish artist fellow Waldek—all discreetly hinted that Sean would be able to get him back in.

Neither his father or mother had mentioned it exactly. But they had said, and often if gently during the days of the wake and funeral, that, however terrible the tragedy, he was now able to start his life all over again.

Was that all Liz had been, and Lise and Brian—obstacles to his starting his life again?

And then there had been Maria, slim and aristocratic in a black crepe dress, gold and silver hair falling around her face, her Rembrandt eyes sparkling ice-blue as though in winter, sunlight behind her glasses; Maria, now with a self-possession born of success and tragedy.

His wife buried only a few days, and now he was already thinking about another woman, a woman about whom he knew nothing, really. *I love you, Maria. I've never stopped loving you.*

He reached for the phone to call her. It rang before he could pick it up.

"Yes, Waldek, I'm sure she's in the apartment. No answer? Yes, I'm concerned too. I'll call my sister, she's staying at the Drake, just a block away. Not at all . . . thanks for calling."

The pain was worse. It was harder to breathe. She didn't have much time. Her life swept by. . . . First Communion, Tom's lips and hands at Twin Lakes, the terrible failure of the wedding night, the later delights, Hugh's birth, the paintings, Hugh's first Mass, the terrible quarrel with Tom.

If only I could find my rosary. It's in my purse in the hallway. I'll never touch it again. I'll never touch Tom again. Dear God, one more chance.

There was so much left to do, good-byes to say, love to repeat, pardons to ask. No time. All right, God, I'm not ready, but You can have me. But please help me to say a last prayer before I leave.

Then one last, desperate word torn from her shattered heart, for Tom and for God and for everyone. . . .

"Love!"

There was light now and someone waiting, then footsteps, and strong arms, and then nothing at all. . . .

CHAPTER
FORTY-THREE

1980-1981

A letter from Liz was waiting for him when he returned to Lexington. It was postmarked from St. Maarten the day of the crash.

Hugh hesitated before opening it. He didn't want a message from the grave, especially not after his mother's flirtation with death.

Peggy was recovering now. According to the doctors, she was out of danger. Yet who could promise that she wouldn't have another attack tomorrow?

Also, as Marge had bluntly said, it might well be in Hugh's hands whether she lived or not. Marge had wanted a decision about the priesthood before he returned to prison.

And he had all but given it, saying he would write to the cardinal as soon as he got back.

Liam was the one who'd saved Peggy's life. What a scene it must have been, the hulking Irishman in his shirt-sleeves, mother-in-law in his arms, running at full speed down Chestnut Street and across Chicago Avenue in a snowstorm with the wind howling in from the lake.

The doctors in the emergency room at Northwestern Hospital said she would have been dead in a few more minutes. "Not many of us would have had the presence of mind to do what your brother-in-law did," the woman cardiological resident told him.

Hugh opened the letter from Liz.

*I suppose I must begin this difficult letter at the begin-
ning. I am not going ahead with the divorce unless you
want me to. If you would rather be rid of me, then I
will go quietly and ask only for enough money to take
care of the kids. If you want them—and I can't imagine
you will—I won't fight that either.*

I hope it's not too late for us, but I leave that to you.

*I have been here in the Caribbean for a week with a
lover, the only time I have been unfaithful to you. I
wanted to commit adultery many other times, so I am
guilty of sin by intention anyway. If you are willing to
take me back, I'll never do it again.*

My lover agrees with this decision.

*The first thing Monday morning I will call a psychi-
atrist and set up an appointment. You are a good man
and a wonderful husband. If I am unhappy in our marriage, it must be my fault. I have never been happy in
my life, not in high school, not in the religious life, not
in graduate school, not with you, and not now. If
somone is always unhappy, then the unhappiness is in
their own soul. Strange I should use that word out of
our past. I'm sick emotionally and sick spiritually.*

*I am going to try to find health. I hope you will give
me a chance.*

*Love,
Liz*

Hugh put the letter aside with trembling fingers. The woman
who wrote that letter had always been inside Liz, clear-eyed and
brave. But he'd never broken through to her, never tried to see her,
never permitted himself to be aware of her existence.

The ice around him grew thicker.

Norma Austin dug into the steak vigorously. "I've had to watch
my budget lately; no steaks for an unemployed professional
woman."

"And no jobs," Maria said with genuine sympathy.

"Can you blame them? I was mixed up with something pretty
shady."

"I'll give it to you straight, Norma. I can find you a job, a pretty good one. Or I can put you in jail for perjury. Which will it be?"

The other woman lost interest in her steak. "You found Tim's affidavit? So you must have found the hedge too. I'm so glad. He wanted it to be found if anything happened to him. You know how he was . . . life was a game."

"We have all we need to obtain a full exoneration for Hugh." Maria was making it up as she went. "Your testimony will be a help, but we can do without it. No one is eager to put you in jail. But if you don't cooperate . . ."

"I'll cooperate," Norma said eagerly. "It's been on my conscience. . . . I was so afraid."

"Just trot over to Pete McQueen's office and spill the whole story. And call me tomorrow. I meant it about the job."

Maria Angelica as lady bountiful, she told herself on the way to her swimming pool and essential daily exercise. She would have to cut it short, only twenty-five laps today, because the bank needed her. In love with a bank, of all things.

In the pool she wondered about Tim's affidavit and the "hedge" he'd left with it. Tim had told her about the hedge too. And probably a lot of other people. He was fond of scattering hints. Where and what was it? She'd better try to find out.

Hugh looked out the window on the recreation field, its lifeless brown turf thinly dusted with snow. He saw, however, Twin Lakes in the late nineteen thirties, the lake a sheet of fog-shrouded glass, the lawns wide and green, the pergola a fortress, the clubhouse a feudal castle. He was running down the gravel path toward the lake and his mother, a beautiful young woman waiting for him with open arms. He tripped and fell on the gravel, scraping his knee. His mother picked him up and made the pain go away, pressing him against her and telling him how much she loved him.

When he was not in the chapel praying or, rather, listening, he let his imagination wander through the past, exploring its colors and images. Somehow they seemed to be linked to his still inchoate prayers.

Some of the ice was melting under the hot rays of the happiness that was still locked up inside him. He was beginning to climb out of the pit. But he had a long slow climb back through hell before he could come alive again.

Where could he make that climb better than in the priesthood?

Ronald Harding twisted uneasily in his oversize chair. His handsome face frowned beneath his thatch of white hair.

"I have the information you want, Maria—at least enough of it, I think. However, you won't be able to use it in court."

"I'm not looking for evidence, Ron, just the lay of the land."

They had been almost lovers for a short time, before Maria had decided the merry-widow game was more trouble than it was worth. Ron was one of the most distinguished lawyers in Chicago, but so uneasy in his distinction that he needed unquestioning adoration. So he didn't need Maria.

"Very well, then. I know I can trust you. The Internal Revenue people are not satisfied that Tim Donlon died penniless. They think Tim embezzled millions of dollars from the firm during the years his brother was away. Typically, Tim left clues and puzzles that others would find virtually impossible to solve."

"Too clever by half."

"Ultimately, yes. And, if I may say so, you are more beautiful than ever."

"Always did have a way with words, Ron." Maria returned the smile. "I hope you and Roberta remember me when you put together the wedding invitation list." Roberta was his twenty-four-year-old mistress soon to become his bride.

"Of course, we will," he said amiably.

"The hell you will, but that's all right," Maria muttered to herself as she escaped from his office, half-angry that she was so skilled at resisting temptation.

Warmth, that's what you want. Warmth.

Hugh's memories brought him to Lake Geneva. He and Maria were sailing in the dingy. Maria was struggling unsuccessfully with the jib, laughing as the sail flopped against her face. He jibed into the wind, and the boom came about. Maria scurried to shift her position but not fast enough; the boom hit her in the stomach and, still laughing, she was catapulted over the side. For a second he was afraid she was hurt, might even drown. But before he could plunge into the water to save her, she was clinging to the side of the boat, hair pasted to her skull, Fenwick T-shirt soaked, her laughter undiminished.

The colors of his memories were astonishingly vivid, the white of the sail, the blue of the lake, the bronze of Maria's hair, the black of her shirt—all in the bright hues of an early Technicolor movie.

She was so lovely sitting in the boat, shivering in the cool wind, gasping for breath, and laughing.

Why was God sending him images of Maria in this prison chapel?

Maria had always been a distraction to his priesthood. She still was.

Then he realized, as if it were the first time the thought had occurred to him, that there was no obstacle now to him and Maria. He could have her if he wanted. It was Lake Geneva all over again.

The same agonizing choice.

CHAPTER

FORTY-FOUR

1981

Liam Wentworth flew from London to accompany Maria to Miami, where she spoke with Ben Fowler. He'd made the trip, he admitted, with some hesitation. Marge wanted Hugh to return to the priesthood with all her heart. They all did, as a matter of fact, but Marge particularly.

"It will help his poor mother recover completely if he is back in the priesthood," Liam had explained in one of his rare complete sentences.

"He can't come back with this scandal over his head. Even Sean Cronin couldn't carry that off."

Fowler had refused to return Maria's phone calls; he'd agreed to see them only when some South American friends of Liam Wentworth made certain remarks about finding another Florida financial consultant.

The Fowler house was on a canal in a very expensive new subdivision. Helen answered the door, an unreadable woman who was managing to age gracefully everywhere but in the eyes.

The rumors said she had been Hugh's lover. What could Hugh have seen in her? Maria wondered. Nice figure. . . . Drat it, Maria Angelica, you have no time for jealousy. Stop it.

Ben Fowler, fat and ugly, despite his expensive clothes, was even less friendly, though he was careful not to be disrespectful to the powerful lord.

"There's nothing much I can do to help. I'm sorry that Tim's dead. I'm sorry Hugh's in prison. I stand by my story."

"What if we tell you we have evidence that Hugh was upriver at a place called mir Hassun on the dates of two of those phone calls about which you testified to the grand jury."

"I don't recall any such testimony," Ben said. She'd hit hard with her make-believe evidence, but not hard enough.

"And we have an affidavit from Mrs. Austin denying that Hugh was involved."

"It would be my word against hers, wouldn't it?"

"And we have access to an affidavit from Tim himself charging you with perjury."

Fowler paused thoughtfully. "I'll believe that when I see it."

"You'll see it," Maria exploded.

"Don't want trouble for you. No trial. No public scandal. Just want to clear Hugh." Liam was pulling out all of his own stops. "Quiet word here, quiet word there. No one suffers."

Fowler nodded. "I can understand that. I'm ready to make some discreet representations to the proper authorities when I see that the evidence is leaning toward exoneration. But I'm afraid a document from the Austin woman wouldn't do. She's nothing but a whore."

"Not the only one in the case," snapped Maria, her judgment breaking under the strain.

Liam covered for her. "All will be glad when it's over. Emotions run high. It's time to cool them. We'll be back to you soon."

Helen Fowler showed them to the door. She and Maria stood together for a moment on the canal bank, while Liam searched for their limousine and its driver.

Helen's hands were working nervously. "You won't do anything to Ben, will you?" She watched the placid waters of the canal, not Maria's face.

"Of course not," Maria replied, making a quick and impulsive decision.

"Tim and Liz were here for a day before they left for Saint Maarten. He talked all day about buried treasure."

"Buried treasure?"

"Actually, I think he said 'sunken' treasure."

"Thank you," Maria said warmly. "That might be a great help."

She didn't know how it would be a great help, but Helen deserved something nice in return for her generosity.

"I would have blown it, Liam, if you hadn't been with me," Maria said wearily as they drove back to the airport. "I don't have the nerves for the private-eye role."

"Rum lot, that chap. Half-victory though. Momentum."

On the long bumpy ride from Miami International to O'Hare, Maria thought about Helen Fowler. No woman, she was sure, would give up Hugh without a great deal of pain.

Well, I'm not giving him up this time.

The U.S. Attorney was gazing out of his window, apparently studying the Calder mobile in the plaza below.

"We'll hang you from that thing," Maria said, "either you or Judge Crawford, take your pick."

"You're bluffing, Mrs. McLain." The stocky, cherubic-faced man turned away from the window and faced her, his eyes less certain than his high-pitched voice.

"You can't afford to take the chance that I am, can you? You're hoping the new crowd will reappoint you, though I don't know why anyone would want your job. If I release a story about how you sent a man against whom you didn't have a case to jail, you're finished."

"It was a plea bargain," he sighed. "Judge Crawford broke his word. I've seen the Austin woman's statement. You bring me one more bit of evidence, especially that document from Tim Donlon that she alleges she witnessed, and I'll take action."

"For what do you pray?" Marilyn Henderson asked. She'd "noticed" that Hugh spent much of his time in chapel. Rather gingerly, she tried to talk to him, and now he wanted someone to talk to.

"Forgiveness," he said promptly. "I don't know whether there is anyone who can forgive or whether He wants to forgive me. I don't deserve it, God knows. But, at least, I want it."

She brushed the hair out of her eyes. "We all want forgiveness. I guess the only religious question that matters is whether someone does forgive." She colored faintly. "If he or she does, it must take a lot of time, there's so much to forgive."

Marilyn was now a kind of Father Meisterhorst, though a much better spiritual director than he. And her husband was a very lucky man. Hugh didn't feel any sexual need for her. But he did note that in her own rather understated way she was very attractive.

Sexual longing was not part of his life anymore. Yet now there was a hint, in his response to Marilyn, that he might not be permanently immune to women.

Fast Eddie put aside Hans Küng's *Does God Exist?*

"Good book?" His mother looked up from the socks she was repairing, compulsive behavior out of her past, at which even Paola laughed. "He sure is a cute-looking fellow."

"Mother," Ed said disapprovingly, "you don't say such things about theologians."

"Only if they are as cute as Hans." The boy was a delight. She looked forward eagerly to his every return from the seminary. What if Hugh had come home from Mundelein that often?

"Stonewalled?" Ed had an uncanny ability to read his mother's mind.

"Absolutely."

"Maybe you're looking at it the wrong way. Maybe you are so in love with Hugh . . . "

"I'm not," she said furiously.

"Okay." He shrugged like an Italian fruit vendor. "Have it your way. Anyway, the point is that Tim had to have been more interested in hedging silver than he was in hiding some document. He put the affidavit with the hedge as an afterthought . . . now what do you hedge a short position—that's the right word isn't it?—what do you hedge a silver short with?"

"A silver long," she said promptly. "But he didn't have any contracts or he would have liquidated them and bailed out."

"How do they store silver?" He leaned forward, putting Hans Küng on the coffee table.

"Normally in thousand-ounce ingots, troy ounces." She punched some numbers into her TI hand calculator. "So that's about seventy-seven pounds; five of them are a normal CBT contract. An ingot would be worth, let me see"—more punches in the calculator, which could also furnish her with cosigns if she wanted to build a bridge—"at the present price about ten thousand dollars. Four times that at the top of the run-up. In a few years maybe twenty thousand dollars."

"So you stack two hundred ingots somewhere, that's two million bucks now and a nice investment in the future. Could a man do it? Could he buy something like that and store it away?"

"Sure, he could, in a bank vault somewhere . . . a multimillion-dollar needle in a haystack."

"Not your man Timmy; half the fun of it would be that a person could find it." Ed returned to Hans Küng.

He was only slightly distracted from the great Swiss thinker by his mother's enthusiastic hug.

The Marshals' house in Park Ridge was so neat it made Maria's fastidious housekeeping look sloppy. "We Italians have a hard time keeping things clean," she told the solemn young couple. "All that olive oil coming out of your skin. . . ."

They both smiled self-consciously. It was an awkward conversation. Joseph could not remember any hint in Tim Donlon's conversation about where he might have hid a couple of hundred silver ingots. The three Marshal children watched her with wide, solemn eyes, just like their parents', till they were chased off to bed.

"Will you marry him when he leaves prison?" Kathy asked bluntly.

"Not right after."

Kathy was crying. "He means so much to us. He's our priest, no matter what." She dabbed at her eyes, but the tears didn't stop. "In court he was beaten down, almost dead. You have to bring him back to life."

"Bringing people back from the dead is God's work, hon, not mine."

"If you don't help God bring him back to life, who will?"

"The house at the lake!" Joseph Marshal interjected suddenly. "Mr. Tim talked a blue streak about the house his wife designed in Michigan during the silver run-up. The rate must have risen from two times a month to ten times a week; that figures out to better than one-point-three mentions of the house every day."

Maria hugged them both and raced to the door. "See you at the wedding, kids."

"I think it would be a mistake, Hugh, for you to go back to the priesthood right after you're released." Marilyn Henderson's hair was now tied behind her head in a ponytail, which made her look like a cute teen-ager.

"How else can I obtain forgiveness, unless I rededicate?"

The young woman jumped up from her chair, in an untypical display of passion. "Rededication, bullshit. Rededication is not the answer for you; it's not good psychology and it's not good religion either."

She was disturbingly pretty when she was angry, sexually appealing enough to be classified as a full-fledged temptation. He was half in love with her.

Yet she didn't understand how painful his climb through the upper six circles would have to be.

And no one could climb with him.

CHAPTER FORTY-FIVE

1981

The house Estelle Donlon had designed at Oakland Beach was a vulgar palace.

"I should have a house with a pool." Maria laughed to herself. She sprawled on one of the enormous couches in the sunken living room.

She had persuaded the real estate agent to give her the keys on the pretext that she was looking for a summer place. She couldn't find a trace of either hedge or affidavit. If there were a couple of hundred silver ingots stored in the house, she had missed them. A good idea, but a wild goose chase.

She was momentarily dazzled by the swimming pool in the basement and its attached sauna and hot tub and beach chairs and sunlamps scattered about in sundry indoor patios. It would have seemed sybaritic—and hence extremely appealing to Maria—had Estelle not entirely covered the pine walls with family pictures. Gross, as the kids would say, but wonderfully convenient, especially if you liked to swim in the nude.

The temperature of the water in the pool was, if the thermometer was to be believed, in the low sixties. That was not exactly the bathtub temperature Maria liked, but tolerable. The agent had told her they had to keep the heat up to avoid freezing and they didn't want to drain the pool while the house was on the market.

Maria was tempted to swim twenty or thirty laps. No exercise for a couple of days.

I can't do that. It would be gross to swim in poor Tim Donlon's pool.

Pool!

Maria sat up in the chair. *Sunken treasure!* Why, sure.

She plunged headlong down the stairs to the terrace surrounding the pool, shedding her suit as she went. She flipped on the floodlights and rushed to the water's edge. The pool was made of tile and plastic, but at the deep end there were painted bricks, either for decoration or to protect the base of the pool from structural stress.

At least, that's what you'd think at first.

She tossed the rest of her clothes on the floor, took a deep breath, and dove in.

My God, it's freezing. Sixty-two degrees is a lie.

She touched bottom, poked at the bricks till her lungs hurt and returned to the surface, gasping for breath.

She thought for a moment, heaved herself out of the pool and, heedless of her shivers, rummaged around the room until she found a tool kit in a narrow closet. Then she dove back in, a screwdriver clenched in her teeth.

Only a few scratches at the paint on the bricks and she saw gleaming metal underneath.

Hanging on the side of the pool again, panting and cold, she considered what to do. At least a hundred and fifty bricks, a million and a half dollars. Whose? Hugh's by right, but he'd have to fight Estelle for it.

She pulled herself out of the pool, hunted for a towel in the cabinets on the wall, wrapped herself in a massive bath sheet, and sat under an unlit sunlamp, shivering and thinking.

Somewhere in this room. . . .

Clutching the towel, she ransacked the cabinets, the tool kits, the books on the tables. Nothing. She searched the sauna room. Nothing there either.

Discouraged and still shivering, she returned to the poolside. Maybe Tim had planted the idea of the affidavit in Norma's head as a final trick. Maybe there wasn't any.

I need my glasses to think properly, she thought. Where's my purse? Damn, I'll buy those contacts next week, the cute soft kind.

Towel tied tightly, she climbed the stairs, ignoring her discarded clothing, and found her purse.

If Hugh is interested in me, I'll definitely invest in contacts.

Maria Angelica, you ought to be ashamed of yourself.

Downstairs again, she put on her glasses, discarded her wet towel, and tugged at the door of a cabinet in search of another.

Her eyes glimpsed the wall next to the cabinet—a picture of the whole Tim Donlon family in swimsuits. Fat wife and fat creepy kids.

I wonder. . . .

She forgot about a dry towel and pulled the back off the frame. Nothing.

On the other wall was a small picture. She rushed across the floor, almost slipping on the tiles. Damn, great place to break your neck.

Sure enough, Lake Geneva, all the Donlons, and a skinny blond girl in a Fenwick T-shirt.

She knew what she would find before she even opened the picture.

The first call was to Cardinal Cronin.

Then to the U.S. Attorney. "It's going to be either your head or Crawford's on a silver platter."

Only then did she notice she'd run upstairs without a stitch. Silly impulsive Sicilian.

"You're joking about the silver platter." He laughed uneasily.

"I've never been more serious in my life."

"Who gave you the right to interfere in our family affairs?" Marge exploded as soon as Maria picked up the phone.

"Huh?" Maria said sleepily.

"Do you want Mom to have another heart attack? What do you think it does to her to have our family secrets in newspaper head-lines all over the world . . . *again*?"

"But Hugh is cleared."

"You save him two months or so in jail at the cost of blackening Tim's memory and endangering Mother's health."

"Did Peggy have another attack?" Sleepily she tried to sort out what was happening.

"Not yet, no thanks to you. And it won't do you any good. Hugh's going to be a priest again." Marge hung up.

"Not if I can help it," Maria said.

Judge Donlon was ushered into her office.

"You did hang the picture here," he said tentatively, taking account of Peggy's watercolor on the wall.

Maria was sitting at her desk, poised, erect, competent as well as beautiful, fingers on the keyboard of her computer terminal. Not bad for a hasty pose. "And no one even suggests that it's me. So much for an old woman's vanity."

"I've come to apologize for the call you received from Killarney. Liam told me about it. He was more angry than I would have believed possible."

"No need to apologize." She waved her hand as if in absolution.

"Yes, there is. Marge is a passionate person, like the rest of us. But, unlike the rest of us, she rarely holds her feelings in. Even as a child . . ."

"I can't hold a grudge, Your Honor. You know that. You're all wonderful people, even Marge, though tell her the next time she wants to shout, please call me in the daytime so I can shout back. Now, give me that copy of your book that you're carrying. I can hardly wait to read it."

Judge Donlon solemnly made the presentation.

Maria responded as though she had been given a rare work of art.

"How's Peggy?" she asked at length, sensing that the visit involved more than the book.

"Fine. Marge exaggerated. My wife had a serious heart attack, but she has recovered quite well. There's no reason to think she won't live for a long time yet. Naturally, it goes without saying that a happy resolution of Hugh's situation would ease her mind. . . ."

So that's it. Well, I love her too. But I'm not about to give up as easily as I did the last time.

"Will she see me . . .? I mean, I've wanted to visit her, but I didn't know . . ."

"Of course she will."

"Ask her," Maria insisted.

      o   o   o

First the cardinal, then Monsignor Martin. Maria was dismayed. Sean Cronin had pulled no punches.

"He should be a priest, Maria; he did wonderful work under impossible circumstances in Lakeridge. He was a superb priest-scholar. He never should have left us. We need him back."

Maria wished she could see his face. Phone conversations with those in authority unnerved her. Sicilian intuitions didn't take to telephonic vibes.

"I don't think he was ever happy as a priest, Your Eminence—Sean—and don't tell me we're not supposed to be happy. I know we are."

"I think he was happy much of the time. Maybe not. . . . Anyway, all I ask is that you give him a chance to make up his mind. Fight fair."

"You think God is on your side. What if you're wrong?"

The cardinal hesitated. "It won't be the first time, Maria. And maybe God is on your side. Still, I want him back. Give us a chance."

Maria had made no promises, especially not the promise of a fair fight.

They weren't fighting fair. Why should she?

As soon as she left the bank, she went to St. Mark's. Monsignor Martin had said Steven's funeral Mass and sustained her through the years of grief. She had no closer friend in all the world.

And now he was harder on her than the cardinal.

"How can you stand in God's way?" He extended his hands dramatically.

"How can you be sure I'm not God's way? Why is your side automatically right?"

"He was ordained a priest forever, Maria."

At the door, as she was leaving, a final plea: "Will you stop loving me if I win, Monsignor Xav?"

"No, Maria." The pastor shook his head. "But I'll be disappointed in you. Terribly disappointed."

At home she called Ed.

"Xav is partly old school; you have to understand that," he said evasively.

"Will *you* be disappointed in me?" Maria persisted in her search for reassurance.

Ed laughed softly. "No way I'll ever be disappointed in you, Mom."

Peggy looked healthy enough and indeed quite pretty, sitting by the window gazing on the lake and the city, her painting tools in hand.

It was the city, blazing with red, not fire, not blood, some other kind of red.

"Best yet. No more pale pastels?"

"Odd red, isn't it? I think it might be love, but that seems presumptuous."

"I hope you'll forgive me." Bank president or not, Maria had lost her cool with this great lady.

"Nothing to forgive, my dear. I'm the one who should be asking. . . ."

"Maybe we mothers take on too much responsibility for our children. We have them only for a few years, then we give them back to God." It was a sermon she'd heard from Ed; why not use it now. "He forgives our mistakes."

Peggy was silent, watching the real city, not the passion-inflamed one in her watercolor.

"I do hope you're right . . . it would be so much easier."

"Peggy"—Maria was seized by an impulsive notion—"why don't you and I say a decade of the rosary together? On those pearl beads."

"What a wonderful idea, Maria; you always have such wonderful ideas. I keep this rosary close all the time. I didn't have it when I needed it. Of course, God sent Liam anyway, which was interesting, wasn't it? Here, you lead. . . ." She passed the beads to Maria.

On the elevator leaving the building, Maria realized she'd been upstaged. She laughed. Wonderful woman. I may lose to you again, but this time it will be after a fight.

And I won't fight fair.

BOOK
SIX

"Into thy hands, I commend my spirit."

CHAPTER
FORTY-SIX

1981

Hugh Donlon left the Federal Correctional Institution at noon on a gray Friday in March. The grass was turning green in Kentucky, although it was only the week before Palm Sunday.

He felt the same fear he had experienced as a young priest leaving the seminary: Institutional life was not pleasant, but it was orderly and predictable. The world outside was risky and uncertain.

He'd been edgy the week before his release. Much of the progress he'd made through prayer and conversation with Marilyn had been undone. The ice sheet around his emotions had thickened. He'd quarreled bitterly with her when she breathlessly congratulated him on his exoneration. Their last interview had been cold and formal.

He'd told his family not to come to meet him at the prison—just send a limo to take him to the airport in Louisville.

A gauntlet of TV cameramen and reporters flanked the walk between him and the shaded windows of the Cadillac. He took a deep breath. The air of freedom didn't smell any different.

A pretty young black woman jabbed a microphone at him. "How does it feel to be out of prison, Mr. Donlon?"

"Better."

"Are you happy that your name has been cleared?"

"I'm sorry my brother's reputation has been clouded." He edged toward the limo.

"Are you going back to the commodity business now that the sanctions have been lifted?"

"No fixed plans. Perhaps I'll teach somewhere."

No questions about the priesthood.

A red-bearded reporter leaned in front of him as he reached the car. "Will you contest your sister-in-law's claim to the silver?"

"What good is the silver?" He opened the door.

He sank into the plush cushion and closed the door. He did not need to see to know who was there, in tinted sunglasses, trim black suit, frilly white blouse, and gold and silver hair.

"While you're in a forgiving mood, do I merit absolution for salvaging your reputation?"

He kissed her lightly on the cheek. "No one can stay angry at you, Maria."

How would he tell her that he was going to return to the priesthood?

"Don't feel you have to talk," Maria said. "I'm in no rush to hear about what it was like. I'll give you five more minutes of morose silence before I start to ask questions. Like my sunglasses? They're called Mafiosa Carissima. . . ."

"Hey, that's the wrong turn."

The limo was going north on I-75 instead of west toward Louisville on I-64.

"We're not going to the airport till Monday morning," Maria said, every inch a bank president who had made up her mind. "This is bluegrass country. There's a resort up in the hills where you're going to be a kept man for the next two and a half days. Can't have you returning to Chicago looking all gray and ex-convictlike. You can call Peg when we get there."

Behind the tinted glasses, she was watching anxiously, a waif lurking behind Her Grace the President.

"Do I get a choice?"

"Nope." She dusted her hands. "No way. You're kidnapped for the weekend."

Gethsemani Abbey the resort was not, as Tim would have said. But it would do—spring flowers, rolling fields, a tumbling stream, neatly cut lawns, and the turf a veritable blue.

"I bet they dye the grass. Don't worry; I've already checked us in."

In their luxurious suite Hugh called his mother. As they talked he watched Maria hustling around the parlor, opening curtains, checking the bottle of champagne in its ice bucket by the sliding glass terrace door, fluffing her hair in the mirror, replacing the sunglasses with oblong-shaped, golden-framed reading glasses.

Beyond the door the sun, which had broken through the clouds, washed the hills and fields and endless white fences.

Not very subtle, Maria.

"I'm fine. I hope you don't mind my taking the weekend off."

The glasses matched her hair. That's not very subtle either, dear.

"Yes, it will be a busy ... yes, I guess we both have risen from the dead."

Maria made a face.

"You'll live to be a hundred. . . ."

Maria took off her black jacket. The frilly blouse was sheer, as was the bra underneath.

"Yes, it will be wonderful to see Fionna and Graine and little Seamus."

By now totally distracted, Hugh bid his mother good-bye and turned to consider his captor.

"Would you believe that she and I said a decade of the rosary together last week and at my suggestion? Anyway, there are two bedrooms in this suite. On that side, sir, is your room, and over here is mine." She smiled. "Any other arrangements you may choose to make will be a matter of free substitution."

Hugh was saved from finding a response by the arrival of a sumptuous steak dinner, with a 1967 red Bordeaux to follow the champagne.

"How can I tell you ... ?"

"A toast to freedom!" Maria uncorked the champagne with a single push of the thumb and splashed the frothy elixir into two glasses.

"That . . ." He sighed, clinking glasses with her. "The past . . ."

"Shh." She cut him off. "For the next sixty hours you're free."

Maria carried the conversational ball as they ate, the stand-up comic doing her desperate routine.

Then, suddenly, she stopped. "It's wonderful to see you laughing again, darling," she said seriously.

The waif lurked behind the clown. Maria was more vulnerable than she appeared. She was risking her life for his with reckless disregard of the near-certainty that she would lose.

"I appreciate what you're doing, Maria." He gripped his dessert spoon bravely.

"You look so lean and silver and distinguished. But you have to get rid of that prison pallor . . . and no more excess pounds. I like men with tight stomach muscles."

With the shock of recognition of her vulnerability came affection, sweet and languid. He didn't deserve her concern but he enjoyed it.

"It wasn't really a prison. I even had a woman social worker, a nice young kid."

"I don't want to hear about her . . . I suppose you had a fight with her before you left."

"How did you know?"

Affection led to tenderness, a longing to protect and care for her.

She waved her hand, dismissing the question as absurd. "That's how you Donlons handle problems with people; you pick a fight so you won't fall in love with them. But, as I said, I don't want to hear about her. . . . How old was she?"

Inevitably, affection and tenderness ignited desire—gasoline on the sparks.

With other women—even with Maria in the hunting cabin and on the beach—Hugh had felt the collapse of ramparts and the fury of a raging torrent pushing him away from his commitments.

But now he felt simply drawn, drifting slowly toward her on a deep and peaceful river, floating to a refuge where he belonged, floating home. What other word could describe this union, but love?

He rose from his chair, took the dessert spoon from her hand, placed it on the table, and lifted her to her feet. "I love you, Maria," he said.

He took her in his arms, bruising her lips with furious kisses. Her lips were as hungry as his.

His trembling fingers were clumsy and the fabric of her blouse became tangled with the chain of her glasses.

"The blouse is designed only for looking, too thin for much else," she apologized, laughing and trembling at the same time. "Mind if I put the glasses away?"

Underneath she was a mass of cream-colored lace, sheer nylon, and elastic.

She tried to help him, unbuttoning his shirt at the same time.

Finally she stood before him naked—solemn and clear-eyed—a woman giving herself wholly and without conditions. She unwound her hair and let it fall.

"Your room or mine?" she asked.

"Yours," he replied.

Hugh was grave, but he was not in charge. Maria was a cheerful and lighthearted lover. They would love one another on her terms and that meant laughter. Their union after twenty-seven years was not solemn high liturgy but farce.

When he awoke, lying on her bed, Hugh saw Maria standing above him, hands on her hips, golden and glowing in the late afternoon sun, wearing only her glasses and the plain gold cross at her throat.

"You like?"

She was proud of herself, proud of her smooth, sleek body with its compact, flawlessly shaped breasts, trim waist, and slender haunches. From modest bride to naked countess. . . .

"I like very much." He leaned back on his pillow. "But . . ."

"Now, I hear that you love me, but you still are obliged to go back to the priesthood because you must do penance for your sins and your family expects it and if you don't Peggy will have another heart attack. Go ahead and say it." She folded her arms. "I don't believe a word of it. And neither do you."

"I must seek forgiveness."

"That's nonsense. Remember your sermon at Marge's wedding? Forgiveness is there to begin with. It's given, just as it was given to that poor woman in the Bible they were going to stone to death."

"A naked woman quoting scripture?"

"Why not? It gets attention. Titian—"

"What does he have to do with it?"

"His painting of sacred and profane love. Profane is a stodgy old prude with all her clothes on and Sacred is like me." She raised her arms. "Except she's not wearing glasses."

He circled her waist with his fingers and drew her close. She put her hands on his head, Sacred love offering her benediction. His fingers moved up to her breasts. Holding one in each hand, he kissed them, first one, then the other, with infinite delicacy. She sighed and her eyes dilated with pleasure.

God in heaven, how he loved her. The only one he'd ever loved. Then he drew back once more.

"Maria . . . I must climb out of hell . . . I can't. . . ."

"No, you don't. You can't escape that way. You should stretch up your hands to God." She recaptured his hands. "And let Him pull you out." She pulled him back to her. "This way."

He wrapped his arms around her.

"Why do you bother with me?" he asked.

Her eyes filled with tears. She leaned her head against his shoulder. "Because I love you, you crazy so and so. I've always loved you and always will, no matter how much you hide from me."

For the first time in four decades, tears spilled out of Hugh Donlon's eyes, tears of agony and pain, of frustration and disappointment, of failure and despair. Maria's arms enveloped him. He buried his head against her chest, his tears washing her breasts, a child in his mother's arms sobbing as though his body would tear itself apart.

When he entered her again, after long and delicate preparation, she said in a voice that was fading into a moan, "If we make a girl baby, we can call her Margaret Mary," and then in a final sigh, "Peggy for short."

And so it was that, close to a monastery named after a garden in which Jesus wept, but not in it, Hugh Donlon forgot about his glacier and experienced peace and happiness.

When Hugh awoke, the sky was turning from black to gray. For a moment he didn't know where he was, only that he had never in his life felt so happy.

Then he remembered.

My God, what have I done? I came out of prison planning to return to the priesthood. And in a couple of hours I'm in bed with a woman.

For a moment he was seized with reflexive guilt. But as quickly the mood passed.

He slipped back into a half sleep, basking in pleasant sensations to which he tried not to give a name. He did not possess; he was possessed. How delicious it was to be possessed. . . .

Another emotion, disturbing but not unpleasant, something to do with being possessed. . . . What was it . . . ?

Something like the tiny unease as a sail flaps helplessly against the mast, looking for a freshening breeze . . . what if he should never make it to shore?

Fear.

Could he be afraid of Maria?

He was fully awake again. Yes, indeed; he was in terror of his captor. He must escape from her. He searched for the strength to heave himself out of bed.

The lovely captor was sleeping peacefully beside him, so slender as to seem ethereal, one childlike hand holding a sheet at her waist. I do fear her, but I don't want to escape from her either

Life had perfected her as a gift, a prize to be given without regard to whether she would suffer or not, a giving mixture of submissiveness and laughter, innocence and hunger. Once more, against his will, he felt a compulsion to protect her. His lips went to her breast again, his teeth gently touching her skin.

She opened her eyes and stretched a hand to the back of his head, holding it in place. Her smile was a smile of complete adoration, a mother nursing a mildly troublesome boy child.

In the sweet taste of her flesh everything else was forgotten and there remained only love and hope.

Hugh had not been convinced, but this time, at least, he did not try to slam shut the door that let in the light.

Hugh took Piedmont 609 from Louisville to Chicago. Maria had business in Louisville, or so she said.

Jack Howard, Marge, Liam, Fionna and Graine and a grinning Seamus met him at O'Hare.

"Am I ever proud of my big brother," Marge gushed as she hugged him. She was an attractive matron now, but no match for her sleek Italian competitor.

"Good show," said Liam. "Jolly good."

"Back in and back in to stay." Jack Howard could hardly contain his happiness.

Both Hugh's nieces called him Father Hugh as they shyly shook hands with him. Seamus called him Uncle.

Maria phoned Kathy Marshal from the airport. As the phone rang she watched the old woman in the glass-covered *U.S. News* ad next to the phone booth. That's me. After seven years of celibacy I forgot what sex could do to you.

In the car on the way to the airport his withdrawn silence, like a teen-age boy who had decided that after all he was not going to the prom, chilled her. She had played for high stakes and lost.

"Operation Resurrection is in trouble, honey. Start spinning the prayer wheels," she said to Kathy.

She should have known better. At her age and with her history, sex couldn't be a casual ploy. Now she was deeply in love, physically a captive if not to Hugh then to her self-constructed need for him.

She recalled their last union in the early hours of the morning. When he was thrusting into her in the final uncontrollable fierceness of his passion, Maria felt like her helpless body was filled with a spring storm—driving rain, rampaging thunder, and jagged bolts of lightning crackling through her body and soul, igniting explosions at every nerve end and in every dark corner of her personality. The unbearable thunderbolts came faster and faster—God how she loved him—and then combined into a single massive outburst of sound and light that momentarily blanked out all sensation and left her floating in a cloud somewhere between heaven and earth, soaked in the storm's cooling rain.

"Maria Angelica"—she shook her head at the woman in the *U.S. News & World Report* ad—"you are about to get yourself badly hurt."

The unspoken assumption that Hugh would, of course, return to the active ministry continued at his parents' condominium. His father's handshake was brisk and businesslike; his mother's tears were brief.

"You look great," Hugh said to her. "Young enough to be my sister."

"Why shouldn't I look great? Just sitting here all day, dabbing with my paints while your poor father waits on me hand and foot? And now those two lovely girls . . . how did we earn such wonderful granddaughters?"

It was all earned, good and bad, Hugh thought.

The judge took her hand. "The doctors are very pleased, Hugh.

Your mother will have to slow down a little and avoid big emotional highs and lows, but she'll outlive us all."

The mute appeal in all their faces was unmistakable. Make it be the way it used to be.

As he was leaving for his motel room at the airport—no place else available and he didn't want to stay with them—his father asked tentatively if he had an appointment with the cardinal.

Poor wonderful people, wanting him to be a priest again and wanting him to be free.

"Jack Howard says the boss wants to see me on Friday," he said easily. "Never say no to a cardinal."

Marge was blunter on Tuesday night when he ate dinner with her and Liam at L'Escargot in its new Allerton Hotel location.

"How hard will it be to get back in?"

"If Sean wants me, I can get back in." Hugh didn't want any further controversy. "But I'll probably end up with a long term of penance in a monastery."

"One prison to another, fool Church," Lord Kerry huffed.

"I might like it in a monastery," Hugh said.

"That wouldn't be good at all." Marge dismissed the notion abruptly. "You might have to put up with it for a couple of months, so long as you could come home on weekends. Mom deserves some good news. You know how much your going back to the priesthood means to her and Dad."

"We'll see what the cardinal has to say."

"Jack Howard says the priests are delighted at your coming back. They think it's a major victory for the Church."

"Grand show," said Liam, the friendly local Irish wolfhound.

Had Tim, Liz, Brian, and Lise died simply so that his mother and father might have a happy old age and the Church a great victory?

Monsignor Xav Martin invited Hugh to a late dinner at St. Mark's after the Holy Thursday liturgy. Hugh didn't attend the Mass; the renewal of priestly vows was something he wanted to avoid.

Pat Cleary joined Xav and his associate, Jack Howard, at the dinner table. It was obviously a dinner in Hugh's honor.

"You'll see the boss tomorrow?" Xav asked expansively.

"Before the Good Friday services."

"To celebrate the end of your descent into hell?" Jack asked.

"I'm not sure it's finished. I still have to climb out."

"It will take time," Pat Cleary said, his usual serenity marred by a small frown.

You know too much about me, Pat Cleary.

"It's wonderful to have you back," Xav persisted, "like old times."

"I can't imagine why." Hugh didn't remember the old times.

They recounted them at considerable length, praising his priestly work and his importance to their lives.

"I never realized. . . ." Hugh was touched, in spite of himself.

"You would if you'd listened." Xav lifted a silver eyebrow.

"I suppose." Hugh wanted to be more enthusiastic in his response to their affection.

"Are you going to come back?" Jack finally blurted the blunt question.

Pat Cleary frowned, less enthusiastic than the others, perhaps because he knew the kinks and crannies of Hugh's mind.

"Yes," Hugh said simply, surprised.

His friends cheered and sang the *"Ad Multos Annos"* hymn, wishing him many years in the priesthood. Yet he was not convinced.

On his way to the rectory Hugh was careful to avoid Ashland, the street on which Maria lived, though he had looked up her address in the phone book before going to St. Mark's.

Somehow he was now at the corner of Ashland at the end of Maria's block. A light in a window halfway down the street might be hers.

Maria's house in the new, new neighborhood, he thought. There had been so many houses in his life—the tiny rooms behind her father's store, Mason Avenue, Lake Geneva, the constricted Hyde Park apartment, the richly furnished but empty home in Kenilworth, the den of iniquity off Rush Street, Tim's grotesque Gothic manor with the pool and sauna bath . . .

. . . and now a seemingly ordinary suburban home on an ordinary suburban street. With a light on in the bedroom window.

Neat, feminine, but not pretentious. Efficient for sleeping and for anything else.

Deceptively, dangerously ordinary.

It was a warm evening for so early in spring; the smell of a coming rainstorm was in the air, humid and fertile.

He must force himself to avoid Maria for now.

He rolled up the car window, started the engine, and turned on the windshield wipers.

For all her chivalrous laughter, Maria was deadly serious about him, grimly determined to remake him in the image of what she thought he ought to be. If he were to be Maria's man, he would have to change—a drastic and painful transformation. And no excuses allowed.

No one in his life, not even his mother, had ever wanted him with such single-minded desire. He was flattered.

And terrified.

The cardinal's secretary enthusiastically welcomed Hugh at the front door and showed him into Sean's study. Hugh waited for a half hour, thinking of Maria and his mother. He loved both of them. How sad that, no matter what he did, he would hurt one.

Sean swept in, eyes glowing, shook Hugh's hand firmly, and tossed his clerical collar and vest on a chair. His white tailor-made shirt contrasted with the sunburst colors of the study.

"Sorry to be late, Hugh. The good old days when a bishop didn't have to listen are no more. Now the bullshit piles up to the top of your mitre in a half hour. Dialogue with nuns is the worst of all. They have read all the right books. . . . But never mind that. You look great. Welcome home."

"It's good to be back."

"Good Friday, so by rights I shouldn't offer you a drink. Why don't we both have a glass of Perrier and pretend we're members of the elite?"

He poured two glasses of sparkling water and then, before Hugh could begin, launched into a monologue.

"I can persuade my Polish friend to take you back. I may have to store you away at the seminary for a few months. He'll give in, though, and say something like 'Cronin, you're too much' and wink a frosty blue eye at me. I can do it, Hugh, and I want to do it. I want you back. I don't like to lose priests from the active ministry and I delight in reclaiming them, especially when they're men like you."

"I understand," Hugh said.

The cardinal held up his hand. "No, you don't, Hugh; no, you don't. I want you back, but I'm not the Holy Spirit. If you want to marry that blond Sicilian tiger, I'll be happy to officiate at the wedding. She claims she's God's will for you and, damn it, she may be right. I can't tell. Only you can. You have a wild card to play, and you'd better play it your way."

He considered Hugh very carefully over the top of his glass.

"No matter what you do, you're a priest of this archdiocese and never forget it."

"It's so hard to know . . ." Hugh stammered. "Should I have been a priest in the first place? Should I have left? Should I return now?"

"Why can't you have a vocation in the active ministry for a while and then a different vocation? I want you back, Hugh, but I want you back only if you're convinced it's the best way for you to go. Either way, you're a priest. The choice is between active ministry and being a priest in some other way no one has yet quite figured out—representing the Church and, yes, ministering for the Church in whatever world you're in."

"I think I need more time." How much he'd sounded like Maria.

"Take it." Sean glanced at his watch. "I'd better run."

"I'll join you in church. I have a lot to think about."

There was a wild gleam in the cardinal's eyes. "That was the general idea."

Hugh listened passively to the Good Friday readings, walked forward to kiss the cross, and then later, even though he had not been shriven for the last weekend's activities, returned to the altar to receive Holy Communion.

After the services were over, he retrieved his Hertz car in the parking lot across State Street from the cathedral and drove west on Chicago Avenue through the area where the Gold Coast was reaching for the river, daintily avoiding the monstrosity of the Cabrini-Green housing project, Chicago's latest version of "Little Hell."

Beyond the river a red light stopped him in the shadow of an old Polish church with a great bulbous green dome. He would drive west another block into the setting sun, then join the light Good Friday rush-hour traffic on the Kennedy back to the O'Hare Marriott.

The melody of the *"Vexilla Regis"* sung in Latin at the cathedral during the veneration of the cross haunted him:

> *Vexilla Regis Prodeunt:*
> *Fulget crucis Mysterium,*
> *Qua vita mortem pertulit,*
> *Et morte vitam protulit.*
>
> *Quae Vulneratae lanceae*
> *Mucrone diro, criminum*
> *Ut nos lavaret sordibus,*
> *Manavit unda, et sanguine.*

Already washed clean? Like Maria's image of God reaching down for outstretched arms and pulling you out of the pit?

The hell of the apostles' creed, the hell of Good Friday, was not the hell of the damned. It was Sheol, where the Patriarchs waited for Jesus to come and collect them. . . .

He was no Patriarch, however.

Only a lost soul.

He remembered a film from childhood, a movie in which Ray Milland played a charming and sinister Satan who led his victims to the island of Almas Perditas—the Isle of Lost Souls. Maybe that's where he belonged.

That was self-pity, he told himself firmly. Salvation was never impossible, no matter how low you sank.

He should drive on to O'Hare. Yet he could still turn left on Milwaukee Avenue, ride by the gigantic heart on the wall of the Polish Roman Catholic Union of America, and then west on Augusta Boulevard through the old Polish neighborhood turned barrio and end up in River Forest.

Maria's sons were in Charleston to spend Easter with their grandmother.

Was it really fornication, this sin he had not confessed? It had not seemed to be. . . . Sacred Love she called herself . . . the first step in a lifelong union?

He hardly knew her—two weeks at Lake Geneva, a few encounters scattered over a quarter-century, a weekend fling. . . . Yet he loved her with the certain knowledge that she was the love of his life. How could he give her up again?

The light changed and he turned north on Milwaukee Avenue. All right, he would enter the Kennedy at Division Street.

Two blocks before Division, however, he turned west on Augusta. The rented Citation bumped through the colorful barrio; the two flat buildings were painted red and yellow and blue and pink, more like Venice than Chicago.

Farther west, he drove through the tired homes of the city's limits, faceless residences lacking both the color of the barrio and calm security of the suburbs; they represented the dull end of the dream of respectability that St. Ursula had offered the Irish in the 1920s and the 1930s, when no one imagined the eventual affluence of Oak Park and River Forest.

He didn't even notice Mason Avenue as he passed it. The old neighborhood where everything started no longer existed. As he crossed Austin Boulevard and entered the gracious, quietly integrated streets of Oak Park, he wished only that he were young again, his life just beginning.

Harlem Avenue was the boundary between Oak Park and River Forest, a very proper street, neatly separating the rich from the richer. He should himself be proper and turn right on Harlem and drive north to O'Hare.

But the Citation stubbornly refused to go along. It went straight on into River Forest.

At Ashland, Maria's street, he stopped the car. This was the point of no return. The bare trees were shining red in the setting sun.

He turned the car around, pointing it toward Harlem.

Halfway down the block to the right he saw two women kneeling on the sidewalk. They were huddled over a small crumpled heap in front of a Dutch Colonial house.

Someone sick? Perhaps they wanted a priest? Let them call St. Mark's. It was only a few minutes away. He turned right into Ashland, not sure exactly what he'd done.

There was Maria, and another woman, apparently comforting a dying old man or woman.

"It's Granny Monaghan," Maria called when she saw him. "She lives right down the street with her great-grandchildren."

Maria was clad in jeans and a silver Fenwick Windbreaker with "Maria!" stitched in black above the pocket. She was chewing bubble gum and wearing her oblong glasses.

The old woman was over eighty, thin, frail, yet with a hint of great beauty and power from long ago.

"It's all right, Granny," Hugh said, rushing to her side, the words coming back with astonishing ease. "I'm a priest. I'm here to help. God loves you, Granny. He's coming to take you home."

"Ah, no, Father"—remnants of a thick Irish brogue—"God will never forgive me; I'm the greatest sinner that ever was. During the Black and Tan Wars and the Troubles, I committed the most terrible sins. I'm an evil old woman; I'm going to hell for certain."

Her eyes closed, her breath stopped for a moment and she seemed to have died, then the poor little chest moved again.

"What's her first name?" Hugh whispered urgently.

"Grace, I think," Maria said.

"You're sorry for all the sins of your life, Grace Monaghan?" He held her hand fiercely; he would not let her die until she was ready.

"I am, Father, I am. It's too late; I'll never be forgiven." She moaned as though she were already among the damned.

"Stop that, woman," Hugh ordered sternly. "I'll not have you talking that way about God, and yourself on your way to join Him. He's forgiven everyone already, and that's a fact. God loves us. . . ."

There was a momentary shrewd gleam in her faded eyes.

"He's a tricky one, isn't He?"

"Lovers are always tricky, Grace, you know that."

"There's truth in that, right enough; quick, now, Father"—her voice was strong and firm—"give me absolution; say the words; He's coming for me; He wants me now; I'll not escape from Him this time."

The old woman tried to sit up, reaching out her arms to embrace an invisible lover.

"I absolve you from all your sins in the name of the Father and of the Son and of the Holy Spirit and by the power granted to me I impart to you the blessing of the Pope and a full pardon for everything you've done wrong in your whole life."

"He's here now, Father, and Himself smiling like a young man in the hedges of Galway." The last rays of the sun caught the old woman's weathered face. For a moment she smiled ecstatically, then slumped forward, unconscious, perhaps dead.

A young priest next to Hugh pushed the oils into his hand. "Go ahead, Father Donlon. You finish."

With a trembling finger, Hugh traced the sign of the cross on her parchment-dry forehead. "Through this most holy anointing and His most tender mercy may God forgive all your sins."

"Jesus, Mary, and Joseph be with me on my last journey," said the young priest.

"Into Thy hands I commend my spirit," repeated the two kneeling women.

"God the Father who made us . . ."

"Into Thy hands I commend my spirit."

"God the Son who saved us . . ."

"Into Thy hands I commend my spirit."

"God the Holy Spirit who loves us . . ."

"Into Thy hands I commend my spirit."

County Galway was long ago and far away. Yet Grace Monaghan had gone home.

As dusk spread, Hugh felt a burst of light and warmth engulf him, drawing him toward the same Love who had crept out of the hedge in front of Maria's house to take Grace Monaghan home.

It was an implacable and impulsive Love, one that forgave without being asked, never turned away from the beloved, and wanted only that the beloved surrender to Love and be happy.

A Love like Maria.

Hugh tried to flee from the Lover's majestic instancy and unperturbed grace, escape from it, hide from it, turn away from it. There was no exit.

"Joe Machowiak, Father. That was beautiful." The young priest extended a beefy paw. The heat and light that had possessed Hugh and drained him momentarily had passed without anyone's noticing.

Someone had come to take Grace Monaghan home and brushed lightly against Hugh as the two of them went by. His life would never be the same.

Maria was watching him. She had never seen him act as a priest for the dying before. Her smile said she was prepared to be a good loser.

Maria.

Her house loomed behind her—trimly painted gables, warm

yellow brick, a soft light in the parlor window, the kindly glow of dusk reflected in the other windows. A house he had never entered. Yet he knew it well enough—neat, clean, warm, unconventional furniture, and flamboyant decorations. A pleasant house, inviting, reassuring, comforting. And once you went into its light you never left. Mason Avenue, Lake Geneva, Bethlehem.

The fire department and the doctor arrived, and a granddaughter and her children. The young priest led them in a decade of the rosary. Then it was over, the ambulance with Grace Monaghan's earthly remains departed, everyone else went home, only Hugh and Maria were left standing silently under the streetlight.

"Coming in?"

"If I may."

"Of course, you may. For a visit?"

"To stay, if you'll let me."

"Be my guest." She gestured dubiously toward the doorway, like a motel owner who was not sure whether a potential client was serious. Her Rembrandt eyes, barely visible in the glow of the streetlight, were clouded with tears.

They walked silently to the door, close yet far enough apart so their hands didn't touch. Maria opened the door. Light from the parlor framed her in the doorway, just as she had been framed at Lake Geneva.

"Sure?" she asked hesitantly, holding the door open.

"I'm sure," he said.

He touched her face, tilted her jaw slightly, caressed her cheek with his thumb.

The ancient Greek Easter greeting leaped out of his memory, an explanation for everything.

"Christ is risen, Maria, alleluia."

"Bet you think I don't know the answer to that." The Maria of raspberries and cream had come back. "He is risen indeed, alleluia!"

A PERSONAL AFTERWORD

Why would a priest write a novel about a man who breaks his vows of celibacy and leaves the active exercise of the priesthood? Am I opposed to celibacy? Do I approve of those who leave the active ministry? Am I trying to justify my own planned departure?

To answer the last three questions in reverse order. I do not intend to resign from the priesthood, nor will I leave even if the powers-that-be try to throw me out. I make no judgments about individuals who leave the active ministry or about those who stay; I can only judge myself. Finally, I am in favor of celibacy, though I also think it might be useful to experiment with limited-term service in the priesthood, a much better strategy, it seems to me, than the abandonment of the celibate tradition.

As to the first question, my story is only secondarily about one man's struggle with a priestly vocation. Like all religious stories this tale is primarily a story of God. The stories of God in the Jewish and Christian scriptures are often both secular and "unedifying." The Joseph and David cycles and the parables of Jesus were stories of God that profoundly scandalized those who heard them. If they don't shock us today, the reason is perhaps that we have heard them too often and do not listen to them.

They are stories of adultery, betrayal, incest, family conflict, rivalry, and envy, of treacherous servants and traitorous brothers, of foolish mothers and indulgent fathers, of unjust judges and incredibly soft-hearted judges, of treasure hunters and crafty merchants, of angry kings and crooked stewards, of impudent workmen and obsessive gardeners, of hardworking housewives and clever investors, of dizzy teen-age girls and angry teen-age boys, of feasts and parties, wars and marriages, life and death.

There is not a character or incident in my story, I think, without a scriptural counterpart and not a story in scripture that would not shock us if we listened to it carefully.

Stories of God are designed to disconcert, to open us up to the power of God's shocking love and to disclose to us new ways of living in the world with the illumination and power that comes from that love.

The parables of Jesus were instruments of controversy. In the parables Jesus tried to persuade the crowds of the attractiveness of his picture of God; he told his stories not to teach doctrinal propositions about the nature of God but to portray, as winningly as he could, how God acts. His are tales not of who God is but how God behaves.

In addition to being both secular and disconcerting, the parables of Jesus are comic; indeed they are comedies of grace. Those who try to deal with God by bargaining, by demanding favor to which they have earned a right through their own good deeds, by winning his mercy and forgiveness through their own efforts—the early Laborers in the Vineyard, the Brother of the Prodigal Son, those who accuse the Woman Taken in Adultery (a story that was probably originally a parable)—are confounded and fall on their faces. While those who have no right to mercy or love—the Laborers of the Eleventh Hour, the helpless robbery victim saved by the Good Samaritan, the Prodigal Son, the Woman Taken in Adultery—are astonished to be swept up in irresistible and overwhelming grace. In the Kingdom of Mercy, there is always comic surprise as Grace has the last laugh on Justice.

And that, says Jesus, is the way God acts.

The doctrinal basis for my story of how God acts is contained in Hugh Donlon's sermon about First Grace (on p. 90) and in the hymn "*Vexilla Regis*," which echoes in Hugh's mind as he drives by the Polish Church on Chicago Avenue; it is documented in the Canon #179 of the Second Council of Orange, which is quoted below.

Although most readers will find it easy to absorb the religious symbols or "sacraments" (realities that reveal the presence of grace, the presence of God in action) that bind this story together, perhaps the images ought to be made explicit for those who are unfamiliar with symbols or stubbornly refuse to see them—most notably Catholic reviewers, who will fail to comprehend the parallel with the Catholic sacraments: water, wind (spirit), breast (food and drink), light, descent and ascent, an open door, house, and woman (especially two lovely women, Peggy and Maria, who represent opposing views of how God acts and for that matter what the Church ought to be).

It also should be noted that Hugh's priesthood is a "sacrament" for him, as well as for others. It reveals to him that the God of grace he preaches to others is not the God of justice who dominates his personal life. The priesthood finally forces him to turn his own word on himself and to realize that the worst sin in his life was to exempt himself from grace.

So, light-years away from them in skill, my comedy of grace seeks to do, however ineptly, what the parables of Jesus did—tell a story of how God acts. Perhaps the reader will be disconcerted by my imagining that God may act like Maria and Maria like God. Comedians both and masters of graceful surprise, God and Maria are, as the theologians would say, "correlates" of one another.

Perhaps the reader who can imagine Maria as a sacrament of God and a revelation of how God works, will then be able to see new ways of living in the light of a story of a God who, like Maria, is illusive, reckless, vulnerable, joyous, unpredictable, irrepressible, unremittingly forgiving, and implacably loving.

THE SECOND COUNCIL OF ORANGE ON THE GRATUITY OF GOD'S LOVE

If anyone says that mercy is divinely conferred upon us when, without God's grace, we believe, will, desire, strive, labor, pray, keep watch, study, beg, seek, knock for entrance, but does not profess that it is through the interior infusion and inspiration of the Holy Spirit that we believe, will, or are able to do all these things in the way we ought ... he contradicts the words of the apostle: "What hast thou that thou has not received?" and "By the grace of God I am what I am."

(The Latin text of this canon is contained in Denzinger et al., "Enchiridion Symbolorum" #376. The English translation is from Clarkson et al., "The Church Teaches" #546.)